KIM
HARRISON

LYNSAY
SANDS

KELLEY
ARMSTRONG

LORI
HANDELAND

Dates from Hell

AVON BOOKS
An Imprint of HarperCollins*Publishers*

This is a collection of fiction. Names, characters, places, and incidents are products of the authors' imagination or are used fictitiously and are not to be construed as real. Any resemblance to actual events, locales, organizations, or persons, living or dead, is entirely coincidental.

AVON BOOKS
An Imprint of HarperCollins*Publishers*
10 East 53rd Street
New York, New York 10022-5299

Undead in the Garden of Good and Evil copyright © 2006 by Kim Harrison
The Claire Switch Project copyright © 2006 by Lynsay Sands
Chaotic copyright © 2006 by Kelley Armstrong
Dead Man Dating copyright © 2006 by Lori Handeland
ISBN-13: 978-0-06-085409-6
ISBN-10: 0-06-085409-X
www.avonbooks.com

First Avon Books paperback printing: April 2006
First Avon Books special printing: November 2005

Avon Trademark Reg. U.S. Pat. Off. and in Other Countries, Marca Registrada, Hecho en U.S.A.
HarperCollins® is a registered trademark of HarperCollins Publishers Inc.

Printed in the U.S.A.

20   19   18   17   16   15   14   13   12

DATING IS A MONSTER!

KIM HARRISON

takes us to the Hollows, where living vampire/homicide cop Ivy Tamwood, investigating a string of very nasty murders, finds herself caught between two very different men, who put every dating principle she holds dear to the ultimate test.
Undead in the Garden of Good and Evil

LYNSAY SANDS

gives the power to shape-shift to a most resourceful woman, who uses it to her wickedly sexy advantage at her high school reunion.
The Claire Switch Project

KELLEY ARMSTRONG

enters the Otherworld to help a beautiful half-demon tabloid reporter escape a disastrous blind date by giving her a hot lead . . . that leads her to an even hotter werewolf jewel thief.
Chaotic

LORI HANDELAND

gives the term "dating hell" a whole new meaning, when a Manhattan literary agent out on her first date in months, is forced to choose between a sexy devil and the rogue demon hunter who's out to destroy him.
Dead Man Dating

Also by Kim Harrison

THE OUTLAW DEMON WAILS
FOR A FEW DEMONS MORE
A FISTFUL OF CHARMS
EVERY WHICH WAY BUT DEAD
THE GOOD, THE BAD, AND THE UNDEAD
DEAD WITCH WALKING

Also by Lynsay Sands

BITE ME IF YOU CAN
A BITE TO REMEMBER
A QUICK BITE
TALL, DARK & HUNGRY
SINGLE WHITE VAMPIRE

Also by Kelley Armstrong

HAUNTED
INDUSTRIAL MAGIC
DIME STORE MAGIC
STOLEN
BITTEN

Also by Lori Handeland

DARK MOON
HUNTER'S MOON
BLUE MOON

CONTENTS

Undead in the Garden of Good and Evil

Kim Harrison

1

Phone cradled between her shoulder and ear, Ivy Tamwood scooped another chunk of chili up with her fries, leaning over the patterned wax paper so it wouldn't drip onto her desk. Kisten was bitching about something or other, and she wasn't listening, knowing he could go on for half her lunch break before winding down. The guy was nice to wake up to in the afternoon, and a delight to play with before the sun came up, but he talked too much.

Which is why I put up with him, she mused, running her tongue across the inside of her teeth before swallowing. Her world had gone too quickly from alive to silent on that flight back home from California. *My God, was it seven years now?* It had been unusual to foster a high-blood living vampire child into a sympathetic camarilla, taking her from home and family for her last two years of high school, but Piscary, the master vampire her family looked to, had become too intense in his interest in her before she developed the mental tools to deal with it, and her parents had intervened at some cost, probably saving her sanity.

I could keep Freud in Havana cigars all by my lone-

some, Ivy thought, taking another bite of carbs and protein. Twenty-three ought to be far enough away from that scared sixteen-year-old on the sun-drenched tarmac to forget, but even now, after multiple blood and bed partners, a six-year degree in social sciences, and landing an excellent job where she could use her degree, she found her confidence was still tied to the very things that screwed her up.

She missed Skimmer and her reminder that life was more than waiting for it to end so she could get started living. And while Kisten was nothing like her high school roommate, he had filled the gap nicely these last few years.

Smiling wickedly, Ivy gazed through the plate-glass wall that looked out on the floor of open offices. Weight shifting, she crossed her legs at her knees and leaned farther across her desk, imagining just what gap she'd like Kisten to fill next.

"Damn vampire pheromones," she breathed, and pulled herself straight, not liking where her thoughts took her when she spent too much time in the lower levels of the Inderland Security tower. Working the homicide division of the I.S. got her a real office instead of a desk in the middle of the floor with the peons, but there were too many vamps—both living and undead—down here for the air circulation to handle.

Kisten's tirade about prank phone calls ended abruptly. "What do vamp pheromones have to do with humans attacking my pizza delivery crew?" he asked in a lousy British accent. It was his newest preoccupation, and one she hoped he'd tire of soon.

Rolling her chair closer to her desk, Ivy took a swig of her imported bottled water, eyes askance on the boss's closed door across the large room. "Nothing.

You want me to pick up anything on the way home? I might be able to wing out of here early. Art's in the office, which means someone died and I have to go to work. Bet you first bite he's going to want to cut my lunch short"—she took another sip—"and I'm going to take it off the end of my day."

"No," Kisten said. "Danny is doing the shopping today."

One of the perks of living atop a restaurant, she thought, as Kisten started in on a shopping list she didn't care about. Pulling her plate of fries off her desk, she set them on her lap, being careful to not spill anything on her leather pants. The boss's door opened, catching her eye when Art came out, shaking hands with Mrs. Pendleton. He'd been in there a full half hour. There was a stapled pack of paper in his hands, and Ivy's pulse quickened. She'd been sitting on her ass going over Art's unsolved homicides for too long. The man had no business being in homicide. Dead did not equal smart.

Unless being smart was in manipulating us into giving the undead our blood. Ivy forced herself to keep eating, thinking the undead targeted their living vampire kin more out of jealousy than maintaining good human relations, as was claimed. Having been born with the vampire virus embedded into her genome, Ivy enjoyed a measure of the undeads' strengths without the drawbacks of light fatality and pain from religious artifacts. Though not in line with Art's abilities, her hearing and strength were beyond a human's, and her sense of smell was tuned to the softer flavors of sweat and pheromones. The undeads' need for blood had been muted from a biological necessity to a bloodlust that imparted a high like no other when sated . . . addictive when mixed with sex.

Her gaze went unbidden to Art, and he smiled from across the wide floor as if knowing her thoughts, his steady advance never shifting and the packet of paper in his hand moving like a banner of intent. Appetite gone, she swiveled her chair to put her back to the room. "Hey, Kist," she said, interrupting his comments about Danny's recent poor choice of mushrooms, "change of plans. By the amount of paperwork, it's one of Art's cleanup runs. I won't be home till sunup."

"Again?"

"Again?" she mocked, fiddling with a colored pen until she realized it telegraphed her mood and set it down with a sharp tap. "God, Kisten. You make it sound like it's every night."

Kisten sighed. "Leave the paperwork for tomorrow, love. I don't know why you bust your ass so hard. You're not moving up until you let Artie the Smarty go down on you."

"Is that so," she said, feeling her face warm and the chili on her tongue go flat. Tossing her plate to her desk, she forced herself to remain reclining with her booted feet spread wide when what she wanted to do was hit someone. Martial arts meditation had kept her out of civil court until now; self-control was how she defined herself.

"You knew the system when you hired in," he coaxed, and Ivy tugged the sleeves to her skintight black pullover from her elbows to her wrists to hide her faint scars. She could feel Art crossing the room, and adrenaline tickled the pit of her stomach. *It was a run,* she told herself, but she knew Art was the reason for the stir in her, not the chance to get out of the office.

"Why do you think I wanted to work with Piscary instead of the I.S.?" Kisten was saying, words she had heard too many times before. "Give him what he wants. I don't care." He laughed. "Hell, it might be nice having you come home wanting to watch a movie instead of ready to drain me."

Reaching to her desk, she finished her water, wiping the corner of her mouth with a careful pinky. She had known the politics—hell, she had grown up in them—but that didn't mean she had to like the society she was forced to work within. She had watched it end her mother's life, watched it now eat her father away, killing him little by little. It was the only path open to her. And she was good at it. Very good at it. That's what bothered her the most.

She stiffened when Art fixed his brown eyes to the back of her neck. Undead vamps had been looking at her since she had turned fourteen; she knew the feeling. "I thought you stuck with Piscary because of his dental plan," she said sarcastically. "His dentals in your neck."

"Ha, ha. Very funny," Kisten said, his good humor doing nothing to ease her agitation.

"I like what I do," she said, putting a hand up against the knock on her open door. She didn't turn, smelling the stimulating, erotic scent of undead vampire in her doorway. "I'm damn good at it," she added to remind Art she was the reason they had pulled his murder-solved ratio up the last six months. "At least I'm not delivering pizzas for a living."

"Ivy, that's not fair."

It was a low blow, but Art was watching her, and that would unnerve anyone. After six months of working with her, he had picked up on all her idiosyncrasies, learning by reading her pulse and breathing patterns exactly what would set her rush flowing. He had been using the information to his advantage lately, making her life hell. It wasn't that he wasn't attractive—God, they all were—but he had been working the same desk for over thirty years. His lack of ambition didn't make her eager to jump his jugular, and being coaxed into something by way of her instincts when her thoughts said no left a bad taste in her mouth.

Even worse, she had realized after the first time she had come home hungering for blood and finding Piscary waiting for her that the master vampire had probably arranged the partnership knowing she'd resist—and Art would insist—the end result being she'd be hungry for a little decompression when she got home. The sad thing was she wasn't sure if she was resisting Art because she didn't like him or because she got off on the anticipation of not knowing if it would be Piscary, Kisten, or both that she'd be calming herself with.

But her weakness was no reason to bark at Kisten. "Sorry," she said into the hurt silence.

Kisten's voice was soft, forgiving, since he knew Art was playing hard on her. "You gotta go, love?" he asked in that lame accent. *Who was he trying to be, anyway?*

"Yeah." Kisten was silent, and she added, "See you tonight," that curious tightening in her throat and the need to physically touch someone settling more firmly inside her. It was the first stage of a full-blown bloodlust, and whether it stemmed from Kisten or Art didn't matter. Art would be the one trying to capitalize on it.

"Bye," Kisten replied tightly, and the phone clicked off. He said it didn't bother him, but he was alive as she was, with the same emotions and jealousy they all had. That he was so understanding of the choices she had to make made it even worse. She often felt they were like children in a warped family where love had been perverted by sex, and the easiest way to survive was to submit. Her invisible manacles had been created by her very cells and hardened by manipulation. And she didn't know if she would remove them if she could.

Ivy watched her pale fingers as she set the phone down. Not a tremor showed. Not a hint of her rising agitation. That was how she kept them away—placid, quiet, no emotion—a skill learned while working summers at Pizza Piscary's. She had learned it so well that only Skimmer knew who she really wanted to be, though she loved Kisten enough to show him glimpses.

Carefully removing all emotion from her face, she swiveled her chair, boot tips trailing along the faded carpet. Art was standing to take up half her doorway, with a packet of stapled paper in his long fingers. Clearly they had a run. By the amount of paperwork, it couldn't be pressing. Probably cleanup from before she became his partner and started following behind him with her dust broom and pan.

"I'm eating," she said, as if it wasn't obvious. "Can it wait a friggin' ten minutes?"

The dead vampire—at least fifty years her senior on paper, her contemporary by appearances—inclined his head in a practiced motion to convey a sly sophistication mixed with a healthy dose of sex appeal. Soft black curls fell to frame his brown eyes, holding her attention. His small, boyish features and his tight ass made him look like a member of a boy band. He had the same amount of personality, too, unless he made an effort. But God, he smelled good, his aroma mixing with hers to set in play a series of chemical reactions that whipped her blood and sexual libido high. "I'll wait," he said, smiling.

Oh joy. He'd wait. Art's practiced voice sent a trail of anticipation down her back to settle at the base of her spine. Damn it all to hell, he was hungry. Or maybe he was bored. He'd wait. He'd been waiting six months, learning the best way to manipulate her. And she knew she'd more than enjoy herself if she let him.

Bloodlust in living vampires was tied to their sex drive, an evolutionary adaptation helping ensure an undead vampire would have a willing blood supply to keep him or her sane. Being "bidden for blood" imparted a sexual high; the older and more experienced the vampire, the better the rush, the ultimate, of course, being blood-bidden by a powerful undead undead.

Art had been dead for four decades, having passed the tricky thirty-year ceiling where most undead vampires failed to keep themselves mentally intact and walked into the sun. Why Art was still working was a mystery. He must need the money since he certainly wasn't good at his job.

The vampire breathed deeply as he stood on her threshold, pulling in her mood the way she inhaled a rare fragrance. Sensing her rising agitation, Art rocked into motion, rounding her desk and easing himself down in her leather office chair in the corner. Her face blanked as her pulse quickened. Art was the only person to ever sit there. Most people respected her attempts to avoid office friendships—if her sharp sarcasm and outright ignoring them weren't enough. But then, Art didn't like her for her personality but for the reputation he had yet to get a taste of.

Eyes on her immaculate desk, Ivy exhaled. He was dead, and she was alive. They were both vampires driven by blood: she sexually, he for survival. A match made in heaven—or hell.

Art reclined, smiling, with his long legs crossed and an ankle on one knee, managing to look powerful and relaxed at the same time. He brushed his hair back, trailing his fingers suggestively across his face kept at a clean-shaven tidiness as he tried to blend in with the younger crowd who would be more receptive to what he offered.

A shiver of anticipation rose through her. It didn't make any difference that it came from Art pumping the air full of pheromones rather than true interest. The desire to satiate herself was as much a part of her as breathing. Inescapable. *Why not get it over with? The gossip was because she was resisting, not because it was expected.* And that was why he sat there in his expensive slacks and shirt with his two-hundred-dollar shoes and that confident bad-boy smile. The dead could afford to be patient.

"Tying off some of your loose ends?" she said dryly, glancing at the packet of papers and leaning back. She wanted to cross her arms over her chest, but instead put her boot heels up on the corner of her desk. *Confident. She was in control of herself and her desires.* Art could turn her into a pliant supplicant if he bespelled her, but that was cheating, and he would lose more than face, he'd lose the respect of every vamp in the tower. He had to bid for her blood. Playing on her bloodlust was expected, but bespelling her would piss Piscary off. She wasn't a human to be taken advantage of and the paperwork "adjusted." She was the last living Tamwood vampire, and that demanded respect, especially from him.

"Homicide," he said, his teeth a white flash against his dark skin that hadn't seen the sun in decades. "We can get there before the photographer if you're done with your . . . lunch."

She allowed a sliver of her surprise to show. A homicide wouldn't come with that much information. Not anymore. She had pulled their solved ratio high enough that they were often among the first on the scene. Which meant they'd get an address, not a file. As her eyes returned to the papers he had set over his crotch, he moved them so she was looking right where he wanted her to. Irritation flickered over her. Her eyes rose to meet his gaze, and his smile widened to show a glimpse of teasing fang.

"This?" he said, standing in a graceful motion too fast for a human. "This is your six-month evaluation. Ready to go? It's clear across the bridge in the Hollows."

Ivy stood, part habit and part worry. Her work had been textbook exemplary. Art didn't want her moving up the ladder and out from under him, but the worst scenario would be a reprimand, and she hadn't done anything to warrant that. Actually the worst would be that he'd give her a shitty review and she'd be stuck here another six months.

Her job in homicide was a short stop on the way to where she belonged in upper management, where her mother had been and where Piscary wanted her to be. She had expected to be on this floor for six months, maybe a year, working with Art until her honed skills pulled her into the Arcane Division, and then to management, and finally a lower-basement office. Thank God her money and schooling let her skip the grunt position of runner. Runners were the lowest in the I.S. tower, the cops on the corner giving traffic tickets. Starting there would have put her back a good five years.

Confident and suave, Art brushed by her, his hand trailing across the upper part of her back in a professional show of familiarity that no one could find fault with as he guided her out of her office. "Let's take my car," he said, plucking her purse and coat from behind her door and giving them to her. A jingle of metal pulled her hand up in anticipation, and she caught his keys as he dropped them into her waiting palm. "You drive."

Ivy said nothing, her faint bloodlust evaporating in concern. That he was pleased with her evaluation meant she wouldn't be. Arms swinging as if unconcerned, she walked beside him to the elevators, finding herself in the unusual position of meeting the faces of the few people eating at their desks. She hadn't made friends, so instead of sympathy, she found a mocking satisfaction.

Her tension rose, and she kept her breathing to a measured pace to force her pulse to slow. Whatever Art had scrawled on her evaluation was going to keep her here—her family name and money had pulled her as far as they could. Unless she played office politics, this was where she was going to stay. *With Art? The luscious-smelling, drop-dead gorgeous, but lackluster Art?*

"Well, screw that," she whispered, feeling her blood rise to her skin and her mind shift into overdrive. That was not going to happen. She would work so well and so hard that Piscary would talk to Mrs. Pendleton and get her out of here and where she belonged.

"That's the idea," Art murmured, hearing only her words, not her thoughts. But Piscary wasn't going to help her. The bastard was enjoying the side benefits of her coming home frustrated and hungry from Art's attempts at seducing her blood. If she couldn't handle this alone, then she deserved the humiliation of picking up after Art the rest of her life.

They halted at the twin sets of elevators in the wide

hallway. Ivy stood with her hip cocked, frustrated and listening to the soft conversation filtering in from the nearby offices. Art *was* attractive—more so given the pheromones, God help her—but she didn't respect him, and letting her instincts rule her conscious thought, even to move ahead, sounded like failure to her.

Leaning closer than necessary, Art pushed the UP button. His scent rolled over her, and while fighting the pure pleasure, she watched his eyes go to the heavy clock above the doors to check that the sun was down. She could feel his confidence that the sun would rise with him getting his way, and it pissed her off.

Her booted foot tapped, and her image in the double silver doors did the same. Behind her, Art's reflection watched her with a knowing slant to his pretty-boy features. *He was an ass. A sexy, powerful, conceited, ass.* Because of who she was, it was assumed that she would rise in status by way of her blood, not her skills or knowledge. It was how business was done if you were a vampire. Always had been. Always would be. There were papers to sign and legalities to observe when a vamp set his or her sights on anyone other than another vampire, but having been born into it, she fell under rules older than human or Inderland law. That she had been conditioned to enjoy giving her blood to another left her feeling like a whore if it ended with her being alone. And she knew it would with Art.

As her mother had said, the only way out was to give them what they wanted, to sell herself and keep selling until she reached the top where no one would have a claim on her. If she did this, she would be promoted out from under Art and someone a little smarter and more depraved would be her new partner. Everyone would want a taste of her on her way up. God, she might as well break off her fangs and become an un-claimed shadow. But she had grown up with Piscary and found that the more powerful and older the vam-pire, the more subtle the manipulation, until it could be confused with love.

Taking a slow breath, she touched the ponytail she had put her hair in this afternoon, pulling the band out and shaking the black waist-length hair free. It and her brown eyes were from her mother. Her six-foot height and pale skin she got from her father. Accenting her Asian heritage was an oval face, heart-shaped mouth, thin eyebrows, and a leggy body toned by martial arts. No piercings apart from her ears and a belly button ring Skimmer had sweet-talked her into while high on Brimstone after finals, kept as a reminder. *Twenty-three, and already tired of life.*

Art was gazing at her reflection beside his, and his eyes flashed black when she melted her posture from annoyed to sultry. God, she hated this . . . but she was going to enjoy it, too. *What the hell was wrong with her?*

Pulling away from Art, she set her back casually against the wall and put one foot behind her, balancing it on a toe as they waited for the lift. "You're a fool if you think I'm going to let an evaluation keep me in this crappy job," she said, not caring if the people in earshot heard. They probably had a pool going as to where and when he'd break her skin.

Art moved with an affected slowness, eyes pupil-black. He knew he had her; this was foreplay. Her eyes closed when he placed the flat of his arm beside her head, leaning to whisper in her ear, "I like you follow-ing behind me, tying off my loose ends. Picking up my slack. Doing my—paperwork."

He smelled like leaf ash, dusky and thick, and the

scent went right to the primitive part of her brain and flicked a switch. Her breath caught, then came fast. She hesitated, then with a feeling of self-loathing she knew would fade and return like the sun, she breathed deeply, bringing his scent deep inside, coating her dislike for him with the sweet promise of blood ecstasy, silencing her desire to avoid him with the quick, bitter lust for blood. She knew what she was doing. She knew she would enjoy it. Sometimes, she wondered why she agonized over it. Kisten didn't.

Letting his keys drop to the carpet with her coat and purse, she curled an arm around his neck and pulled him close, an inviting sound lifting through her, realigning her thoughts, shutting down her reasoning to protect her sanity. "What do you want to change my evaluation?"

She sensed more than saw his smile widen as she leaned forward. His earlobe was warm when she put her lips on it, sucking with just a hint of pressure from her teeth. He slid his fingers along her collarbone to rest atop her shoulder, easing his fingers under her shirt. Eyes closing at the growing warmth, her muscles tensed. He exhaled against her, a soft promise to bring her to life with an exquisite need, then satisfy it savagely.

The elevator dinged and slid open, but neither of them moved. Art breathed deeply when the doors closed, an almost subliminal growl that touched the pit of her soul. "Your paperwork is above reproach," he said, his fingers moving to grip the back of her neck.

A jolt of blood-passion lit through her. Without thought, she jerked him forward into her, spinning them until Art's back hit the wall where hers had been. Breath fast, she met his hunger-laced eyes with her own. She felt her jaw tighten and knew her eyes had dilated. *Why had she put this off? It was going to be glorious. What did she care if she respected him? Like he respected her? Like any of them did?*

"And my investigative skills are phenomenal," she said, maneuvering a long leg between his and hooking her foot behind his shoe, tugging until their hips touched. Adrenaline zinged, promising more.

Art smiled, showing his longer canines that death had given him. Hers were short by comparison, but they were more than sharp enough to get the job done. Undead vamps loved them. She likened it to how a sexual pervert loved children. "True," he said, "but your interpersonal skills suck." His smile widened. "More accurately, you don't."

Ivy chuckled low, deep, and honestly. "I do my job, Artie."

The vampire pushed from the elevator, and together they found the opposite wall. Ivy's jaw clenched as he tried to physically manipulate her, making her feel as if she was moving on animal instinct. She had been putting this off so long that it might last all night if she let it.

"This isn't about your job," Art said, his fingers tracing the trails he wanted his lips to follow, but there was a strict policy against bloodletting in the tower. She could tease and flirt, drive him crazy, let him drive her to the brink, but no blood. Until later.

"It's about putting your time in," he continued, and Ivy shivered when his lips touched her neck. *God help her, he'd found an old scar.* Pulse hard and fast, she pushed him away and around again so he was between her and the wall. He let her do it.

"I am putting my time in." Ivy put a hand to his

shoulder and shoved him back. He hit the wall with a thump, black eyes glinting from behind his black curls. "What is my evaluation going to say, Mr. Artie?" She leaned into his neck, taking a fold of skin between her lips and tugging. Her eyes closed, and as her own bloodlust pulsed through her, she forgot that they were standing in the elevator hallway, deep underground, amid the hum of circulation fans and electric-lit black.

Art rode the feeling she knew she was instilling in him, letting it grow. He had been dead long enough to have gained the restraint to string the foreplay out to their limits. "You're argumentative, closed, and refuse to work in a team environment," he said, his voice husky.

"Oh . . ." She pouted, gripping the hair at the base of his scalp hard enough to hurt. "I'm not bad, Mr. Artie. I'm a good little girl . . . when properly motivated."

Her voice had an artful lilt, playful yet domineering, and he responded with a low sound. The bound heat in it hit her, and her fingers released. She had found his limit.

He moved so quickly, she sensed more than saw the motion. His hand abruptly covered hers, forcing her fingers back among the black ringlets at his neck and making them close about them again. "Your evaluation is subjective," he said, his eyes stopping her breath as time balanced. "I decide if you're promoted. Piscary said you'd be a worthwhile hunt, pull me up in the I.S. hierarchy as you resisted, but that you'd give in and I'd have a better job *and* a taste of you."

At that, Ivy paused, jealousy clouding her. Art was conceited enough to believe Piscary was giving her to him when the truth was Piscary was using Art to manipulate her. It was a compliment in a backward way, and she despised herself for loving Piscary all the more, craving the master vampire's attention and favor even as she hated him for it.

"I am giving in," she said, anger joining her blood-lust. It was a potent mix most vamps craved. And here she was, giving it to him. The only thing they liked more was the taste of fear.

But Art's domineering smile surprised her. "No," he admonished, using his undead strength to force her back to the elevators. Her back hit hard, and she inhaled to catch her breath. "It's not that easy anymore," he said. "Six months ago, you could have gotten away with a nip and a new scar I could brag about, but not now. I want to know why Piscary indulges you beyond belief the way he does. I want everything, Ivy. I want your blood *and* your body. Or you don't move from that shitty little office without dragging me with you."

Fear, unusual and shocking, trickled through her and gripped her heart. Art sensed it, and he sucked in air. "God yes," he moaned, his fingers jerking in a spasm. "Give this to me . . ."

Ivy felt her face go cold, and she tried to push Art off her, failing. Blood she could give, but her blood and body both? She had flirted with insanity the year Piscary had called her to him, breaking her, lifting her to glorious heights of passion her young body could scarcely contain before dropping her soul to the basest of levels to pay for it, to make her kneel for more and do anything to please him. She knew it had been a studied manipulation, one practiced on her mother, and her grandmother, and her great-grandmother before that until he was so good at it that the victim wept for the abuse. But that didn't stop her from wanting it.

True to his word, she got as good as she gave. And

she almost killed herself from the highs and lows as Piscary carefully built within her an addiction to the euphoria of sharing blood, warping it, mixing it with her need for love and her craving for acceptance. He had molded her into a savagely passionate blood partner, rich in the exotic tastes that evolve in mixing the deeper emotions of love and guilt with something that, at its basest, was a savage act. That he had done it only to make her blood sweeter didn't matter. It was who she was, and a guilty part of herself gloried in the abandonment she allowed herself there that she denied herself everywhere else.

She had survived by creating the lie that sharing blood was meaningless unless mixed with sex, whereupon it became a way to show someone you loved him or her. She knew that the two were so mixed up in her mind she couldn't separate them, but she had always been in a position to choose who she would share herself with, avoiding the realization that her sanity hung on a lie. But now?

Her eyes fixed on Art's black orbs, taking in his mocking satisfaction and checked bloodlust. He would be an exquisite rush, both beautiful and skilled. He would let her burn, make her weep for his pull upon her, and in return she would give him everything he craved to find and more—and she would wake alone and used, not cradled among sheltering arms that forgave her for her warped needs, even if that forgiveness was born in yet more manipulation.

Jaw clenching, she shoved Art away and moved to get her back from the wall. He fell back a step, surprised.

She did not want to do this. She had protected herself with the lie that blood was just blood, and had been prepared for the mental pain of whoring that much of herself. But Art wanted to mix blood with her body. It would touch too closely to the truth to keep the lie that held her intact. She couldn't do it.

Art's lust shifted to anger, an emotion that crossed into death where compassion couldn't. "Why don't you like me?" he questioned bitterly, jerking her to him. "I'm not enough?"

Ivy's pulse hammered as they stood before the elevators, and she cursed herself for her lack of control. *He was enough. He was more than enough to satisfy her hunger, but she had a soul to satisfy, too.* "You have no ambition," she whispered, instincts pulling her into his warmth even as her mind screamed no. Art's jaw trembled, and his heady scent sang through her, starting a war within her. *What if she couldn't find a way past this?* She had always been able to avoid a test between her instinct and willpower by walking away, but here that wasn't an option.

"Then you aren't looking deep enough." Art gripped her shoulder until it hurt. "Either I get a taste of why Piscary indulges you, or you take me up with you, promotion by promotion. I don't care, Ivy girl."

"Don't call me that," she said, fear mixing with the sexual heat he was pulling from her. Piscary called her that, the bastard. If she gave in, it would start her on the fast track at work but kill what kept her sane. And if she held to her lie and refused, Art had her doing his dirty work.

Art's smile became domineering as he saw her realize the trap. That Piscary had probably arranged the situation to test her resolve only made her love the master vampire more. She was warped. She was warped and lost.

But her very familiarity with the system she had

been born into would save her. As she stilled her panic, her mind started to work, and a wicked smile curled the corner of her lips. "You forgot something, Art," she said, tension falling from her as she faked passivity and hung in his grip. "If you break *my* skin without *my* permission, Piscary will have you staked."

All she had to do was best her hunger. She could do that.

He gripped her tighter, his fingers pressing into her neck where the visible scars of Piscary's claim had been hidden with surgery. The scars were gone, but the potent mix of neuron stimulators and receptor mutagens remained. Piscary had claimed her, sensitized her entire body so that only he could make it resonate to past passions with just his thoughts and pheromones, but she still felt a spike of desire dive to her groin at the thought of Art's teeth sinking cleanly into her. She had to get away from him before her bloodlust took over.

"You knew that, didn't you?" she mocked, her skin tingling.

"You'll enjoy it," he breathed, and the tingles spun into heat. "When I'm done with you, you'll beg for more. Why would you care who bit who first?"

"Because I like to say no," she said, finding it difficult to keep from running her fingernail hard down his neck to bring him alive with desire. She could do it. She knew exactly how exhilarating the feeling of domination and utter control over a monster like him would feel. Her fear was gone, and without it, the bloodlust returned all the harder. "You take my blood without my acquiescence, and I'll get you bumped down to runner," she said. "You can coerce, you can threaten, you can slice your wrist and bleed on my lips, but if you take my blood without me saying yes, then you—lose."

She leaned forward until her lips were almost touching his. "And I win," she finished, pulse fast and aching for him to run his hand against her skin.

He pushed her away. Ivy caught her balance easily, laughing.

"Piscary said you'd resist," he said, his eyes black and tension making his posture both threatening and attractive.

God, the things she could do with this one, she thought in spite of herself. "Piscary is right," she said, cocking her hip and running her hand provocatively down it. "You're in over your head, Art. I like saying no, and I'm going to drive you into taking me without my permission, and then?" She smiled, coming close and curling her arms about his neck and playing with the tips of his curly hair.

Eyes black with hunger, Art smiled, taking her fingers in hers and kissing the tips. The hint of teeth against her skin brought a shiver through her, and her fingers trembled in his grip. "Good," he said, voice husky. "The next six months are going to be pure hell."

Instinct rose and gathered. Licking her lips, she pushed him from her. "You've no idea."

He retreated to the wall beside the elevator. With a friendly ding, the elevator door opened as he bumped the call button. He stepped into the elevator, still wearing that shit-grin. "Coming?" he mocked, looking too damn good to resist in the back of the elevator.

Feeling the pull, she swooped for his keys beside her purse. Her pulse was faster than she liked, and she felt wire-tight from hunger thrumming through her. *Damn it, it was only nine. How was she going to get to the end of her shift without taking advantage of the mail boy?*

"I'm taking my cycle," she said, throwing his keys at

him. "I'll meet you there. Better put your caps on. I want out of this crappy job, and I'd say you've got a week. You won't be able to resist once I put my mind to it."

Art laughed, ducking his head. "I'm older than you think, Ivy. You'll be begging me to sink my teeth by Friday."

The door closed and the elevator rose to the parking garage. Ivy felt her eyes return to normal as the circulation fans pulled away the pheromones they had both been giving off. One week, and she'd be out from under him. One week, and she'd be moving to where she belonged.

"One week, and I'll have that bastard taking advantage of me," she whispered, wondering if at the end of it, she would be counted the winner.

I went an entire two weeks saying no to Piscary, once, Ivy thought as she idled into the apartment complex's parking lot on her cycle's momentum. Art didn't have a shit's chance in a Cincy sewer.

Feeling a flush of confidence, she parked her bike under a streetlight so the assembled I.S. officers could get a good look. It was a Nightwing X–31, one of the few things she had splurged on after getting her job at the I.S. and a paycheck that wasn't tied to Piscary or her mother. When she rode it, she was free. She wasn't looking forward to winter.

Engine rumbling under her provocatively, Ivy took in the multispecies-capability ambulance and the two I.S. cruisers, their lights flashing amber and blue on the faces of gawking neighbors. The U.S. health system had begun catering to mixed species shortly after the Turn, a natural step since only the health care providers who were Inderlanders in hiding survived the T4–Angel virus. But law enforcement had split, and after thirty-six years, would stay that way.

The FIB, or human-run Federal Inderland Bureau, wasn't here yet. Art wasn't here yet, either. She wondered who had called the homicide in. The man in the back of the I.S. cruiser in pajama bottoms and handcuffs? The excited neighbor in curlers talking to an I.S. officer?

Art wasn't the only thing missing, and she scanned the lot for the absent I.S.'s evidence collection van. They wouldn't show until Inderland involvement was confirmed, and while many humans lived across the river to take advantage of the lower taxes in the Hollows, to think that this was strictly a human matter was a stretch.

The man in the car was in custody. If he had been an Inderlander, he'd be in the tower by now. It seemed they had a human suspect and were waiting for the FIB to collect him. She'd probably find the crime scene almost pristine, with only the people removed to help preserve it.

"Idiot human," she muttered, her foot coming down to balance her weight as she shut off her cycle and slid the key into the shallow pocket of her leather pants to leave the skull key chain dangling. She knew what she'd find in his apartment. His wife or girlfriend dead over something stupid like sex or money. Humans didn't know where true rage stemmed from.

Fixing her face into a bland expression to hide her disgust, she removed her helmet and took a deep breath of the night air, feeling the humidity of the unseen river settle deep in her lungs. The man in the back of the cruiser was yelling, trying to get her attention.

"I didn't mean to hurt her!" he cried, muffled through the glass. "It wasn't me. I love Ellie. I love Ellie! You gotta believe me!"

Ivy got off her cycle. Clipping her ID to her short leather jacket, she took a moment to collect herself, concentrating on the damp night. The man's fear, not his girlfriend's blood he was smearing on the windows, pulled a faint rise of bloodlust into existence. His face was scratched, and the welts were bleeding. The man was terrified. Locking him in the cruiser until the FIB picked him up was for his own safety.

Her boot heels making a slow, seductive cadence to draw attention, Ivy walked to the front door and the pool of light that held two officers. Spotting a familiar face, Ivy let some of the tension slip from her and her arms swing free. "Hi, Rat," she said, halting on the apartment complex's six-by-eight common porch. "Haven't you died yet?"

"It's not for lack of trying," the older vamp said, his wrinkles deepening as he smiled. "Where's Art?"

"Biting himself," she said, and his partner, a slight woman, laughed. The living vamp looked right out of high school, but Ivy knew it was a witch charm that kept her that way. The woman was pushing fifty, but the disguise was tax deductible since she used her looks to pacify those who needed . . . pacifying. Ivy nodded warily to her, and got the same in return.

The faint scent of blood coming from the hallway sifted through her brain. It wasn't much, but after Art's play for her, her senses were running in overdrive. "Is the body still in there?" she asked, thinking the situation could be useful. Art hadn't been up long and his resistance would be lower. With a little planning, she might tip him into making a mistake tonight, and she stifled a shudder of anticipation for what that actually meant.

Rat shrugged, eyeing her speculatively. "Body's in the ambulance. You okay?"

His teeth sinking deep into her, the salt of his dusty blood on her tongue, the rush of adrenaline as he drew from her what made her alive . . . "I'm fine," she said.

"Vampire?" she questioned, since they usually left bodies for the morgue unless there was a chance it might decide it was well enough to get up.

Rat's expressive face went hard. "No." His voice was soft, and she took a pair of slip-on booties that his partner extended to her. "Witch. Pretty, too. But since her staked-excuse of a husband was encouraged to ignore his rights and confessed to beating her up and strangling her, they moved her out. He's a paint job, Ivy. Only good for draining and painting the walls."

Ivy frowned, not following his gaze to the man shouting in the cruiser. *They moved her?*

Rat saw her annoyance and added, "Shit, Ivy. He confessed. We got pictures. There's nothing here."

"There's nothing here when I say there's nothing here," she said, stiffening when the recognizable rumble of Art's late-model Jaguar came through the damp night. Damn it, she had wanted to be in there first.

Ivy's exposed skin tingled, and she felt a wash of self-disgust. God help her, she was going to use a crime scene to get Art off her back. Someone had died, and she was going to use that to seduce Art into biting her against her will. How depraved could she be? But it was an old feeling, quickly repressed like all the other ugly things in her life.

Handing her purse to Rat, she got a packet of evidence bags and wax pencil in return. "I want the collection van here," she said, not caring that Rat had just told her to collect any evidence she thought pertinent herself. "I want the place vacuumed as soon as I'm out. And I want you to stop doing my job."

"Sorry, Ivy." Rat grinned. "Hey, there's a poll started about you and Art—"

Ivy stepped forward, coiled arm extending. Rat

blocked it, grabbing her wrist and pulling her off balance and into him. She fell into his chest, his weight twice hers. His partner snicked. Ivy had known the strike would never land, but it had burned off a little frustration.

"You know," Rat breathed, the scent of his partner's blood fresh on his breath from an earlier tryst, "you really shouldn't wear those high-heeled boots. They make your balance suck."

Ivy twisted and broke from him. "I hear they hurt more when I crotch-kick bastards like you," she said, the fading adrenaline making her head hurt. "Who else has been in there?" she asked, thinking a room stinking of fear would be just the thing to tip Art into a mistake. He was currently standing by the cruiser, looking at the human and letting his blood-ardor grow. *Idiot.*

Rat was rubbing his lower neck in invitation. God, it had started already. By sunup, they'd all think she was in the market to build up the IOUs necessary to reach the lower basement and she'd be mobbed. Imagining the coming innuendos, suggestions, and unwanted offers, Ivy stifled a sigh. *Like the pheromones weren't bad enough already?* Maybe she should start a rumor she had an STD.

"The ambulance crew," the vampire was saying. "Tia and me to get him out. He was crying over her as usual. A neighbor called it in as a domestic disturbance. Third one this month, but when it got quiet, she got scared and made the call."

Frowning, Ivy took a last breath of clean night air, and stepped into the hall. Not too many people to confuse things, and Rat knew not to touch anything. The room would be as clean as could be expected. And *she* wasn't going to sully it.

The tang of blood strengthened, and after slipping on the blue booties, she bent to duck under the tape across the open door. She stopped inside, taking in someone else's life: low ceilings, matted carpet, old drapes, new couch, big but cheap TV, even cheaper stereo, and hundreds of CDs. There were self-framed pictures of people on the walls and arranged on the pressboard entertainment shelves. The feminine touches were spotty, like paint splatters. The victim hadn't lived here very long.

Ivy breathed deeply, tasting the anger left in the air, invisible signposts that would fade with the sun. Blue booties scuffing, she followed the scent of blood to the bathroom. A red handprint gripped the rim of the toilet, and there were several smears on the tub and curtain. Someone had cut his scalp on the tub. The pink bulb gave an unreal cast, and Ivy shut off the exhaust fan with the end of her wax pencil, making a mental note to tell Rat that she had.

The soft hum stopped. In the new silence, she heard the soft conversation and laugh track of a sitcom coming from a nearby apartment. Art's satisfied voice filtered in from the hallway, and Ivy's blood pressure rose. Rat had said the man had strangled his wife. She'd seen worse. And though he hadn't said where they found the body, an almost palpable anger flowed over the bedroom's doorjamb, broken about the latch with newly painted-over cracks.

Ivy touched the hidden damage with a finger. The bedroom had the same mix of careless bachelor and young woman trying to decorate with little money to spend. Cheap frilly pillows, pink lace draped over ugly lampshades, dust thick on the metal blinds that were never opened. No blood but for smears, and they were likely the suspect's. Pretty clothes in pink and white were strewn on the bed and floor, and the closet was empty. She had tried to leave. A black TV was in the corner, the remote broken on the floor under a dent in the wall smelling of plaster. On the carpet was Rat's card and a Polaroid of the woman, askew on the floor by the bed.

Forcing her jaw to unclench, Ivy pulled the air deep into her, reading the room as if the last few hours of emotion had painted the air in watercolors. Any vampire could.

The man in the car had hurt the woman, terrified her, beat her up, and her magic hadn't stopped him. She had died here, and the heady scents of her fear and his anger started a disturbing and not entirely unwelcome bloodlust in Ivy's gut. Her fingertips ached, and her throat seemed to swell.

The sound of Art's scuffing steps cut painfully through her wide-open senses. A thrill of adrenaline built and vanished. Eyes half lidded, she turned, finding a seductive tilt to her hips. Art's eyes were almost fully dilated. Clearly the fear of the man outside and its echo still vibrating through the room were tugging on his instincts. Maybe this was why he continued to work homicide. Pretty man couldn't get his fangs wet without a little help, maybe?

"Ivy," he said, his voice sending that same shiver through her, and she felt a dropping sensation that said her eyes were dilating. "I make the call for the evidence van, not you."

Posture shifting, Ivy stepped to keep him from getting between her and the door. "You were busy jacking off on the suspect's fear," she said lightly. She moved as if to leave, knowing if she played the coy victim it would trigger his bloodlust. As expected, Art's pupils went wider, blacker. She felt his presence rise up behind her, almost as if pushing her into him. He was pulling an aura, not a real one, but simply strengthening his vampiric presence.

Art snatched her arm, domineering and possessive. Teasing, she feigned to draw away until his grip tightened. "I call the van," he said, voice dangerous.

"What's the matter, Art?" she said languorously, pulling her wrist and his hand gripping it to her upper chest. "Don't like a woman who thinks?" Sexual tension lanced through her. Enjoying it, she put a knuckle between her lips, letting it go with a soft kiss and a skimming of teeth. Piscary had made her who she was, and despite his experience, Art didn't have a chance.

"You think I'm going to lose it over a fear-laced room and a pair of black eyes?" he said, looking good in his Italian suit and smelling deliciously of wool, ash, and himself.

"Oh, I'm just getting started." With her free hand, she took Art's fingers off her wrist. He didn't stop her. Smiling, she ran her tongue across her teeth, hiding them even as they flashed. The fear in the room flowed through her, inciting instincts older than the pyramids, screaming unhindered through her younger body. She stiffened at the potent rush of blood rising to her skin. She expected it, riding and enjoying it. It wasn't the scent of blood, it was the fear. *She could handle this. She controlled her bloodlust; her bloodlust didn't control her.*

And when she felt that curious drop of pressure in her face as her eyes dilated fully, she turned to Art, her paper-clad boots spread wide as she stood in the middle of the room stinking of sex and blood and fear, lips parted as she exhaled provocatively. A tremble lifted through her, settling in her groin to tell her what could follow if she let it. She wouldn't give him her blood willingly, and that he might forcibly take it was unexpectedly turning her on.

"Mmmm, it smells good in here," she said, the adrenaline high scouring through her because *she* was in control. She was in control of this monster who could kill her with a backhanded slap, who could rip out her throat and end her life, who could make her powerless under him—and who couldn't touch her blood until she allowed him, bound by tradition and unwritten law. And if he tried, she'd have his ass and a better job both.

Pulse fast, she took a step closer. He wanted her—he was so ready, his shoulders were rock hard and his hands were fists to keep from reaching for her. His inner struggle was showing on his face, and he wasn't breathing anymore. There was a reason Piscary indulged her. This was part of it, but Art would never taste it all.

"Can't have . . . this," she said, her hand sliding up from her inner thigh, fingers spread wide as they crossed her middle to her chest until they lay provocatively to hide her neck. She felt her pulse lift and fall against them, stirring herself as much as Art. Her eyes were on the vampire before her. He would be savagely magnificent. She exhaled, imagining his teeth sinking into her, reminding her she was alive with the promise of death in his lips.

Almost . . . it might be worth letting him have his way.

Art read her thought in the very air. In a flash of motion too fast for her to follow, he moved. Ivy gasped, her core pulsing with fear. He jerked her to him. His hand gripped the back of her neck, the other twisted her arm painfully behind her. He hesitated as he caught himself, his eyes black and pained with the control needed to stop. She laughed, low and husky.

"Can't have this," she taunted, wishing he would take it as she lolled her head back to expose the length of her neck. *Oh God. If only he would . . .* she thought, a faint tickling in her thoughts warning her a war had started between her hunger and will.

"Give it to me," Art managed, his voice strained, and she smiled as he started to weaken. "Give this to me . . ."

"No," she breathed. Her pulse lifted under his hand, and her eyes closed. Her body demanded she say yes, she wanted to say yes. *Why,* she thought, hunger driving through her as she found his hard shoulders, *why didn't she say yes? Such a small thing . . . And he was so deliciously beautiful, even if he didn't stir her soul.*

Art sensed her falter, a low growl rising up through him. He pressed her to him, almost supporting her weight. With a new resolve, he nuzzled the base of her neck.

Ivy sucked in her air, clutching him closer. Fire. This was fire, burning promises from her neck to her groin.

"Give this to me," he demanded, his lips brushing the words against her skin. His hand slipped farther, edging between her coat and shirt, cupping her breast. "Everything . . ." he breathed, his exhalation filling her, making her whole.

In a breathless wave, instinct rose, crushing her will. *No!* she panicked even as her body writhed for it. It would turn her into a whore, break her will and crack the lie that kept her sane. But with a frightened jolt, Ivy realized her lips had parted to say yes.

Reality flashed through her, and with a surge of fear, she kneed him in the crotch.

Art let go, falling to kneel before her, his hands covering himself. Not waiting, she fell back a step and snapped a front kick to his jaw. His head rocked back and he hit the floor beside the bed. "You stupid bitch," he gasped.

"Ass," she panted, trembling as her body rebelled at the sudden shift of passions. She stood above him, fighting the desire to fall on him, sink her teeth into him while he knelt helpless before her. Damn it, she had to get out of this room. Two unrequited plays for her blood in one night was pushing it.

Slowly Art lost his hunched position and started to chuckle. Ivy felt her face flame. "Get off the floor," she snapped, backing up. "They haven't vacuumed yet."

Still laughing, Art rolled onto his side. "This is going to be one hell of a week," he said, then hesitated, eyes on the carpet just beyond the bedspread knocked askew. "Give me a collection bag," he said, reaching into his back pocket.

Bloodlust still ringing in her, Ivy came forward, pulled by his intent tone. "What is it?"

"Give me a bag," he repeated, his expensive suit clashing with the ugly carpet.

She hesitated, then scooped up the bags from where they had fallen. Checking the time, Ivy jotted down the date and location before handing it to Art. Still on the floor, Art reached under the bed and rolled something shiny into the light with a pen from his pocket. With an eerie quickness, he flicked it into the bag and stood. The growing brown rim about his pupils said he was in control, and smiling to show his teeth, he lifted the bag to the light.

Seeing his confidence, Ivy felt a flash of despair. It had been a game to him. He had never been in danger of losing his restraint. *Shit,* she thought, the first fingers of doubt she could do this slithering about her heart.

But then she saw what he held, and her worry turned to understanding—and then true concern. "A banshee tear?" she asked, recognizing the tear-shaped black crystal.

Suddenly the words of the distraught man in the car had a new meaning. *I didn't mean to hurt her. It wasn't me.* Pity came from nowhere, making the slice of low-income misery surrounding her all the more distasteful. He probably *had* loved her. It had been a banshee, feeding him rage until he killed his wife, whereupon the banshee wallowed in her death energy.

It was still murder, but the man had been a tool, not the perpetrator. The murderer was at large somewhere in Cincinnati, with the alibi of time and distance making it hard to link her to the crime. That's why the tear had been left as a conduit. The banshee had targeted the couple, followed them home, left a tear when they were out, and when sparks flew, added to the man's rage until he truly wasn't capable of resisting. It wasn't an excuse; it was murder by magic—a magic older than vampires. Perhaps older than witches or demons.

Art shook the bag to make the black jewel glitter before letting his arm drop. "We have every banshee on record. We'll run the tear through the computer and get the bitch."

Ivy nodded, feeling her pupils contract. The I.S. kept close tabs on the small population of banshees, and if one was feeding indiscriminately in Cincinnati, they could expect more deaths before they caught her.

"Now, where were we," Art said, slipping an arm about her waist.

"Bastard," Ivy said, elbowing him in the gut and stepping away. But the strike never landed, and she schooled her face to no emotion when he chuckled at her a good eight feet back. God, he made her feel like a child. "Why don't you go home after the sun comes up," she snarled.

"You offering to tuck me in?"

"Go to hell."

From the hallway came the sounds of soft conversation. The collection van was here. Art breathed deep, bringing the scents of the room into him. His eyes closed and his thin lips curled upward as he exhaled, apparently happy with what he sensed. Ivy didn't need to breathe to know that the room stank of her fear now, mixing with the dead woman's until it was impossible to tell them apart.

"See you back at the tower, Ivy."

Not if I stake you first, she thought, wondering if calling in sick tomorrow was worth the harassment she'd get the next day. She could say she'd been to the doctor about her case of STD—tell everyone she got it from Art.

Art sauntered out of the room, one hand in his pocket, the other dropping the banshee tear onto the entering officer's clipboard. The werewolf's eyes widened, but then he looked up, eyes watering. "Whoa!" he said, nose wrinkling. "What have you two been doing in here?"

"Nothing." Ivy felt cold and small in her leather pants and short coat as she stood in the center of the room and listened to Art say good-bye to Rat and Tia. She forced her hands from her neck to prove it was unmarked.

"Doesn't smell like nothing," the man scoffed. "Smells like someone—"

Ivy glared at him as his words cut off. Adrenaline

pulsed, this time from worry. She had contaminated a crime scene with her fear, but the man's eyes held pity, not disgust.

"Are you okay?" he asked softly, his clipboard held to himself as he obviously guessed what had happened. There was too much fear in here for just one person, even a murdered one.

"Fine," she said shortly. Psychic fear levels weren't recorded unless a banshee was involved. That she hadn't known one was, wasn't an excuse. She'd get reprimanded at the least, worse if Art wanted to blackmail her. And he would. Damn it, could she make this any easier for him? Flushed, she scooped up the rest of the collection bags and gave them to the Were.

"I don't know how you can work with the dead ones," the man said, trying to catch her eyes, but Ivy wouldn't let him. "Hell, they scare my tail over my balls just looking at me."

"I said, I'm fine," she muttered. "I want it vacuumed, dusted, and photographed. Don't bother with a fear level profile. I contaminated it." She could keep quiet about it, but she'd rather suffer an earned reprimand than Art's blackmail. "Keep the tear from the press," she added, glancing at it, small and innocuous on his clipboard. "The last thing we need is the city in a panic, calling us every time a high schooler cries over her boyfriend."

The man nodded. His stubble was thick, and stifling the thought of how it would feel to rake her fingers and then her teeth over it, Ivy strode from the room, fleeing the stink of the dead woman's fear. She didn't like how it smelled exactly like her own.

Ivy passed quickly through the living room and into the hallway, trying not to breathe. She should have planned this, not made a fool of herself by acting on impulse. Because of her assumptions, Art had her by the short hairs. Avoiding him the rest of her day was going to be impossible. Maybe she could spend it researching banshees. The files were stored in the upper levels. Art might follow her, but the Inderlander ratio would be slanted to witch and Were, not only reducing the pheromone levels, but also making it easier to pull out early since the entire tower above ground emptied at midnight with their three to twelve shift. Only the belowground offices maintained the variable sunset to sunrise schedule.

Wine, she thought, forcing herself to look confident and casual when she emerged on the stoop and found the lights of a news crew already illuminating the parking lot. She'd pick up two bottles on the way home so Kisten would be drunk enough not to care if she hurt him.

3

Even with her intentions to leave at midnight, the sun was up by the time Ivy was idling her bike through the Hollows's rush-hour traffic, winding her way to the waterfront and the spacious apartment she and Kisten shared above Piscary's restaurant. That she worked for the force that policed the underground he controlled wasn't surprising or unintentional, but prudent planning. Though not on the payroll, Piscary ran the I.S. through a complicated system of favors. He still had to obey the laws—or at least not get caught breaking them lest he get hauled in like anyone else. It reminded Ivy of what Camelot had probably really been like.

Her mother had worked in the top of the I.S. hierarchy until she died, and Ivy knew that was where she and Piscary wanted Ivy to be. Piscary dealt in gambling and protection—on paper, both legal ways to make his money—and the master vampire had more finesse than to put her where she'd have to choose between doing what he wanted and what her job required. The corruption was that bad.

Or that good, Ivy thought, checking to see that the guy behind her was watching before she slowed and turned left into the restaurant's parking lot. If it hadn't been for the threat of Piscary coming down on aggressive vampires in backstreet justice, the I.S. wouldn't be able to cope. She was sure that was why most people, including the FIB, looked the other way. The I.S. was corrupt, but the people actually in charge of the city did a good job keeping it civilized.

Ivy slowed her bike by the door to the kitchen and cut the engine, scanning the empty lot. It was Wednesday, and whereas any other day of the week the restaurant would be emptying out of the last stragglers, today it was deserted. Piscary liked a day of rest. At least she wouldn't have to dodge the waitstaff and their questions as to why her eyes were half dilated. She needed either a long bubble bath before bed, or Kisten, or both.

The breeze off the nearby river was cool and carried the scent of oil and gas. Taking a breath to clear her mind, she pushed the service door open with the wheel of her bike. It didn't even have a lock to let the produce trucks make their deliveries at all hours. No one would steal from Piscary. For all appearances he obeyed the law, but somehow, you'd find yourself dead anyway.

Purse and twin wine bottles in hand, she left her bike beside the crates of tomatoes and mushrooms and took the cement steps to the kitchen two at a time. She passed the dark counters and cold ovens without seeing them. The faint odor of rising yeast mixed with the lingering odors of the vampires who worked here, and she felt herself relax, her boots making a soft cadence on the tiled floor. The scent brought to memory thoughts of her summers working in the kitchen and, when old enough, on the floor as a waitress. She hadn't been innocent, but then the ugliness had been lost in the glare of the thrill. Now it just made her tired.

Her pulse quickened when she passed the thick door that led to the elevator and Piscary's underground apartments. The thought that he would meet her with soothing hands and calculated sympathy was enough to bring her blood to the surface, but her irritation that he was manipulating her kept her moving into the bar. He wouldn't call her to him, knowing it would cause her more mental anguish to come begging to him when she could take no more, desperate for the reassurance that he still loved her.

It was comfortingly silent in the restaurant proper, and the low ceilings and dim atmosphere seemed to follow her into the closed-party rooms in the back. A wide stairway behind a door led to the private second floor. Her hand traced the wall for balance as she rose up the wide, black-wood stairs, eager to find Kisten and an understanding ear that wasn't attached to a manipulating mind.

She and Kisten lived in the converted apartment that took up the entire top floor of the old shipping warehouse. Ivy liked the openness, arbitrarily dividing it into spaces with folding screens and strategically placed furniture. The windows were spacious and smeared on the outside with the dirt and grime of forty years. Piscary didn't like being that exposed, and this granted the two of them a measure of security.

Wine bottles clinking, Ivy set them on the table at the top of the stairs, thinking she and Kisten were like two abused children, craving the attention of the very person who had warped them, loving him out of desperation. It was an old thought, one that had lost its sting long ago.

Shuffling off her coat, she set it and her purse by the wine. "Kist?" she called, her voice filling the silence. "I'm home." She picked the bottles back up and frowned. Maybe she should have gotten three.

There was no answer, and as she headed back toward the kitchen to chill the wine, the scent of blood shivered through her like an electrical current. It wasn't Kisten's.

Her feet stopped, and she breathed deeply. Her head swiveled to the corner where the deliverymen had put her baby grand last week. It had dented her finances more than the bike, but the sound of it in this emptiness made her forget everything until the echoes faded.

"Kist?"

She heard him take a breath, but didn't see him. Her face blanked and every muscle tightened as she paced to the couches arranged about her piano. The dirty sunshine pooling in glinted on the black sheen of the wood, and she found him there, kneeling on the white Persian rug between the couch and the piano, a girl in tight jeans, a black lacy shirt, and a worn leather coat sprawled before him.

Kisten lifted his head, an unusual panic in his blue eyes. "I didn't do it," he said, his bloodied hands hovering over the corpse.

Shit. Dropping the bottles on the couch, Ivy swung into motion, moving to kneel before them. Habit made her check for a pulse, but it was obvious by her pallor and the gentle mauling on her neck that the petite blond was dead despite her warmth.

"I didn't do it," Kisten said again, shifting his trim, pretty-boy body back a few inches. His hands, strong and muscular, were shaking, the tops of his fingernails red with a light sheen. Ivy looked from them to his face, seeing the fear in his almost delicate features that he hid behind a reddish blond beard. A smear of blood was on his forehead behind his brown bangs, and she stifled an urge to kiss it away that both disgusted and intrigued her. *This is not who I wanted to be.*

"I didn't do it, Ivy!" he exclaimed at her continued silence, and she reached over the girl and brushed his too-long bangs back. The gentle swelling of black in his gaze made her breath catch. God, he was beautiful when he was agitated.

"I know you didn't," she said, and Kisten's wide shoulders relaxed, making her wonder if that was why he was upset. It wasn't that he had to take care of Piscary's mistake, but that Ivy might think he had killed her. And somewhere in there, she found that he loved her.

The pretty woman was Piscary's favorite body type with long fair hair and an angular face. She probably had blue eyes. *Shit, shit, and more shit.* Mind calculating how to minimize the damage, she asked, "How long has she been dead?"

"Minutes. No more than that." Kisten's resonant voice dropped to a more familiar pitch. "I was trying to find out where she was staying and get her cleaned up, but she died right here on the couch. Piscary . . ." He met her eyes, reaching up to tug on a twin pair of diamond-stud earrings. "Piscary told me to take care of it."

Ivy shifted her weight to her feet, easing back to sit on the edge of the nearby couch. It wasn't like Kisten to panic like this. He was Piscary's scion, the person the undead vampire had tapped to manage the bar, do his daylight work, and clean up his mistakes. Mistakes that were usually four foot eleven, blond, and a hundred pounds. Damn it all to hell. Piscary hadn't slipped like this since she had left to finish high school on the West Coast.

"Did she sign the release papers?" she asked.

"Do you think I'd be this upset if she had?" Kisten arranged the small woman's hair as if it would help. God, she looked fourteen, though Ivy knew she'd be closer to twenty.

Ivy's lips pressed together and she sighed. So much for getting any sleep this morning. "Get the plastic wrap from the piano out of the recycling bin," she said in decision, and Kisten rose, tugging the tails of his silk shirt down over the tops of his jeans. "We open in eight hours for the early Inderland crowd, and I don't want the place smelling like dead girl."

Kisten rocked into motion, headed for the stairs. "Move faster, unless you want to have the carpet steam cleaned!" Ivy called, and she heard him jump to the floor from midway down.

Tired, Ivy looked at the woman's abandoned purse on the couch, too emotionally exhausted to figure out how she should feel. Kisten was Piscary's scion, but it was Ivy who did most of the thinking in a pinch. It wasn't that Kisten was stupid—far from it—but he was used to having her take over. Expected it. Liked it.

Wondering if Piscary had killed the girl on purpose to force Kisten to take responsibility, Ivy stood with her hands on her hips, her eyes going to the filthy windows and the river hazy in the morning sun. It sounded just like the manipulative bastard. If Ivy had succumbed to Art, she would have spent the morning at his place—not only obediently taking the next step to the management position Piscary wanted for her, but forcing Kisten to handle this alone. That things hadn't gone the way he planned probably delighted Piscary;

he took pride in her defiance, anticipating a more delicious fall when she could fight no longer.

Warped, ruined, ugly, she thought, watching the tourist paddleboats steam as they stoked their boilers. Was there any time she hadn't been?

The sliding sound of plastic brought her around, and with no wasted motion or eye contact, she and Kisten rolled the woman onto it before her bowels released. Crossing her arms over her like an Egyptian mummy, they wrapped her tightly. Ivy watched her hands, not the plastic-blurred face of the woman, trying to divorce herself from what they were doing as they passed the duct tape Kisten had brought around her like lights on a Christmas tree.

Only when she had been transformed from a person to an object did Kisten exhale, slow and long. Ivy would cry for her later. Then cry for herself. But only when no one could hear.

"Refrigerator," Ivy said, and Kisten balked. Ivy looked at him as she stood bent over the corpse with her hands already under the woman's shoulders. "Just until we decide what to do. Danny will be here in four hours to start the dough and press the pasta. We don't have time to ditch the body *and* clean up."

Kisten's eyes went to the blood-smeared rug. He lifted a foot and winced at the tacky brown smear on it, tracked downstairs and back again. "Yeah," he said, his fake British accent gone, then took the long bundle entirely from Ivy and hoisted it over his shoulder.

Ivy couldn't help but feel proud of him for catching his breath so quickly. He was only twenty-three, having taken on Piscary's scion position at the age of seventeen when Ivy's mother had accidentally died five years ago and abdicated the position. Piscary was active in his control of Cincinnati, and Kisten had little more to do than tidy up after the master vamp and keep him happy. Stifling her tinge of jealousy that Kisten had the coveted position was easy.

Piscary's savage tutorial had made her old before she had begun to live. She wouldn't think about what she was doing until it was over. Kisten hadn't yet learned the trick and lived every moment as it happened, instead of over and over in his mind as she did. It made him slower to react, more . . . human. And she loved him for it.

"Is there a car to get rid of?" she asked, already on damage control. She hadn't noticed one in the parking lot, but she hadn't been looking.

"No." Kisten headed downstairs with her following, his vampire strength handling the weight without stress. "She came in with Piscary right around midnight."

"Off the street?" she asked in disbelief, glad the restaurant had been closed.

"No. The bus station. Apparently she's an old friend."

Ivy glanced at the woman over his shoulder. She was only twenty at the most. How old a friend could she be? Piscary didn't like children, despite her size. It was looking more and more likely Piscary *had* orchestrated this to help Kisten stand on his own. Not only planned it, but built in the net of the woman's cryptic origins in case Kisten should fall. The master vamp hadn't counted on Ivy catching him first, and she felt a pang of what she would call love for Kisten—if she knew she could feel the emotion without tainting it with the desire for blood.

Ivy caught sight of Kisten's grimace when she moved to open the door to the kitchen. "Piscary killed her on purpose," he said, adjusting the woman's weight on his shoulder, and Ivy nodded, not wanting to tell him about her own part in the lesson.

Tucking a fabric napkin from the waiting stack into her waistband, she yanked up the handle of the walk-in refrigerator and slid a box with her foot to prop it open. Kisten was right behind her, and in the odd combination of moist coldness Piscary insisted his cheese be kept at, she moved a side of lamb thawing out for Friday's buffet, insulating her hands with the napkin to prevent heat marks from making it obvious someone had moved it.

Behind the hanging slab was a long low bed of boxes, and Kisten laid the woman there, covering the blur of human features with a tablecloth. Ivy had the fleeting memory of seeing a similar bundle there once before. She and Kisten had been ten and playing hide-and-seek while their parents finished their wine and conversation. Piscary had told them she was someone from a fairy tale and to play in the abandoned upstairs. Seemed like they were still playing upstairs, but now the games were more convoluted and less under their control.

Kisten met her eyes, their deep blue full of recollection. "Sleeping Beauty," he said, and Ivy nodded. That was what they had called the corpse. Feeling like a little girl hiding a broken dish, she moved the slab of lamb back to partially hide the body.

Cold from more than the temperature, she followed him out, kicking the box out of the way and leaning against the door when it shut. Her eyes went to the time clock by the door. "I'll get the living room and stairs if you take the elevator," she said, not wanting to chance running into Piscary. He wouldn't be angry with her for helping Kisten. No, he'd be so amused she had put off Art again that he would invite her into his bed, and she would quiver inside and go to him, forgetting all about Kisten and what she had been doing. God, she hated herself.

Kisten reached for the mop and she added, "Use a new mop head, then put the old one back on when you're done. We're going to have to burn it along with the rug."

"Right," he said, his jaw flushing as it clenched. While Kisten filled a bucket, Ivy made a fresh batch of the spray they wiped the restaurant tables down with. Diluted, it removed the residual vamp pheromones, but at full strength, it would break down the blood enzymes that most cleaning detergents left behind. Maybe it was a little overkill, but she was a careful girl.

It would be unlikely to have the woman traced here, but it wasn't so much for eliminating her presence from a snooping I.S. or FIB agent as it was avoiding having the restaurant smell like blood other than hers and Kisten's. That might lead to questions concerning whether the restaurant's mixed public license, or MPL, had been violated. Ivy didn't think her explanation that, no, no one had been bitten on the premises—Piscary had drained a woman in his private apartments—and therefore the MPL was intact, would go over well. From the amount of aggravation Piscary had endured to get his MPL reinstated the last time some fool Were high on Brimstone had drawn blood, she thought he'd prefer a trial and jail to losing his MPL again. But the real reason Ivy was being so thorough was that she didn't want her apartment smelling like anyone but her and Kisten.

Her thoughts brought her gaze back to him. He looked nice with his head bowed over the bucket, his light bangs shifting in the water droplets being flung up as it filled.

Clearly unaware of her scrutiny, he turned the water off. "I am such an ass," he said, watching the ripples settle.

"That's what I like about you," she said, worried she might have made him feel inadequate by taking over.

"I am." He didn't look at her, hands clenching the rim of the plastic bucket. "I froze. I was so damn worried about what you were going to say when you came home and found me with a dead girl, I couldn't think."

Finding a compliment in there, she smiled, digging through a drawer to get a new mop head. "I knew you didn't kill her. She had Piscary all over her."

"Damn it, Ivy!" Kisten exclaimed, lashing the flat of his hand out to hit the spigot, and there was a crack of metal. "I should be better than this! I'm his fucking scion!"

Ivy's shoulders dropped. Sliding the drawer shut, she went to him and put her hands on his shoulders. They were hard with tension, and he did nothing to acknowledge her touch. Tugging into him, she pressed her cheek against his back, smelling the lingering fear on him, and the woman's blood. Eyes closing, she felt her bloodlust assert itself. Death and blood didn't turn on a vampire. Fear and the chance to *take* blood did. There was a difference.

Her hands eased around his front, fingers slipping past the buttons to find his abs. Only now did Kist bow his head, softening into her touch. Her teeth were inches from an old scar she had given him. The intoxicating smell of their scents mixing hit her, and she swallowed. The headiest lure of all. Her chest pressed into him as she breathed deep, intentionally bringing his scent into her, luring fingers of sexual excitement to stir along her spine. "Don't worry about it," she said, her voice low.

"You'd be a better scion then I am," he said bitterly. "Why did he pick me?"

She didn't think this was about which one of them was his scion but his stress looking for an outlet. Giving in to her urge, she lifted onto her toes to reach his ear. "Because you like people more than I do," she said. "Because you're better at talking to them, getting them to do what you want and having them think it was their idea. I just scare people."

He turned, slowly so he would stay in her arms. "I run a bar," he said, eyes downcast. "You work for the I.S. You tell me which is more valuable."

Ivy's arms slipped to his waist, pressing him back into the edge of the sink. "I'm sorry for the pizza delivery crap," she said, meaning it. "You aren't running a bar, you're learning Cincinnati, what moves who, and who will do anything for whom. Me?" Her attention went to the wisp of hair showing at the V of his shirt. "I'm learning how to kiss ass and suck neck."

His gaze hard with self-recrimination, Kisten shook his head. "Piscary dropped a dead girl in my lap, and I sat over her and wrung my hands. You walked in and things happened. What about the next time when it's something important and I fuck it up?"

Running her hands up the smooth expanse of silk to his shoulders, she closed her eyes at the deliciously erotic sensation growing in her. Guilt mixed with it. She was ugly. All she had wanted to do was console Kisten, but the very act of comforting him was turning her on.

The thought of Art and what had almost happened hit her. Between one breath and the next, the muscles where her jaw hinged tightened and her eyes dilated. *Shit. May as well give in.* Feeling like a whore, she opened her eyes and fixed them on Kisten's. His were as black as her own, and a spike of anticipation dove to her middle. *Warped and twisted. Both of them. Was there any way to show she cared other than this?*

"You'll handle it," she whispered, wanting to feel her lips pulling on something, anything. The soft skin under his chin glistened from the thrown-up mist, begging her to taste it. "I save your ass. You save mine," she said. It was all she had to offer.

"Promise?" he said, sounding lost. Apparently it was enough.

The lure was too much, and she pulled herself closer to put her lips softly against the base of his neck, letting his pulse rise and fall teasingly under her. She felt as if she was dying: screaming because they needed each other to survive Piscary, pulse racing in what was going to follow, and despairing that the two were connected.

"I promise," she whispered. Eyes closed, she raked her teeth over skin but didn't pierce as her fingers lifted through the clean softness of his hair.

Kisten's breath came fast, and with one arm he picked her up and set her on the counter, forcing his way between her knees. She felt her gaze go sultry when his hands went behind her hips, edging over the top of her pants. "You're hungry," he said, a dangerous lilt to his voice.

"I'm past hungry," she said, twining her hands behind his neck as if bound. Her voice was demanding, but in truth she was helpless before him. It was the bane of the vampire that the strongest was the most in need. And Kisten knew the games they played as well as she did. Her thoughts flitted to Sleeping Beauty in the refrigerator, and she shoved away the loathing that she wanted to feel Kisten's blood fill her not ten minutes after a woman had died in their apartment. The self-disgust she would deal with later. She was eminently proficient at denying it existed.

"Art bothering you again?" he said, his almost delicate features sly as he slipped a hand under her shirt. The firm warmth of his fingers was like a spike through her.

"Still . . ." she said, stifling a tremor to entice the feeling to grow.

His free hand traced across her shoulder and her collarbone to slide up the opposite length of her neck. "I'll have to write a letter and thank him," he said.

Eyes flashing open, Ivy yanked him to her, wrapping her legs around him, imprisoning him against her. His hands were gone from her waist, leaving only a cool warmth. "He wants my blood and my body," Ivy said, feeling her lust for Kisten mix with her disgust for Art. "He's getting nothing. I'm going to drive him into taking my blood against my will."

Kisten's breath was against her neck, and his hands were at the small of her back. "What's that going to get you?"

A smile, unseen and evil, spread across her as she looked over his shoulder to the empty kitchen. "Satisfaction," she breathed, feeling herself weaken. "He promotes me out from under him to keep my mouth shut or he becomes the laughingstock of the entire tower." But she didn't know if she could do it anymore. He was stronger than she had given him credit.

"That's my girl," Kisten said, and she sucked in her breath when he bent his head, his teeth gently working an old scar to send a delicious dart of anticipation

through her. "You're *such* a political animal. Remind
me never to cross stakes with you."

Breathless, she couldn't answer. The thought of having to deal with the contaminated scene flitted past,
and was gone.

"You'll need practice saying no," Kisten murmured.

"Mmmm." Eyes open, she found herself moving
against him as his hands pulled her closer. His head
dropped, and her hands splayed across his back curled
so her fingers dug into him. Kisten's lips played with
the base of her neck, moving ever lower.

"Could you say no if he did this?" Kisten whispered,
grazing his teeth along her bare skin while his hands
under her shirt traced a path to her breast.

The two feelings were joined in her mind, and it felt
as if it was his teeth on her breast. "Yes . . ." she
breathed, exhilarated. He worked the hem of her shirt,
and she gripped the hair at the base of his skull, wanting more.

"What if he made good on his promise?" he asked,
dropping his head, and she froze at the wash of a silver
feeling cascading to her groin when he set his teeth where
his fingers had been. It was too much to not respond.

Pulse racing, she jerked his head up. It could have
hurt, but Kisten knew it was coming and moved with
her. She never hurt him. Not intentionally.

Lips parted, she tightened her legs around him until
she nearly left the counter. And though she buried her
face against his neck, breathed in his scent, and
mouthed his old scars, she didn't break his skin. The
self-denial was more than an exquisite torture, more
than an ingrained tradition. It was survival.

The truth was that she was very nearly beyond
thought, and only patterns of engraved behavior kept

her from sinking her teeth, filling herself with what made him alive. She lusted to feel for that glorious instant total power over another and thus prove she was alive, but until he said so, she would starve for it. It was a game, but a deadly serious one that prevented mistakes made in a moment of passion. The undead had their own games, breaking the rules when they thought they could get away with it. But living vampires held tight to them, knowing it might be the difference in surviving a blood encounter or not.

And Kisten knew it, enjoying his temporary mastery over her. She was the dominant of the two, but unable to satisfy her craving until he let her, and in turn he was helpless to satisfy himself until she agreed. His masculine hands pushed her mouth from his neck, forcing his own lips against her jugular, rising and falling beneath him. Her head flung to the ceiling, she wondered who would surrender and ask first. The unknowing sparked through her, and feeling it, a growl lifted from her.

Dropping her head, she found his earlobe, the metallic diamond taste sharp on her tongue. "Give this to me," she breathed, succumbing, uncaring that her need was stronger than his.

"Take it," he groaned, submitting to their twin desires faster than he usually did.

Panting in relief, she pulled him closer, and in the shock of him meeting her, she carefully sank her teeth into him.

Shuddering, Kisten clutched her closer, lifting her off the counter.

She pulled on him, hungry, almost panicked that someone would stop them. Blessed relief washed through her at the sharp taste. Their scents mixed in her brain, and his blood washed into her, making them one, rubbing out the void that loving Piscary and meeting his demands continually carved into her. His warmth filled her mouth, and she swallowed, sending it deeper into her, desperately trying to drown her soul somehow.

Kisten's breath against her was fast, and she knew the exquisite sensations she instilled in him, the vamp saliva invoking an ecstasy so close to sex it didn't matter. His fingers trembled as they traced her lines and reached for the hem of her shirt, but she knew there wasn't time. She was going to climax before they could work themselves much more.

Breathless and savage from the sensations of power and bloodlust, she pulled back from him, running her tongue quickly over her teeth. She met his eyes, pupil-black. He saw her teetering.

"Take it," she breathed, desperate to give him what he needed, craved. It wouldn't make amends for the savagery of the act, but it was the only way she could find peace with herself.

Kisten didn't wait. A guttural sound coming from him, he leaned in. Sensation jerked through her, the instant of heady pain mutated almost immediately into an equal pleasure, the vampire saliva turning the sting of his fangs into the fire of passion.

"Oh God," she moaned. Kisten heard, and he dug harder, going far beyond what he usually did. She gasped at the twin sensations of his teeth on her neck and his fingernails on her breast. Body moving with his, she pulled his hand from where he gripped the back of her neck and found his wrist. She couldn't . . . bear it. She needed everything. Everything at once.

His mouth pulled on her, and with elation filling her, she bit down, slicing into old scars.

Kisten shook, his grip faltering as sexual and blood

rapture filled them both. He pulled away from the counter, and her legs tightened around his waist.

She heard in his breathing that he was going to reach fulfillment, and content that they would end this with both of them satisfied, she abandoned all thought. Everything was gone, leaving only the need to fill herself with him, and she took everything he gave her, not caring he was doing the same. Together they could find peace. Together they could survive.

Ivy's grip tightened, and she sank her teeth deeper. Kisten responded, a low rumble rising up through him. It sparked a primitive part of her, and fear, instinctive and unstoppable, jumped through her. Kisten felt it, gripping her aggressively.

She cried out, and with the pain shifting to spikes of pleasure, she climaxed, her pulse a wild thrum under Kisten's hand, and in his mouth, and through him. He tensed, and with a last groan, his lips left her as he found the exquisite mental orgasm brought on by satiating the hunger and blood.

No wonder she was screwed up, she thought, even as her body shook and rebelled at the rapturous assault. *Evil or wrong didn't matter. She couldn't resist something that felt so damn good.*

"Kist," she panted when the last flickers faded and she realized she still had her legs wrapped around him, her forehead against his shoulder and her body trying to figure out what had happened. "Are you okay?"

"Hell yes," he said, his breathing haggard. "God, I love you, woman."

As his arms tightened around her, an emotion she seldom felt good about filled her. She loved him more than she would admit, but it was pointless to plan for a future that was already mapped out.

Slowly he settled her back on the counter, his muscles starting to shake. The rim of blue about his pupils was returning, and his lips, still reddened from her blood, parted and his eyebrows rose. "Ivy, you're crying."

She blinked, shocked to find she was. "No, I'm not," she asserted, swinging her leg up and around to get him out from between them. Her muscles protested, not ready to move yet.

"Yes, you are," he insisted, grabbing a cloth napkin and pressing it to his wrist, and then his neck. The small punctures were already closing, the vampire saliva working to stimulate repair and fight possible infection.

Turning away, she slipped from the counter, almost stumbling in her need to hide her emotions. But Kisten grabbed her upper arm and turned her back.

"What is it?" he said, and then his eyes widened. "Shit, I hurt you."

She almost laughed, choking it back. "No," she admitted, then closed her eyes, trying to find the words. They were there, but she couldn't say them. She loved Kisten, but why did the only way she could show him involve blood? Had Piscary completely killed in her how to comfort someone she loved without it turning into a savage act? Love should be gentle and tender, not bestial and self-serving.

She couldn't remember the last time she had slept with someone without blood. She didn't think she had since Piscary first turned his attentions fully to her, warping her until any emotion of caring, love, or devotion stimulated a bloodlust that seemed pointless to resist. She had carefully built the lie to protect herself that blood was blood and sex-and-blood was a way to show she loved someone, but she didn't know how much longer she could believe it. Blood and love had become so intertwined in her that she didn't think she *could* separate them. And if she had to admit that sharing blood was how she expressed her love, then she'd have to admit she was a whore every time she let someone sink his or her teeth into her on her way to the top. *Was that why she was forcing Art into taking her against her will? She had to submit to rape in order to keep herself sane?*

Kisten's eyes roved the kitchen, and she saw his nose widen as he took in their scent. They'd endure a ribbing from the entire staff for having "relieved their vampiric pressures" in the kitchen, but it would cover up the smell of the corpse, at least. "What is it then?" he asked.

Anyone else would have been pushed aside and ignored, but Kisten put up with too much of her crap. "All I wanted to do was comfort you," she said, dropping her head to hide behind the curtain of her hair. "And it turned into blood."

Making a soft sigh, Kisten took her in a slow, careful embrace. A shiver lifted through her when he gently kissed away the last of the blood from her neck. He knew it was so sensitive as to almost hurt and would be for a few more minutes. "Hell, Ivy," he whispered, his voice telling her he knew what she was not saying. "If you were trying to comfort me, you did a bang-up job."

He didn't move, and instead of pulling away, she stayed, allowing herself to accept his touch. "It's what I needed, too," he added, the smell of their scents mingling inciting a deep contentment instead of a dire need now that the hunger had been satisfied.

She nodded, believing him though she still felt ashamed. *But why is that the only way I know how to be?*

4

I vy swiveled her chair, rolling the banshee tear
safe in its plastic bag between her fingers and wondering if it was magic or science that enabled a banshee
to draw enough emotional energy through the gem to kill
someone. Science, she was willing to believe. A science
so elaborate and detailed that it looked like magic. Res-
onating alpha waves or something, like cell phones or ra-
dio transmissions. The files hadn't been clear.

The office chatter coming in her open door was light
because of the ungodly hour. She was working today
on the upper-tower schedule, having a three-thirty afternoon appointment to talk to a banshee who had
helped the I.S. in the past. That it would get her out of
here at midnight was a plus, but it was still damn early.

Mood souring, Ivy leaned back in her chair and listened to the quiet, the usual noises sounding out of
place because of their sparseness. The office atmosphere had changed, the glances she caught directed at
her having gone from bitter to sympathetic. She didn't
know how to react. Apparently the word had gone out
that Art had made a real play for her blood, causing her

not only to contaminate a crime scene but also to almost succumb. And whereas she could have taken comfort in the show of sympathy, she felt only a resentful bitterness that she was the object of pity. How in the hell was she going to get rid of Art if she couldn't say no to him? It was a matter of pride, now.

Ivy's eyes lifted to the humming wall clock. Art was tucked underground, and knowing he wouldn't be coming in for several hours gave her a measure of peace. She'd like to stake the bastard. *Maybe that's what Piscary wanted her to do?*

Over the ambient office noise of keyboards and gossip, she heard her name spoken in a soft, unfamiliar voice. Focusing, Ivy listened to someone else give directions to her office. Ivy set the tear beside her pencil cup with its colored markers, turning to her door when the light was eclipsed.

Her breath to say hello hesitated as she evaluated the woman, forgetting to invite her in. She'd never met a banshee before, and Ivy wondered if they all had that disturbing demeanor or if it was just Mia Harbor.

She was wearing a dramatic calf-length dress made of strips of sky blue fabric. It would have looked like rags if the fabric wasn't silk. The cuffs of the long sleeves ran to drape over her fingertips, and it fit her slight figure perfectly. Her severely short hair was black, cut into downward spikes and iced with gold, completely contrary to her pale complexion and meadowy attire but somehow harmonizing perfectly. Dark sunglasses hid her eyes. Small, petite, and agelessly attractive, she made Ivy feel tall and gawky as she stood in her doorway, the expression on her delicate features shifting from question to a tired acceptance.

Ivy realized she was staring. Immediately she stood, hand extended. "Ms. Harbor," she said. "Please come in. I'm Officer Tamwood."

She moved forward, her dress furling about her calves. Her hand was cool, with a smooth strength, and Ivy let go as soon as it was polite. The confidence of her grip caused Ivy to place her somewhere in her sixties, but she looked twenty. *Witch charm,* Ivy wondered, *or natural longevity?*

"Please call me Mia," the woman said, sitting in Art's chair when Ivy indicated it.

"Mia," Ivy repeated, sinking back down behind her desk. She considered asking the woman to call her by her first name, but didn't, and Mia settled herself with a stiff formality.

Unusually uncomfortable, Ivy leafed through the report to hide her nervousness. Banshees were dangerous entities, able to draw enough energy from people to kill them, much like a psychic vampire. They didn't need to kill to survive, able to exist on the natural sloughing off of emotion from the people around them. But that didn't mean they wouldn't gorge themselves if they thought they could get away with it. She had never had the chance to talk to one before. They were a dying species as public awareness grew about this innocent-looking but highly dangerous Inderlander race.

Like black widow spiders, they generally killed their mate after becoming pregnant. Ivy didn't think it was intentional; their human husbands simply lost their vitality and died. There had never been much of a population of them anyway—every child born was female, and the magic needed to conceive outside one's species made things difficult.

"I make you nervous," Mia said, sounding pleased.

Ivy glanced at her and then back to the papers. Giving up trying to maintain her stoic demeanor, she leaned back in her chair, setting her hands in her lap.

"I won't be *taking* any emotion from you, Officer Tamwood," Mia said. "I don't need to. You're throwing off enough nervous energy and conflicted thoughts to sate me for a week."

Oh joy, Ivy thought sourly. She took pride in suppressing her emotions, and that Mia not only felt them but was sopping them up like gravy wasn't a pleasant thought.

"Why am I here?" Mia asked, pale hands holding her tiny blue-beaded purse on her lap.

Ivy gathered herself. "Ms. Harbor," she said formally, seeing Mia grimace when Ivy made an effort to calm herself. "I'd like to thank you for coming to see me. I have a few questions that the I.S. would be most grateful if you can help me with."

A sigh came from Mia, chilling Ivy—it sounded like the eerie moan of a lost soul. "Which one of my sisters killed someone?" she asked, looking at the tear in its evidence bag.

Ivy's prepared speech vanished. Relieved to be able to sidestep the formalities, she leaned forward, the flat of her forearms on the desk. "We're looking for Jacqueline."

Mia held out a hand for the tear, and Ivy pushed it closer. The woman let go of her purse and took the bag, slipping a white nail under the seal.

"Hey!" Ivy exclaimed, standing.

Mia froze, looking at Ivy over her sunglasses.

Breath catching, Ivy stopped her vamp-fast reach for the evidence bag and rocked back. The woman's eyes were the shockingly pale blue of a near albino, but it was the aching emptiness that halted Ivy. Unmoving, her heart pounded at the raw hunger they contained, chained by an iron-laced restraint. The woman was holding a hunger whose depths Ivy had only tasted. But Ivy had learned enough about restraint to see the signs that her control was absolute: her lack of emotional expression, the stiffness with which she held herself, the soft preciseness of her breathing, the careful motions she made as if she would lose control if she moved too fast and broke through the envelope of her aura and will.

Shocked and awed by what the woman confidently contained, Ivy humbly sat back down.

A smile quirked Mia's face. The snap of the seal breaking was loud, but Ivy didn't stop her, even when she shook the tear into her palm and delicately touched it briefly to her tongue. "You found this at the crime scene?" she asked, and when Ivy nodded she added, "This tear is not functioning." Ivy took a breath to protest, and Mia interrupted, "You found this in a room stinking of fear. If it had been working, every wisp of emotion would have been gone."

Surprised, Ivy struggled to keep her emotions close. That the room reeked of fear when she entered hadn't made it to her report. Since she had contaminated it, it seemed pointless. That might have been a mistake, but amending her report to include it would look questionable.

Mia dropped the tear back into the bag. "It wasn't Jacqueline who killed. It wasn't any of my sisters. I'm sorry, but I can't help you, Officer Tamwood."

Ivy's pulse quickened. Thinking Mia was protecting her kin, she said, "The man admits to killing the victim, but doesn't know why he did. Our theory is Jacqueline left the tear knowing there was the chance domestic violence would cover her crime. Please, Mia. If we don't find Jacqueline, an innocent man will be sentenced for murdering his wife."

The crackle of the broken seal was loud, and Ivy wondered what the black crystal tasted like. "A tear older than a week won't function as a conduit for emotions," Mia said. "And while that tear is Jacqueline's"—she tossed the bag to the desk—"it is at least three years old."

Wondering how she was going to explain why the original seal was broken, Ivy frowned. This had been a waste of time. Just as well she hadn't told Art about it. "And you know that how, ma'am?" she said, frustrated. "You can't date tears."

From behind her black glasses, Mia smiled to show her teeth, her canines a shade longer than a human's. "I know it's at least that old because I killed Jacqueline three years ago."

Smooth and unhurried, Ivy rose and shut the door. The hum of a copier cut off, and Ivy returned to her desk in the new silence, trying to maintain her blank expression. She watched the woman, reading nothing in her calm. Silently she waited for an explanation.

"We are not a well-liked group of people," Mia said bluntly. "Jacqueline had become careless, falling back on old traditions of murdering people to absorb their death energy instead of taking the paltry ambient emotions that Inderland law grants us."

"So you killed her." Ivy allowed herself a deep breath. This woman was scaring the shit out of her with her casual admission of so heinous an act.

Mia nodded, the hem of her dress seeming to shift by itself in the still air. "We police ourselves so the rest of Inderland won't." She smiled. "You understand."

Thinking of Piscary, Ivy dropped her eyes.

"We aren't substantially different from each other," the woman said lightly. "Vampires steal psychic energy, too. You're just clumsy about it, having to take blood with it as a carrier."

Head moving slowly in acceptance, Ivy quashed her feelings of guilt. Generally only vampires knew that a portion of a person's aura went with the blood, but a banshee would, seeing as that's what they took themselves. A more pure form of predation that stripped the soul and made it easy to break it from the body. A person could replace a substantial amount, but take too much aura too quickly, and the body dies. Ivy had always thought banshees were higher on the evolutionary ladder, but perhaps not, seeing as vampires used the visible signs of blood loss to gauge when to stop. "It's not the same," Ivy protested. "No one dies when we feed."

"They do if you feed too heavily."

Ivy's thoughts lighted on the body in Piscary's refrigerator. "Yes, but when a vampire feeds, they give as much emotion as they get."

And though Mia didn't move, Ivy stiffened when the slight woman seemed to gather the shadows in the room, wrapping them about herself. "Only living vampires with a soul give as well as take," she said. "And that's why you suffer, Ivy."

Her voice, low and mocking, shocked Ivy at the use of her given name.

"You could still find beauty amid the ugliness, if you were strong enough," Mia continued. "But you're afraid."

Ivy's stomach clenched and her skin went cold. It was too close to what she had been searching for, even as she denied it existed. "You can't find love in taking blood," she asserted, determined to not get upset and unwittingly feed this . . . woman. "Love is beautiful, and blood is savagely satisfying an ugly need."

"And you don't need love?"

"That's not what I'm saying." Ivy felt unreal, and she gripped the edge of her desk. "Blood isn't a way to show you love." Ivy's voice was soft, but inside she was screaming. She was so screwed up that she couldn't comfort a friend without tainting it with her lust for blood. To mix her need for love and her need for blood corrupted love and made it vile. Her desire to keep the two separate was so close to her, so vulnerable, that she almost choked when Mia shook her head.

"That's not who you want to be," she taunted. "I see it. It pours from you like tears. You lie to yourself, saying that blood and love are separate. You lie saying sanity exists in calling them two things instead of one. Only by accepting that can you rise above what your body demands of you, to live true to who you want to be . . . with someone you love, and who is strong enough to survive loving you back."

Shocked, Ivy froze. This slight woman sitting before her was pulling from Ivy her most desperate, hidden desires, throwing them out for everyone to see. She wanted to control the bloodlust . . . but it felt so damn good to let it control her. And if she called it love, then she had been whoring herself half her life.

As she stared at Mia's knowing smile, memories filled her: memories of Piscary's touch, his praise, of his taking everything from her and saying it was proof of her devotion and love, and her flush of acceptance, of finding worth in being everything he wanted. It was as raw as if it happened last night, not almost a decade ago. Years of indulgence followed, as she found that the more dominating she was, the more satisfaction she craved and the less she found. It was a cruel slipknot that sent her begging for Piscary to give her a feeling of worth. And though she never found it, he had turned the pain sweet.

Now this woman who could sip misery from another as easy as breathing wanted her to accept that the dichotomy that had saved her sanity was a hollow truth? That she could find beauty in her cravings by calling it love?

"It is not love," she said, feeling as if she couldn't breathe.

"Then why do you resist Art?" she accused, a hint of a smile on her face and one eyebrow raised tauntingly. "The entire floor is thinking about it. You know it's more than a casual act. It's a way to show your love, and to give that to Art would mean you were a demimonde; no—a whore. A filthy, perverted slut selling herself for a moment of carnal pleasure and professional advancement."

It was so close to what she had been thinking herself that Ivy clenched her jaw, glad the office door was closed. She felt her eyes dilate, but the memory of Mia's leashed hunger kept her sitting. She knew that Mia was provoking her, inciting her anger so she could lap it up. It was what banshees did. That they often used truth to do so made it worse. "You can't express love in taking blood," Ivy said, her voice low and vehement.

"Why not?"

Why not? It sounded so simple. "Because I can't say no to blood," Ivy said bitterly. "I need it. I crave it. I *want* to satisfy it, damn it."

Mia laughed. "You stupid, whiny little girl. You want to satisfy it because it's tied to your need for love. It's too late for me. I can't find beauty in satisfying my needs since anyone a banshee loves dies. You can, and to see you so selfish makes me want to slap you. You are a coward," she accused. "Too frightened to find the beauty in your needs because to do so would admit that you were wrong. That you have been fooling yourself for most of your life, lying that it has no importance so you can indulge yourself. You are a whore, Ivy. And you know it. Stop deluding yourself that you aren't."

Ivy felt her eyes flash entirely to black, pulled by anger. "You need to leave," she said, muscles so tense, it took all her restraint to keep from striking the banshee.

Mia stood. She was alive and vibrant, her smooth face flushed and beautiful—an accusing angel, hard and uncaring. "You can live above your fate," she mocked. "*You* can be who you want to be. So Piscary warped you. So he broke you and remade you to be a pliant source of emotion-rich blood. It's up to you to either accept or deny it."

"You think I like being like this?" Ivy said, standing when her frustration spilled over. "That I like anyone with long teeth able to take advantage of me? This is what I was born into—there's no way out. It's too late! Too many people expect me to be the way I am, too many people force me to be the way they want me to be." The truth was coming out, pissing her off.

Mia's lips were parted and her face was flushed. Her eyes were lost behind her sunglasses, and the gold in her short black hair caught the light. "That is the excuse of a lazy, frightened coward," she said, and Ivy tensed, ready to tell her to shut up but for the memory of the leashed hunger in her eyes. "Admit you were wrong. Admit you are ugly and a whore. Then don't be that way anymore."

"But it feels too good!" Ivy shouted, not caring if the floor heard her.

Mia trembled, her entire body shuddering. Breath fast, she reached for the back of her chair. When she brought her gaze up from behind her sunglasses, Ivy realized that the air was as pure and pristine as if the argument hadn't happened. Pulse fast, Ivy breathed deeply, finding only the hint of Mia's perfume and the softest trace of her sweat. *Damn. The bitch was good.*

"I never said it would be easy," Mia said softly, and Ivy wondered exactly what the hell had just happened. "The hunger will always be there, like a thorn. Every day will be worse than the previous until you think you won't be able to exist another moment, but then you'll see the filth in your eyes trying to get out—and if you're strong, you'll find the will to put it off another day. And for another day, you will be who you want to be. Unless you're a coward."

The humming of the wall clock grew loud in the new silence, almost deep enough to hear Mia's heartbeat, and Ivy stood behind her desk, not liking the feelings mixing in her. "I'm not a coward," Ivy finally said.

"No, you're not," Mia admitted, subdued and quiet. Satiated.

"And I am not weak of will," Ivy added, louder.

Mia inhaled slowly, her pale fingers tightening on her purse. "Yes, you are." Ivy's eyes narrowed, and Mia's mien shifted again. "Forgive me for asking," she said, sounding both embarrassed and nervous, "but would you consider living together?"

Ivy's gut tightened. "Get out."

Mia swallowed, taking off her sunglasses to show her pale blue eyes, her pupils carrying a familiar swelling of black that made her look vulnerable. "I can make it worth your while," she said, her eyes running over Ivy as if she was a past lover and moistening her lips. "My blood for your emotion? I can satisfy everything you need, Ivy, and more. And you could kindle a child in me with the pain you carry."

"Get—out."

Head bowing, Mia nodded and moved to the door.

"I am not weak of will," Ivy repeated, shame joining her anger when Mia crossed the small office. Mia opened the door, hesitating to turn and look at her.

"No," she said, a gentle sadness in her ageless features. "You aren't. But you do need practice." Dress furling, the woman left, the click, click of her heels silencing the entire floor, the fluorescent lights catching the highlights in her hair.

Angry, Ivy lurched to the door, slamming it shut and falling back into her chair. "I am not weak of will," she said aloud, as if hearing it would make it so. But the idea she might be wiggled in between thought and reason, and it was too easy to doubt herself.

Her boot heels went up onto her desk, ankles crossed. She didn't want to think about what Mia had said—or what she offered. Eyes closed, Ivy took a breath to relax, forcing her body to do as she told it. She hadn't liked Mia using her, but that's what they did. It was Ivy's own fault for arguing with her.

Again, Ivy inhaled, slower to make her shoulders ease. She could ignore everything but what she wanted to focus on if she tried—she spent a great deal of her life that way. It made her quick to anger, depressed her appetite, and caused her to be overly sensitive, but it kept her sane.

Ivy's eyes opened in the silence, falling upon the tear. As inescapable as shadows, her mind fastened on it, desperately seeking a distraction. Disgust lifted through her at the torn bag. *How was she going to explain the broken seal to Art?*

Leaning forward, she felt her muscles stretch as she pulled the bag closer, and in a surge of self-indulgence, shook the tear into her palm. A moment of hesitation, and she touched it to her tongue. She felt nothing, tasted nothing. With a guilty motion, she dropped it back in and pressed the seal shut, tossing it to her desk.

The tear was three years old, found in a room stinking of fear. A banshee hadn't been responsible. The man had murdered his wife with a plan already in place to shift the blame. Where had he gotten a tear? A tear three years old, no less?

Three years. That was a long time to plan your wife's murder. Especially when they had been married only eight months, according to Mr. Demere's file. *Long-term planning.*

Ivy leaned forward in a spike of adrenaline and fingered the bag. Vampires planned that long. Jacqueline had a record. Only a vampire who worked for the I.S. would be in a position to know she was dead, unable to clear her name. And only an I.S. employee would have access to a tear swiped from the old-evidence vault. A tear no one would miss.

"Holy shit," Ivy softly swore. This went to the top.

Dropping the tear, Ivy reached for the phone. Art would crap his coffin when he found out. But then a thought struck her, and she hesitated, the buzz of the open line a harsh whine.

The apartment had been full of fear—anger and fear that should have been soaked up by the tear but wasn't— fear that Art had covered up with her own emotions.

The buzz of the phone line turned to beeping, and

she set the phone back in the cradle, the acidic taste of betrayal filling her thoughts. Art had used her to muddle the psychic levels in the room. The guy from the collection van had commented on it when he had come in, blaming it on her after he saw the banshee tear, not knowing she had only added to what was already there. No one documented psychic levels unless a banshee was involved, and they hadn't known until after she contaminated the scene. "After Art stole and planted the tear," she muttered aloud. Art, who was so dense he couldn't find his pretty fangs in someone's ass.

Plucking a pen from her pencil cup, she tapped it on the desk, wanting to write everything down but resisting lest it come back to bite her. *Maybe not so dense after all.* "Motive . . ." she breathed, enjoying the adrenaline rush and feeling as if it cleansed her somehow. Why would Art help plan and cover up a murder? What would he get out of it? Being undead, Art was moved only by survival and his need for blood.

Blood? she thought. Had the suspect promised to be Art's blood shadow in exchange for the opportunity to murder his wife? *Didn't sound right.*

Her lips curled upward and she smiled. Money. Art's rise in the I.S. had stopped when he died and was no longer a potential source of blood. Without the currency of blood for bribes, he couldn't rise in the vampiric hierarchy. He was existing on the interest from his postdeath funds, but by law he couldn't touch the principal. If the suspect gave Art a portion of his wife's insurance money, it might be enough to move Art up a step. That the undead vampire had openly admitted he wasn't adverse to using Ivy to pull him up in the ranks only solidified her belief that he was having money problems. Undead vampires didn't work harder than they had to. That Art was working at all said something.

Pen clicking open and shut so fast it almost hummed, Ivy tried to remember if she had ever heard that Art had died untimely. He'd been working the same desk over thirty years.

Jerking in sudden decision, she dropped the pen and pulled out the Yellow Pages, looking for the biggest insurance ad that wasn't connected to one of Cincinnati's older vamp families. She would call them all if she had to. Pulse quickening, she dialed, using the suspect's social security number to find out his next payment wouldn't be due until the fifteenth. It was for a hefty amount, and she impatiently kept hitting the star button until the machine had a cyber coronary and dumped her into a real person's phone.

"Were Insurance," a polite voice answered.

Ivy sat straighter. "This is Officer Tamwood," she said, "and I'm checking on the records of a Mr. and Mrs. Demere? Could you tell me if they upped their life insurance recently?"

There was a moment of silence. "You're from the I.S.?" Before Ivy could answer, the woman continued primly. "I'm sorry, Officer Tamwood. We can't give out information without a warrant."

Ivy smiled wickedly. "That's fine, ma'am. My partner and I will be there with your little piece of paper as soon as the sun goes down. We're kind of in a hurry, so he might skip breakfast to get there before you close."

"Uh . . ." the voice came back, and Ivy felt her eyes dilate at the fear it held. "No need. I'm always glad to help out the I.S. Let me pull up the policy in question."

Ivy tucked the phone between her ear and her shoulder, picking at her nails and trying to get her eyes to contract.

"Here it is!" the woman gushed nervously. "Mr. and Mrs. Demere took out a modest policy covering each of them shortly after getting married . . ." The woman's voice trailed off, sounding puzzled. "It was increased about four months ago. Just a minute."

Ivy swung her feet to the floor and reached for a pen.

"Okay," the woman said when she returned. "I see why. Mrs. Demere finished getting her degree. She was going to become the major breadwinner, and they wanted to take advantage of the lower payment schedule before her next birthday. It has a payout of a half million." The woman chuckled. "Someone was a little enthusiastic. A data entry degree won't get her a good enough job to warrant that kind of insurance."

A zing of adrenaline went through Ivy, and the pen snapped. "Damn it!" she swore as ink stained her hand and dripped to the desk.

"Ma'am?" the woman questioned, a new wariness to her voice.

Staring at the blue ink on her hand, Ivy said, "Nothing. My pen just broke." She dropped it in the trash, and using her foot, she opened a lower drawer and snatched up a tissue. "It might be in your company's best interest to misfile any claim for a few weeks," she said as she wiped her fingers. "Could you give me a call when someone tries to process it?"

"Thank you, Officer Tamwood," the insurance officer said cheerfully over the sound of a pencil scratching. "Thank you very much. I've got your number on my screen, and I'll do just that."

Embarrassed, Ivy hung up. Still trying to get the worst of the ink off her, she felt a stirring of excitement.

It wasn't in any report that the tear wasn't functioning. This had possibilities. But she couldn't go to the basement with her suspicions; if Art had promised someone down there a cut of money, her suspicions would go nowhere and she'd look like a whiny bitch trying to get out of giving Art his due blood. That she was doing just that didn't bother her as much as she thought it would.

Balling up the inkstained tissue, Ivy reached again for the phone. Kisten. Kisten could help her on this. Maybe they could have lunch together.

5

The muted sounds of the last patrons being ushered out the door vibrated through the oak timbers of the floorboards, and Ivy relaxed in it, finding more peace there than she'd like to admit. Extending her long legs out under the piano, she picked up her melted milkshake and sipped through the straw as she planned Art's downfall. Before her on the closed lid were written-out plans of contingencies, neatly arranged on the black varnished wood. Below her, Piscary's living patrons stumbled home in the coming dawn. The undead ones had left a good hour ago. The scent of tomato paste, sausage, pasta, and the death-by-chocolate dessert someone had ordered to go drifted up through the cracks.

The light coming in the expansive windows was thin, and Ivy looked from her pages set in neat piles and stretched her laced fingers to the distant ceiling. She was usually in bed this time of day—waiting for Kisten to finish closing up and slide in behind her with a soft nibble somewhere. More often than not, it turned into a breathless circle of give and take that left them content in each other's arms as they fell asleep with the morning sun warming their skin.

Focus blurring, Ivy plucking at the itchy fabric of her lace shirt, her thoughts returning to Mia. Banshees were known for inciting trouble, often hiring themselves in to a productive company and putting old friends at each other's throats with a few well-placed words of truth, whereupon they would sit back and lap up the emotion while everything fell apart. That they usually did this with the truth made it worse. She loved Kisten, but to call it love when she took his blood? That was savage need. There could be no love there. Eyes dropping to the papers surrounding her, she pushed at them as if pushing away her thoughts, bringing her hand up to slide a finger between her neck and the collar of itchy lace.

Ivy felt like a vamp wannabe, dressed in tight jeans and a black stretchy shirt with a high collar of peekaboo lace and an open, low neckline. A pair of flat sandals finished the look. It wasn't what she would have picked out for framing her partner for homicide, but it was close to what Sleeping Beauty had on.

She had been here at the piano for hours, having called in sick after meeting Kisten for lunch, blaming it on bad sushi. Kisten wasn't convinced putting Art in jail by dumping Piscary's mistake in his apartment was a good way to get promoted, but Ivy liked its inescapable justice. Going to the I.S. would gain her nothing but their irritation for interfering. True, Mr. Demere wouldn't be going to jail for murdering his wife, but that didn't mean he was going to walk away from it. She'd take care of him later when he thought he had escaped unscathed.

It surprised her that she was enjoying herself. She liked her job at the I.S., working backward from where someone else's plan went wrong to catch stupid people making stupid decisions. But plotting her own action to snare someone in her own net was more satisfying. She was headed for management, but she'd never stopped to ask herself if it was something she wanted.

And so after she had discussed it with Kisten, he had reluctantly bought her car for cash, and she had gone shopping with the untraceable money. She had felt ignorant at the first charm outlet she had gone into, but the man had become gratifyingly helpful once she showed him the money.

Fingers cold from her melted shake, Ivy set the wet glass on a coaster and reached for the sleep amulet safe in its silk bag. She had wanted a potion she could get Art to drink or splash on him, but the witch refused to sell it to her, claiming it was too dangerous for a novice. He had sold her an amulet that would do the same thing, though, and she felt the outlines of the redwood disk on its cord carefully through the bag, satisfied it would work. The man had cautioned her three times to be sure there was someone there to take it off her or she'd sleep for two days before the charm spontaneously broke for safety reasons.

A second, metallic amulet would give her the illusion of blond hair and take off about eight inches of height, making her closer to the size and look of Sleeping Beauty. She didn't know how witches in the I.S. managed to make any money, seeing as the two charms had cost as much as her car, and she wondered if the witch had upped the price because she was a vampire.

She had been sitting here writing out contingencies for nearly two hours, and she was growing stiff. The I.S. tower had cleared out by now, and Art was home.

He had called her cell phone shortly after sunset, feeling her out as to what she was doing avoiding him, and with her charms literally in her hand, she had agreed to a date with him. Sunup. His place.

Agitated, Ivy clicked her pen open and shut, imagining he had probably spent his time in the office talking himself up big as to his plans for tonight. Her eyes fell on the purple stains in her cuticles from breaking her pen earlier, and she set it down.

A creak on the stairway brought her heart into her throat. She hadn't told Piscary what she was doing, and only he or Kisten would be coming up. But then her eyes went to the windows and she berated herself. Piscary would never come up here so close to sunrise.

Determined to keep her back to the stairs, she hid her unease behind turning off the table lamp and shuffling her papers, but she didn't think Kisten was fooled—he was grinning from behind his reddish blond beard when she looked up. Eyebrows rising, she sent her gaze across his shiny dress shoes, up his pinstripe suit, and to the tie he had loosened.

"Who are you trying to be?" she asked sharply, rarely seeing him in a suit, much less a tie.

"Sorry, love," he said, using that British accent. "Didn't mean to startle you."

He bent to slip a hand around her waist and give her a soft tug, but she ignored him, pretending to study her papers. "I don't like your accent," she said, releasing some of her tension in a bad mood. She smelled someone on him, and it made things worse. "And you didn't startle me. I smelled you and some tart halfway up the stairs. Who was it? That little blond that's been coming in here every payday to make black eyes at you? She's early. It's only Thursday."

Fingers sliding from her, Kisten edged a step away. Eyes down, he picked up a paper. "Ivy . . ."

It was low and coaxing, and her jaw clenched. "I'm doing this."

"Ivy, he's an undead." With a soft sound, he sat beside her on the piano bench. "If you make a mistake . . . They're so damn strong. When they get angry, they don't even pretend to remember pity."

They both knew that all too well. Her pulse quickened, but she kept her face impassive. "I won't make a mistake," she said, scratching a notation on her paper.

Kisten took the pen from her and set it atop her papers. "All you have is a few witch charms and the element of surprise. If he has any idea that you might betray him, he's going knock you out and drain you. And no one will say anything if you went down there looking to tag him. Even Piscary."

Ivy pulled her fingers from his as if unconcerned. "He won't kill me. If he does, I'll sue his ass for unlawful termination."

Clearly unhappy, Kisten opened the piano. The light made shadows on him, throwing his faint scars into sharp relief. "I don't want you to get hurt," he said, spreading his fingers to hit almost an entire octave, but he made no sound. "And I don't want you dead. You won't be any fun that way."

Her eye twitched, and she forced it to stop with pure will. If things went right, Art would be really pissed. If things went wrong, Art would be really pissed and in a position to hurt her. "I don't want to die, either," she admitted, tucking her feet under the bench.

Kisten struck a chord, modifying it into a minor that sounded wrong. As the echoes lifted through the brightening room, she cursed herself for being so addicted to blood that it was such an overriding factor in her life. Mia had said all it took was practice to say no. Ivy had always scorned living vampires who abstained from blood, thinking they were betraying everything they were. Now she found herself wondering if this was why they did it.

The eerie chord ended when Kisten lifted his foot from the pedal and reached for the blue silk pouch.

"Careful," Ivy warned, gripping his wrist. "It's already invoked and will drop you quicker than tequila."

Dark eyebrows high, Kisten said, "This?" and she let go. "What does it do?"

Hiding her nervousness, Ivy bent back over her paper. "It gets Art off my neck." He held it from the drawstring like it was a rat. Clearly he didn't like witch magic either. "It's harmless," she said, giving up on her last-minute planning, "Just bring Sleeping Beauty when you get my call."

Kisten leaned backward, touching the front pocket of his slacks. "I've got my phone. It's on vibrate. Call me. Call me a lot."

Ivy allowed herself a smile. Setting the pen aside, she stood, gingerly wedging the amulet safe in its bag into a pocket. Kisten turned on the bench to keep her in view, and she tucked a placebo vial of saltwater down her bustier-enhanced cleavage. The man at the charm outlet had insisted she take the vial since it could do double-duty as a quick way to permanently break the sleep charm if she spilled it on the amulet. The cool spot it made caused her to shift her shoulders until the glass warmed. Kisten was wearing a shit-grin when she brought her head up. "How do I look?" she asked, posing.

Smiling, he drew her to him. "Mmmm, dressed to

kill, baby," he said, his breath warming her midriff since he was still sitting on the piano bench. "I like the shirt."

"Do you?" Eyes closing, she let the mingling of his scent with hers stir her bloodlust. Her hands ran aggressively through his hair, and when his fingers traced the outlines of her buttocks and his lips moved just under her breast, she wondered if finding love in blood might be worth the shame of having lied to herself, of letting others tell her who she was, and letting them make her into this ugly thing. Feeling the rise of indecision, she pulled away. "I've got to go."

Kisten's face was creased in worry, and as he ran a hand through his hair to straighten it, she found herself wanting to arrange his tie. Or better yet, rip it off him. "I'm going to change, then I'll be right behind you," he said. "Your wine is downstairs on the counter."

"Thanks." She hefted her duffel bag with its change of clothes and hesitated. She wanted to ask him if he thought it was possible to find love in sharing blood, but shame stopped her. Sandals loud on the hardwood floor, she walked to the stairs, feeling as if she might never walk this floor again. Or that if she did, she'd be changed beyond recognition.

"Burn those papers for me?" she called, and got an "Already ahead of you" in return.

The restaurant had emptied of patrons, and the soft chatter of the waitstaff was pleasant as she passed the bar. Music was cranked in the kitchen over the sounds of the oversized dishes being hand washed, and everyone was enjoying the span between Piscary becoming unavailable and quitting time. Like children left home alone, they laughed and teased. Ivy liked this time the best, often lying in bed and listening, never telling anyone she could hear. Why the hell couldn't she join in? Why was everything so damn complicated for her?

Grabbing a bottle of Piscary's cheapest wine in passing, she gave a high-five to the pizza delivery guy coming in the receiving dock/garage as she went out. She couldn't help but notice that the kitchen atmosphere was radically different from the one she found in the I.S. tower. The office held pity; the kitchen was sly anticipation.

Shortly after opening this afternoon, the entire staff knew there was a body in the refrigerator. They also knew Kisten was in a good mood. And with her change in her work patterns, they knew she was up to something. Maybe Kisten had it right.

The wine went into the duffel bag, which she then strapped to the back of her cycle. Swinging on to it, she started it up, eyes closing at the power beneath her as she put her helmet on. Waving to the second delivery guy pulling in, she idled into the rush hour traffic. It would soon slack off as humans took over Cincinnati, calling it theirs alone until noon when the early-rising Inderlanders began stirring.

Ivy felt insulated in her helmet, the wind tugging at her hair a familiar sensation. She was alive, free, the smooth movement of the earth turning under her instilling a peace she couldn't readily find. Wishing she could just get on the interstate and go, she sighed. It would never happen. Her need for blood would follow her, and without Piscary providing protection as her master, she would be taken by the first undead vampire she ran into. There was no way out. There never had been. Mia's invitation surfaced, and Ivy tasted it in her thoughts, trying it on before dismissing it as a slow, pleasant way to suicide.

The sun was rising as she crossed the bridge into Cincinnati. She was late. Art would be either pissed or still glowing from the men's-club talk of the day. The thought that she was a whore flitted through her before she quashed it. She wasn't going to sell herself to move up the corporate ladder. She could resist Art long enough to knock him out, and then she'd nail his ass to the wall and use it to make a new ladder.

Pulse quickening, she took a sharp right, weaving in and out of traffic until she reached Fountain Square. The plaza was empty, and she found a parking spot near the front of the belowground garage. Nervousness crept into her as she shut off her cycle. A moment with a small mirror and a red lipstick, and she was ready. Leaving her helmet on the seat, she fumbled for her duffel bag and headed to the rectangle of light with more confidence than she felt. There was no reason for her anxiety. She'd planned sufficiently.

A furtive glance to make sure no one was watching, and she found the charmed silver that would change her appearance. She pulled the tiny pin out of the watch-sized amulet to invoke the disguise, tossed the pin aside, and laced the metallic amulet over her head. This one didn't need to touch her skin, just be on her person. The witch had said it worked using her own aura's energy, but she really hadn't cared beyond what she needed to make it function properly.

An eerie feeling rippled over her, and Ivy shuddered, her sandals grinding the street grit. It wouldn't make her look like Sleeping Beauty—that was illegal, she had been primly told—but with the clothing, hair, and attitude, it would be close enough.

She squinted in the brighter light when she came out onto the sidewalk and headed for the bus stop. Witch magic was powerful shit, and she wondered if no one realized the potential it had, or if no one cared, seeing as witches didn't try to govern anything but themselves, quietly going about their business of blending with humanity.

The bus was pulling up as she got there—precisely as she had timed it—and she was the third one on, dropping a token in before finding a seat and putting her duffel bag to prevent someone from sitting beside her. She had a swipe card, but using a token would add to her anonymity.

Jostled, she watched the city pass, the professional buildings giving way to tall thin homes with dirt yards the size of a Buick. Her clenched jaw eased when the yards got nicer and the paint jobs fresher as the house numbers rose. By the time she reached Art's block, the salt-rusted, dented vehicles had been replaced by late-model, expensive cars. She watched Art's house pass, waiting two blocks before signaling the driver she wanted off. It wasn't a regular stop, but he pulled over, letting irate humans on their way to work pass him as she said, "Thank you" in a soft voice and disembarked.

She was walking before the door shut behind her. Free arm swinging, she hit her heels hard to attract attention. Warming, she shortened her pace to accommodate her smaller look. The clip-clack, clip-clack cadence was unnatural, and she dropped her head as if not wanting to be seen when she heard a car start.

At Art's house, she hesitated, pretending to check an address. It was smaller than she expected, though well-maintained. Her parents had a modest mansion built with railroad money earned by her great-grandfather, the elaborate underground apartments added after her great-grandmother had attracted Piscary's attention.

Art couldn't have much of a bedroom; the footprint for the two-story house was only fifty-by-thirty.

Swinging her duffel bag to her front, she took the stairs with a series of prissy steps. Thirty years ago, the house would have been low high-class, and it was obvious why Art needed the money. His interest income when he died had been sufficient to keep him at low high-class—of the seventies. Inflation was moving him down in the socioeconomic ladder. He needed something to pull himself up before he slid into poverty over the next hundred years.

There was a note on the door. Smirking, she pulled it from the screen and let it fall to the bushes for the forensics team to find. "Late, am I?" she muttered, wondering if he had the front miked. Pitching her voice high, she called, "Art, I brought wine. Can I come in?"

There was no answer, so she opened the door and entered a modest living room. The curtains were drawn and a light was on for her. She wandered into the spotless kitchen with a dry sink. Again there were leather curtains, hidden behind a lightweight white fabric to disguise them. Leather curtains couldn't protect an undead vamp from the sun, but boarding up the windows was against the city ordinances. Another note on an interior door invited her down.

Her lip curled, and she started to wish she had arranged this during night hours so she didn't have to play this disgusting game. Crumpling the note, she dropped it on the faded linoleum. She took off the charmed silver amulet, shivering when something pulled through her aura. Her hair lost its corn yellow hue, and she hung the amulet on the knob so Kisten would know where she was.

Knocking, she opened the door to find a downward leading stair and music. She wanted to be annoyed, but he'd done his research and it was something she liked—midnight jazz. A patch of cream carpet met her, glowing under soft lights. Gripping her duffel bag, she called, "Art?"

"Shut the door," he snarled from somewhere out of sight. "The sun is up."

Ivy took three steps down and shut the door, noting it was as thick as coffin wood and reinforced with steel with a metal crossbar to lock it. There was a clock stuck to its back, along with a page from the almanac, a calendar, and a mirror. Her mother had something similar.

Again Ivy wanted to belittle him, but it looked professional and businesslike. No pictures of sunsets or graveyards. The only notation on the calendar about her was "date with Ivy." No exclamation points, no hearts, no "hubba-hubba." *Thank God.*

She touched her pocket for the sleep amulet and looked down her cleavage for the fake potion. Relying on witch magic made her nervous. She didn't like it. Didn't understand it. She had had no idea witch magic was so versatile, much less so powerful. They had a nice little secret here, and they protected it the same way vampires protected their strengths: by having them out in the open and shackled by laws that meant nothing when push came to shove.

Sandals loud on the wooden steps, she descended, watching Art's shadow approach the landing. The faint scent of bleach intruded, growing stronger as she reached the floor. She kept her face impassive when she found him, glad he was still wearing his usual work clothes. If he had been in a Hugh Hefner robe and holding a glass of vodka, she would have screamed.

Ignoring him watching her, she looked over his belowground apartments. They were plush and comfortable, with low ceilings. It was an old house, and the city had strict guidelines about how much dirt you could pull out from under your dwelling. They were in what was obviously the living room, a wood-paneled hallway probably leading to a traditional bedroom. Her eyes went to the lit gas fireplace, and she felt her eyebrows rise.

"It dries the air out," he said. "You don't think I'm going to romance you, do you?"

Relieved, she dropped her duffel bag by the couch. Hand on her hip, she swung her hair, glad it was back to its usual black. "Art, I'm here for one thing, and after I'm done, I'm cleaning up and leaving. Romance would ruin my entire image of you, so why don't we just get it over with?"

Art's eyes flashed to black. "Okay."

It was fast. He moved, reaching out and yanking her to him. Instinct got an arm between them as he pulled her to his chest. Her pulse pounded, and she stared when he hesitated, her naked fear striking a chord with him. It was a drug to him, and she knew he paused so as to prolong it. She cursed herself when her own bloodlust rose, heady and unstoppable. She didn't want this. She could say no. Her will was stronger than her instincts.

But her jaw tightened, and he smiled to show his teeth when she felt her eyes dilate against her will. Lips parting, she exhaled into it. The savage desire to force her needs on him vibrated through every nerve. Mia was wrong. There could be no love here, no tenderness. And when Art forced her closer and ran his teeth gently across her neck, she found herself tense with anticipation even as she tried to bring it under control. *Concentrate, Ivy,* she thought, her pulse quickening in her conflicting feelings. She was here to nail his coffin, not be nailed.

He knew she wouldn't say yes to him until he pulled her to the brink where bloodlust made her choices. And even as she thought no, she gripped his shoulder, poised as he ran his hand down her hips and eased to the inside of her thighs, searching. A rumbling growl came from him, shivering through her. His hands became possessive, demanding. And she willed the feeling to grow, even when self-loathing filled her.

How had it come on so fast? she thought. Had she been wanting this all along, teasing herself? Or was Mia right in that she had refused Art because giving in would prove she knew she could find love in the ugliness, but was too cowardly to fight for it?

Art carefully hooked a tooth into the lace of her collar and tore it, the sound of the ripping fabric cutting through her. His teeth grazed her, promising, and she lost all thought but how to get him to sink them, to fill her with glorious feeling proving she was alive and could feel joy, even if she paid for it with her self-respect.

Art didn't speak as he stood, holding her against him, the demanding pressure in his lips, his fingers, his very breathing, waking every nerve in her. He hadn't bespelled her; he hadn't needed to. She was willing to be everything he wanted, and a tiny part of her screamed, drowned out by her need to give to him and to feel in return, even though she knew it was false.

His fingers rose from his grip upon her waist, tracing upward with a firm insistence until they found her chin and tilted her head. "Give this to me," he whispered, his fingers among her hair. "This is mine. Give it . . . to me."

It was haggard, almost torn by the need in him that her tortured willingness had sparked. The thought that she was buying empty emotion rose like bubbles to pop against the top of her mind. Mia had said she could live above the bloodlust. Mia didn't know shit, didn't know the exquisite pleasure of this. She wanted his blood, and he wanted hers. What difference did it make how she would feel in the morning? Tomorrow she could be dead and it wouldn't matter.

And then she remembered the leashed hunger Mia contained and counted it stronger than her own. She remembered the scorn in Mia's voice, calling her a whiny little girl who could have everything if she had the courage to live up to her greater need for love. Even if she did have to taint it with bloodlust.

Ivy's heart pounded as she tried to find the will to pull away, but the lure of what he could fill her with was too strong. She couldn't. It was ingrained too deeply. It was what she was. But she wanted more, damn it. She wanted to escape the ugliness of what she really was.

As she struggled with herself, she found Art's mouth with her own, drawing his lips from her neck and putting them on hers. The salty electric taste of blood filled her, but it wasn't hers. Art had cut his own lip, sending her into a dizzy lust for the rest of him.

Gasping, she pushed away. *It would stop here.*

She fell back, fingers fumbling for the vial. Eyes black, Art gripped her wrist, the tiny glass bottle exposed. Ivy flushed hot as she stood, her arm stretched between them.

Hunched from the pain of breaking from her, Art wiped his mouth of his blood. He let go of her, and she stumbled back. In Art's hand was the vial.

"What's this?" he asked, wary but amused when he unscrewed the top and sniffed at it.

"Nothing," she said, truly afraid even as her body ached at the interruption.

He sucked in her fear, his eyes going blacker and his smile more predatory. "Really."

Panicking that he would drop it and come at her again, she fumbled in her pocket, bringing out the real charm, invoked but quiescent in its silk pouch.

Art's eyes went to it, and before he could think, she jumped at him. Arm moving in a quick arc, Art flung the contents of the vial at her. Heavy droplets, warm from her body, struck her like shocks from a whip. Adrenaline pounding to make her head hurt, she forced her muscles to go slack. She collapsed as if she'd run into a wall, falling to where he had been standing a second earlier. The carpet burned her cheek, and she exhaled as if passing out.

From across the room, she heard him shift his feet against the carpet, trying to figure out what had happened. She forced her breathing to slow, feigning unconsciousness. It had to work. If not, she had only an instant to escape.

"I knew you'd try something," Art said, going to the wet bar and pouring himself something. The undead didn't need to drink, but it would cleanse his cut lip. "Not as clever as Piscary said you'd be," he said amid the heavy clink of a bottle against glass. "Did you really think I wouldn't have you followed on your shopping?"

Ivy clenched her stomach muscles when a dress shoe edged under her and flipped her over. Forcing herself to remain flaccid, she kept her eyes lightly shut as her back hit the carpet. He might bite her anyway, but fear and desire tainted the blood with delicious compounds, and he'd rather have her awake. Heart pounding, she loosened her fingers and let the pouch slip from them. Curiosity could put the cat in the bag when force could not.

"I'm forty-two years dead," he said bitterly. "You don't survive that long if you're stupid." There was a slight hesitation, and then, "And what the hell was this supposed to do?"

Ivy heard him pick up the silk pouch and shake the amulet into his hand. She tensed, springing to her feet as he exhaled. He was still standing, his eyes losing their focus when she shot her hand out, curling his slack fingers around the amulet before it could slip from him.

With a sigh, he collapsed, and she went down with him, desperate to keep the amulet in his grip. They hit the carpet together, her arm wedged painfully under her.

"You can survive that long if you're stupid *and* lucky," she said. "And your luck's run out, Artie."

Slowly Ivy shifted her legs under her into a more comfortable position, her hand still gripped around Art's fingers. Hooking her foot in the handle of her duffel bag by the couch, she dragged it closer. With one hand, she opened it to pull out a plastic-coated metallic zip-strip the I.S. used to bind ley line witches to keep them from escaping by jumping to a ley line. Art couldn't use ley line magic, but the strip would hold the amulet to him. At the sound of the plastic ratcheting against itself to pinch the amulet between his palm and the strip, she relaxed.

Exhaling, she got to her feet. Drawing her foot back, she kicked him. Hard. "Bastard," she said, wiping his spit off her neck. Limping, she went to the stereo and clicked it off. She'd never be able to listen to "Skylark" again. She rummaged in her duffel bag, and upon finding her phone, headed for the stairs. Three steps from the top, and she had enough bars. She hit speed-dial one, struggling to listen and take off her disgusting shirt simultaneously.

"Ivy?" came Kisten's voice, and she pinched the phone between her shoulder and her ear.

"He's down. Bring her in," she said.

Without waiting for an answer, she ended the call, adrenaline making her jumpy. Shaking, she stripped off her clothes and slipped into her leather pants and a stretch-knit shirt, wiping her neck free of Art's scent with a disposable towelette that then went into the contractor garbage bag she shook out with the sharp crack of thick plastic. She considered the lacy shirt for an instant, then dropped it in, too. Her sandals went into her duffel bag.

Barefoot, she crouched by Art. Lifting his lips from his gums, she sucked up blood and saliva with a disposable eyedropper, putting a good quarter inch into the empty saltwater vial. Done, she opened the wine, sat on the raised hearth, and with the hissing flames warming her back, took a long pull. It was bitter, and she grimaced, taking another drink, smaller this time. Anything to get rid of the lingering taste of Art's blood in her mouth.

Toes digging into the carpet, she looked at Art, out cold and helpless. Witch magic had done it. God, they could be a serious threat in Inderland politics if they put their mind to it.

The sound of feet upstairs brought her straight, and she set the bottle aside. It was Kisten, thumping down the stairs with a large cardboard box in his arms. Ivy looked, then looked again. He had changed into an institutional gray jumpsuit, but that wasn't it.

"You're wearing the charm," she said, and he flushed from under his new blond bangs. He was shorter, too, and she didn't like it.

"I always wanted to know what I'd look like blond," he said. "And it will help with the repairman image." Grunting, he set down the box with Sleeping Beauty in it. "God almighty," he swore as he stretched his back and looked at Art with the amulet strapped to his palm. "It smells like a cheap hotel down here, all blood and bleach. Did he wing you?"

"No." Ivy handed him the bottle, unwilling to admit how close Art had come.

Kisten's Adam's apple bobbed as he drank, and he exhaled loudly as he lowered the bottle. His eyes were bright and his smile was wide. *Just one big joke to Kisten,* Ivy thought, depressed. She had acted just in time. If she hadn't dropped Art, she would have said yes to him—even when she hadn't wanted to. Mia was right. She needed more practice.

"Where do you want to put her?" Kisten said cheerfully.

A shrug lifted her shoulders. "The bathtub?"

Clearly enjoying himself, he lifted the box and headed into the paneled hallway. "Holy Christ!" he shouted, faint from the wall between them. "Have you seen his bathroom?"

Tired, Ivy rose from the hearth, trying not to look at Art sprawled on the floor. "No."

"I'm going to put her in the hot tub."

"He's got a hot tub?" That would explain the scent of chlorine, and Ivy went to see, her eyebrows rising at the small tub flush with the floor. Kisten had turned it on, and though it wasn't warm yet, tiny bubbles swirled in the artificial current. Putting Sleeping Beauty in that was going to make a mess, but it would help remove any traces of Piscary and blur that she had been stuck in the refrigerator for a day. Not to mention a dripping wet corpse was harder to get rid of than a dry one. Art wasn't smart enough to manage it before the I.S. knocked on his door.

Kisten had gone respectfully silent, and keeping the woman in the box, they worked at getting her out of the plastic and duct tape. Jaw clenched, Ivy worked her out of her clothes, handing them to Kisten one by one to be sprayed with the de-enzyme solution from the bar to remove Piscary's scent. The bottle was heavy as it hit Ivy's palm, and with Kisten's help, they sprayed her down as well, taking extra care with the open wounds.

Disturbed, she met Kisten's eyes in the silence, and together they slipped Sleeping Beauty into the water, wedging the corpse between an edge and the railing. While Kisten tidied, Ivy went back for the wine and a glass.

Carefully keeping her prints off it, Ivy pressed Sleeping Beauty's hand around the glass several times before adding a few lip prints. She dribbled some wine into the woman's mouth, then the glass, which she set at arm's length. There wouldn't be any in her stomach, and there wouldn't be any of her blood in Art's system either, but it was a game of perception, not absolutes. Besides, all she needed to do was eliminate any evidence of Piscary.

Kisten had the vial of Art's spit, and crouching by the tub, she took a sterile swab and ran it through the woman's open wounds. Finished, she stood, and together they looked down at her.

"She had a nice smile," Kisten finally said, gaze flicking to Ivy. "You okay with this?"

"No, I'm not okay with this," Ivy said, feeling empty. "But she's dead, isn't she. We can't hurt her anymore."

Kisten hesitated, then grabbed the box and maneuvered his way out. Ivy picked up the heavy-duty shears he had left and tucked them behind her waistband. Looking at the woman, she crouched to brush the long hair from the corpse's closed eyes. An impulsive "thank you," slipped from Ivy's lips, and, flustered, she stood.

Sickened, she backed out of the room. This was ugly. She was ugly. The things she did were ugly, and she didn't want to do them anymore. Her stomach was cramping when she found Kisten standing above Art, and she forced herself to look tall and unbothered. The broken-down box and plastic wrap were already in the trash bag, along with everything else. "You sure you don't want me to move him upstairs?" he asked. "They might call it a suicide."

Ivy shook her head, checking the bottom of the woman's shoes and setting them by the stairway. "Everyone's going to know what I did, but as long as there is no easy evidence, they'll let it go as me thinking outside the box. No one likes him anyway. But if I kill him, they'll have to do a more thorough investigation."

It was perfect in so many ways. Art would be cited for Piscary's homicide and end up in jail. She would get to write her own six-month review. No one would mess with her for a while, not wanting a dead body showing up in their bathroom. She was a force not to be taken lightly. The thought didn't make her as happy as she thought it would.

Kisten seemed to notice, since he touched her arm to bring her eyes to his. She blinked at the color of his

hair and the fact that he was shorter than she, even if it
was an illusion. It was a damn good illusion. "You did
all right," he said. "Piscary will be impressed."

She hid her face by leaning to scoop up the duct
tape. That Piscary would be proud of her lacked the expected thrill, too. For a moment, only the sound of the
tape being unwound and wrapped about Art's wrists
and ankles rose over the hiss of the propane fireplace.
The tape wouldn't stop him, but all they needed was to
get to the stairs.

"Ready?" Ivy asked when she tossed the tape into
her duffel bag and took out her boots.

Kisten turned from his last-minute wipe down of fin-
gerprints. "All set."

As she sat on the hearth and laced her boots, Ivy
looked over the room. The scent of chlorine was growing stronger as the water warmed, hiding the odor of
dead girl. She wanted a moment with Art. Why the hell
not? She'd earned a little gloating. Let him know she
caught him covering up a murder. "Wait for me in the
van," she said. "I'll be right there."

Kisten grinned, clearly not surprised. "Two minutes," he said. "Any longer than that, and you're playing with him."

She snorted, giving him a swat on the ass as he
started up the stairs with her duffel bag and the trash.
His blond hair caught the light, and she watched until
he vanished in a flash of morning sun. Still she waited
until the faint sound of the van starting up met her before she turned Art's hand palm up and cut the strip
with the shears. Tucking them behind her waistband,
she stepped back and teased the amulet off his hand
and into its little bag.

For a panicked moment she thought she had killed

him, but her fear must have scented the air since Art jerked, his eyes black when they focused on her. He tried to move, his attention going to the duct tape about his wrists and ankles. Chuckling, he wedged himself into an upright position against the couch, and Ivy's face burned.

"Piscary thinks so much of you," he said condescendingly. "He needs to wipe the sand from his eyes and see you as the little girl you are, playing with boys too big for her."

He tensed his arms, and Ivy forced herself to stay relaxed. But the tape held and she bent at the waist to look him in the eyes. "You okay?"

"This isn't winning you any friends, but yes, I'm okay."

Satisfied she hadn't hurt him, she rose and plucked up the wine bottle and gave it another pull, the heat of the fire warming her legs. "You've been a bad boy, Art," she said, hip cocked.

He ran his eyes over her, going still when he realized she was wearing her usual leather and spandex. His face abruptly lost its emotion. "Why is my hot tub going? What day is this? Who was here?"

Again he pulled against the tape, starting a rip. Ivy set the bottle down and moved closer, sending her wine breath over him to shift his silky black curls. It didn't matter if her presence was placed here. The entire I.S. tower knew where she was this morning. "I'm not happy," she said. "I came over here to make good on our arrangement, and I find another girl down here?"

Art shifted his shoulders, arms bulging. "What the hell did you do, Ivy?"

Smiling, she leaned over him. "It's not what I did, Artie. It's what I found. You need to be more careful with your cookies. You're leaving crumbs all over your house."

"This isn't funny," he snarled, and Ivy moved to the stairway.

"No, it isn't," she said, knowing that the tape would last as long as his ignorance. "You have a dead girl in your hot tub, Artie, and I'm out of here. The deal is off. I don't need your approval to move into the Arcane Division. You're going to jail." Adrenaline struck through her when she turned her back and her foot touched the lowest stair. The door was open and ambient sunlight was leaking in. He couldn't put one foot on them without risking death. She almost hoped he would.

"Ivy!" Art exclaimed, and she turned at the sound of ripping tape.

Pulse pounding, she hesitated. She was safe. It was done. "You made one mistake, Art," she said, taking in his anger. "You shouldn't have tried to use me to cover up that witch's murder," she said, and the color drained from him. "That pissed me off." Giving him a bunny-eared "kiss-kiss" she turned and took the stairs with a slow, taunting pace.

"This isn't going to work, Ivy!" he shouted, and her pulse leaped at the sound of the tape ripping, but she had reached the top and it was *far* too late. She smiled as she emerged into his kitchen. He was stuck down there with that corpse until the sun went down. If he called in help to get it out, it would damn him faster. An anonymous tip from a concerned neighbor was going to bring someone knocking on his door within thirty minutes. "No hard feelings, Art," she said. "Strictly business." She went to shut the door so he wouldn't get light sick, hesitating. "Really," she added, closing the door on his scream of outrage.

Scooping up her duffel bag from where Kisten had left it, she sauntered out the front door and down the steep walk to the street. Kisten was waiting, and she slipped into the passenger-side seat, throwing her bag into the back. She imagined the fury belowground, glad she could walk away. It didn't matter if anyone saw her leave. She was supposed to be here.

"Two minutes on the nose," Kisten said, leaning over to give her a kiss. He was still wearing her disguise amulet, and she caught him looking at himself and his hair. "Are you okay, love?" he asked, hitting his new accent hard and fussing with his bangs.

Rolling down the window, she put her arm on the sill as he drove away and the sun hit her. The memory of being unable to say no to Art resounded in her, and the lure of the bloodlust. Saying no had been impossible, but she had stopped him—and herself. It had been hard, but she felt good in a melancholy way. It wasn't the glorious shock of ecstasy, but more like a sunbeam, unnoticed when you first find it, but its warmth growing until you felt . . . good.

"I'm all right," she said, squinting from the morning sun. "I like who I am today."

6

Ivy dropped the empty box on her desk and sat before it, swiveling her chair back and forth until someone walked past her open door. Adopting a more businesslike mien, she looked over her office. Her eyebrows rose, and she plucked her favorite pen from the cup and then tossed the empty box into the hall. The thump silenced the gossip, and she smirked. They could have everything. All she wanted was her favorite pen. Well, and a pair of thicker leather pants. And an updated map of the city. A computer would be helpful, but they wouldn't let her take the one she'd been using. Some really comfortable boots. Sunglasses—mirror sunglasses.

A soft knuckle-knock at her open door brought her head around, and she smiled without showing her teeth. "Rat," she said companionably. "Come to see me off?"

The large officer eased into her office, a manila folder in his hand. "I won the pool," he said, ducking his head. "I've got your, ah, transfer papers. How you doing?"

"Depends." She leaned across her desk, biting her finger coyly. "What's the word on the street?"

He laughed. "You're bad. No one will be looking at

you for a while." Brow pinching, he came in another step. "You sure you don't want to work Arcane? It's not too late."

Ivy's pulse quickened at the lure of bloodlust she knew she couldn't resist. "I don't want to work in the Arcane anymore," she said, eyes lowered. "I need to get out from underground. Spend some time in the sun."

The officer slumped, the folder before him like a fig leaf. "You're ticking them off with this rebellious shit. This isn't Piscary's camarilla, it's a business. They had a late meeting about you this morning in the lowest floor."

Fear slid through her, quickly stifled. "They can't fire me. There was no evidence that I had anything to do with that girl in Art's tub."

"No. You're clear. And remind me to stay on your good side." He grinned, but it faded fast. "You did contaminate that crime scene, and they're almost ignoring that. You should lay low for a while, do what they want you to do. You have your entire life and afterlife ahead of you. Don't screw it up your first six months here."

Ivy grimaced, flicking her attention past him to the outer offices. "They're already blaming my demotion on my—lapse. They can't punish me twice for the same thing." The reality was she was being demoted because she refused to move up to the Arcane. That was fine by her.

"Publicly," he said, making her agitated. "What happens behind closed doors is something else. You're making a mistake," he insisted. "They can use your talents down there."

"Don't you mean a new infusion?" Rat winced, and she held up a hand and leaned back into her chair, well aware it put her in a position of power with him standing. "Whatever. I won't be manipulated, Rat. I'd rather take a pay cut and go where I don't have to worry about it for a while."

"If only it was that easy." Rat dropped the folder on her desk as if it meant something. "Ah, I thought you'd like to see your new partner's file."

In a smooth, alarmed motion, Ivy sat up. "Whoa. Put your caps on. I agreed to move upstairs, but no one said anything about a partner."

Rat shrugged, his wide shoulders bunching his uniform. "They can't give you a pay cut, so you're pulling double duty chaperoning a newbie for a year. Intern with two years of social science and three years pulling familiars out of trees. Management wants her under someone with a more, ah, textbook technique before they instate her as a runner, so she's all yours, Ivy. Don't let her get you killed. We like you ju-u-u-ust the way you are."

The last was said with dripping sarcasm, and her face hot, Ivy pushed the folder away. "She's not even a full runner? I've worked too hard for my degree to be a babysitter. No way."

Rat chuckled and pushed it back with a single, thick-knuckled finger. "Yes way. Unless you want to move down to Arcane where you belong."

Ivy almost growled. She hated her mother. She hated Piscary. *No, she hated their control over her.* Slowly she pulled the folder to her and opened it. "Oh my God," she breathed as she looked at the picture, thinking it couldn't get any worse. "A witch? They partnered me with a witch? Whose bright-ass idea was *that*?"

Rat laughed, pulling Ivy's eyes from her "partner's" picture. Slumping back, she tried not to frown. Though it was clearly meant to be a punishment, this might not be a bad thing. A witch wouldn't be after her blood, and the relief of not having to fight that would be enough to compensate for the extra work that having such a weak partner would engender. *A witch? They were laughing at her. The entire tower was laughing at her.*

"You said management doesn't want her on her own. What's wrong with her?" she asked and Rat took her shoulder in a thick hand and drew her reluctantly to her feet.

"Nothing," he said, grinning. "She's impulsive is all. It's a match made in heaven, Ivy. You'll be best friends before the week is out: going shopping, eating chocolate, catching chick-flicks after work. You'll love it! Trust me."

Ivy realized she was clenching her jaw, and she forced her teeth apart before she gave herself a headache. Her partner was a flake. She was partnered with a girly-girl flake who wanted to be a runner. This was going to be pure hell. Rat laughed, and seeing no other option, Ivy dragged the folder to her, tucked it under her arm, and headed for the door with Rat, leaving her old office and its comforting walls behind for an open office with pressboard walls and bad coffee.

It was only for a year. How bad could it be?

Born and raised in Tornado Alley, KIM HARRISON now resides in more sultry climates. The bestselling author of *Dead Witch Walking; The Good, the Bad, and the Undead;* and *Every Which Way But Dead,* she rolls a very good game of dice, hangs out with a guy in leather, and is hard at work on the next novel of the Hollows.

For more information, go to *www.kimharrison.net.*

The
Claire Switch
Project

Lynsay Sands

1

"A *bunny.*" **The disgust John Heathcliffe poured** into those two words made Claire Beckett roll her eyes as she rinsed out and refilled the water bottle from the rabbit cage. He wasn't finished with his bitching, however, and continued, "I don't know why we can't—"

"You *do* know why, John," Kyle Lockhart countered with what Claire considered the patience of a saint. He didn't raise his head from the report he was reading, but added, "Because we have to follow safety procedures. We test it on animals to ensure that it's safe *before* we let it anywhere near humans."

Claire glanced toward John as she moved back to the rabbit cage, noting the irritation that flashed across his face. John, apparently, didn't appreciate Kyle's patience, but then she suspected there was little John appreciated about Kyle. Claire knew he resented Dr. Cohen putting Kyle in charge of the lab. John felt it should have been he. Both men were in the last stage of attaining their doctorates and it made their relationship somewhat competitive, at least on John's part. Kyle didn't seem to have the same issues, but then he was the one in charge.

"We've already tested it on a dozen mice and rats and now three bunnies," John pointed out impatiently as Claire reset the water bottle in the rabbit cage.

"Yes," Kyle agreed. This time he did glance up from the reports as he added pointedly, "And the first couple of those animals ended up a puddle of mush."

John waved that away as unimportant. "Only the first few, and that was because we were giving them too much juice. We fixed that. We now know the amount needed per pound. We—"

"We are testing it on the rabbit, John," Kyle said firmly. "And then we'll test it on a bigger animal, like a—"

"Yes, yes," the other man said impatiently. "We'll test it on half a dozen bunnies, then half a dozen cats, and then another half a dozen dogs, and then monkeys, and then, and then, and then . . . I'll be an old man before we test it on an actual human. *If* I'm still alive," he said with disgust. "What use is it testing it on these animals anyway? They can't tell us what it's like. They don't understand what we've done to them, and they can't follow commands and try to change. They—"

"They can tell us if it's safe by surviving the procedure," Kyle countered shortly. "They can tell us what damage—if any—the procedure does to them physically by our following and testing them over the years."

"Years," John muttered. "Stupid, safe science."

"Yeah," Kyle said dryly as he closed the file and got to his feet. "Sucks huh?"

Claire bit her lip to keep from laughing and raised her eyebrows in question as Kyle turned his sky blue eyes her way.

"Claire, I need to go give Dr. Cohen the latest test results of our subjects. Would you mind getting Thumper out of his cage and strapping him into place while I'm gone? We'll start when I get back."

"Yes, Kyle." Claire turned back to the cage as he headed out of the lab, but her eyes immediately found him in the rectangular mirror on the wall over the cage. Her gaze dropped over Kyle in his long white smock. He looked so sexy in the smock. She wouldn't mind playing doctor/patient with him, she thought. Then her eyes moved to her own reflection, and she sighed as she took in the familiar features under the mop of red hair she had scraped back into a ponytail. She'd been told she was pretty more than a time or two in her life, and had a certain amount of confidence in her looks, but they didn't seem to matter to Kyle. He treated her more like a buddy or kid sister than a woman.

"Yes, Kyle," John mimicked nastily. "Thank you, Kyle. Bend me over the counter and—"

"You are such a jerk sometimes, John," Claire interrupted as she reopened the rabbit cage. She managed to use bored tones despite her irritation and embarrassment. If the man knew he was getting to her, he'd be like a dog with a bone. She knew that from experience. John had become increasingly rude since she'd refused his invitation to dinner two months ago. He'd decided her refusal was because she "had the hots" for Kyle. Which was true, but Claire had no idea how he knew that.

"Come on, Thumper," she cooed, scooping the white rabbit out of the cage. "There's nothing to be scared of."

"Right," John agreed as he moved to the panel that controlled the destabilizer. "We're just going to zap you with a molecular destabilizer that will turn you into a puddle of goo."

Claire glared at his back as she closed the cage door, then turned her attention to Thumper. Petting the rabbit soothingly, she said, "Don't listen to him. That hasn't happened for a long time, not since we figured out we were using too much juice. You'll be fine."

Claire continued to whisper soothing nonsense to the rabbit as she carried him into the experiment chamber. It was a small room, built in the center of the wide back wall of the lab. The chamber was only ten feet square, its front and side walls made of protective glass to allow viewing. This was where the molecular destabilizer waited. It looked like nothing more interesting than an X-ray machine, but it wasn't photons of electromagnetic interference that this machine shot out.

The automatic door shushed open for Claire, then closed behind her with the same soft sound as she carried Thumper to the table under the destabilizer. Setting the rabbit on the surface, she began to strap him down.

For some reason, this part of her job always bothered Claire. She didn't like strapping the animals down. Of course, they always panicked and began to struggle at this point, but she couldn't blame them, she wouldn't like to be strapped down, either. Then too, they were probably picking up on some of her nervousness. As she worked, Claire found her eyes flickering nervously up to the funnel-shaped projector the destabilizer beam came out of. She was always nervous around the thing, afraid it would suddenly start spitting its beam at her, which of course it couldn't do. Someone would have to turn it on for that to happen.

That thought made Claire glance over her shoulder and through the glass to the control panel. John was there, frowning and muttering to himself as he worked out the necessary calculations for the proper amount of power to use with Thumper. It was a very weight-specific process, needing a specific amount of power per pound of the animal. Too little and nothing would happen, too much and . . . but that had only happened with the first couple of trials.

Sighing, she turned back to Thumper and continued fixing the straps, making sure they were firmly in place, but not so tight they'd harm him. Despite her reservations about working so close to the destabilizer itself, Claire enjoyed her job. This was an exciting field to work in, this experiment on the cutting edge. They had used research on chameleons, as well as various changes natural in nature, such as gas turning into liquid when under pressure, and liquid to solid when cold. Putting it all together they had created their destabilizer, hoping that it would bring about cellular changes that would allow other animals to effect tonal changes that could act as camouflage. In effect, creating a chameleon rabbit, or a chameleon mouse, rat, dog, and—eventually—a chameleon human.

Finished with Thumper, Claire turned to head out of the room, pausing when John's voice came over the intercom.

"Claire, Thumper isn't aligned under the projector. Go back and fix it."

Frowning, she turned and moved back to the table to peer at the rabbit. He looked to be in the right position to her.

"Are you sure?" Claire asked, knowing John would hear her through the open intercom. "He looks right from here."

"The camera is only showing his lower half." She could hear the irritation in his voice. "Maybe it's the camera that's off kilter."

Claire glanced up, peering at the destabilizer itself.

"The camera is on the far side of the projector," John announced. "Take a look at it for me, will you?"

Claire frowned. As far as she could see, there was no way to get to the far side of the projector without crawling over the table.

"The table slides back," he said helpfully. "Just slide the table backward, then crawl under the projector and look up on the other side for a small camera. It should be aligned with the projector. If it isn't, I'll need Kyle to pick up some special tools on his way back from Dr. Cohen's office so I can adjust it."

She pushed gently on the table Thumper was strapped to. As John had said, it slid easily backward, leaving the floor under the destabilizer clear. Claire stared at the space, reluctant to fill it. She really didn't like the idea of climbing right under the projector. It would put her in the direct path of the destabilizing beam.

"Which is perfectly safe so long as it isn't on," she assured herself.

"Hello! I'm waiting here," John said testily.

Sighing, Claire dropped to her knees and crawled into the space where the table had been. Once under the projector, she raised her head and peered up. Claire spotted the camera at once, but it didn't look out of line to her.

"It looks fine," she said with a frown. "It—"

The words died in her throat as a white beam suddenly shot out of the destabilizer's projector. It hit her with a jolt, and Claire suddenly found herself unable to move or even scream. It felt exactly what she imagined being hit by lightning would be like. A quick crack of agony shot through her, hitting seemingly every nerve ending, then she went numb and unconsciousness claimed her.

* * *

"Claire?"

The voice sounded urgent and upset, but it took a moment before Claire could move or open her eyes in response. When she did, it was to find herself staring up at Kyle Lockhart. His blond hair was endearingly tousled, something she'd rarely seen since high school. His sky blue eyes were crinkled with concern, and his mouth a firm line in his chiseled face.

"Kyle?" Claire breathed.

"Oh, thank God." He closed his eyes briefly, then opened them just as quickly and straightened. "Come on, let's get you up."

Claire peered around as Kyle helped her to her feet. They were still in the experiment chamber, but by the front wall, as far from the molecular destabilizer as possible. The white beam that had shot such teeth-jarring pain into her was still pouring from the projector.

"This way." Kyle began to usher her to the door, but Claire glanced back toward the beam and frowned as she recalled what had happened.

"The destabilizer went off somehow while I was checking the camera," Claire said as he urged her out of the room. She shuddered at the recollection of the beam jolting through her body.

"John is the 'somehow,'" Kyle said grimly.

"John?" Claire asked sharply as he led her to a lab chair and eased her into it. "You mean he *deliberately* zapped me?"

"Yeah. The bastard was determined to try his human trials and must have decided you would be the test subject. The jerk."

Kyle placed a hand on her forehead and used his thumb to pull one eyelid up. He peered into her eye for

a moment, then shifted his hand to the other side to re-
peat the process.

"Your eyes are a little dilated," he said with a frown.
"How's your vision?"

"Fine," Claire assured him. The moment he removed
his hand from her forehead, she turned her head to
glance toward the control panel, looking for John. The
dark-haired man was out cold on the floor in front of
the machine.

"What happened to him?" she asked, more out of
curiosity than any real concern. It was hard to feel concern for the man after what he'd done.

"I knocked him out," Kyle muttered as he took her
pulse.

Claire's eyes shot to his face in surprise. John was
six feet tall and handsome in his own way, but he had
the body of a scientist, long and lean. He also had the
studious nature of a scientist and wasn't the kind of
guy who ran around getting into fights.

Kyle shrugged uncomfortably under her startled
glance.

"I came back in and saw what he was doing and
punched him," he said almost apologetically. "Then I
ran in to the experiment chamber to pull you out from
under the beam."

"You *punched* him?" Claire asked, still marveling
over the fact.

"It was just . . . instinct," Kyle explained with embarrassment. "I was . . . upset."

"Oh," Claire said huskily. "Thank you."

Kyle shrugged and avoided her eyes by staring at his
watch as he took her pulse, but then his lips twisted
with displeasure and he said, "It's my fault. I should
have realized John would try a stunt like that. He's

been crabbing about the animal trials from the start and insisting we need to do human trials."

"It's not your fault," Claire said quickly. "I've heard all his complaining, but didn't expect him to pull a stunt like this, either."

Kyle nodded, but she could tell he still felt responsible.

"Your pulse is a little fast, but not alarmingly so." He straightened and peered at her. "How do you feel?"

Claire paused and considered. She felt a little shaky, but then she'd been knocked out by the beam. Other than that, however, she felt pretty much normal.

"I feel fine," Claire said at last. "I don't feel different or anything."

Kyle hesitated, his gaze moving around the lab, then asked, "Do you think you're up to walking?"

When Claire nodded, he urged her back to her feet. "Come on, then. This has been more than enough for the day. Let's get out of here."

Claire couldn't have agreed more. She felt fine, but didn't want to stay in the lab. And she definitely didn't want to be there when John woke up. If he said a single word to her, Claire might be tempted to commit bodily harm on the jerk. He could have killed her with that stunt.

Kyle took her arm, eyeing her closely. He was just opening the door when Claire suddenly recalled the poor rabbit still strapped to the table in the experiment chamber.

"Wait." She paused and turned back. "What about Thumper?"

"Oh." Kyle glanced toward the glass-walled room. After a hesitation, he said, "Wait here" and hurried over to the control panel to switch off the destabilizer, then continued on to the small room.

Claire watched him unstrap the animal, smiling as she saw his lips moving as he petted and soothed the rabbit. Like herself, Kyle tended to murmur and coo nonsense to the lab animals, and she knew he got just as distressed when something went wrong. It was only John who treated them like blocks of wood.

Thoughts of the other man drew her attention to his unconscious form and she scowled. John Heathcliffe had done some rotten things in the time she'd known him, but today had taken the cake. It wasn't just that she could have been killed, but who knew what effects the destabilizer could have on her?

The door to the experiment chamber opened with a soft swish, and Claire glanced over, relieved to be distracted from her thoughts. Kyle was quick about putting Thumper in his cage and then he hurried to join her at the door.

"What are we going to do about him?" Claire asked, nodding toward John's still form.

"Leave him. I'd call security, but . . ." Kyle hesitated, then admitted, "I'm worried about Dr. Cohen's reaction if he learns you were exposed to the molecular destabilizer."

It was all he had to say. If anyone found out, Claire could expect to be kept here in the lab in her very own cage—though it would probably be a sterile white room rather than an actual cage. She would be subjected to hundreds of tests and asked a million questions every day to see just how her mind had been affected by exposure to the destabilizer.

No, thank you. Claire didn't know what effect her exposure would have on her, but no matter what it was, she'd rather not be locked up while it happened.

"You don't think John will tell?" she asked anxiously.

"And risk being banned from the scientific community?" Kyle asked with a snort. "Not to mention being arrested for assault, because that's what it was." He shook his head. "No. He'll keep his mouth shut."

Relief soaking through her, Claire nodded and allowed Kyle to take her arm and lead her out of the lab.

They didn't run into anyone on the way down to the parking garage. Claire was so unsettled by the whole experience that they were in Kyle's car before she remembered her own vehicle.

"What about my car?" Claire asked as Kyle started the engine of his little red car.

Pausing, he glanced in the direction of her parking spot, a small frown playing about his lips, then he shook his head. "I don't think it's a good idea for you to be driving just now. In fact, I don't want you to be alone. I was planning on taking you home with me so I could keep an eye on you for at least tonight, preferably the weekend. But if nothing happens and you continue to seem fine, I'll bring you by to pick up your car tomorrow morning."

When she nodded her agreement, Kyle added, "Fortunately, it's Friday, so you'll have the weekend to recover before we have to decide what—if anything—to tell Dr. Cohen about this."

"I thought we didn't want him to know?" Claire asked with a frown. "I mean, if nothing has happened . . ."

"I don't want John to get away with this," Kyle said solemnly. "We could tell Dr. Cohen that he *tried* to turn the destabilizer on you and I arrived as he did it and knocked him out. That you managed to throw yourself out of the way when you heard it power up."

Claire blinked with a sudden realization.

"What is it?" Kyle asked.

"I *didn't* hear it power up," she said slowly, perplexed by the fact. Usually the soft hum started while she strapped down the animal, then built to a high-pitched whine as she left the room.

"He must have powered it up before you went in," Kyle said thoughtfully, and his expression became even more forbidding. "The bastard must have planned to try this all along. He was just waiting for a time when I was out of the lab." Kyle cursed. "I never should have—"

Claire placed her hand over his on the steering wheel and patted him soothingly. "You couldn't know. It's fine. Let's just go."

Blowing his breath out, Kyle nodded and shifted the car into gear, then backed out of his parking spot.

"You're okay with staying over tonight?" Kyle asked once they were out of the parking garage.

"Yes." Claire nodded. "To tell you the truth, if something's going to happen, I'd rather not be alone."

Kyle gave a nod, and fell silent, leaving Claire to worry over what might result from the experiment. Nothing much had appeared to happen yet to the animals they'd tested it on. If put in front of a white background, some of them lightened in color, like a chameleon taking on its surroundings, but it didn't happen to all the animals and it didn't happen regularly. This didn't seem to bother Kyle. Claire supposed he was just happy it happened at all. As John had pointed out, the animals didn't understand what was done to them so simply might not be using their full abilities. She did understand, however, and supposed that was why John had broken all the rules and exposed her to the destabilizer.

Claire peered down at her hands, the only part of her body that wasn't covered by clothing and that she could see at the moment. She stared at where they rested in her lap, but they looked the same as always to her. Her skin wasn't suddenly lightening to match the white smock she wore. For a moment, she considered trying to make them lighten, but then changed her mind. She was almost afraid to find her exposure had had some effect.

"Here we are."

Claire glanced up and felt herself relax. They were pulling into the driveway of the home Kyle shared with his twin sister, Jill. It was an old Victorian house on the edge of the city, their childhood home. Kyle and Jill had inherited it jointly when their parents died in a car accident some years back. The twins got along well enough that they'd decided to live there together until one of them married. At which point, they'd either sell the house and split the profits, or one of them would buy the other out.

Claire had been in the charming old house many times over the years. She and Jill had been best friends since grade school. Claire had slept over countless times as a teenager and still did. It was a second home to her, and she wasn't surprised to feel relief ease through her as Kyle parked the car in the drive.

"Jill's home early," Kyle commented with a frown. "I wonder what's up."

Claire shook her head, her eyebrows drawing together with concern. After the accident that had taken their parents' lives, Kyle had taken his half of their parents' insurance money and invested it. Jill had used her half to purchase a little clothing store downtown. It was doing well, mostly because Jill was a very dedicated store owner, willing to put in long hours to make it work. She usually started early and worked late. Her being home in the middle of the day was unusual.

Kyle slid out of the car and started around to her side, but Claire opened the door and stepped out before he could get there to open it for her. She smiled faintly as he took her arm to walk her to the door, noting the worry still visible in his eyes as he peered her way. His concern was sweet . . . and encouraging to Claire. She'd had a crush on him all through high school. It had blossomed into something more since she'd started working with him. Unfortunately, despite Jill's assertions to the contrary, Claire suspected he thought of her as nothing more than a buddy and coworker. She wished it was otherwise.

"Jill?" Kyle called out as they entered the house.

"Kyle?" Jill's voice came from the living room. Her tone suggested she was just as surprised at his arrival home in the middle of the day as they had been to know she was here.

"Yeah. Are you okay?" Kyle led Claire up the hall. "You aren't sick or something, are you?"

"Or something."

Claire frowned at the weariness evident in Jill's voice. As they entered the living room, she stepped around Kyle and peered at her friend. Jill sat balled up in a corner of the couch, her shoulders slumped and posture dejected. She was pale, her eyes red-rimmed, and she held a freshly opened container of ice cream . . . always a bad sign.

"What's wrong?" Claire asked with concern as she moved to sit beside her on the couch.

"What are you doing here?" Jill asked with surprise.

"Never mind that," Claire said. "Tell us what's wrong."

"Nothing," Jill said, then sighed and admitted, "Actually, I just got dumped."

"What?" Claire asked with amazement. Jill had been seeing a store owner named Ted Leacock for the last six months. Claire knew her friend had thought it was "the real deal." That she'd found the man she would marry and raise babies with.

"Yeah," Jill held up the container of Ben & Jerry's ice cream. "So I came home for lunch."

"Oh, honey." Claire hugged her with sympathy.

Jill shrugged. "Plenty of good men out there, and right now Ben and Jerry are being *very* sympathetic."

Kyle shifted and Claire glanced his way to see a myriad of emotions cross his face, anger for his sister, a frown of concern, then discomfort.

"Well," he said finally. "You can't just eat ice cream, Jill. I'll see about lunch."

Claire watched him leave the room, then glanced back to Jill as the blond slid a spoonful of ice cream into her mouth.

"I'm sorry, Jill," she said quietly.

Jill shrugged. "Better now than later."

"You're too good for him anyway."

"I thought you liked him?" Jill asked with a frown.

"I did. He seemed nice," Claire said quickly. "Though he obviously had bad taste if he broke up with you . . . and you deserve a guy with good taste. A super guy."

"Super guy, huh?" Jill smiled briefly, then sighed. "He wasn't as nice as we thought, anyway. It seems I wasn't the only woman he was dating."

"What?" Claire asked with surprise, then understanding crossed her face. "All those late nights working?"

"Yeah. It seems he was *working* on a couple of other

girls. Trying to decide who would be the winner in the 'Ted's wife lotto.' I apparently made it to the final two, but the other finalist won out."

"What?" Claire repeated with amazement.

Jill grimaced. "It was apparently close. So close, in fact, that he couldn't bring himself to break the news to me until now. A week before the wedding to the winner."

Claire opened her mouth, but Jill forestalled her with "Please don't say what again."

Claire closed her mouth, frowned, then shook her head. "But you two went away last weekend."

"Yes. And have been sleeping together for the last four of the six months we've been dating." Jill grimaced. "I guess I should be glad I wasn't the winner. Who needs a jerk like that for a husband?"

Claire nodded. "He'll never be faithful. Oh, honey. I *am* sorry." She gave her another hug.

"I guess I'll have to go to the grocery store," Kyle announced coming back into the living room. "We'll need lunch and supper."

"I thought you two were going to the school reunion tonight?" Claire reminded him, peering over Jill's shoulder. She had decided not to go herself, but the twins had planned to attend, and Claire was sure that getting out would be the best thing for her friend.

Jill snorted at the idea. "Like I'm going to the reunion without a man on my arm? You have got to be kidding. Magda would spend the entire night insulting me . . . the bitch," she added on a sniff.

"And I'd rather not leave you alone," Kyle said. He was speaking to Claire, but his concerned gaze was bouncing between her and his sister. "I need to keep an eye on you for at least twenty-four hours, though the whole weekend would be better."

Jill stiffened in Claire's arms, then pulled back to peer at her.

"Why? What's happened?"

Claire merely grimaced, while Kyle said, "John zapped her with the destabilizer."

"What?!" Claire winced at the shriek as Jill peered from her to Kyle and asked, "How? Was it an accident?"

"No," Kyle said grimly,

"You're kidding?" Jill looked outraged. She was one of the very few people privy to their experiments and what they entailed. "How?"

Sighing, Claire shook her head. "I had strapped in the bunny and started out of the room, but he sent me back to check on the camera. He said it was offline and told me how to move the table so I could kneel under it and check the camera alignment. Once I was there, zap," she finished with a shrug.

"So that's how he did it," Kyle murmured, and she realized he hadn't known how John had got her under the camera and therefore under the beam.

"The toad!" Jill said with disgust, tossing the ice cream carton on the coffee table.

"Yeah." Claire sighed. Really, it was unconscionable. She could have been killed and was just lucky Kyle had got her out before any damage was done.

"Dangerous toad," Kyle said grimly. "He was tired of running trials and decided to speed the experiment along."

Ben & Jerry—and even Ted—briefly forgotten, Jill caught Claire by the arms and looked her over as if expecting to find her glowing green and falling to pieces. "Are you okay?"

"I'm fine," Claire assured her firmly. "Really. I don't feel bad at all."

"Well, you aren't suddenly turning the same color as the couch or anything," Jill murmured, eyes narrowed.

Claire glanced toward the paisley couch and muttered, "Thank God."

"Still, Kyle's right, we can't leave you alone this weekend," Jill said firmly.

Claire shrugged, uncomfortable with all the concern.

"Although I'm not going to be any fun tonight," Jill added with a grimace, then brightened, her expression that of someone who's just had an idea. "You two could go to the reunion together, though. That way Kyle could go and still keep an eye on you."

Claire flushed, knowing Jill was playing matchmaker. Her friend had known about Claire's crush on Kyle for years and thought they would be perfect together. As far as Jill was concerned, the only thing keeping them apart was their own shyness. Claire didn't doubt for a minute that Jill was trying to push them together, and while she appreciated it, one glance at Kyle's reluctant expression told her it wasn't working.

"Well, I'm not certain it's a good idea to take Claire anywhere until we're sure she's okay," Kyle said slowly. Turning, he moved back up the hall toward the front door, saying, "Keep an eye on her while I go to the grocery store. Okay, Jill?"

"I won't take my eyes off her," Jill promised.

2

"**H**e is *so* not interested in me," Claire bemoaned as the door closed behind Kyle.

"Yes, he is," Jill said with exasperation. "I've been telling you that since we were all twelve. He's crazy about you, Claire."

"Yeah right," she snorted. "That's why he jumped at the chance to go to the reunion with me tonight."

Jill tsked with disgust and snapped the lid back on the container of Ben & Jerry's. "You two are so pathetic. Honestly. You've adored him for years, and he's been following you with calf eyes just as long, yet neither of you has the balls to do anything about it. When he comes back, you should just follow him into his room, jump his bones, and get it over with. I bet the two of you wouldn't surface until Monday . . . if then."

Claire imagined what would happen if she followed Jill's advice. She imagined Kyle coming home, putting away the groceries in the kitchen, then going to his room for something. She would follow, close the door, then . . . then . . .

Then what? Did she throw off her clothes and wait for him to do something? The only problem was, he'd likely assume her behavior was a result of being subjected to the destabilizer. Then he'd start checking her pulse and such.

What if she just walked in, closed the door, then kissed him? Claire bit her lip at the idea. He'd probably blame that on the destabilizer, too. He'd think her brain had been destabilized by the exposure. Blowing her breath out on a sigh, she shook her head. "If he were interested, he'd have done something about it."

"Like *you* have?" Jill asked archly, taking the ice cream with her as she stood up. "What makes you think he's any less shy than you are? Besides, he's in a much more delicate spot than you. He's your supervisor at the lab. Asking you out could be considered sexual harassment."

Claire frowned over that as Jill carried the ice cream out to the kitchen. She'd appreciated Kyle getting her the job at the lab. While he'd gotten his bachelor of science and continued on for his master's and doctorate, Claire—to avoid costing her parents too much money—had stopped with her bachelor's. Since then, she'd taken courses toward her own master's at night, while bouncing from contract position to contract position during the day to support herself and her further education. Then, last year, Kyle had gotten her a job in the lab where he was interning under Dr. Cohen. At the end of this year, she would have her master's and Kyle his doctorate. Now, Jill's comment made Claire wonder if she should have taken the position in the lab after all.

"The mail's here. God, they deliver later and later all the time."

Claire glanced toward Jill as she returned to the living room carrying a stack of mail.

"Bill, bill, bill," Jill muttered, leafing through the envelopes. She paused at a magazine, stared at the cover, then heaved a depressed sigh. "I bet Ted would have picked me for his wife if I looked like her."

"You're better off without him," Claire murmured.

"Yeah, but if I looked like her, I probably would have been the *dumper* rather than the *dumpee*," she pointed out, dropping the magazine on the coffee table. "It's always better to be the dumper."

Claire peered down at the magazine, noting who was on the cover. Brooke Jordan, one of the world's most popular—not to mention successful—models. Tall, leggy, slim, and gorgeous, the woman exuded both beauty and sex appeal in megawatts. Men all over the world would kill to be with her, and women all over the world would kill to be her. Apparently, that included Jill.

And me, Claire acknowledged to herself, then said aloud, "Well, I wish we both looked like her. Then you could dump Ted and maybe I could get Kyle. I bet he wouldn't be so shy if I looked like her."

Jill made a clucking sound and propped her hands on her hips as she glared down at her. "He likes you just the way you—"

Claire glanced up in question at the way Jill suddenly cut herself off mid-sentence. The blond appeared frozen, her mouth still open, and eyes wide with shock. Claire felt herself go stiff in reaction as concern welled up within her. "What is it?"

"Oh . . . my . . . God!" The words were drawn out and spaced apart for emphasis.

"What?" Claire asked, getting to her feet. She

peered down at herself in a panic, afraid she'd suddenly taken on the paisley pattern of the couch, but her hands were still her hands. She peered back to Jill. "What?"

"You look like . . . *her,*" Jill said faintly.

"What?" Claire asked, her heart beating wildly in her chest. "I look like who her?"

"Like what's-her-name. You look like that model, that—" Jill snatched up the magazine off the coffee table and shoved it in her face. *"Her!"*

Claire peered down and found herself staring at the photograph of Brooke Jordan. She shook her head slowly with disbelief. "I can't—I don't—"

"The hell you don't!" Jill grabbed Claire by the arm with her free hand to drag her across the living room. She was muttering the whole way. "I can't believe this. I just can't believe it. Oh my God, this is incredible. Do you realize how incredible this is?"

Claire just stumbled along behind her, anxiety and confusion rife in her head. She *couldn't* look like the model. It was impossible. Jill was playing a joke on her. That thought gave her some relief from the welter of emotions whirling through her head. Of course! That was it! Jill was playing a joke.

"Here!" Jill slammed through the bathroom door. She tossed the magazine on the counter, then shoved Claire in front of the mirror.

Claire stared at herself. And stared. Jill wasn't playing a joke. Claire was staring into the mirror, but the stunned face looking back was Brooke Jordan's. She tentatively touched her face. It felt normal, both in that her fingers felt like they were touching skin and her skin felt the fingers touching them, but it wasn't her face she was looking at and those gorgeous chestnut waves were not her hair, either. Claire was a natural redhead.

"You look exactly like her. *Exactly*," Jill breathed with awe. "Right down to her clothes."

Claire blinked, then switched her gaze to her body. At first, she didn't understand what Jill was talking about. She was still wearing the white smock and black pants she'd left work in. Then Claire noticed the pink collar of a T-shirt was visible under the open neckline of her white blouse and smock.

"What . . . ?" Bewildered, Claire stripped off the smock and unbuttoned several buttons of her white blouse. Underneath was the same pink T-shirt Brooke Jordan had been wearing on the magazine cover.

"Are you wearing her capri pants too?" Jill reached for the waist of her black dress pants, but Claire danced instinctively away, then paused and undid them herself.

"Holy Jeez," Jill breathed as baby blue linen was revealed poking up from under her white lace panties. "You're wearing her capri pants, too."

"I can't be," Claire said faintly, then finished stripping her own clothes away until she stood there in a pink T-shirt, blue capri pants and Brooke Jordan's face. She stared at herself in the mirror with bewilderment.

"You're a dead ringer."

"But how?" Claire asked faintly. "This doesn't make sense."

"Of course, it does. It makes perfect sense. It's the destabilizer," Jill said triumphantly, then tilted her head and asked, "Do you think Kyle would let me try it out? Just imagine what I could—"

"It can't be the destabilizer," Claire argued. "It's supposed to cause a chameleon effect. The ability to change skin tone, not *shape*."

Jill paused to consider that, then suggested, "Well maybe you haven't really changed shape. Maybe you're still under there and it's just like a painting over your skin."

Catching Claire by surprise, Jill suddenly reached out and began to feel her face. A frown immediately tugged at her lips. "This doesn't feel like your face."

"What do you mean?" Alarmed by the statement, Claire put her own hands to her face once more, but this time doing more than just touching her cheeks. She began to explore her face like a blind person examining features.

"Your nose should be turned up," Jill pointed out. "You have the cutest little turn at the end, but Brooke has a straight nose, kind of Roman. Your nose feels Roman now. I guess it isn't just a chameleonlike painting on your face."

Claire immediately shifted her fingers to her own nose. It *didn't* feel like her nose. It was too straight.

"You've actually changed shape," Jill said, then brightened. "Like a shape-shifter. The destabilizer made you a shape-shifter! How did you do it?"

"I didn't," Claire said faintly as she tried to absorb what had happened to her. "John did."

"Not that!" Jill said swiftly, then waved to her face and body. "This. How did you . . . you know . . . shift?"

"I don't know," Claire admitted, glancing down at herself with bewilderment. "I just stared at the picture thinking that Kyle might be more interested in me if I looked like her . . . and wishing that I did . . . look like her, I mean."

"I've told you and told you, Claire. Kyle likes you as you are," Jill insisted, then paused, frowned, and amended, "Well, he *did* like you . . . as you were."

Claire blinked at the correction, anxiety crowding in at what it suggested.

"Never mind." Jill waved the problem of Kyle away and snatched up the magazine she'd tossed on the counter. "Here, look at another model and see if you can do it again."

"I don't think I can," Claire admitted. "I don't know how I did it the first time."

"Just try," Jill insisted, leafing through several pages before settling on a short-haired blond. "Here. Do her."

"Jill, I—"

"Try," Jill ordered.

Claire hesitated, then peered down at the blond. She was beautiful, with full red lips and big green eyes. Claire took the magazine from Jill and concentrated on the picture, trying to put herself in the same frame of mind she'd been in earlier while looking at Brooke . . . Trying to drum up the same longing to be so beautiful and attractive to the opposite sex . . . To Kyle.

"Oh my Gawd!!" Jill squealed suddenly.

Concentration broken, Claire glanced up. "Did it work?"

Kyle's sister nodded dumbly.

Claire turned to the mirror and found herself staring at yet someone else's face; this time, the blond with short cropped hair and large red lips. Her body shape and clothing had also changed, her breasts appearing larger as they pushed up out of the strapless black blouse she was now wearing with black satin pants.

"How do you do the clothes?" Jill asked with amazement, reaching out to touch the pants.

"I don't know," Claire admitted. "It must be me. I mean the pink T-shirt and capri pants were *under* my own clothes."

"You mean . . . like this is *you*?" Jill asked, touching the satin. "Your cells?"

"It must be," Claire repeated faintly. It was the only thing that made sense. They weren't really clothes at all, just her body shifting and changing color to look like them. The chameleon effect was there after all. It just wasn't alone—the ability to shift her shape was there as well.

Jill nodded slowly, then stiffened and said, "Hang on!"

She glanced around with confusion as Jill rushed out of the bathroom. Claire had no idea where the other woman was going, but couldn't seem to care much at the moment. Her poor mind was struggling to accept her new abilities. She peered at herself in the mirror with fascination until she heard Jill cursing and the sound of thumping and drawers and door slamming in the room across the hall, Jill's bedroom.

Claire started out of the bathroom, then paused to snatch up her clothes. The last thing she needed was for Kyle to come home and stumble over her bra and panties in the bathroom.

"What on earth are you doing?" Claire asked with amazement as she entered Jill's room to find it in chaos. Jill was a whirlwind, rushing about her room, searching drawers and closets and tossing things willy-nilly. "What are you trying to find?"

"I had a magazine here," Jill explained, kneeling to look under her bed. "I know I put it—aha!"

Claire raised her eyebrows at this triumphant cry as Jill dragged a magazine out from under the bed and got back to her feet. It was a celebrity magazine, she saw as Jill began to leaf through it. Suddenly, her friend paused, folded the magazine over, and thrust it forward.

"Try this."

Claire tossed her clothes on the bed and took the magazine. She peered down at the picture it was open to and blinked, then glanced up, asking with disbelief, "Brad Cruise?"

Jill nodded. "Yes."

"But he's a guy," Claire protested, which was something of an understatement. Brad Cruise wasn't just a guy. He was *the* guy. He was the male equivalent of Brooke Jordan. He was also the biggest action movie star of their time, raking in double-digit millions for each role he took. The most familiar face in film, Brad Cruise was the man women lusted after and *men* would kill to be.

"No. Really? I hadn't noticed," Jill said sarcastically, then smacked her in the forehead and said, "Duh!"

Claire rolled her eyes and shoved the magazine back at her. "I can't do it."

"Oh, come on. How do you know until you try? You've changed into Brooke and the blond, you *can* do this," Jill said encouragingly.

"I shifted into Brooke and the blond by *wanting* to be them," Claire argued. "They're women; beautiful, successful women. Brad is a guy. G . . . U . . . Y. Guy. Male. A man. The opposite sex. I have no desire to be a man."

"Think Freud. Think penis envy," Jill said quickly.

"I *don't* have penis envy," Claire assured her.

"Oh, come on," Jill pleaded. "Just try. Just— imagine it. Being Brad Cruise; feted and adored by everyone. Rich beyond your wildest dreams. Just try. Please. For me."

Claire blew her breath out with exasperation, then sighed. "Fine. I'll try. For you."

"Thank you, thank you, thank you!" Jill gave her a

quick hug, then stepped back, nodded, and said with excitement, "Go on . . . Do it."

Claire shook her head and peered down at the picture, sure she wouldn't be able to do it. For one brief moment, she'd had a real longing to look like Brooke. As for the blond, Claire had even managed a little excitement and interest in looking like her, but Brad Cruise . . . ? She just didn't really have any desire to become him, though she supposed it might be interesting. Sighing inwardly, she concentrated on the picture, noting the features, the shape, the . . .

"Holy shit."

Claire glanced up when Jill breathed those two words. One look at her wide, round eyes was enough to make Claire head back to the bathroom to peer at herself in the mirror.

"Wow," Claire breathed as she stared at Brad Cruise's reflection looking back at her. Rugged good looks, short, tousled light brown hair, and the same black suit the man had worn in the magazine photo. It was as if he'd stepped right out of the page and into the room. Only he hadn't. It wasn't Brad Cruise she was staring at, it was herself.

"Yeah." Jill sighed, following her into the bathroom. "Wow."

Claire's gaze narrowed at the sudden spark in her friend's eyes; a spark that was usually reserved for members of the opposite sex.

"Oh yeah." Jill walked around Claire, her eyes sweeping over her body in the suit. "This is incredible. You look just like him."

"Yeah," Claire agreed dryly. "I *look* like him, but it's still *me* in here."

Jill stopped behind her and peered at their reflection

in the mirror. "Oh, wow, look!! It's me and Brad Cruise. I gotta get a picture of this. All those women at the reunion tonight would just eat their hearts out."

"I thought you weren't going," Claire reminded, then shook her head as Jill started out of the room, but her friend had barely taken a step into the hall before stopping abruptly and whirling back.

"What?" Claire asked warily.

"I have an idea," Jill said slowly.

Claire noted the mounting excitement on her face and began to shake her head. Excitement and ideas were a bad mix with Jill. "No."

"You don't even know what it is," Jill protested.

"I don't need to, Jill. I know that look. It's the look that always got me in trouble when we were teenagers," Claire said. Her mouth tightened when Jill's shoulders drooped and her face took on a pathetic, dejected cast. It was the look that always got her. Knowing she would regret it, Claire sighed and asked, "What is it?"

Jill hesitated, then blurted, "Be my date for the reunion tonight?"

Claire blinked. "What?"

"Be my date. Like that," Jill explained, gesturing to her Brad Cruise guise.

"Oh no, no, no, no, no," Claire said, shaking her head.

"Oh yes, yes, yes, yes, yes," Jill countered quickly, then clapped her hands together as if in prayer and begged, "Please? Please Claire? It could be fun."

"Fun?" she echoed with disbelief.

"Yes, fun. Just think about it," Jill said. "Magda the bitch would eat her heart out. For once in life, we would have it over her."

Claire grimaced at the idea of Magda the bitch. A Barbie doll look-alike with blond hair and boobs, she'd had everything . . . Except personality, compassion, and heart. Magda had been a devoted subscriber to the belief that when you looked as good as she did, you just didn't have to be nice. More than that, she'd gone out of her way to be cutting and cruel to anyone she'd felt beneath her on the food chain . . . which had been everyone in the school who wasn't male and on the football team. Claire seriously doubted the woman had improved with age. The idea of Magda's distress if Jill walked into the reunion on the arm of Brad Cruise really had some charm to it.

"And then there's Ted," Jill said, adding to her argument. "He'd eat his heart out, too."

"Ted?" Claire asked with confusion. "He didn't even go to our high school. Why would he be there?"

"He'll be there with Magda. It's why he had to end it today rather than wait until the very last minute, like the day of the wedding . . . or maybe months after," she added.

"*Magda* won the 'Ted's wife lotto'?" Claire asked with horror. "*She* was the other finalist?"

Jill nodded, stone-faced. "After he told me he was dumping me, I was foolish enough to ask if he couldn't at least attend the reunion with me tonight and he told me about Magda."

"I can't believe he told you about Magda," Claire gaped. "He's got some balls, that guy. What if you tell her everything tonight?"

Jill snorted. "He knows I won't. Magda would just sneer and point out that she—of course—won him from me and I was a loser . . . *again*."

Magda had made something of a hobby of stealing other girls' boyfriends in school. She'd stolen Jill's prom date a week before the prom, then gone on to steal Claire's prom date on the actual night of the prom after he and Magda were crowned Prom King and Queen.

Claire pressed her lips together, then nodded. "Okay. We'll do it. We'll go to the reunion and rub Magda and Ted's face in it. But only because I love you like a sister, and only this once."

"Only this once," Jill agreed, then squealed and hugged her. "Oh, you're the greatest."

Claire smiled wryly as she patted Jill's back. "Yeah, yeah. Now, we have another problem."

"What's that?" Jill asked, pulling back to peer at her.

"How do I change back into myself?" Claire asked quietly.

Jill stared at her blankly, then frowned. "You . . . well . . ." She brightened suddenly. "I have tons of pictures of you. You can look at one and turn back."

Jill rushed out of the room, leaving Claire to turn and survey herself in the mirror. In the picture of Brad Cruise, he'd had a serious case of five o'clock shadow going on. Claire now had that case herself. Curious, she lifted a hand and ran it over her cheek and chin, grimacing at the scrape of short hair against her fingers. Man, this was so weird . . . but kind of cool.

"Here." Jill hurried back in and started to hold out a picture, then pulled it back. "Wait, first try to do it without the picture."

"Without it?" Claire asked with surprise.

"Well, sure. I mean it *is* your body. Just close your eyes and concentrate on being you again. Just think 'I want to be me,'" Jill suggested.

"Isn't that a song?" Claire asked with amusement.

"Will you concentrate," Jill said with irritation. "Just try to change."

Sighing, Claire closed her eyes and concentrated on being herself. She didn't have a picture to think of; she didn't need one. She had lived with her face and body for years.

"Ooops."

Claire blinked her eyes open as she felt a soft towel being wrapped around her.

"I guess the clothes you were wearing really *were* you," Jill said with a shrug, holding the towel together until Claire reached up to take over the task.

Jill had wrapped a bath towel around her shoulders. Claire shifted it under her arms and wrapped it around herself sarong style. She was completely and utterly nude under the towel, which meant that the pink T-shirt and blue capri pants, the black satin dressy outfit, and the man's black suit *had* been purely her. That seemed kind of weird.

Both women stiffened at the sound of the front door opening.

"I'm back! Claire? Jill?"

Claire was the first to break out of her surprise. Suddenly aware of her nudity, she quickly pushed the bathroom door closed.

"Hello?" Kyle apparently heard the door close, his voice now came from somewhere in the hall.

"Yes?" Claire called. "Hello."

"Claire?" Kyle asked, his voice now right outside the door.

"Yes."

"Are you okay? What are you doing?"

Hearing the worry in his voice, she said quickly, "I'm fine. I'm . . . I'm in the bath."

When Jill's eyebrows rose at her choice of activity, Claire gestured to her attire. She was in a towel and her clothes were in Jill's bedroom, Claire could hardly tell Kyle she was just using the loo. He might wait in the hall until she came out so that he could see for himself that she was okay. He seemed terribly worried about her, and had every right to be. The destabilizer *had* affected her after all.

"Bath?" Kyle sounded surprised, then asked, "Where's Jill?"

Claire's eyes widened on her friend.

"She's . . . er . . ."

"At the store," Jill suggested in a whisper.

"She's at the store," Claire said dutifully.

"Damn it. She was supposed to watch you," Kyle sounded irritated. "What if something had happened?"

"She only went a minute ago . . . to the corner store. She'll be right back," Claire assured him. "She could hardly watch me in the bath any more than you would."

"Right."

Claire heard Kyle's sigh through the door. Silence followed, then he cleared his throat and said, "Maybe that's for the best. I wanted to ask you something."

Claire and Jill raised their eyebrows at each other.

There was more throat-clearing, then Kyle said, "I was wondering . . ."

"Yes?" Claire prompted when he hesitated, and found herself taking a step closer to the door as she waited.

"Look," he said abruptly. "Would you go to the reunion with me tonight?"

Claire froze, sure her heart briefly stopped, then she swallowed and asked, "So you can watch me? Or as your date?"

There was a moment of silence, then Kyle asked, "Would you be interested in being my date?"

Claire hesitated, afraid to say yes and then learn that it wasn't what he'd intended.

"You don't have to answer that. It isn't fair when I haven't given you any indication of my feelings," he said before she could decide how to answer him. "Look, I really suck at this kind of thing. I'm great with beakers and bunnies, but personal relationships are just kind of beyond me in some ways . . . But . . . Claire, I like you. I've liked you for the longest time. Since we were twelve years old and you were pestering me about the science kit my parents bought me for Christmas. I even almost asked you out in high school, but you were dating that football guy."

"Jack," Claire murmured, thinking she would have dumped Jack in a heartbeat if Kyle had said a word. Especially since he was the one who had abandoned her for Magda on prom night.

"Yeah, Jack," Kyle muttered, sounding jealous even now.

Claire smiled and lifted a hand to the door, running her finger lightly over the wooden surface and wishing it was he.

"Then . . ." Kyle paused before offering a vague "Well, something happened that made me wait."

"What?" Claire asked curiously.

"I'll tell you another time," Kyle promised. He cleared his throat. "So, to answer your question, what I'm interested in here is a date."

Claire sucked in her breath, hardly able to believe he'd said it.

"Claire?"

"Yes," she breathed.

"Yes?"

Claire could hear the grin in his voice and found herself smiling, too, until movement made her glance toward Jill. The blond was shaking her head frantically in a definite negative gesture.

"No?" Claire asked Jill with bewilderment.

"No?" Kyle said sharply through the door, obviously having heard her speak.

"No!" Claire cried. She hadn't meant the word for him at all. "I mean yes."

"Which is it?"

"Yes to going to the reunion, and no I wasn't talking to you when I said no," Claire explained.

"Who were you talking to then?" She could hear the frown in his voice and scrambled to think of an excuse.

"I—myself," she said quickly, then added, "I saw I had a broken nail and . . . er . . . said no because . . . well, because I didn't want it to be broken," Claire finished lamely.

"Oh . . . I see." It didn't sound like he saw. It sounded like he thought her a fruitcake.

Claire frowned over the possibility. She didn't want him to think she was a fruitcake. Or a freak, she added unhappily as she considered what she could now do. Kyle might not think it as cool as she and Jill did. He would probably find it exciting, scientifically. He'd want to study her and test her and . . . She'd become a lab animal to him instead of a prospective girlfriend.

"Well, I'll let you get back to your bath," Kyle said, interrupting her grim thoughts, then he offered, "We'll go over to your place after you're done your bath to pick up some clothes, if you like?"

"Okay," Claire said quickly, shrugging her worries away. She wouldn't tell him about the destabilizer's effect. At least, not until she saw how this date went. If it went well . . . well, she might wait a couple months. If

it went badly, she might wait forever. Claire had no desire to become a lab rat.

"Okay," Kyle said. There was silence for a minute,
then Claire heard his footsteps moving away. Once the
sound had faded, Claire turned away with a little sigh.
She was going on a date with Kyle. Finally, after all
these years, she—

"You can't go with him."

Claire blinked and peered at Jill blankly. "What?
Why?"

"You promised to be *my* date."

3

"Kyle Lockhart and Claire Beckett!" Maureen Brighton beamed as they approached the registration table at the entrance to the reunion. "Wow, you both look great."

"So do you, Maureen," Claire said with a smile as Kyle accepted the blank name tags the brunette held out. While he bent to write their names on them, she chatted with Maureen. The brunette had been one of the nicer girls on the cheerleading squad with Claire, Magda and her crew being the not so nice ones.

When another couple came up to the table, Claire stepped away to make room for them and peered curiously around. The reunion was being held in Murphy High School's smaller gymnasium. A suitable spot, Claire supposed as she glanced over all the well-dressed people maneuvering around under the streamers and decorations inside. She didn't care where it was held, Claire was just glad to be here.

At last, Claire Beckett was having her first date with Kyle Lockhart. There were several points this afternoon and evening when she hadn't thought it would happen. Jill had been the first stumbling block with her determination to hold Claire to her promise to be her date as Brad Cruise. Fortunately, after several moments of Claire pathetically pleading to be free of her promise so she could go with Kyle, Jill had come up with an alternative they could both live with. She'd proposed that Claire keep both dates; with Jill as Brad Cruise and with Kyle as herself. First, she would enter on Kyle's arm as herself, then after half an hour, she would excuse herself to use the ladies' room and slip out to the parking lot, where Jill would be waiting. She would change into Brad in the car, then reenter the reunion with Jill. Claire was to switch back and forth all night. Simple.

"Yeah right," Claire muttered to herself unhappily. This was going to be the date from hell . . . or the double date from hell.

"Did you say something?" Kyle asked, catching her comment as he finished at the registration table and joined her.

Claire forced a smile, but shook her head as she reached for the name tag he was holding out. She accepted it, then froze as she saw it was a pin-on name tag.

Oh, this was bad, Claire thought faintly. In order to do the quick change between herself and Brad Cruise, Claire had borrowed a black satin strapless gown from Jill. However, she wasn't wearing it now. She'd showered, done her hair and makeup, then donned the gown only to have Jill take a picture with her digital camera. They'd printed it, then Claire had used it to shape-shift into herself. That had been Jill's idea and Claire had thought it brilliant at the time. It saved her having to worry about stashing her dress somewhere while she was Brad. Unfortunately, it also meant that Claire had nowhere to pin her name tag. There was no way she was poking it through *her,* her skin or her cells or whatever.

She wasn't sure exactly what it was, but it was part of her and she so *wasn't* harpooning herself with a name tag.

"Do you need a hand? Shall I put it on for you?" Kyle asked, noting that she was still just staring at the pin.

"No," Claire said sharply, then forced another smile and said more calmly, "No, I don't want to put holes in Jill's satin gown. Do they have stick-on name tags?"

"Oh, I don't know." He turned to the table to ask Maureen, swiveling back a moment later to say, "Apparently if you slide the label out of the clear casing, the label itself peels off its backing."

"Oh, good," Claire breathed and set to work taking the label apart.

"There we are." Kyle smiled as she finished with the pin and slapped the label onto the black satin of her chest, which really was her chest, Claire realized, and hoped it wouldn't hurt to peel it off.

"Shall we?"

Shrugging off the concern of removing the name tag, Claire smiled. She placed her hand on the arm he offered and allowed him to lead her into the reunion. Once through the doors, Claire peered around at the tables set everywhere. They were covered with maroon-colored tablecloths and had silver and maroon centerpieces. These were the school colors, and most of the decorations carried them. With the lighting low as it was and all the decorations hanging about, it was easy to forget it was a gymnasium. Someone had decorated it with the same moonlight, stars, and heavenly aspect theme as at their prom some ten years ago.

"It feels strange to be back here, doesn't it?" Kyle said with a wry smile.

"Yes," Claire agreed and gave a small shake of her head as she peered over the people milling about, wondering who they all were. "I'm torn between feeling old because I don't recognize anyone, and yet feeling like a teenager again. I'd almost expect old Mr. Hardwick to come marching up and ask for my book report."

Kyle chuckled at her words, but frowned slightly as he peered around. "Everyone looks so different. Surely we haven't changed as much as everyone else appears to have?"

"Maybe," Claire said, peering at him. Kyle had aged well, growing into his looks and his body. He'd been much thinner when he was young, almost gawky. As had she, Claire supposed, but merely said, "Do you recognize anyone?"

"Not really. But there were a lot of— Oh, I spoke too soon. I do recognize someone."

"Who?" Claire asked curiously, following his gaze.

"Magda Richardson at two o'clock and closing in on us like a shark," he announced, then added, "I apologize in advance for any nastiness she may spew our way."

"Why should *you* apologize?" Claire asked with surprise.

"Because Magda has gone out of her way to be rude to me and anyone I was with since she cornered me in the science lab in grade twelve and tried to trade kisses for help with homework. I refused."

"Magda hit on you in high school?" Claire asked with shock.

"Yeah. But I think she just wanted help with her science project. Still, she wasn't too pleased when I said, 'Thanks, but no thanks.' The few times I've run into her over the last ten years, she's been sure to be rude." He frowned. "Is that Ted with her? I thought he broke up with Jill because he was marrying some—"

"Magda was the 'Ted's wife lotto' winner," Claire

informed him dryly as she noted the smug look on the man's handsome face as they approached. Kyle, of course, hadn't been privy to the news when Jill had shared it with her.

"You're joking," Kyle said, half with disgust and half with disbelief.

"I wish I were," Claire muttered under her breath as the other couple reached them.

"Well, if it isn't Murphy High's very own science geeks," Magda drawled, looking down her nose at them. "So you two twits finally got together."

"Magda," Kyle greeted her dryly. "Charming as ever, I see."

"Charm is overrated, Kyle," Magda informed him sweetly. "Honesty is in now." She tightened her hold on Ted's arm and dragged him forward. "I should introduce my fiancé, Ted Leacock. He's an important business owner here in town."

"Important?" Kyle asked dryly, not bothering to extend his hand in greeting. "As it happens, Ted and I are well acquainted."

"You are?" Magda didn't look pleased at this news, but Ted Claire was more interested in watching. The man with incredible balls had lost his smug look and was starting to appear a tad nervous. It seemed while he'd been sure Jill would keep their relationship quiet, he hadn't considered Kyle in the equation.

"Yes. We've met at least once a week for the last six months when he came to pick up my sister for dates, or weekends away," Kyle announced calmly, then smiled at Magda. "Of course, they're broken up now. I guess that means you're marrying Jill's castoff."

Dead silence fell between the four of them, during which Magda's face flushed with a mounting fury.

When Ted's mouth began to work silently like a fish out of water, Kyle took Claire's arm and said, "We should circulate, but it was so nice seeing you. I do hope the two of you are as happy as you deserve to be."

Claire bit her lip at the double-edged comment as Kyle led her away. A glance over her shoulder showed Magda had turned furiously on Ted and was now berating him something fierce. If he wasn't such a jerk, Claire might almost have felt sorry for the man.

Shaking her head, she turned to Kyle and murmured, "You handled that beautifully. Ted lost his smug look in a hurry."

"Yes, but Jill will be upset with me, I suppose," he said on a sigh.

"I don't think she will. You put both of them in their place with the 'Jill's castoff' crack," Claire said with amusement. "Besides, she has a special date herself tonight, one that should finish setting Magda and Ted on their ears."

"Really?" Kyle asked with interest. "Who?"

Claire bit her lip and hesitated, unsure how to answer. He was going to be shocked enough when he saw Jill enter—seemingly on the arm of Brad Cruise. In the end, Claire decided to let Jill deal with it and shook her head. "You'll see soon enough."

Kyle peered at her closely. For a minute, she feared he might press the issue, but he apparently decided to let it go. He merely asked if she'd care for a drink, then moved toward the bar.

Claire peered around at the other attendees as she waited. At least half the tables were filled. No doubt most of the attendees would show up over the next half hour before she slipped out to the parking lot. Jill and her "date" would probably be nearly the last, if not *the* last people to arrive, which was just as Jill wanted it. If everyone was seated for the meal when they entered, it meant absolutely *everyone* would see who—or who they would believe—was on her arm as she sashayed in.

Claire took a deep breath and tried not to let panic overwhelm her as she thought about what was to come. She and Jill had discussed it in detail before she'd left with Kyle for the reunion, trying to cover every possible problem with their plan. The first issue to crop up was her voice. While Claire could make herself *look* like Brad Cruise, nothing she could do would make her *sound* like the man. They had decided she wasn't to talk. Jill would claim she—he, Claire corrected herself, *he*—Brad Cruise—had a bad case of laryngitis. Claire had also insisted on no autographs; it was one thing to pretend to be Brad Cruise at a school reunion, and quite another to indulge in forgery by signing his autograph for a couple hundred people.

"They didn't have Châteauneuf-du-Pape, so I got you Montepulciano."

Claire glanced up and smiled as Kyle offered her a glass of wine. "Thank you."

Kyle nodded, his eyes moving over her solemnly as he took a sip of his own drink. Lowering the glass, he asked, "How do you feel? Any ill effects from this afternoon?"

Claire shook her head quickly and told herself she wasn't lying as she took a sip of wine. After all, being able to shape-shift wasn't necessarily an "ill effect," was it? Sighing, she lowered her glass and glanced around. The tables had been set up around the outside of the large room, leaving a wide space to dance in, and couples were out there now sweeping along to a ten-year-old love song.

"Would you like to dance?" Kyle asked, following her gaze.

Claire hesitated and nearly said no, but it would have been a lie. She really *would* like to dance, she was just afraid of stumbling and making a fool of herself. Deciding to be brave, she nodded.

Kyle took her wine and set it on a table next to them. He then took Claire's arm and led her out onto the center of the floor.

Claire was as tense and sweaty as a teenager as Kyle took her in his arms. She hadn't been this nervous with a man in a long time, but then none of the men she'd dated had meant as much to her as Kyle did. She was so wired up it took a moment for her to notice that they fit perfectly together, her body matching itself to his as if fitting into a puzzle slot.

"We fit together perfectly," Kyle whispered by her ear.

Claire stiffened in surprise at his verbalizing her thoughts, then lifted her head to peer at him. He stared back, his gaze traveling over her face in a caress that she could almost feel. Her lips parted slightly of their own accord when his eyes settled there and Claire felt her breathing become more swift and shallow with anticipation. She was finally, finally going to be kissed by Kyle Lockhart, Claire thought, almost faint at the prospect. But, rather than kiss her, Kyle used a hand to urge her head back to his chest.

Claire sighed and tried to relax against him, but her mind was on the fact that he'd passed up the perfect opportunity to kiss her.

Why? She wondered. What was wrong with her? Was it her figure? Perhaps if she had larger breasts . . .

Claire stumbled in the dance and blinked in surprise as her neck was suddenly forced to bend farther forward to keep her head on Kyle's chest. For a moment she didn't understand what had happened, then she realized her breasts had suddenly grown between them, like two balloons inflating.

"Er . . . Claire?" Kyle said uncertainly, apparently noticing something was amiss.

"Oh God," Claire breathed and squeezed her eyes closed, thinking *Go away, go away, go away.*

"Claire?" Kyle pulled back and she forced her eyes open, relieved to find her chest normal-sized again.

"Yes?" She raised her head to his, but Kyle was peering at her cleavage with confusion.

After a moment, he shook his head. "I thought—"

"Kyle! Is that you?"

Claire and Kyle broke apart to peer at the excited man suddenly standing beside them.

"It *is* you!" the man said. He had boyish good looks and a full head of dark hair, but was almost painfully short at a couple of inches less than five feet. It was his height that helped Claire to recognize him right away.

"Bobby Loth," she said, happy for the distraction.

"Claire! You remember me!" he said with surprised pleasure.

"Of course, I do." Claire smiled. Bobby had been in the science club with them; intelligent and good-humored, he'd been a good friend in high school.

"Who could forget you, Bobby?" Kyle asked lightly. "How are you, old friend."

"Good." Bobby beamed as they shook hands, then stepped back to catch the arm of a petite brunette waiting shyly a step behind him. "This is my wife, Meredith. Meredith, this is Kyle and Claire."

Claire and Kyle smiled and said hello. The four of them stood talking on the dance floor for several minutes, before moving to collect their drinks and settle at a table together. The conversation continued, but Claire was slightly distracted as she kept one eye on the wire-covered clock on the wall. As pleasant as she found the interlude with Bobby and his wife, Claire just couldn't relax. It was almost a relief when it was time to leave. At least it meant an end to her tense waiting.

Excusing herself—ostensibly to visit the ladies' room—Claire slipped from the table and made her escape.

"Right on time," Jill said cheerfully as Claire slid into the front passenger seat of her car a moment later. She was obviously looking forward to what was to come. Claire wasn't. There were too many things that could go wrong.

"Thanks," she murmured as Jill handed her the photos. She handed back the snapshot of herself, then took the picture of Brad Cruise they'd ripped out of the magazine and hesitated as she squinted at it in the dark. "I don't suppose you brought a flashlight or something?"

"No, I didn't think of it. Just a minute." Jill dug through her purse briefly, then held out a small item.

"A lighter?" Claire asked with surprise as she took it. "You don't smoke."

"Ted smoked cigars once in a while and always forgot his lighter."

"Oh." Claire glanced around nervously, but the parking lot appeared empty. She flicked the lighter on and concentrated on the picture once more.

"Perfect."

The one word from Jill a moment later told Claire she'd finished the change. She let the lighter go out with relief. It had started to get warm under her thumb, distracting her, but she'd feared letting it go out before she was done.

"Okay?" Claire asked, lifting her head.

Jill flicked the interior car light on just long enough to look her over, then flicked it back off to avoid attracting attention.

"As I said, perfect," she assured her. "Come on."

Sighing, Claire slid out of the car and walked around to meet her, then handed back the magazine photo for her to put away.

"Take my arm, like a gentleman," Jill instructed as they started toward the entrance to the school.

Claire took her arm, and mentally reminded herself that she was now a man, so she should pull out chairs, take Jill's arm, and all those other little courtesies.

"What are you doing?"

Claire glanced at Jill with surprise. "What do you mean?"

"You're swaying your hips."

"No, I'm not."

"Yes, you are. You're walking like a girl."

"I *am* a girl," Claire said with irritation.

"Not tonight you're not," Jill said firmly. "Think manly, try to swagger. And don't talk."

"Anything else?" Claire asked dryly.

"Yes." Jill patted her hand and said, "Thank you . . . By the way, how is the date with Kyle going?"

"Good . . . until I had to come out here," Claire said, then recalled the incident with Magda and Ted and quickly related it to Jill who—fortunately—wasn't upset.

The registration table was empty when they reached the gym. They truly were going to be the last to enter. Jill paused outside the closed gym doors, took a deep breath, then glanced at her and said, "Show time. Just smile and nod and agree with anything I say. Okay?"

Against her better judgment, Claire nodded her agreement, then added, "Just don't leave me alone."

"Like I'd abandon Brad Cruise in the same room with a bimbo like Magda on the loose," Jill said dryly, then pushed through the door. Still holding her arm, Claire pushed her own door open and entered with her, noting that everyone was now seated and servers were moving through the tables delivering the first entrée.

"Perfect," Jill whispered, pausing just inside the doors to peer around. Their entrance had not gone unnoticed. Several people had turned their way to see who had entered, then more people looked toward them as the first people nudged those next to them. A loud whispering began to move through the crowd, most of it made up of the name "Brad Cruise."

Claire forced herself to keep her head upright and not flinch and shrink behind Jill. She couldn't have anyway; Jill was now sailing forward, forcing Claire to accompany her.

"Where are we going to sit?" Claire asked, bending her head to Jill's ear so she wasn't overheard.

"We're sitting with Kyle."

"What?" Claire's eyes widened in horror. "But—"

"That way we can distract him from noticing you're gone, so you don't have to turn back so soon."

Claire thought this was a very bad idea, but it was too late to stop it; they were already halfway to the table where Kyle sat gaping at their approach. And no wonder, she supposed. It must be a bit disconcerting to see your sister enter the reunion on the arm of the biggest film star in the world.

"Where are Magda and Ted?" Jill asked as they neared the table where Kyle, Bobby, and Meredith sat in a frozen tableau.

"I don't know," Claire murmured, her gaze swiveling to the right, then pausing as she found the pair several tables over from their own. The couple were gaping openmouthed, but then everyone was, Claire thought as she whispered to Jill to look to their right. When she did, Jill's shoulders straightened and a look of satisfaction crossed her face that made Claire glad she'd agreed to this. She just hoped she still felt that way at the end of the night.

"Magda is ready to shriek and Ted looks like he just ate his shorts," Jill said, glancing at Claire with amusement. The amusement vanished abruptly, and she forced them to a halt not three feet from the table.

"What is it?" Claire hissed urgently as she noted the alarm on her friend's face.

Jill hesitated, then turned to fully face her. She put one hand on Claire's chest and leaned up as if to kiss her. Claire instinctively turned her head to the side to avoid the kiss and hissed, "No kissing. I'm still Claire."

"Right," Jill murmured, then Claire gasped as Jill took her hand away, ripping the Claire name tag away with it, as she added wryly, "No need to advertise it though."

The name tag had remained when she had changed. It was little things like this that were likely to catch them up in this charade, Claire thought grimly, but merely caught Jill's arm in her hand as the blond continued on to the table.

"Sorry we're late," Jill sang gaily as Kyle got to his feet.

"Jill," Kyle greeted, but his gaze was locked on Claire . . . or "Brad" really, she supposed. His expression was a combination of confusion and suspicion, then he turned his gaze to his sister to say, "I didn't think you were coming tonight."

"Brad changed my mind," she said lightly.

"Jill, is that you?" Bobby Loth got to his feet as well

to greet her, and Claire had no doubt Jill was grateful for the distraction. The blond turned quickly to greet the man and be introduced to Meredith, which—unfortunately—left Claire alone to face Kyle.

"Kyle Lockhart," he introduced himself and held out his hand.

Claire automatically put her hand in it, forgetting that she was supposed to be a guy and should be giving a firm handshake. She barely held back her wince as his hand squeezed her own.

"And you are?" Kyle asked when she kept her mouth shut.

Much to Claire's relief, Jill had been paying attention and suddenly whirled back saying, "Oh Kyle, you know who this is. Unfortunately Brad has a bad case of laryngitis, which is why I wasn't sure I would be coming after all when Ted bowed out, but Brad bravely agreed to accompany me."

Claire blinked as Jill pressed a kiss to her cheek, then allowed her to urge her to a seat at the table. Jill had the good sense to seat her between herself and Meredith, keeping her away from Kyle and his questions. Claire felt herself relax a little as Meredith offered her a shy smile, until she quietly asked if "Brad" could sign her table napkin. Before Claire could panic too much, Jill leaned around Claire/Brad to say, "I'm sorry, Meredith. The one promise I had to make to get Brad here was that he wouldn't have to sign autographs. He hurt his wrist on set a couple weeks ago and he's trying to rest it up before he starts a new movie next week."

"Oh, I think I heard something about that," Meredith said with understanding. "Didn't you fall off a horse while filming your last movie and land badly on your wrist?"

Claire turned blankly to Jill, who nodded solemnly and told Meredith, "He was lucky it was just a sprain and he didn't break it."

Claire inwardly shook her head as Meredith cooed sympathetically. Honestly, where did they find out all this stuff? And why waste their time on it? The only thing she knew about Brad Cruise was that he was rich, good-looking, and an actor. Jill and Meredith seemed to know all sorts of details about him.

"You don't have name tags."

Claire stiffened at Kyle's sharp comment, but Jill merely turned to smile at her brother. "The registration table was empty when we got here. I guess we were a bit late."

Kyle nodded and Claire was just starting to relax again when he said, "But it looked like it was a name tag you ripped off . . . Brad's chest as you approached the table."

Claire felt her eyes widen in alarm. They hadn't been far from the table when Jill had noted the Claire name tag and ripped it off. Had Kyle seen and been able to read it before his sister could take it away?

"Brad was at a press conference before picking me up and still had his star pass on," Jill lied glibly. "I removed it."

"Hmmm." Kyle was silent for a minute, then glanced to the side. "I wonder what's holding Claire up?"

"Oh, you know women's washrooms, they always have a terrible line. She's probably still waiting to get into a stall."

Kyle turned his head slowly back and Claire felt the hair rise on the back of her neck at the look in his eyes. She'd seen it before. It was his "aha!" look and she nearly closed her eyes with a groan when he said, "Did I mention she'd gone to the ladies' room?"

Jill looked taken aback for a minute, then improvised with "I just assumed. Where else would she be?"

Much to Claire's relief, Bobby leaned toward Kyle then, claiming his attention, but she was tense now and impatient to get to the bathroom and return as Claire. They had agreed that she would stay through the entrée as Brad, then Jill would remind him he had to make a phone call and she could escape to change back. The entrée couldn't come quick enough for her.

Claire only grew more impatient to escape as the next twenty minutes passed. A few of their braver ex-classmates began to approach the table, eager to tell "Brad" how much they enjoyed his movies and requesting autographs. Jill did an excellent job of fending them off for her, but it was disconcerting to have people—mostly women—gushing to her about how "wonderful" he was. It was a great relief when Jill finally said, "Oh Brad, you were supposed to call your agent. Maybe you should do it now before the main course arrives."

"How can he make a phone call? I thought he had laryngitis," Kyle commented.

Claire had just closed her hand around the pictures Jill had passed to her under the table and started to get to her feet, but froze like a deer in headlights at this comment.

"Yes, of course. I'd better go with him then, hadn't I?" Jill said sweetly.

"He knows," Claire hissed as they headed for the exit at the back of the gymnasium, knowing the washrooms were in the side hall.

"No he doesn't," Jill assured her. "How could he? Kyle doesn't have any idea the destabilizer can do this. It's only supposed to cause a chameleonlike effect, remember? He's just freaked out that I have a date with a big star."

Claire was about to remind her that she didn't *really* have a date with a big star, when Jill suddenly cursed and began to urge her to move faster.

"Ted and Magda are closing in," she hissed.

"Great," Claire muttered as they hurried out of the gym. They hadn't gone far when Ted called out after them.

Gritting her teeth, Jill gave her a push. "Go on, I'll handle them."

Hand tightening on the pictures she still clutched, Claire hurried for the bathrooms, slowly becoming aware of the tap of high-heeled shoes following her. She glanced over her shoulder, expecting to find Jill had only paused long enough to make some quick excuse, then had followed, but instead, found that Jill had been stopped in the hall by Ted and it was Magda trailing after her.

The Barbie doll look-alike gave her a sultry smile and picked up speed in an effort to catch up. Claire just panicked. Her heart lodged itself in her throat, and she broke into a run for the last few feet, and sped into the bathroom. Relaxing a little once the door swung shut behind her, Claire slowed to a walk and glanced around, relieved to find the bathroom was empty.

She walked into the first empty booth, and started to close the stall door, then heard the bathroom door open again. Surprised, Claire paused, blinking at Magda as the woman hurried into the bathroom. The blond's steps didn't even slow; Magda rushed forward and straight into the booth, placing one hand on Claire's chest and forcing her back against the stall wall as she closed and locked the stall door with her other hand.

4

"**O**h Brad."

Claire stared in horror as Magda pressed eagerly up against her.

"I saw you notice me when you came in with Jill, and felt sure you'd want me. How clever of you to lead me to the ladies' room."

Oh dear, Claire thought faintly. She'd unthinkingly entered the ladies' room rather than the men's room and Magda was taking that as a come-on. And she couldn't talk to explain otherwise.

Catching at Magda's hands as they wandered over her wide "Brad Cruise" chest, Claire used the only avenue of communication she had open to her and shook her head firmly. She then tried to slip past her to unbolt the door and get out; however, Magda wasn't cooperating.

Laughing as if she thought "Brad" was playing games, Magda shook her hands free to again run them over "Brad's" body. "Don't worry. Ted will keep Jill busy. He's been steaming ever since we saw you arrive. Let them have their fun. We can have our own. I promise I'll show you a better time than that homely little wannabe ever could."

Claire stiffened, indignant on her friend's behalf. Magda was a cow, a man-stealing cow, she decided grimly, then found her ability to think buried under an avalanche of shock as Magda suddenly kissed her. For one moment, Claire was so stupefied she couldn't think. When her brain did manage to function again, the only thing it spat out was the fact that in high school, the boys had all claimed Magda was an *awesome* kisser. Claire was no expert, but to her, Magda's kiss was limp and sloppy. Wait till Jill heard, she thought, then regained enough sense to begin to struggle.

Claire didn't have to struggle hard this time. While she had been distracted by Magda's kiss, the other woman had slid her hand down to where Brad's groin should have been . . . and got the surprise of her life.

Breaking the kiss, Magda said with shock, "You don't have a penis!"

"Yeah, well you're a rotten kisser," Claire growled in as manly a voice as she could manage. She then shoved her away, pushing her in the only direction available to her, toward the toilet. Unfortunately for the blond, it had obviously been cleaned recently and the toilet seat had been left up. Magda shrieked as she landed with a splash, then began to thrash and struggle to get out.

Claire didn't wait to see if she did. Unbolting the door, she hurried from the stall and straight out of the bathroom. She didn't hesitate or glance around, but charged straight out of the women's washroom and across the hall into the men's room, then into the first open stall she saw.

Slamming the booth door closed, Claire leaned her

forehead against it and took several deep breaths, then groaned. This was bad. Magda would go out and tell everyone that Brad didn't have a penis and Jill would be upset and—

"Claire? Brad?"

Stilling at the sound of Jill's voice, Claire unbolted the door, opened it, and dragged Jill inside. "We have a problem."

"What happened?" Jill asked anxiously as she relocked the stall door. "I saw Magda follow you into the ladies' room."

"She kissed me," Claire blurted with disgust, then added, "And she is a *really* bad kisser. All those guys in high school must have been lying their heads off. They probably hadn't even kissed her, because there is no way they would have thought what she gave me was a good kiss."

Jill stared at her blankly and then burst out laughing.

"Go on, laugh," Claire muttered. "But you won't be laughing when you hear the rest."

Jill stopped at once, her eyes narrowing warily. "What?"

"She grabbed me, only there was nothing to grab."

Jill blinked, slow to comprehend. "You mean . . ." Her gaze dropped to "Brad's" groin.

"Yes."

Jill frowned. "You mean, you don't have a 'package'?"

"Was there a package in the picture?" Claire asked dryly, then answered herself, "No. There were pants. I have pants. No package."

"Oh, that's just wrong," Jill said unhappily and then dug around in her purse, coming up with a black marker. "Give me the picture."

Perplexed, Claire handed over the pictures she'd

been clutching through all this and watched in amazement as Jill put a noticeable bump in Brad's pants in the magazine photo. "What are you—?"

"There! Now concentrate on the picture and give yourself a package."

"I'm supposed to be turning back to myself, Jill. I'm here with Kyle tonight, too."

"Not till we clear this matter up," she said firmly. When Claire opened her mouth to argue, Jill added, "You agreed to be *my* date first."

Sighing, Claire lowered her head and concentrated on the picture, giving herself a definite bump where Brad's package should have been.

"Nice," Jill said with approval, then turned to unlock the stall door. "Now we'd better get out of here before another guy comes in and sees us. Everyone would think we were having sex or something."

Jill had opened the stall door, but now paused as if reconsidering how bad an idea it would be for everyone to think she was having sex in the bathroom with Brad Cruise. Claire gave her a determined push forward. She just wanted to get this over with so she could get back to her date.

"What is it?" Jill asked as they left the men's room.

Claire followed her gaze to her new bump and shrugged. "A bump. Just a bump."

"Yeah, but what's it look like under there?" Jill reached for the zipper of her trousers, but Claire knocked her hand away.

"There is no *under* there. Under there is me, remember? This is me. There are no clothes. It's really all just *me*."

"Right," Jill said slowly and gave an abrupt nod. "We need to find a picture of Brad naked."

"What?" Claire asked with disbelief and then snapped, "Do not even think it."

"Oh please," Jill pleaded. "Just once. You could keep your mouth shut and I could have my fantasy night. You'd never have to buy me a birthday gift or Christmas present ever again." She tried the pitiful expression that always worked on Claire, but this time she wasn't falling for it. This whole Brad nonsense was ruining her date with Kyle, a date she'd waited forever for. She was all out of sympathy.

"You've lost your mind," Claire snapped impatiently. "These are *my* lips, *my* eyes looking out, and *my* brain. I am not Brad Cruise and neither am I a lesbian, and I am *so* not having sex with you."

Jill sighed, giving up the attempt to talk her into it. "Yeah . . . I get it. Too bad though." She suddenly reached out to poke at the lump. "Where does it feel like I'm poking you?"

"My leg," Claire answered.

"Really?" She poked some more. "That's kind of weird, isn't it? I guess it means that leg cells were used to make up the lump and—"

"Jill! Magda was just telling Maureen and me—"

Claire and Jill glanced over with surprise as Meredith rushed out of the women's room with Maureen on her heels. Her words had died abruptly and she gaped as she spotted Jill standing there with her hand on "Brad's package."

"What?" Maureen peered over Meredith's shoulder with curiosity at her sudden silence, then said, "Oh," as she took in what appeared to be Jill caught feeling up the superstar.

"Sorry," Jill said, retracting her hand as Claire

flushed with embarrassment. "I was . . . er . . . talking to Brad. What is it Magda was saying?"

Meredith hesitated, exchanging a glance with Maureen, then she grabbed Jill's arm and pulled her several feet away. The three women went into a huddle and began to whisper in earnest.

Claire shook her head, wondering if this night would ever end. As abruptly as it had started, the huddle broke apart. Meredith and Maureen threw Claire/Brad almost leering smiles as they rushed off back toward the gymnasium.

"Well?" Claire asked as Jill returned to her side. "What did they say?"

"That Magda kissed you in the women's washroom and felt you up and you had no package."

"Shoot. I was afraid of that." Claire sighed. "What did you say?"

"That Magda was just jealous. That she dragged you into the bathroom, threw herself at you, kissed you and you said she was a lousy kisser and gave her the brush off and she's jealous so she's spreading false stories."

"Smart," Claire said with a smile.

"Yeah. It helps that Brad Cruise did that full frontal nudity scene in the British movie he did last year. There was a definite package there."

Claire blinked. "That was like a split second on the screen, too fast to see anything."

"You've never heard of pause?" Jill asked, arching one eyebrow.

"You *paused* it to see him nude?" she asked with disbelief.

"Me and twenty million other women. Why do you think the DVD sold so well?"

"Dear God," Claire muttered. "I am *so* seeing a side of you I didn't know about."

"Sure you knew about it," Jill countered. "You know me better than anyone. Maybe it's just different because you're a guy now. Kind of."

"Could be." Claire sighed and promised herself she would never again slag men for being pigs. Women could be just as bad. "Now that the crisis is handled, can I change back into me?"

"Yeah, go on."

Claire turned back to the men's room with relief, only to stiffen as she noted the door was cracked open. As she stared, it opened the rest of the way, revealing the man who had been listening to everything.

"Kyle!" Claire squawked and then covered her mouth with horror at having given the gig away.

Kyle arched his eyebrows sternly, but merely said, "I find it hard to believe that neither of you thought to check to see if you were alone in the bathroom before talking so freely. Anyone might have heard you."

"But how did you get here?" Jill asked with dismay. "We left you at the table."

"I followed."

"When? I didn't see you," Jill said with bewilderment.

"You were busy talking to Ted when I slipped by. Telling him you weren't interested in his offer to start dating again," he added dryly.

"He had the balls to ask you out again?" Claire asked with amazement, then smiled. "So you got to be the dumper after all."

"It wasn't as much fun as I thought it would be," Jill told her morosely. "Really, he turned out to be a major greaseball."

Claire started to pat her back in sympathy, then gave

a startled bleat as Kyle suddenly tugged her into the men's room.

"Hey!" Jill followed them, but Kyle just dragged Claire into a booth and slammed the door in his sister's face.

"Would you care to explain?" he asked as he bolted the door.

Claire opened her mouth, but he forestalled her by saying, "On second thought, don't bother. I heard enough to understand. I gather the destabilizer had an effect after all?"

"Did it!" Jill snorted from outside the booth even as Claire nodded.

Kyle tossed a glare toward the door, but merely asked, "More than the chameleon effect?"

"Yes," Claire said reluctantly. "I can shape-shift."

"I take it you discovered this while I was at the grocery store?"

Claire nodded again.

"And you didn't tell me when I came back."

Claire eyed him warily. Kyle's expression was blank; no emotion showing at all, but there was something in his voice that suggested he wasn't at all happy.

"Why?" he finally asked, allowing his anger to now show.

"Because she didn't want you to see her as a lab rat," Jill answered from outside the booth when Claire hesitated.

"A lab rat?" Kyle unlocked the door and jerked it open to glare at his sister.

Jill immediately squeezed inside, forcing Claire to move between the toilet and one wall of the booth.

Kyle hesitated, then pushed the stall door closed and

bolted it again. "What do you mean she didn't want me to see her as a lab rat?"

"Well, you're a scientist," Jill pointed out with a shrug, as if that said it all. Then she added, "And you'd *finally* just asked her out after the two of you have mooned over each other for years. Claire didn't want to spoil it by telling you what had happened. She was afraid the scientist in you would start to see her as an experimental subject rather than a date."

Kyle hesitated for a moment, then opened the door again and pushed his sister out.

"Hey! You can't leave me out here," Jill protested as he locked the door again. "What if someone comes in?"

"Then get out of the men's room," Kyle suggested.

There was a moment of silence, then the tap of Jill's high heels moved into the booth on their right as she said, "Not on your life, brother. This is partially my fault and I am not leaving you two alone to screw things up."

Kyle rolled his eyes and sighed, but turned to Claire and said, "I may be a scientist, Claire, but I could never see you as just an experiment. I *am* a man, too."

A snort came from overhead, drawing their attention to the fact that Jill had apparently mounted the toilet to look over the top of the stall.

"Will you leave us alone?" Kyle asked with exasperation.

"Not till I straighten this out," Jill insisted. "I love you two too much to see you ruin this chance."

Kyle opened his mouth to snap at her, then seemed to change his mind. "Okay, say what you have to say and then go."

Jill nodded her satisfaction, and turned to Claire. "See, he isn't as stupid as most men. He knows women are better at communication and lets me talk."

Claire bit her lip to keep back a laugh and nodded solemnly.

"So, Kyle," Jill turned her attention to her brother. "Claire's liked you forever. I've listened to her moan over you since we were twelve, and if you think it's easy hearing someone rhapsodize over your brother, think again. But she was my friend and she liked you, so I put up with it. And Claire." She turned to Claire now. "Kyle has been secretly lusting after you for just as long. He's had a snapshot of you in his wallet since he started carrying a wallet, and he has another bigger picture of you hidden in his top drawer at home."

"How did you know—" Kyle began, but Jill cut him off.

"Today, you"—she glared at her brother—"finally had the nerve to ask her out, and Claire accepted. Unfortunately, she'd already agreed to help me out tonight. The only fair solution was to do both. She didn't want to," Jill added. "She just wanted to go out with you, but I blackmailed her into it by threatening to tell you about her new . . . er . . . abilities. Okay? Now kiss and make up."

There was a moment of silence as Kyle surveyed Claire/Brad, then he raised his eyes to his sister and said succinctly, "Out."

Jill opened her mouth as if to protest, then seemed to think better of it and shrugged. "I'll be waiting in the hall."

She disappeared from the top of the booth and they heard the tap of her heels as she exited the stall and left the men's room.

Kyle sighed with relief and turned to Claire.

She stared up at him wide-eyed, her palms suddenly sweaty at the idea of his finally kissing her, but after a hesitation, Kyle cleared his throat and shook his head. "I know it's you in there, but do you think you could change back to yourself now? I really don't want to kiss you as Brad."

"Oh." Claire jerked up the pictures she still held in her hand and switched the snapshot of her to the top. She hesitated, suddenly shy, but then bowed her head and concentrated on the picture.

"Wow," Kyle breathed and Claire relaxed and peered down at herself to see she was back in the black satin dress. She was herself again. Claire glanced up.

"There you are," he said gently and lifted his hand to caress one cheek, then before she was quite ready, his mouth dropped to cover hers.

Claire stilled, her heart thumping in her chest as Kyle kissed her, then she released a little moan and relaxed against him. For one moment, she'd feared what would happen. What if his kiss wasn't all she'd imagined it would be? Reality would be hard pressed to compare to more than ten years of fantasy, but there was nothing to fear. Unlike Magda, Kyle knew how to kiss. His mouth was firm on hers, slanting over her own and sending her pulse racing as he slid his tongue out to urge her mouth open.

She opened for him, welcoming him in with an excited gasp that died abruptly as the bathroom door opened outside the stall. They both stood frozen, listening for Jill's tapping shoes, but there was no tapping.

Releasing her, Kyle moved to the door and peered out at the room beyond through the crack between door and stall. Claire guessed by his frown, and the fact that he didn't berate Jill, that someone else had entered the bathroom. A man, she presumed since it was a men's room.

Kyle turned back and raised a finger to his lips to warn her to silence, then a stall door farther down the row squeaked as it was opened. Kyle waited until it had closed, then unlocked their door, and led her quickly out of the stall.

"You changed back!" Jill cried on spotting them.

"Of course, she did," Kyle said with irritation. "She's my date too."

"Yes, but—" Jill said, then hesitated, her expression calculating before she said, "I'll make a deal with you. She changes back to Brad so that we can leave together, then she's all yours for the rest of the night."

Claire's eyes widened with surprise. "You don't want me to continue being your date too?"

"No. There's no need to carry on the charade. Everyone's seen me with Brad Cruise. That's all I wanted. Besides, it's ruining your date." She glanced from Claire to Kyle. "And it's not like you can talk anyway. So it's like a serious instance of show and tell. Well I've shown, and told them enough. I can go home happy now."

Claire felt Kyle relax beside her and knew he was feeling the same relief now coursing through her.

"Then, too," Jill added with an evil grin, "they'll all just think I went home to have hot monkey sex with Brad Cruise anyway. And if they don't, I'll be sure to spread the rumor myself."

"Hot monkey sex?" Claire echoed with disbelief. "I've got news for you, Jill, I've seen two monkeys have sex and it's *not* pretty."

"She's right," Kyle informed his sister. "Not pretty at all."

"Oh God!" Jill shook her head with despair. "Honestly, the pair of you deserve each other. You're both pathetic. Sex between *any* species is not pretty. It's not *supposed* to be. It's—" She stopped abruptly, then said, "Eww! You mean like you two have stood there and *watched* monkeys have sex? That's sick!"

Claire and Kyle exchanged glances, but Kyle spoke first. "I saw them at University when I was working as a T.A. in the lab. I didn't stand there and watch, but I saw enough."

"Well, I *did* watch," Claire admitted with a bit of embarrassment. "But it was part of my job at the time, we were studying . . ." She paused and shook her head. "Never mind. Let's get me changed and get you and Brad out of here, so Kyle and I can have our date."

"Good idea." Jill led her into the empty women's washroom, and into a stall.

"Hey!" she protested when Kyle squeezed in with them.

"I want to see," Kyle said.

"Well, get up on the toilet seat then," Jill ordered after a hesitation. "That way if anyone enters and peers under the stall door it won't look so weird. They'll just see that two women are in here."

"And that's not weird?" Kyle asked with disbelief.

"Not as weird as two women and a man," she pointed out dryly. "We could just be gossiping, or comforting one another over something. Just get on the toilet," she finished when he stared in doubt.

Shrugging, Kyle carefully maneuvered himself to stand on the toilet seat and Jill relaxed and turned to Claire. "Okay, go for it."

Claire lifted the pictures and switched her own to the bottom so that Brad Cruise smiled back at her. She cast an almost apologetic glance Kyle's way, then turned her attention to the picture. Claire had barely begun to concentrate on the magazine photo when the outer bathroom door opened. Jill half jerked around toward the stall door at the sound, bumping Claire's hand. She gasped with alarm as the pictures slipped from her fingers. They shot down like paper airplanes, curving to the side on a draft and sliding under the divider between the stalls.

Instinct made Claire bend to grab for them, but then she froze as the door to the neighboring stall suddenly opened. Hissing with alarm, Jill caught at her arm to bring her upright even as Claire saw that she was now wearing the black blazer of Brad Cruise. It seemed she'd managed to change into Brad that quickly. Amazing, she thought, retracting her suit-covered arm before it could be seen. Claire straightened once more and the three of them exchanged slightly embarrassed grimaces as they waited for the woman to finish her business and leave.

All three breathed a sigh of relief when the toilet next door finally flushed and the door opened. Claire immediately bent and peered at the floor in the next stall, frowning when she saw that there was only one picture there now. It was the snapshot, she saw, and it had come to rest near the opposite side of the next stall, too far away for her to reach it at the moment.

"Where's the other one? Where's Brad?" Jill asked in a bare whisper against her ear and Claire shrugged her confusion.

"What is it?" Kyle hissed from his perch on the toilet. They straightened and whispered the explanation to him. All three stared at each other blankly, each trying to sort out where the picture might have gone as they listened to the sound of water running in the sinks in the main part of the bathroom, then Jill's eyes widened. Lifting her eyebrows in question, she jerked a thumb toward the door.

Claire stared at her, taking a minute to realize she was suggesting the woman who had entered must have picked it up. Frowning over the possibility, Claire moved to press her face to the crack on one side of the door. Jill promptly crowded up next to her to peer out the crack on the other side.

Claire had a pretty good view of the girl through the crack as she turned off the taps and walked over to the hand drier, good enough to see that she wasn't carrying any pictures in her hand. There didn't appear to be any pockets in the form-fitting black dress the woman was wearing either, she noted.

Claire was about to pull away from the crack and kneel to give the floor of the next booth a more thorough look over, when Kyle gave a "psst." Both she and Jill glanced over their shoulders to find he'd stood up on the toilet to look out at the room. Obviously he'd seen something they'd missed, for he was gesturing down toward his feet. Claire glanced down, didn't see anything and glanced back up to find Kyle pointing toward the door.

Claire turned back to her crack and peered out, this time focusing on the woman's legs, then feet. At first she didn't see anything, then as the girl finished at the hand drier and turned to walk out of the room, her eyes widened incredulously at the sight of the folded magazine photo stuck to the bottom of one high-heeled shoe.

5

"**T**hat is so me," Claire muttered as the door closed behind the girl with the picture-bearing shoe.

"What do you mean?" Kyle asked, stepping off the toilet. It left him standing behind her, his chest against her back in the small space.

"*I'm* usually the girl with the toilet paper trailing behind her on her way out of the bathroom," Claire explained with a wry twist of her lips.

"Yeah well, she's walking out with my date under her heel," Jill said with disgust. "Kind of like Magda with Ted under her thumb."

"Maybe," Kyle commented. "But I can't think of a guy more deserving of Magda than Ted. God, what an arrogant ass he turned out to be."

"Yeah," Claire agreed. "And I thought *I* had bad taste."

"Thank you very much," Kyle said with amusement and Claire flushed.

"I meant other than you, of course," she amended. "Most of the guys I've dated—aside from you—have been total turds like Ted."

"Thank you very much for pointing out what bad taste *I* have," Jill said shortly.

"Oh, that's not what I meant," Claire said quickly.

"Yeah. He had me fooled, too, Jill," Kyle assured her.

Slightly mollified, Jill sighed and gestured Claire out of the way. "Back up. I'll go get the other picture. God! Why couldn't it have been *your* picture she walked out with?"

"Well I'm glad it was Brad," Claire countered, backing into the small bit of space between the toilet and the side wall to leave room for Kyle and Jill to juggle around and get the stall door open. "I'm already Brad Cruise."

"Hardly," Jill snorted, managing to struggle her way out of the booth.

Claire frowned as the stall door swung closed on her back, then turned to Kyle to ask, "What does she mean, 'hardly'?"

Kyle hesitated, his expression pained.

Jill's voice came from the stall next door. "You're only half changed."

Claire's head jerked sideways at the announcement and then she tugged the stall door open and hurried to the mirror over the sink to peer at her reflection.

"Oh my God," Claire breathed with horror. Some of the features staring back at her were her own. She was looking at her green eyes and her little turned-up nose, but they rested above Brad Cruise's mouth and chin with the five o'clock shadow. Her hair was a strange mix of short light brown hair and long red waves, and her body . . . well . . . it was a mishmash of Brad and Claire. She had the jacket and pants from his suit, but the pants ended above her knees and she also had boobs. They didn't go well with the bulge between her legs that was his "package."

"This is a nightmare," she breathed, no longer caring which picture it was so long as it was a whole somebody. She could not leave the bathroom looking like this, and while she could turn back to herself without a picture, she would be naked.

"It's all right," Kyle murmured, slipping out of the stall to pat her back as he met her gaze in the mirror. "We'll fix it with the other picture."

"Oh dear."

Claire turned sharply toward the stalls as Jill came out with the remaining picture in hand. "Oh dear, what?"

"Nothing. It'll be fine," Jill said quickly, suddenly picking at the picture, then she paused and said, "Oh no."

"Oh no? Don't say 'oh no.'" Claire started forward to take the picture, but Jill suddenly frowned at her as if just realizing she was out of the stall.

"What are you doing?" she cried. "Get back in the stall! Someone could see you." Holding the picture out of Claire's reach, she grabbed her with her free hand and wrestled her into the stall, then slammed the door behind them and sighed.

"Jill?" Kyle asked from the other side of the door and she grimaced, then opened the door again and waved him in. She waited until they were all situated in their original places again before locking the stall door once more.

"Tell me," Claire ordered grimly.

Jill sighed, then held out the snapshot. Claire snatched it from her hand, peered down and nearly bit off her own tongue. The picture had landed facedown on a wad of gum. The girl who had used the stall must have stepped on it because it had really been worked into the picture. When Jill had tried to pick it away, the image itself had ripped off the photo backing.

"Hell," Kyle muttered.

"It will be all right," Jill assured them both as she turned to the door. "Wait here."

"Wait here?" Claire grabbed at her arm with alarm. "Where are you going?"

"The corner store is only a couple minutes away. I'll get a fan magazine with a picture of Brad in it and be right back," she assured her.

"Brad? What about *her*? Do you have another picture of her?" Kyle asked with concern.

"No. Unfortunately, we only took the one snapshot," Jill admitted and Kyle turned back to Claire.

"Can you do it without the picture?"

"No," she said on a sigh.

"Have you tried?" Kyle asked and Claire smiled faintly, thinking he sounded just like his sister earlier that day when she'd been coaxing her to be Brad Cruise.

"She can turn back into herself, but she'll end up naked without a picture to look at," Jill announced.

"Naked?" Kyle's gaze flickered over her in such a way she thought he might be picturing her that way. And might not necessarily think it was a bad thing.

"What time is it?" Claire asked suddenly.

"I don't know. Why?" Jill asked with confusion.

"I was just wondering how much of this double date from hell I've spent in the bathroom," she admitted, and Kyle, who had glanced at his wristwatch, now let it drop to his side without telling the time. That long, she thought with a sigh.

"Look, you two wait here and I'll go get a magazine at the store," Jill repeated.

"No. Enough of this nonsense," Kyle said. "She's not turning back into Brad. She's supposed to be Claire now."

"Well she isn't Claire now, and surely a full Brad is better than a Brad with boobs for getting her out of here?" Jill pointed out. "We can leave, then I'll take her home and she can change into herself and put on the dress and come back to finish the date with you."

While the twins continued to argue, Claire peered down at herself with a frown, recalling the incident on the dance floor when she'd accidentally made her boobs grow and then shrink. Could she do it again? Squeezing her eyes closed, she concentrated on making them go away and leaving her flat-chested.

"Oh man that is so awesome!"

Claire blinked her eyes open at Jill's words and peered down to find her chest flat.

"Can you make them grow?" Jill asked curiously.

"I believe she did on the dance floor tonight," Kyle said dryly, and Claire felt herself flush.

"It was an accident," she admitted.

"Do you know how cool this is?" Jill asked with disbelief. "A boob job without silicone or surgery. Oh Kyle, can I get zapped, too?"

"Jill!" Claire cried, staring at her with disbelief.

"No," Kyle said firmly at the same time.

Jill chose to respond to Kyle's answer, asking a plaintive "Why not?"

"We don't know what side effects there are," he said as if explaining things to a child. "There could be all sorts of repercussions to this kind of molecular alteration. Her cells are now unstable, they might—"

When he paused abruptly, Claire finished what he was reluctant to say. "They might yet break apart altogether and leave me a puddle of goo."

They were all silent for a minute, then Jill asked, "You're kidding, right?"

Kyle reached out to caress Claire's cheek, then cleared his throat and changed the subject. "You did that without a picture. Do you think you could change yourself back to yourself in a dress without a picture?"

Claire hesitated, not at all certain she could manage the trick. Her boobs were . . . well . . . her boobs. But he was talking about the whole body.

"Never mind," Kyle said suddenly. "I don't want you to do too much shifting until we're sure that it doesn't cause the cells to destabilize further."

"You mean her switching back and forth tonight might have been dangerous?" Jill asked with dismay.

Claire frowned at the possibility. It was something she hadn't considered.

"I don't know," Kyle admitted. "This is all new ground and I'm not sure what could happen. Nothing has happened to the animals so far, but they've only been changing color, not shifting their shapes."

Jill looked briefly stricken that this favor Claire had done her might have been dangerous and harmful, then she shook her head. "That's it then, switch back to yourself."

"I'll be naked," Claire pointed out with alarm.

"You can wear Kyle's suit jacket," Jill suggested.

"I am not walking out of here wearing nothing but Kyle's suit jacket," Claire said emphatically.

Kyle cleared his throat and said, "I'm afraid there are only two choices here . . . No, three," he corrected himself.

"Which are?" Claire asked warily, sure she wouldn't like any of them.

"One: you and I can stay here and wait while Jill drives home and fetches you some clothes."

Claire grimaced at the suggestion. Too many embarrassing situations could come out of that. They were two men in a women's washroom, after all. Well, one and a half men, she supposed.

"Two: you can leave here as you are," Kyle continued, but his expression suggested this wasn't really an option at all. Having seen herself, Claire had to agree, so she didn't even bother to comment. Instead, she prompted, "Or?"

"Or, three: you can change back to yourself and leave here naked with my jacket on," he finished with a shrug.

"No offense," Claire said unhappily. "But those options all suck."

Turning away, she leaned her head against the cool metal of the stall wall and tried to think of something herself.

"What?" Jill asked when Claire suddenly stiffened. "You have an idea?"

"Maybe. What if you went and got one of the phoebuses and I shifted into one of the teachers, I could leave here, then we could go get another present-day photo of me and—" She paused at the thunderous expressions on the faces of both Lockharts. They looked furious that she would even suggest the extra shift. "Never mind. Okay, Kyle give me your jacket."

All three of them were forced to shift and bend and juggle about to allow him to remove the suit coat, and then to do so again as she donned it. They were all hot and sweaty and relieved when it was done.

"Okay, shift," Jill instructed once Claire had the jacket on over her Brad/Claire body.

Claire closed her eyes and concentrated on being herself.

"Honest to God, Claire. You're the only woman I know who could make a man's jacket look sexy."

Claire blinked her eyes open at Jill's words.

"Am I me?" she asked, glancing down at herself, eyebrows rising at just how short the jacket was on her. Dear God, she wasn't going to be bending over any time soon.

"Oh yeah, you're you," Kyle said huskily, and Claire flushed under his admiring glance.

"Oh please," Jill said. "Let's get out of here. I can smell the hormones starting to ooze out of the two of you. And while I love you both, I'd rather not think of either of you naked doing the wild thing, especially not together." She ended her comment with a delicate little shudder of distaste that made both Claire and Kyle grimace.

"Go check and be sure the hall is empty first, Jill," Kyle suggested.

"Oh right. Be right back." She had barely slid from the stall when Kyle turned Claire into his arms and covered her mouth with his.

Claire gasped in surprise at the abrupt action and Kyle took advantage of her open mouth and thrust his tongue inside.

"Oh God!" Jill's exclamation drew them apart. "Can't you at least wait until you get her to the car?"

Claire flushed as they turned to face Kyle's sister, and Jill shook her head.

"The coast is clear if you want to leave. Or the two of you could just do it right here in the girls' bathroom and get it over with. Honestly!" Turning, she stomped back to the door muttering, "He waits forever to finally ask her out, then he's all over her. Mr. Octopus. Hands everywhere. It really is the quiet ones you have to watch."

Biting her lip, Claire hurried after Jill, aware that

Kyle was at her back. She could feel his gaze traveling over the back of her bare legs and was grateful the jacket covered at least her behind.

"Damn," Kyle muttered several moments later as they stared at the third exit door they'd approached since leaving the washroom. This, like the two before it, was chained shut.

"The door by the gymnasium must be the only one they left open tonight," Jill suggested.

"They should have a second door unlocked in case of fire," Kyle said with a frown.

"Maybe they do, on the other side of the gym," Claire suggested.

Both Kyle and Jill peered at her, their gazes sliding over her skimpy wear. They had managed to avoid being seen so far. The first door they had tried had been the only one with any real risk of being seen. The last two were down halls no one had any real business being down, including themselves under normal circumstances.

"The gym bisects this end of the school," Kyle pointed out. "The only way to get to the other side is through the gym."

"Or across the stage," Claire said.

Kyle blinked. "I forgot about the stage," he acknowledged. The small gymnasium was used for plays as well as sports, or had been when they'd attended Murphy High.

"It's curtained off tonight." Jill began to grin. "We can sneak across it to the other side and slip out unseen."

"Okay." Kyle took an arm of each of them and turned back the way they'd come.

Luck seemed to be on their side, and they reached the door to the back of the stage unseen. All three of them sighed with relief as they slipped into the dark alcove at the foot of the stairs leading onstage . . . until the door closed, leaving them in utter blackness.

"I can't see a thing," Jill complained in a whisper, her hand grabbing at Claire's arm.

"Just wait here a minute until our eyes adjust," Kyle suggested. They waited several minutes, listening to someone giving a speech in the gymnasium itself. From the alcove, the voice was really just a low incomprehensible drone occasionally punctuated by clapping or laughter from the reunion attendees, but it was soothing in its tenor.

"Okay," Kyle said after several useless moments had passed and their vision didn't improve. "I guess this is as good as it gets. I'll lead the way. Claire, you take my hand. Jill, you hold on to Claire."

Claire almost protested that she couldn't hold the jacket closed if both her hands were occupied, but then let the matter drop. After all, it was so dark, no one would be able to see if the coat hung open. She'd just retrieve her hand before they slipped out through the door on the opposite side.

Kyle moved very slowly up the stairs to the stage. Claire followed just as slowly, carefully feeling out each step as she drew Jill behind her. Once on the stage itself, it was less difficult; the flat floor was easier to negotiate. It was also easier to hear the speech being given on the other side of the curtain up here, though Claire was too tense to listen as she blindly followed Kyle's firm hand.

Claire never considered that there might be anything on the stage itself to trip them up. Presumably, Kyle didn't either, for he moved a bit more quickly as they crossed the floor, trading caution for speed. When he suddenly came to a halt with a grunt of surprise, Claire crashed into his back, then stumbled to the side, their handhold briefly broken. Before she could tumble to the stage floor to alert those beyond the curtains that someone was onstage, she crashed into Kyle and his hands closed around her waist, steadying her.

"Sorry," Claire whispered, relaxing against him.

"What happened?" Jill hissed, tightening her hold on her hand.

"We ran into something."

"What?"

"I don't know," Claire whispered.

"Who is that?" a baritone voice asked over her head and Claire stiffened. That wasn't Kyle's voice. The hands around her tightened as if sensing she would try to break free, and Claire began to struggle in earnest, then stilled and blinked as she realized it was growing lighter . . . Fast.

"I give you your Prom King and Prom Queen from 19—" The voice died mid-year and Claire whirled around as the hands holding her suddenly dropped away.

"Oh God," Claire heard Jill breathe as the stage lights suddenly went on, blinding them to the sight of the people staring at them . . . but highlighting them on the stage.

"You're not Claire!"

Claire's hands had gone up to shield her eyes the minute the lights blinked on. Now she turned her head toward that startled comment from Kyle and saw him almost off the stage with Magda by the hand. The blond was wearing a long red robe over her dress and a tiara on her head. She also had a furious expression on her face that said she wasn't pleased.

"Claire?"

She glanced over her shoulder at the man who had

caught her when she'd stumbled and found herself staring at Jack McCarthy, the football player she'd dated in high school. He, too, wore a robe over his suit, but his head was topped by a crown.

Prom King and Prom Queen, Claire recalled the speaker saying. Magda and Jack had been the Prom King and Prom Queen the year they'd all graduated. Obviously they'd been waiting back here in their robes and crowns to be presented to their cograduates. Kyle must have stumbled into one of them, and the moment their hands had broken apart, confusion had set in. He'd ended up dragging Magda offstage, and she'd ended in Jack's arms.

The silence that had gripped the gymnasium suddenly gave way to the roar of shouts and clapping. It was so loud, Claire almost didn't hear Jill's shout. She did however, notice the way she was trying to pull the lapels of Kyle's suit coat closed over her nakedness.

Squealing in horror, Claire finished the task herself and turned her back to the pandemonium in the gymnasium, only to find herself staring at a leering Jack.

"You aged well, babe. Are you still single?" Jack asked, reaching for her.

"No, she isn't," Kyle snarled, suddenly at their side. Snatching her hand, he dragged her quickly offstage, leaving Jill to rush along behind them.

"Well, I'd say that's a reunion no one will forget," Jill gasped as they ran out of the school and hurried across the parking lot.

Claire groaned and felt her already flushed face darken a bit more. She would really rather not think about what had just happened.

"Did you see Magda's face?" Jill added. "She was furious we stole her moment."

Claire groaned again, then sighed as they reached Kyle's car and leaned weakly against the side of it.

"Cheer up, Claire," Jill said, rubbing her back. "This might have been the double date from hell, but Magda had it worse."

"Worse?" Claire asked with disbelief.

"Well sure. First she finds out her fiancé's been cheating on her from Kyle and that she's dating my castoff, then Ted goes and asks me to see him again, then Brad Cruise says she's a lousy kisser and drops her in the toilet, then her crowning moment as the Prom Queen revisited is spoiled when she's dragged offstage. At least you got a standing ovation for your figure. You were a hit."

Claire groaned and dropped her head.

"I don't think that helped, Jill," Kyle said archly. "Get in the car."

"No thanks. You two go on. I'll wait for you at home," Jill announced.

"But—" Claire straightened abruptly, feeling as if she was being abandoned.

"I have my car here and you two need to talk," Jill said firmly as she moved off.

Claire blew a breath out and glanced at Kyle. He didn't say anything, but merely unlocked and opened the passenger door of his car for her to get in, then closed it behind her. Biting her lip, she watched him move around to the driver's side to slide behind the wheel.

A moment of silence filled the dark interior and then Kyle gave a short laugh.

"What?" Claire asked warily.

"I was just thinking that you were two-timing me tonight with my own sister."

Claire grimaced. "It was more like a double date where I was both Brad and Claire."

"This night would have gone much easier if you'd just told me what was going on," Kyle pointed out.

"I know." Claire bowed her head.

"But you didn't trust me not to immediately rush you back to the lab and treat you like Thumper," he said quietly.

"No," Claire said quickly. "I mean, not really. I was just afraid you'd think I was a freak, or that you'd . . ."

"See you as an experimental subject rather than as yourself," he finished quietly.

Claire sighed, unable to deny it.

"That would never happen, Claire," Kyle said solemnly. "We've known each other too long for me to think of you as anything but the beautiful, intelligent young woman you are."

Claire felt tears well in her eyes, but forced them away, and quickly changed the subject to one she'd been wondering about all night. "You said you'd tell me why you didn't ask me out when we were in high school," she reminded him.

Kyle grimaced, then admitted, "Actually, it's because your father had a talk with me and asked me not to."

"My *father*?" Claire asked with surprise.

Kyle nodded. "He said it was obvious the two of us liked each other and that we were very compatible and would probably make a good team, but he cautioned me that I might want to wait until we were both out of school to start up anything with you. That we already knew we liked each other, so if we found we had passion together, we might do something unfortunate and become pregnant, or marry impulsively and destroy the possibility of two promising careers. He also wanted you to gain some independence and learn you could stand on your own two feet rather than move from living with your parents to living with a husband."

"Daddy said that?" she asked with outrage. Claire couldn't believe her own father had interfered in her love life that way. She was definitely going to have a chat with the man.

"He was right, Claire," Kyle said quietly. "It was better this way. You'll have your master's soon and I my doctorate. You experienced independence and know that if you aren't happy, you can leave and take care of yourself. You've also dated other men and I've dated other women, so we'll never wonder what we were missing out on."

Claire blinked. "That sounds rather long-term, Kyle."

"Yeah, it does, doesn't it?" He smiled wryly, then took her hands and said, "Look, Claire, I've known you since you were a skinny little twelve-year-old brat with braces. More than long enough to know I love you. I've always loved you."

"You *love* me?" Claire asked with pleased surprise.

"Yes."

"I love you, too," she said happily.

Kyle leaned forward and kissed her and Claire felt her heart thrill at the passion that again exploded between them. They definitely had some chemistry going on there, which was good to know, she thought, and then felt Kyle's hand slide beneath the jacket to find and cup one breast. Claire moaned and arched against him as his lips began to travel down her neck.

"Oh Kyle," she breathed, clutching at his shoulder with one hand as the other started doing a little traveling of its own.

"Oh Claire," he gasped, shifting around and trying

to find a better position for them both without the stick shift and steering wheel to get in the way. They were both panting, half with excitement, half with frustration, when he reached past her and pulled the lever to let the upper part of her seat down.

Claire gasped as she suddenly slammed backward in the front seat and then simply began to crawl backward, leading him into the backseat where the steering wheel and stick shift wouldn't be a problem. Kyle growled and followed, tugging the sides of his jacket aside to leave her exposed to him as he joined her on the backseat. Then he paused, and glanced around, blinking at the sight of the already fogged window. He frowned and reluctantly offered, "We could go back to the house."

"Too far," Claire muttered, reaching for him. She then paused and smiled wryly as she realized they were so eager for each other that they were about to make love in the back of a car like a pair of teenagers. Shaking her head, she said, "Daddy was right."

"Oh yeah," Kyle admitted wryly, stretching himself so he lay half on her and half on the seat and then he kissed her again.

Shuddering and moaning, she arched against him again, then gasped with excitement as his hand found and cupped the center of him. Moaning into his mouth, she shifted her hips upward into the touch, then reached to find him as well, smiling against his mouth as he groaned in response to her own hand covering him.

He was already hard, but his erection was still growing and she blinked her eyes open in surprise as his more than healthy erection continued to grow under her hand. And grow. And grow.

Dear God, she thought faintly, she'd hit the jackpot. The man was *really* well endowed.

Kyle broke their kiss and moved his mouth to her ear to murmur, "Did I mention the destabilizer ray was still on when I ran into the experiment chamber to drag you out? I discovered the effect it'd had and my new abilities in the parking lot of the grocery store this afternoon when I went to get groceries."

Claire's eyes widened at this news. "You mean you're *doing* this? You're shifting to make it bigger?"

He nodded, then caught the lobe of her ear in his teeth and sucked lightly. "Anything for my lady's pleasure."

"But Kyle," she cried. "You shouldn't be shifting. What about the possibility of destabilizing the cells further, to the point of breakdown?"

Kyle straightened with a sigh. "I don't really think that's likely. Mostly I just didn't want to have to share you with Jill anymore tonight," he said, then added with a wry smile, "Getting you naked was also a consideration."

Claire narrowed her eyes on him. "Kyle, you may be able to fool Jill with that, but I'm as savvy on the experiment as you are. I know there is some worry that—"

"Some small worry," he acknowledged. "But very small, and you're worth the risk."

"Oh, Kyle," Claire breathed, pulling him back down toward her. "That's just the sweetest thing ever."

Epilogue

Five years later

I can't believe Kyle agreed to babysit," Jill said as they got out of the car.

Claire laughed as she led the way around to the trunk to unload the goods they'd bought. "He knew I wanted a special dress for the graduation next week. I have to look good when I become Dr. Claire Lockhart."

Jill smiled faintly at her obvious pride in finally achieving her doctorate, but shook her head. "Still . . ."

"Oh, come on," Claire chided. "Kyle's a great dad. He loves little Beth."

Jill snorted. "He *loses* little Beth every time he babysits and it drives him wild."

Claire laughed again, the laugh of a wife and mother who was happy and satisfied. It was five years since their high school reunion and her first date with Kyle Lockhart. Four years since she'd become Mrs. Claire Lockhart, and two years since they'd had their first child. Claire was now three months pregnant with their second child and already couldn't wait for Beth's little brother or sister to be born. She was hoping for a boy.

Nothing would make her happier than giving Kyle a son to go with his daughter.

"Kyle!" Claire yelled as she led Jill into the house. "We're back!"

A childish giggle answered her from the end of the hall and Claire started slowly forward, carefully scanning the floor as she moved toward the kitchen. She was nearly at the kitchen door when she stopped abruptly and shook her head.

"You little dickens," Claire chided. "Are you playing hide and seek with your daddy again?"

The uneven bit of floor she'd noted gave another little giggle and suddenly shifted into a naked baby girl with curly strawberry blond hair and big blue eyes.

"Claire!" Kyle came rushing down the stairs, his hair and clothes a tousled mess, his eyes slightly frantic and a diaper and pink dress in hand. "I can't find Beth. She shed her clothes and is hiding on me again. She—"

He paused, blinking abruptly as he noted the child standing, leaning against her mother's knee.

"Oh, Beth," Kyle breathed with relief, hurrying forward to scoop her up into his arms. "Naughty girl, scaring Daddy like that."

When his daughter's only response was to giggle, Kyle shook his head and bent to kiss Claire softly on the lips.

"I love you," he breathed by her ear before straightening.

"And I love you," Claire assured him.

She watched with a soft smile as Kyle moved off down the hall, reprimanding their daughter as he went.

Five years had passed since the day they'd both been exposed to the destabilizer. They'd managed to keep their secret and still see John Heathcliffe lose his position for his "attempt" to test the destabilizer on a human. And, so far—much to their relief since they'd passed their condition on to their child—there didn't appear to be any terrible side effects to the exposure to the destabilizer. If anything, it tended to make life more than a little interesting.

CHAOTIC

Kelley Armstrong

For Alexander and Marcus,
who keep my life "chaotic"
but in a good way.

1

"**S**o what kind of stories do you cover?" he asked, bathing my face in champagne fumes. "Bat Boy Goes to College? Elvis Shrine Found on Mars?" He laughed without waiting for me to answer. "God, I can't believe people actually buy those rags. Obviously, they must, or you wouldn't have a job."

My standard line flew to my lips, something about tabloids functioning as a source of entertainment, not news, quirky pieces of fiction that people could read and chuckle over before facing the horrors of the daily paper. I choked it back and forced myself to smile up at him.

"I did a Hell Spawn feature once," I said, as brightly as I could manage. "That's *True News*'s version of Bat Boy. I covered his graduation from kindergarten. He was so cute with a little mortarboard perched on his horns . . ."

I crossed my fingers under my cocktail napkin and prayed for "the look," the curl of the lip, the widening of the eyes as they frantically searched for an escape. Escape would be *so* easy—a crowded museum gala,

everyone in evening wear—come on, Douglas, just excuse yourself to use the bathroom and conveniently
forget where you left me . . .

He threw back his head and laughed. "Hell Spawn's
kindergarten graduation? Now that's a fun job. You
know what the highlight of my workweek is? Nine
holes of golf with the other AVPs."

See, now that was the problem with guys like
Douglas—they weren't evil. Boring, boorish and bor-
derline obnoxious, but not so awful that you could jus-
tify abandoning them. So you were stuck hoping
they'd be the ones to declare the date a dud, and beg
off early.

Dinner had been a mistake. I should have insisted
we meet here, at the party, so if things didn't go well,
we'd have only been sentenced to a couple hours of
each other's company. But he invited me to dinner first,
and even as I'd been thinking *No!* my mouth had done
the right thing, the polite thing, and said, "Sure, dinner
would be great."

I'd spent forty-five minutes at the table by myself,
fending off sympathetic "you've been stood up" looks
from the servers and watching my salad wither on the
plate. Then Douglas had arrived . . . and I'd spent the
next hour listening to him complain about the cause of
his lateness, some corporate calamity too complex for
my layperson's brain to comprehend. It wasn't until we
were here at the opening of the museum's new wing
that he'd even gotten around to asking what *I* did for a
living.

"So what's the weirdest story you've ever covered?"
he asked.

I laughed. "Oh, there would be plenty of contenders
for that one. Just last week I had this UFO—"

"What about celebrities?" he cut in. "Tabloids cover that, right? Celebrity gossip? What's the best one of *those* stories you've done?"

"Ummm, none. *True News* includes some celebrity stories, but I'm strictly the 'weird tales' girl, mainly paranormal, although—"

"Paranormal? Like ghosts?" Again, he didn't wait for me to answer. "Our frat house was supposed to be haunted. Frederick and I—your brother-in-law and I were frat brothers, but I guess your mother told you that. Anyway, one night . . ."

My poor mother. Reduced to canvassing my sister's husband's college buddies for potential mates for her youngest child. She'd long since gone through every eligible bachelor she knew personally.

"I don't need you to find me dates, Mom," I said the last time, as I'd said the hundred times before. "I'm not so bad at it myself."

"Dates, yes. Relationships, no. I swear, Hope, you go out of your way to find men you wouldn't want to know for more than a weekend. Yes, I know, you're only twenty-six, hardly an old maid, and I'm not saying you need to settle down, but you could really use some stability in your life, dear. I know you've had a rough go of it . . ."

What do you expect? I wanted to say sometimes. *You gave me a demon for a dad.* Of course, that wasn't fair. Mom didn't know what my father was. I'd been born nine months after my parents separated, and grown up assuming, like everyone else, that I was my father's "parting shot" before he'd run off with his nurse.

Only at eighteen had I begun to suspect otherwise, when I'd realized that my feelings of being "different" were more than adolescent alienation.

Douglas finished his haunted frat house story, then asked, "So what kind of education does a tabloid writer need? Obviously you don't go to journalism school for that."

"Actually, I did."

He had the grace to flush. "Oh, uh . . . but you wouldn't need to, right? I mean, it's not real reporting or anything."

I searched his face for some sign of condescension. None. He was a jerk, but not a malicious one. Damn. Another excuse lost. I had a half-dozen girlfriends who wouldn't need a justification for ending this date early, who'd just cut and run. So why couldn't I? I was half-demon, for God's sake. I could be as nasty as I wanted.

I scanned the room. The gala was being held in the reception hall, which was also—as discreet signs everywhere reminded us—available for weddings, parties and corporate events. A jazz trio played in the corner beside a portable parquet dance floor that was small enough to be a solo stage, as if the organizers acknowledged this wasn't a dancing crowd, but felt obligated to provide something. Most of the guests were big business, so the main event here was schmoozing, fostering contacts while basking in the feel-good glow of supporting the arts. Large-scale artifact replicas, such as statues and urns, dotted the room, reminding guests where they were and why . . . although the pieces seemed to be getting more use as coatracks and leaning posts.

"The buffet table looks amazing," I said. "Is that poached salmon?"

"Wild, I hope, but you can't be too careful these days. I had dinner with a client last week, and he'd been to a five-star restaurant in New York the week before, and they'd served farm-fed salmon. Do people

just not read the papers? You might as well eat puffer
fish, which reminds me of the time I was in Tokyo—"

"Hold that thought," I said. "I'm going to grab
something and scoot back."

I bolted before he could stop me.

As I crossed the floor to the buffet, I was keenly
aware of eyes turning my way. A wonderful feeling for
a woman . . . if those eyes are sweeping over her in ad-
miration and envy, not glued to her dress in "what the
hell is she wearing?" bemusement.

It was the dress's fault. It had screamed to me from
across the store, a canary yellow beacon in the rack of
blacks and olive greens and navy blues. A ray of sunshine
in the night. That's how I'd pictured myself in it, cutting a
swath through the darkness in my slinky bright yellow
dress. Ray of sunshine? I looked like a banana in heels.

Sadly, it wasn't my first fashion disaster. The truly
sad part was that I had no excuse for my lack of dress
sense. My mother routinely showed up on the local society papers as a shining example of the well-bred and
well-dressed. My sister had paid her way through law
school by modeling. Even my brothers had both made
the annual "best dressed bachelor" lists before their
marriages disqualified them. It didn't matter. My
whole family could have accompanied me to that store,
told me—yet again—that yellow was the worst color
anyone with dark hair and a dark complexion could
choose, and I'd still have walked out with this dress,
blinded by my sun-bright delusions.

At least I hadn't spilled anything on it. I paused mid-
stride, and looked down at myself. Nope, nothing
spilled yet, and as long as I stuck to white wine and
sauce-free food, I'd be fine.

I picked up a plate and surveyed the table. A roast

duck centerpiece surrounded by poached salmon, mari-
nated prawns on ice, chocolate-covered strawberries . . .
I wasn't hungry, but there's always room for chocolate-
covered strawberries. As I reached for one, my vision
clouded.

Oh God. Not now.

I tried to force the vision back, concentrate on the
present, the buffet table, the smell of perfume circling
the room, the soft jazz notes floating past, focus on
that, keep myself grounded in the—

Everything went dark. Images, smells, and sounds
flickered past, hard and fast, like physical blows. A
forest—the shriek of an owl—the loamy smell of wet
earth—the thunder of running paws—a flash of black
fur—a snarl—teeth flashing—the sharp taste of—

I ricocheted from my vision so fast I had to grab the
edge of the table to steady myself. I swallowed and
tasted blood, as if I'd bitten my tongue.

A deep breath, then I opened my eyes. There, in the
center of the table, wasn't a roast duck, but a newly
dead one, ripped apart, bloodied feathers scattered
over the ice and prawns and poached salmon, steaming
entrails spilling out on the white tablecloth.

I wheeled, smacked into a man standing behind me,
and knocked the plate from his hands. I dove to grab it,
but my charm bracelet snagged on his sleeve, and I
nearly yanked him down with me. The plate hit the
floor, shards of china flying in every direction.

"Oh, I'm *so* sorry," I said.

A soft chuckle. "Quite all right. I'm better off without the added cholesterol. My doctor will thank you."

I fumbled to extricate his sleeve from my bracelet.
He reached down, hand brushing mine, and with a deft
twist, set us free.

As he did, I got my first glimpse of him, and inwardly groaned. If I had to make a fool of myself, it would be in front of someone like this, who looked as if he'd never made a fool of himself in his life. Tall, dark, and handsome, he was elegance personified, marred only by a slight hawkish cast to his face. Every response to my stammered apologies was witty and charming. Every move as we untangled was fluid and graceful. The kind of guy you expected to speak with a crisp, British accent and order his martinis shaken, not stirred.

As a bevy of serving staff rushed in to clean up, I apologized one last time, and he smiled, his last reassurance as sincere as his first, but his gaze grown distant, as if he'd mentally already moved on and, in five minutes, would forget me altogether . . . which, under the circumstances, I didn't mind at all.

As I walked back to Douglas, the working Big Ben replica clock in the middle of the room chimed the hour. Ten o'clock? Already? No, that made sense—with Douglas being almost an hour late for dinner, we hadn't arrived at the gala until past nine.

I hurried over to him. "There's a—"

He cut me short with a discreet nod toward my bodice.

"You have a spot," he whispered.

I looked down to see a dime-sized blob of marinara sauce beside my left breast. Fallout from the buffet table debacle. Naturally. If food flew, I'd catch some, and in the worst possible place.

I thanked him and tried to blot it with my napkin. It grew from a dime to a quarter, and I stretched my purse strap to cover it.

"I was going to say there's a special behind-the-scenes tour of the new exhibit starting now," I said. "I'd love to see it, and it would be a great way to meet people, mingle . . ." . . . *save me from another two hours of your corporate war stories.*

"Speaking of mingling, did you see who's here?" He directed my attention to a group of middle-aged couples wedged between a bronze urn and a terracotta bull.

"Robert Baird," he whispered reverently.

He paused, as if waiting for me to drop and touch my forehead to the floor.

"CEO of Baird Enterprises?" he said.

"Oh, well, if you know him, I guess we could—"

"I don't, but I'm sure you do . . . not directly maybe, but his wife and your mother both serve on the Ryerson Foundation board, and—"

"You thought I could introduce you."

"You would? Thanks, Hope. You're a gem."

"Sure, right after the tour—"

Too late. He was already heading for the Bairds. I sighed, adjusted my purse strap, and followed.

2

Thirty minutes later, the tour was over, the attendees were returning, gushing over the new exhibit . . . and I was still stuck with Douglas and the Bairds. Now that I'd won him an audience, he wasn't leaving until they did.

I began to wonder whether he'd notice if I left. Maybe I could slip away, conduct a little self-guided tour . . .

Douglas put his arm around my waist and leaned into me, as if to take some of the weight off his feet. I bit back a growl of frustration, fixed on my best "gosh, this is all so interesting" smile, and did what I'm sure every other significant other in the group had done an hour ago: turned off and tuned out.

While every other partner's mind slid to mundanities like juggling the children's schedules, planning next weekend's dinner party, or contemplating the report he or she had to write for work, mine went straight to the dark realm of human suffering, evil, and chaos. I can't help it. The moment I let my mind wander, it turns into a dedicated chaos receiver, picking up every nearby trouble frequency.

Unlike the buffet table vision, these weren't mental blackouts. More like semi-dozing, that state right before sleep where you're still conscious, but the dream world starts to encroach on reality. The first thing I saw was a woman sitting at Mrs. Baird's feet, her knees pulled up under her party dress, her makeup running, her shoulders heaving with silent sobs.

As the apparition vanished, I felt my gaze slide to the left, and I knew somewhere down a hall, I'd find a woman, huddled and sobbing in some quiet place. Maybe someone had called with bad news, or maybe she'd seen her husband's hand snake onto another woman's thigh. I never knew the causes, only the outcomes.

"Tonight," a man's voice hissed at my ear. "He had to do it tonight, while the offices are empty."

I didn't bother looking beside me. Instead I let my subconscious draw my attention across the room to two men near the door. One was shaking his head. The other's face was taut as he talked quickly.

The voices faded, and others took their place—angry words, accusations, whimpers, sobs, a Babel of voices joined in the common tongue of chaos. Images flashed, superimposed on reality, burning themselves onto my retinas, an unending parade of chaos in every conceivable form, from grief to rage to sorrow to jealousy to hate. I saw, heard, felt, experienced it all. And the worst of it? Even as my brain rebelled, throwing up every proper reaction: horror, sympathy, and anger, my soul drank it in like the finest champagne, reveling in the sweet taste and the bubbles popping against my tongue and the delicious caress of giddy light-headedness.

Every half-demon has a power, inherited from his or her father. Some can create fire, some can change the weather, some can even move objects with their minds. *This* was mine.

For six years, I'd struggled with my growing "power," this innate radar for chaos, this thirst for it. I'd fought like the most self-aware junkie, knowing my addiction would destroy me, but unable to stop chasing it. Years of dark moods, dark days, and darker thoughts. Then . . . salvation.

Through my growing network of half-demon contacts, someone had found me, someone who could help. I wouldn't say I was surprised. For community support, you can't beat the supernatural world. Most races had formed core groups centuries ago, like the witch Covens, werewolf Packs, sorcerer Cabals . . . When you live in a world that doesn't know you exist, and it seems best to keep it that way, community is a must, for everything from training to medical care.

Half-demons are often considered the least "communal" of the races, but I'd argue the opposite. We may not have a core group or hold meetings or police our own, but the half-demon regional communities encompass everyone in that region, which is more than I can say for the others. Because we lack the family support of the hereditary races, half-demons are always on the lookout for others, and once you're found, a world of support opens up to you. So, when a local half-demon I knew only through a mutual acquaintance called me, I wasn't surprised. And when she asked me to meet with someone who might be able to help me hone and control my powers, I didn't say no.

The meeting had been scheduled for lunch, at a sidewalk café, someplace public and private at the same time, which reassured me from the start. I'd arrived to find just one person at the table, a slight, fair-haired man in his thirties, dressed business casual, like everyone else in the restaurant. Handsome, in a delicate way, well-mannered, with an easy smile and warm brown eyes, Tristan Robard had put me at ease from that first handshake. We'd ordered a pitcher of sangria, chatted about local events, and spent the first half of the meal getting a sense of each other. Then, halfway through lunch, he'd looked up from his salad, met my gaze and said,

"Have you ever heard of the interracial council?"

When I hesitated, he laughed. "They really need a better name, don't they? The Sumerian Council, the Grand Guild, or something like that. That's the problem with trying to be understated . . . if you don't give yourself a fancy name, no one remembers who the heck you are. Get a good name, a clever slogan, a nice logo—" He grinned. "Then people would remember who you are and, more importantly, remember you when they need you."

"Is that . . . It's the delegates council, isn't it? The heads of the various supernatural races—the American ones, at least . . ."

"Exactly. Do you know what the council does?"

I made a face. "Sorry, only the vaguest idea, I'm afraid." I smiled. "Like you said, they need a better marketing plan. They're supposed to help supernaturals, right? General policing, resolving conflicts between groups . . ."

"Protect and serve, that's the council's motto . . . or it would be, if they had one. The problem is that, for about twenty years, they've been slipping so far under the radar that no one knows they're there, so no one reports problems. They're trying to fix that now, and step one is broadening their reach. Recruiting, so to speak."

"New delegates, you mean?"

He laughed. "No, those positions are filled, and far loftier than you or I can aspire to . . . for now, at least. What they're doing instead is creating a network of 'eyes on the ground,' supernaturals willing to join the payroll, look for trouble and, eventually, help them solve it."

My hand clenched around my napkin as I struggled to keep my face neutral. Help look for trouble? Was there anyone better suited for such a task? If I could help—use my power for good—Oh, God, please . . .

I don't think I breathed for that next minute, waiting for him to go on.

"In particular, they want people in careers suited to troubleshooting, like law enforcement officers, social workers, or—" He met my gaze and smiled. "Journalists. And the ideal candidate would be someone not only with a suitable job, but from a race that could prove equally useful, werewolves or vampires for their tracking skills or, maybe"—his smile grew to a grin—"a half-demon with a nose for trouble."

"You mean . . ." The words jammed in my throat.

"On behalf of the council, Hope, I'd like to offer you a job."

And so it began. With Tristan as my contact, I'd been working for the council for eighteen months now. I hadn't been fortunate enough to meet the delegates to thank them personally, but in the meantime, I thanked them with every job I did, putting my all into each task they assigned me, however simple.

Tristan had gotten me the job at *True News*. Not exactly a prestigious position for an up-and-coming journalist, but I knew it would help the council and that was more important than my professional ego. Tabloids *do* stumble on the truth now and then, and it's usually trouble: a careless vampire, an angry half-demon, a power-hungry sorcerer. As Tristan had taught me, my powers were particularly honed for supernatural trouble. So I used my job at the paper to sniff it out.

I was good at my job. Damn good. So after the first year, the council had expanded my duties to cover bounty hunting. Supernaturals who cause trouble often flee. With the right cues, I could find supernaturals even when they *weren't* creating chaos. If they came near my part of the country, I could sniff out the guilty party, then call in the cavalry.

For this, the council paid me, and paid me well, but the best part wasn't the money; it was the guilt-free excuse to quench my thirst for chaos. To help the council, I needed to hone my powers, and to do that, I had to practice. I had a long way to go—I still picked up random visions like that silly one with the duck, who'd probably seen his mother ripped apart by a dog or some such nonsense. But I was improving, and while I was, I had every excuse to indulge in the chaos around me.

So when my mind wandered during the conversation, that's exactly what I did—practiced. I concentrated on picking out specific audio threads and visual images, pulling them to the forefront and holding them there when they threatened to fade behind stronger signals.

The one I was working on was a very mundane marital spat, a couple trading hissed volleys of "you never listen to me" and "why do you always do this?" The kind of fights every relationship falls into in times of stress . . . or so my siblings and friends told me—

relationships, as my mother pointed out, are not my forte. There's too much in my life I can't share, so I concentrate on friends, family, work, and my job with the council, and try to forget what I'm missing. When I hear stuff like this meaningless bickering, ruining what should have been a romantic night together, I'm not convinced that I'm missing anything.

The very banality of the fight made it a perfect practice target. Even at a social function like this, there were a half-dozen stronger sources of chaos happening simultaneously, and my mind kept trying to lead me astray, like a puppy straining on the leash in a new park.

Keeping my focus on the bickering couple was a struggle and—

"You aren't supposed to be back here, sir," said a gruff voice in my ear. "This area is off-limits to guests."

I mentally waved the voice aside like a buzzing mosquito. Back to the couple. The husband was bitching about the wife ordering fish for dinner when she knew he hated the smell of it.

"Which is why I had it when we were out," she snapped. "So I don't stink up the kitchen cooking it and—"

"What the—?"

The same gruff voice, now shrill with alarm. My head shot up, pulse accelerating, body tense with anticipation, as if my mental hound had just caught the scent of fresh T-bone steak.

"No! Please—!"

The plea slid into a wordless scream. One syllable, one split second, then the scream was cut short, and I was left hanging there, straining for more—

I whipped my thoughts back and turned to pinpoint

the source of the chaos. Another jolt, this one too dark, too strong even for me, like that last gulp of champagne when you've already had too much and your stomach lurches in rebellion, the sweetness turning acid-sour.

"Hope?" Douglas's hand slipped from my waist, and he leaned toward my ear to whisper, "Are you okay?"

"Bathroom," I managed. "The champagne."

"Here, let me take you—"

I brushed him off with a smile. Then I made my way across the room, my legs shaking, hoping I wasn't staggering. By the time I reached the hall, the shock of that mental jolt had been replaced with an oddly calm curiosity.

A few more steps, and I began to wonder whether I'd been picking up a "chaos-memory." I often sensed strong residual vibes from events long past, like that dead buffet duck. I'm working on learning to distinguish residuals from current sources, but I'm always second-guessing myself.

I arrived at the end of the hall, where it split into two. To the right I could detect traces of the source that had bitch-slapped me. But I also caught another, fresher source of trouble to the left.

My attention naturally swung left. The chaos-puppy again, far more interested in that squirrel gamboling in plain sight than an old rabbit trail. I gave in to the impulse, already ninety percent convinced that whatever I'd felt had been a chaos-memory.

3

I looked around, then slipped past the sign reminding guests that this area wasn't part of the gala. In
other words: keep out, worded nicely to avoid insulting current and future museum benefactors.

As the sounds of the party faded behind me, the
clicking of my heels grew louder. I stopped, backed
into a recessed doorway, and removed them. Then,
with the shoe straps threaded through my purse strap, I
leaned out of the doorway, looked both ways, crept out,
and padded down the hall.

I'd nearly made it to the end when a flashlight beam
bounced off the walls. I backpedaled, heart tripping. A
security guard's shoes clomped through the next room,
then receded. I started out again.

At the end of the hall, I peeked into the next room.
The chaos signal was stronger now, a siren's call luring
me in. It came from down yet another darkened hallway. As I stepped into the room, a red light blinked. A
surveillance camera. Shit!

Again I scooted into the hall. I crouched nearly to
the floor, then shuffled forward, too low for the camera
to pick up. I craned my head back to look for that light.

There it was, on a video camera lens fixed on the display cases.

Squinting, I visually charted a safe path around the perimeter. Still crouched, face turned from the camera, I started forward. It wasn't easy, moving in the near darkness, through an unfamiliar room dotted with obstacles—priceless obstacles. But I reveled in every terrified heart thump. Part of me wanted to rise above that, to dismiss this as an inconvenient—even silly—part of my job, skulking about dark corridors, avoiding security guards. I blame my upbringing in a world that prized detachment and emotional control. But that only made the thrill that much more precious, the glittering allure of the forbidden . . . or at least, the unseemly.

I made it to the next hall. This time, I had the foresight to look before I strolled in. I needed more practice at this sort of thing. My bounty hunting missions often required some degree of stealth and spying. Another skill I didn't mind having an excuse to hone.

As I peered around the corner, I saw another corridor, this one wide and inviting, with a carpeted floor and benches. Paintings and prints decorated the left wall. The right needed no adornment—it was a sloping sheet of glass overlooking the special exhibit gallery below. I had seen Tutankhamen in that gallery, relics from the *Titanic,* peat bog mummies, and most recently, feathered dinosaurs. Now, if I remembered correctly, it displayed a traveling collection of jewelry.

This second-story viewing hall stretched along two sides of the gallery below. Through the glass, I saw something move on the adjoining side. The pale circle of a face. I eased back, but the face stayed where it was, bobbing only slightly, as if the owner were cleaning the glass. A janitor? Was my trouble alert on the fritz again? I really needed more practice.

A shard of light reflected off the glass on the other side. Again I moved back, expecting the guard with his bouncing flashlight. But by then, my eyes had adjusted enough for me to see a dark figure beneath that pale face, and the light had reflected off a sheet of glass . . . in his dark-gloved hands.

I bit back a laugh. So that's what I'd picked up, not a janitor or some bored partygoer wandering around off-limits areas, but a robbery-in-progress. My gaze still fixed on the would-be thief, I reached into my purse.

My fingers brushed two objects that Tristan insisted I carry at all times: a gun and a pair of handcuffs. Even tonight, he'd been so concerned for my safety that he'd had me meet someone from the security detail before I'd gone to dinner, pass my gun and cuffs to him, and pick them up again inside the gala, circumventing the security at the door. Overkill, but it was sweet of him to care.

I'd rolled my eyes as I'd gone through Tristan's cloak-and-dagger routine with the gun and cuffs, but now I was actually in a position where they could come in handy. *That* would add some excitement to my night. But no. Apprehending a thief wasn't my job, no matter how tempting. Instead, I pulled out my cell phone to call the police. An unexpected positive use for my powers.

Across the way, the thief was climbing over the edge, through the hole he'd cut in the glass. Now this would be interesting. How would he get down? Rappel or lower himself like Tom Cruise in *Mission Impossible*? Curiosity stayed my finger on the phone buttons. I'd just see this, then back out—

The man jumped.

I sucked in a gasp. My God, it was at least thirty feet down. Was he crazy? Surely he'd break—

The man landed on his feet as easily as if he'd hopped off a two-foot ledge.

I put my phone away. No human could make that leap, not like *that*. I knew now why I'd picked up the trouble signal so clearly from so far. A supernatural thief. This was my job after all.

The figure moved across the well-lit gallery. His back was to me as he started working on the security panel.

What was he? Knowing his supernatural race would help. The first time I'd followed a paranormal lead from *True News* without council backup, I'd ended up with second-degree burns from a very pissed-off fire half-demon. My own fault. He'd been torching abandoned buildings, what did I think his demonic power was?

I looked down at the man. No clues there. There never were. Half-demons, witches, sorcerers, werewolves, vampires . . . you couldn't tell by looking. Or, with the vampires and werewolves, I'd *heard* you couldn't tell. I've never met one of either race, both being rare.

He could be a vampire. Vampires had more than their share of thieves—natural stealth combined with invulnerability made it a good career choice.

As he continued working on the security panel, I ran through a few other possibilities, so I'd be prepared. My mental databanks were overflowing with supernatural facts, most for types I had never and maybe would never meet.

Sometimes, poring over my black market reference books, I felt like an overeager army recruit digesting ballistic tables for weapons he'd never fire, tactical manuals for situations he'd never encounter. Yep, I was a keener, devouring everything in an effort to "be all that I could be." The council had taken a chance on me and turned my life around, and damned if I wasn't going to give them all I had to give.

Security system disabled, the man walked to the display and, with a few adroit moves, scooped up three pieces of jewelry as easily as if he'd been swiping loose candy from a store shelf. As he moved, something about him looked familiar. When he did turn, face glowing in the display lights, I let out a silent oath. It was the man I'd crashed into at the buffet table.

The oath was for me—I'd been inches from a supernatural and hadn't noticed. I could blame that silly "dead duck" vision, and the ensuing confusion, but I couldn't rest on excuses. I needed to be better than that.

Jewelry stashed in an inside breast pocket, the man crossed the floor. I pulled the gun from my purse and crept forward, crouched to stay under the glass. When he came through that open window again, I'd—

Wait, how was he going to climb out of it? He hadn't left a rope . . . meaning he didn't plan to exit the way he'd come in. Shit!

I popped my head over the window ledge to see him at the door. It was barred on the inside—vertical metal bars—the extra security hidden from passersby who would see only a closed door.

The man reached one gloved hand through the bars, and pushed the handle. The door opened a crack, any electronic security having been overridden from the panel he'd disabled. Great, but that still left those metal bars—

He took hold of the nearest bar, flexed his hand, and

pulled. As I stared, he pried open a space big enough to slip through and—

Wake up, girl! He's going to get away.

I snapped my hanging jaw shut, and broke into a hunched-over jog. As I moved, I mentally ran through the layout of the museum. Take the first junction and there'd be back stairs to the main level. The stairs led to an emergency exit, but the stairwell itself could be used without tripping a fire alarm, a courtesy to museum-goers who knew their way around and didn't care to cross to the main stairs and elevator.

But even if opening the door didn't set off a fire alarm, did it trigger anything else? Maybe a signal in the security station? I couldn't worry about that. When I hit the doorway, I quickly checked for security cameras, saw none, pushed open the door, and tore down the steps.

4

Pulse racing, I forced myself to slow enough to peek out the main level door first. It opened into a dark hallway. No security cameras in sight. I put on my shoes, stuffed my charm bracelet into my purse, and stepped out.

As I hurried down the hall, I put the finishing touches on my plan. Was it a good plan? Of course not, I needed time for that. The best I could do was concentrate on him, his situation, his certain desire to get the hell out of the museum before the theft was discovered.

Sure enough, I looked around the next corner to see the thief step into the well-lit main hall leading to the front door. Cheeky bastard, waltzing right out the front. He wasn't even hurrying.

I *did* hurry. I raced down the hall, and called "Excuse me!"

He didn't slow . . . or speed up, just tipped his head to a trio of women at the coat check. I picked up my pace. He made it to the door, and paused to hold it open for an exiting elderly couple.

I covered the last few paces at a jog. He saw me then—the yellow dress did it, I'm sure. A friendly smile and nod. He did remember me. I'm sure in his profession, he made it a rule to remember anyone who might be able to identify him later.

"My bracelet," I said, breathing hard, as if I'd chased him from the party. "Charm—my charm bracelet—it snagged—"

"Slow down." His fingers touched my arm, and he frowned in polite concern. "Here, let's step out of the way."

His fingers still resting on my arm, he steered me into a side hall, a scant yard or so in, far enough from the door to speak privately, but not so far from others to alarm me. Damn smooth . . . and damn calm for a guy with a pocketful of stolen jewelry.

"My bracelet snagged on your jacket," I said. "In the buffet line—"

"Yes, of course. It isn't broken, is it?" His frown grew. "I did try to be careful, so I hope—"

"It's gone. I noticed it right away, and I've been trying to find you ever since. It must have been caught on your jacket or slid off into your pocket or—"

"Or, more likely, fell onto the floor. I'm sorry, but if it did catch on me"—he lifted his arms and displayed his sleeves—"it's long since fallen off and it didn't"— another demonstration, reaching into his pockets— "fall in here. It must be on the floor somewhere."

"It isn't. I checked *everywhere*."

Frustration darted behind his eyes. "Then, I would suggest, as reprehensible as the thought is, that someone picked it up with no intention of returning it."

Reprehensible? Amazing, he could say that with a straight face. Then again, I suspected he could say pretty much anything with a straight face.

"You mean someone stole it?" I said.

"Possibly, although, considering the guest list, I realize that's hard to believe."

"Oh, I believe it," I said, letting my voice harden. "I wanted to give you the benefit of the doubt, but your conclusion just proved me wrong. It didn't *fall* into your pocket, did it?"

He chased away his surprise with a laugh. "I believe someone has had one glass of champagne too many. What on earth would I do with a . . . cheap bauble like that."

He faltered on "cheap bauble." The man could spin lies with a face sincere enough to fool the angels, but lying about his specialty gave him pause. Even in that brief moment of untangling my bracelet he recognized it for what it was—a valuable heirloom, each charm custom-made. I was surprised he hadn't tried to nick it in the confusion of our collision.

He continued, "And, if I recall correctly, you bumped into me."

"I *tripped* over you . . . and I'm pretty sure that wasn't an accident."

"You think I tripped—?"

A security guard glanced down the hall.

He lowered his voice. "I assure you, I didn't steal your bracelet, and I would appreciate if you didn't accuse me quite so publicly—"

"You think *this* is public?" I strode past him toward the main hall. "Let's make this public. We'll catch up with that guard, you let him search you, and if I'm wrong—"

He grabbed my arm, his grip tight, then loosening as I turned toward him.

He managed a smile. "I would rather not end my night being frisked. Why don't I help you search for it, and if we don't find it, I'll willingly submit to the search."

I pretended to think it over, then nodded.

"Last time I saw it was when you freed it from your jacket," I said. "Then I went to the cloakroom, to get my scarf to cover this—" I pointed to the marinara spot. "And I noticed the bracelet was gone. Maybe . . ." I paused. "When I was looking for the cloakroom, I walked into the wrong room—it was dark, and I brushed against something."

"Perfect. Let's start there then."

As we walked down the semi-dark hall, music and chatter drifting in from the party beyond, I prayed the door would be open. The room I had in mind was a janitorial closet I'd discovered in fourth grade, when my best friend and I had hidden to avoid our teacher after we'd been caught ducking out of the pottery exhibit and sneaking into the arms and armor one. My fault. I'd loved that gallery, even more than mummies and dinosaurs. Those marvelous, ancient weapons where I could, even at eight, stand in front of the display, close my eyes, and hear the clash of metal on metal, smell the blood-streaked sweat, see the rearing horses, feel the hate, the fear, the panic . . . and feel my own soul rise to drink it in.

At the time, perhaps thankfully, I'd seen nothing wrong with my "fixations," nor had anyone around me—at my mother's insistence—chalking it up to a child's bloodthirsty imagination.

My second visit to the janitorial closet had no such demonic backstory, only the raging hormones of youth. I'd been with a cute boy and a dark closet held infinitely more attraction than even the weaponry exhibits on a tenth-grade field trip.

If the door wasn't open, I had a backup plan, but I really hoped—

"Here," I said.

He waved at the door. "This one?"

I nodded, and he reached for the handle. I slid my hand into my purse, crossed my fingers, and . . .

The door opened.

"Seems to be a janitor's closet," he said. "How far in did you—?"

I pressed the gun barrel against the small of his back. He stiffened, as if recognizing the sensation. At this point, he could call for help, even just cry out, but in my experience, no supernatural likes calling attention to himself . . . either that or our powers make us cocky when others would panic. Whatever the reason, he did as I expected—only sighed, then walked into the closet. I flipped on the light, and closed the door behind us.

Once inside, the man turned to me and smiled. "Nicely done. An excellent trap, and I admit myself caught. My cuff links are gold, and you're welcome to them, but if you'd prefer cash, there's a few hundred in my wallet. No banking or credit cards, I'm afraid."

"I believe you have something more valuable. Check your inside breast pocket. The left side."

Surprise darted behind his blue eyes, but he masked it with a laugh. "Well done again. And, again, I surrender and offer my forfeit. Your choice of the bounty."

He started to reach into his pocket.

"Uh-uh. Hands out," I said. "I don't want any of your 'bounty,' but I think the museum does."

"Ah, museum security, I presume. I believe you might find my offer more . . . lucrative than the pat on the back the museum will give you."

"Nice try. I'm not—"

"Interested in a bribe? I'm impressed, and I'm sure your superiors will be as well. You see, they hired me to test their security system. They didn't inform your team, to test you as well, your efficiency and, if possible, your integrity. You've outdone their expectations, and I will personally recommend you for a bonus—"

"Stuff it. I'm not museum security."

He only gave a small smile, still unfazed. "So this is a citizen's arrest? Very admirable, but police won't appreciate being called for an authorized test of museum security, so I'd suggest you reconsider . . . and I do hope you have a permit for carrying that gun because—"

"I'm not calling the police. As I'm sure you already know, our sort have special ways of handling our special problems, ones better dealt with internally."

Normally this was enough, but he only arched his brows, feigning confusion. "Our sort?"

"The sort who can jump thirty feet and bend metal bars with their bare hands."

"Ah, that. I can explain—"

"I'm sure you can. Save it for the council."

His brows arched. "Council? You don't mean—"

The jingle of the handcuffs as I pulled them from my purse swallowed his last words. I'd heard enough already. He didn't have anything important to say, but would keep saying it, in every possible form, until I either lowered my guard or got so confused I set him free.

"You carry handcuffs in your purse?" He chuckled. "Perhaps when this misunderstanding is cleared up, we can get to know each other better—"

I drowned him out by snapping open the cuffs. He only sighed and held his hands in front of him, as helpful as could be. That, too, is typical. I'd only "arrested" four supernaturals so far, but three of them had done just this, surrendered and let themselves be taken into custody. The council had a reputation for fairness, and even criminals trusted them. As for the fourth arrest, the witch . . . I pushed the thought back. That one had been a lesson to me—not *every* supernatural would come along easily.

"You said council," he said as I fastened the cuffs. "That wouldn't be the interracial council, would it?"

"Had some experience with them, have you? Surprise, surprise."

"And you're a . . . delegate?"

"I'm a bit young, don't you think?" I said as I tested the cuffs.

"No, not really," he murmured. "So you're a . . ."

"Contract agent."

His brows shot up. "Agent? I hope you don't really expect me to believe that."

Figures. He might not be physically fighting back but he sure as hell *was* going to use what—despite his superhuman strength—was obviously his weapon of choice. I took my scarf from my purse.

He continued, "Perhaps that story works with others, but I'm afraid whoever you're working for has underestimated my knowledge of the interracial council. They don't employ—"

I lifted the scarf.

He looked at it. "I'm already cuffed, and I can assure you, I don't need to be bound in any other way."

"Oh, I think you do."

I jammed it into his mouth. His eyes widened. He looked at me, eyes narrowing. Then, with a noise almost like a snarl, he turned his gaze away, and let me tie the scarf.

"Wait here," I said. "I'm going to make a call."

5

One last check to make sure my quarry was secure, then another check—this one outside the door—and I slipped into the hall. I didn't dare go far, not when I wasn't sure of his powers.

He wasn't a vampire. The Samson routine with the metal bars had disapproved that theory. Contrary to some legends, vampires didn't have superhuman strength. My guess was that he belonged to the most complex of races—my own. I couldn't recall a half-demon type with his particular skill set, but we were a varied lot, with plenty of rare and poorly documented types, like my own.

One thing I *did* know. This meeting had been no accident, and I kicked myself for not realizing that the moment Tristan offered me tickets to the gala. Granted, he did that kind of thing often—the perks that came with this job were phenomenal, and I sometimes felt guilty accepting them. I'd told Tristan and, through him, the council, that I didn't need any extras to boost my job satisfaction. But he assured me they were all freebies, like these gala tickets, a gift from a grateful supernatural that would go to waste if I didn't use them. Still, this was the second time Tristan had sent me someplace and I'd "stumbled" onto a supernatural crime in progress.

They were testing me. The council wanted to see how good my chaos nose worked, and I guess I couldn't fault them for that, but when I made that call, I couldn't help snapping at Tristan.

"Okay, okay," he said, laughing. "No more tests. Can you blame us, Hope? You're an Expisco half-demon! We're like kids with a new toy, dying to see what it can do. And you outdid yourself, as always. Karl Marsten, caught by a half-demon rookie agent."

"So the council's been after this guy for a while?"

"They have, which is why I should remind you that you shouldn't take down targets on your own. That's why we provide backup. You're too valuable."

"It wasn't much of a risk. Superhuman strength or not, he didn't even try to fight," I paused. "Those hand-cuffs *will* hold him, won't they? You said they're specially made to hold anything supernatural."

A moment's hesitation. "You cuffed him?"

"So they *won't* hold? Well, he's still in that room anyway. The door's closed and—"

"He can't break the cuffs, Hope. That's not the problem. I thought you knew—didn't you—you usually know what they are."

"Sometimes. This time, I didn't get a vision—"

Oh yes, I had. Standing in line at the buffet, with him behind me, a vision of forest and fur and fangs and blood.

"He's a werewolf," I said.

"And a very dangerous one. You need to subdue him—"

"Should I? If he's dangerous, don't you want me to wait—"

"No time. As charming as Marsten seems, he's a

werewolf, the most brutal and unpredictable kind of supernatural, and now he's cornered, which makes him ten times as dangerous. If he knows it's the council who captured him, he'll do anything to get away—kill anyone in his path."

I swallowed. "Okay, so how do I subdue a werewolf?"

"Disable him. Knock him unconscious. Shoot him if you have to. You don't need silver bullets—"

"I know."

"Don't kill him, just—"

"Disable him. Got it."

I was already hanging up as Tristan promised me a backup team was on the way.

I made it as far as the door, one hand on the knob, the other on my gun, still hidden in my purse. I turned the handle and—

"You there!"

I dropped the gun into my purse and wheeled as a white-haired security guard strode toward me.

"What are you doing in that room?" he said.

Room? Oh, *this* room, the one I was clutching for dear life. I let go of the knob and stepped away. Inside, a broom clattered to the floor. The guard turned toward the door, his eyes narrowing.

"Sorry," I said. "Guess I jostled it too hard. This isn't the coatroom, is—?"

Something clanged against a metal bucket. Then a clacking, like nails against linoleum. Oh God. He'd changed into a wolf. Of course he'd changed into a wolf. What else would a cornered werewolf do?

The guard reached for the handle. In that split second, I saw him pulling open the door, and a wolf leaping at his throat—

I grabbed the knob and held it. "It's jammed, see?" I made a show of jangling it. "That noise, that's what I heard, that's why I was trying to open it. But it's jammed."

"Probably locked."

"Er, no, I don't think—"

"The janitor has the keys—"

"Oh, actually, then, I bet you're right," I said quickly. "It's probably locked. Why don't you go find the janitor. I'll wait here."

The guard started to leave, then paused, and turned. "First, let me try the door. It might just be jammed—"

I backed into the door so fast my head cracked against it. The guard reached to steady me.

"Heels," I mumbled. "I'm always tripping in them."

I stepped forward, and let my knee give way. The guard grabbed my arm as I grimaced.

"My ankle. I think I twisted it."

"We should get you to—"

"Please," I said through my teeth, still grimacing. "I'll wait here."

"All right, just let me try the door first—"

As he turned toward the door again, I had no idea what to do, short of falling to my knees and howling in agony. He reached for the handle. Okay, one pratfall coming up—

Before the guard touched the knob, it turned. The door opened. A figure stepped out. Karl Marsten, fully dressed.

"Well, that was embarrassing," he said with a self-deprecating half-smile. "I could've sworn this was the bathroom, and then the door jammed. Thank you. You saved me from the even more serious embarrassment of having to call for help."

He shook the security guard's hand. Then he turned to me, and with a murmured thank you, a tip of his head, and a smile, he strolled off down the hall. I took a step after him.

"Miss? Do you want me to call a doctor?"

"Doctor? Oh, right. My ankle. No, my . . . date . . . he's a doctor. I'll just—"

I looked up and down the hall. The guard pointed toward the party, in the opposite direction of the one Marsten had taken. Damn. I managed a weak smile and a thank you, and headed back to the gala, tossing in the occasional limp for good measure.

When I reached the party, Douglas was still with the Bairds. I tried making a beeline for the other door, to go after Marsten, but Douglas hailed me. I headed over.

"Sorry," I said. "I was just . . . there's an old friend over there. You stay with the Bairds. I'll just go talk—"

"Friend?" He perked up. "What company does he work for?"

"She's a musician. Classical. With the symphony."

His face fell. "Ah, well, you go on then." He nodded toward the Bairds. "I'm fine here."

I'll bet you are, I thought as I hurried away. *And, by the way, my stomach's fine, too. Thanks for asking.*

When I reached the corner where I'd last seen Marsten, he was gone. I switched on my mental radar to find him before he escaped with the jewelry. Yes, according to Tristan, I had far bigger things to worry about than stolen goods but . . . maybe I'm being naïve, but Marsten hadn't *acted* like a cornered wild beast. I couldn't imagine him ripping through innocent partygoers in a frenzied dash to the exit, especially not when I wasn't picking up any chaos signals to suggest such a thing.

Tristan could be quite a mother hen. As he'd said, I

was valuable. Expisco half-demons were rare, and one willing to work on the side of the white hats was rarer still. So I understood when Tristan did things like this, not letting me in on a takedown, keeping me sequestered from other agents, or overreacting with someone like Marsten. But understanding isn't accepting. I knew my limitations, which were many, and I was careful. Yet I had lost Karl Marsten, and damned if I was going to sit on my butt and wait for the backup team to find him again.

So I practiced my developing bounty hunter skills. I cleared my mind and pulled up the images I'd seen at the buffet table: forest, running, fur, fangs. As I did, I tried, with debatable success, not to chastise myself too much for failing to recognize the meaning of the vision from the start.

I knew little about werewolves. Like vampires, they were rare, and kept to themselves. Unlike vampires, they also policed themselves, meaning the council had no reason to deal with them. I knew only one half-demon who'd ever even met a werewolf . . . and she wasn't all that sure that's what it had been. So I had an excuse for not leaping to "he's a werewolf!" conclusions. But, again, I didn't accept excuses.

After about a minute of mental scanning, I picked up Marsten's frequency. It was faint and flat—meaning he wasn't causing any trouble. Not yet.

I focused on the signal and followed. Down two dark halls, skirting past the gala, down another hall— the same one I started in when I'd first left the party. I reached the fork again. Marsten's trail went left, in the direction of that chaos residual I'd been tracking when his theft had diverted me. He was heading for the back exit.

Still concentrating on his trail, I went down the next corridor, turned the corner—and was smacked by a wave of chaos.

Marsten. Shit! He was—

No, a deeper, calmer part of me replied. *It's not him. It's here. Something happened here. Something recent.*

I'd been hit by two chaos waves, both originating in this area. They had to be connected.

I pushed aside the werewolf images, and focused on this new signal. The voice came again, that gruff voice telling someone he shouldn't be back here. The plea. Then the scream.

When the wave hit me this time, I only rocked on my heels. Half the strength of the slap I'd felt in the main room earlier, even though I was at the apparent locus of the trouble. I filed this away as a lesson in separating residuals from current chaos, then closed my eyes and pivoted, trying to find the exact location—

There, around that next corner. I hurried to it, then walked into a wall of darkness. I braced myself as the visions flashed past.

Metal glinted. A blade winked in a flashlight beam. The flashlight clattered to the floor. A plea. *No! Please—!* The blade sheered down. Hands flew up. Blood sprayed.

I froze the vision there as I panted, my heart racing. I struggled to hold that last thought . . . and wondered why I was holding it.

Blood sprayed.

Blood.

I fumbled in my purse for my keys, took them out, and turned on my penlight. I waved the weak beam over the walls. There. Blood droplets, invisible in the near-darkness.

6

Were the blood drops still wet? I almost reached up to one before snatching my hand back. Look, don't touch, stupid. Standing on my tiptoes, I moved the light closer to the specks. They glistened. Still wet, but drying.

I swung the beam to the floor and found faint smears of blood that would go undetected until they turned on the lights in the morning . . . or noticed they were one security guard short.

So where was . . . ? Follow the trail.

I stopped at a door a few yards away. Tissue over my hand, I turned the knob.

I half-expected a body to fall out on top of me. Too many horror movies, I guess.

The door opened into an office. I shone my flashlight around. Nothing.

As the door closed behind me, I grabbed it and twisted the knob, to make sure it wouldn't lock me inside. Reassured, I eased the door shut, and moved toward the center of the room.

As I walked, I picked up a twinge of trouble. Yes, this had to be the right place. So where was the . . . ?

A booted toe protruded from behind the desk. I hurried to it. The desk faced the wall, with a wide gap for computer cord access behind it, and that's where the killer had stuffed the body. One end of the desk was against the adjoining wall and the other against a metal filing cabinet, so I had to crawl onto the desk to peer behind it.

I shone the flashlight beam into the gap, and bit back a yelp.

I resisted the urge to pull away. With something like this, I was sure the council would expect a report, so I had to get a good look.

A man lay faceup in the gap. His eyes stared at me, wide with that last minute of "I don't believe this is happening" horror. His security uniform shirt was a mess of gaping holes, the edges torn, shredded, unlike anything a knife would do. The flesh beneath the holes looked . . . mangled. Chewed. It looked as if he'd been—

A hand clamped over my mouth.

"Found something you were missing?" a voice hissed.

I kicked backward. My foot connected, but a second arm clamped around my neck, and yanked me off the desk. It spun me around, and I found myself looking into a pair of blue eyes so cold and hard that my heart leaped into my throat. Karl Marsten.

"Did you think I wouldn't smell the body when I walked by?" His voice was as cold and hard as his eyes, all traces of smooth charm gone. "You would have been wiser to let me leave through the front door."

I pulled back my fist and plowed it toward his gut. He caught my hand easily and squeezed. Tears of pain sprang to my eyes. *Oh God, you stupid, stupid—*

He brought his face down to mine, and the thought dried up.

"I'm going to let go," he said, his voice calm. "If you scream, I will crush your fingers. Do you understand?"

I blinked back tears and nodded. He took his hand from my mouth and released the other one just enough to stop the throbbing pain, but still gripped it so tightly that I didn't dare even try to wiggle my fingers.

"I will only ask you this once," he said. "Who do you work for?"

"The—I told you—the—"

"Interracial council," he interrupted. "Is that so? Then tell me, which delegate of the council hired you?"

"I was approached by a representative—"

"Which delegate?"

"He's not a delegate. He works for them."

He exhaled, as if in frustration. "All right, then. Which delegates have you met?"

"None. I only work through my contact—"

He cut me off with a humorless laugh. "Oh, they have you well trained, don't they? I'm sure this story has worked well for you in the past, but it falls a little flat when dealing with someone who actually knows the interracial council, knows most of the delegates, and knows, beyond any doubt, that they do not have employees or recruits or 'agents'—"

A noise from the hall. Voices. Marsten half-turned, his attention diverted just long enough for me to ram my spiked heel into his shin and wrench my hand free.

He grabbed for me. I kicked and lashed out at the same time, my nails clawing his face. He fell back. I ran for the door, threw it open, and raced into the hall.

A split-second decision: run toward the voices or away from them? Running to them might have been safer, but I couldn't—wouldn't—endanger others. I'd already underestimated Marsten once.

I tore down the halls. Marsten's soles squeaked behind me as he wheeled out of the office. That reminded
me that he was in flat dress shoes . . . and I was in
heels—with no hope of outrunning him.

I grabbed the first doorknob I came to. Locked.

I dove for the one across the hall. As my fingers
closed around it, I saw Marsten running toward me.
The handle turned. The door opened. I darted through,
and slammed it.

Even as I turned the lock, I knew I might as well not
have bothered. It was a flimsy household privacy lock,
one that could be snapped by any strong man, let alone
a werewolf.

I reached for my purse but it wasn't on my shoulder.
It must have fallen when Marsten yanked me off the
desk. No purse . . . no gun.

Marsten's footsteps had slowed to a walk. Of course
they had; he didn't need to hurry. I'd trapped myself in
an office with no second door, no windows, no way to
escape.

Blockade the door.

The council backup team was on the way. If I could
slow Marsten down long enough to call Tristan—

The footsteps stopped inside the door. The handle
turned.

Someone laughed—the sound close by—and the
handle stopped turning. A drunken giggle. A voice,
growing closer.

I grabbed the sides of the metal filing cabinet. It
didn't budge. The printer stand? Like that would slow
down a werewolf.

"Oh," someone said near the door. "Didn't see you
there."

"Unless you're staff, this hall is off limits," Marsten said.

"Oh, right, we were just—"

"Lost," the woman giggled.

"Then I suggest you turn around, go back to the end of the hall, and follow the sounds of the party. You can't miss it."

I looked around for something to block the door, but anything big enough was too heavy for me to move. Outside, the man was telling Marsten to mind his own business, but his companion was already moving away, and calling to him to do the same. No time to phone Tristan. I needed—

My gaze rose to the ventilation shaft over the desk.

Oh please. You have *seen too many movies.*

I silenced the inner voice, and climbed onto the desk as Marsten threatened to call security. As much as I appreciated the distraction the couple was providing, I prayed they moved on before Marsten gave up trying to handle them discreetly.

As the woman cajoled her partner away, I quickly unscrewed the ventilation cover with a quarter from a dish of coins on the desk.

"I'm coming, I'm coming," the man slurred, then muttered a parting obscenity at Marsten.

As the man's footsteps faded, I yanked on the cover. One side came free. I tugged again, but the other side caught.

The footsteps were almost gone. Palms sweating, I fumbled for a better hold. The cover popped off with a *ping* that I was sure could be heard throughout the museum. I shoved the cover into the shaft, grabbed the edges, heaved, and managed to get inside up to my breasts. Then I found myself stuck, upper torso in, butt hanging out, legs flailing, arms trembling with the strain of just holding myself up, with no extra strength for hauling the rest of me through.

Goddamn it! I'd been spending three evenings a week at the gym, and I couldn't do better than this?

The door handle turned.

Shit, shit, shit! I'd never make—

"And another thing, asshole," the man's voice boomed from the end of the hall.

One last push, boosted by a wave of relief, and I heaved the rest of my torso into the shaft.

"Come on, Rick!" the woman called. "Do you want me to go back to the party?"

I wriggled and twisted, getting my legs in and my body turned around so I was facing the shaft opening. I tugged the cover from under me, hooked my fingers through the slats, and pulled it into place just as the doorknob twisted, and the lock snapped.

Marsten threw open the door, fast—as if he expected me to be standing there armed with a heavy stapler. Door wide, he paused in the opening, gaze tripping across the room, nostrils flaring.

Nostrils flaring . . . Werewolf . . . He could smell me.

Damn it! I tried to twist around. My shoulder knocked against the metal. A dull thump, but he heard it. Of course he heard it.

Werewolf. Heightened smell, heightened hearing, heightened strength . . .

I knew all this, so why did I keep forgetting until it was too late? I was out of my league. Way out of it, and I would pay for my hubris—

"Let's make this easy," he said, his smooth mask back in place. "You don't want to play hide-and-seek with me. I have all the advantages, and a low tolerance for frustration. So we'll skip the games. If you feel safer in your hidey-hole—" He scanned the room. "You're welcome to stay there. You can hear me, and that's all that matters."

He turned slowly, searching for me even as he said he wouldn't. Bastard.

I shifted my shoulders, testing my space limits again. Too tight. I'd been able to turn around with the vent open but, without that added space, I was stuck. No, not stuck. I could move backward. Awkward, slow, and probably loud, but if it came to that, I would. He'd barely fit in here—if at all—so I could still move faster than he could.

"Whoever you are, you're of no interest to me," he continued. "That means I have no particular desire to hurt you. So you have a choice. Tell me who you're working for, and I'll step aside and let you out this door. Refuse, and I'll use you for leverage. That's not a position you want to be in."

I stayed still and quiet.

"I don't have all night," he said. "Nor do you. When I hear your associates approach—which I'm sure will be soon—I'll sniff you out, and the choice will be made. After that, whether you walk out of here depends on how willing your employer is to negotiate."

I said nothing. As he moved, his nostrils flared, still searching. Then he stopped and smiled. His gaze lifted to the ventilation shaft.

"Ah, there you are."

A quick leap and he was on the desk. As he pulled off the cover, I scrambled backward. I got about five feet before my shoulders hit the sides, stopping me. While I struggled to back up, he peered into the shaft and smiled, his teeth glinting in the dark.

"I do believe you've backed yourself into a corner."

I wriggled, but the shaft had narrowed, and the more I moved, the tighter I wedged myself in.

"Are you going to tell me who you work for?" he said.

"I already did," I snarled.

"And I told you, I know better." His voice was calm, conversational, no trace of the cold fury from earlier. "You're obviously a bright young woman, and quite capable of thinking on your feet, as you proved earlier, so why you insist on sticking to this story—"

"Don't bother. I know who I work for, and nothing you say is going to make me second-guess that—or betray them."

He lifted his hand to his mouth and rubbed it, his gaze searching mine.

"You didn't kill that security guard, did you?" he said.

"Kill—!" I gritted my teeth. "We both know who— and what—killed him, so don't try pinning that on me."

"That spot on your dress. I suppose you'll tell me it isn't blood."

I snorted. "It's the marinara sauce from the damn mussels you threw at me in the buffet line."

"I *threw*—?"

He rubbed his mouth and growled. Or I thought it was a growl, until I saw his eyes dancing and realized he was laughing.

"All right. Here." He reached into the shaft. "Come on out of there. I believe we both have a problem, and we'd best set about resolving it before your 'associates' arrive."

"You really think I'm a fool, don't you?"

He tilted his head, as if considering it. "A fool? Young, yes. Reckless, yes. Naïve, probably. But foolish? No. Not foolish. You—"

A sound from the hall. A door opening, then closing. He swiveled, his eyes narrowing as if tracking something I couldn't hear. His gaze shot to the door handle and he mouthed a silent oath.

"Couldn't lock it, could you?" I said. "That's the problem with breaking things. They tend to stay broken."

He shushed me, grabbed the vent cover, and knocked it back into place. Then he peered through the slats and whispered, "If you want to find out whether I'm lying—and I think you do—stay there and stay quiet."

7

Marsten jumped off the desk and was halfway to the door when it opened. Two men strode in, guns in hand. Part of the council security force. I recognized both from other operations.

I crawled forward, ready to push open the vent. Then I stopped, palms against the cover. I didn't need to eavesdrop to know Karl Marsten was full of shit. I heard the web of lies he'd spun when I'd first confronted him with the theft. He'd say anything to get out of this—to use me to get out of it. Yet there was reason to stay up here, hidden and silent, the perfect position to watch Marsten, and make sure he didn't try anything. Or that's what I told myself.

A man strolled in. Mid-thirties, average height and slightly built, with light brown hair and a delicate, almost feminine face. Tristan, my council contact.

"Ah, Karl," he said. "I didn't know you were a patron of the arts."

"Tristan Robard," Marsten said. "I'd say I should have known, but I'd be lying. After the last time, I thought you'd have the sense to leave me alone. I guess I overestimated you."

Tristan's eyes narrowed.

"I should give you credit, though," Marsten continued. "You have quite a clever setup here. And your young agent. Well done. A beautiful young woman lays the most irresistible traps and, it seems, even I'm not immune." He paused. "Aren't you going to ask where she is?"

"Not terribly worried."

Marsten smiled. "Oh, but you should be. The one problem with using beautiful young women as bait? They make equally irresistible hostages."

"So you have her."

As Marsten nodded, I opened my mouth to call out and let Tristan know I was safe—

Tristan smiled. "As I said, not terribly worried."

I blinked, but shook it off. Of course Tristan would say that. He was a skilled negotiator. He wouldn't let Marsten know he had leverage.

"I don't think your superiors will approve of that attitude," Marsten said. "Oh, but your superiors have nothing to do with this, do they? This is personal. A little boy lashing out because the big bad wolf embarrassed him."

Tristan's jaw set.

"I didn't embarrass you, Tristan," Marsten continued. "You did it to yourself. You offered me a job. I turned it down—respectfully and politely. But that wasn't good enough, because you'd already promised them I'd do it. If I refused, you'd need to explain that you'd over-reached, and there was no way you were doing that, so you came after me. I was happy to let the matter rest—a rejected business proposition, no cause for animosity—but you came after me. *That* was your mistake."

Tristan give a tight laugh. "My mistake? You're the one being held at gunpoint, and you're talking about my mistake? Delusional to the end."

Marsten only shrugged. "If you say so."

Marsten stepped forward, as if ready to go with them. Then he stopped.

"I'll suppose you'll want me to tell you where I hid that security guard you had killed. Backup plan, I presume?"

Tristan said nothing, only reached for his cell phone. Marsten's gaze flicked to the vent shaft, then back to Tristan.

"So you didn't trust your girl to do the job. If she failed, you'd still have a mauled security guard, found at the scene of a jewel theft, a little tale you could take to the interracial council."

Tristan only smiled, gaze still down as he checked messages on the phone. "I think the Pack would be more interested in that story."

"Ah, of course. The werewolf Pack. A clever plan, and one that might have worked . . . if I hadn't been part of the Pack myself for the past two years."

Tristan looked up.

Marsten laughed. "Not very good at doing your homework, are you? That's obvious from that preposterous story you told the girl. Working as an agent for the interracial council? I'm sure Aaron, Paige, Adam, and the other delegates will be thrilled to know they have a team of secret agents working on their behalf."

Marsten caught Tristan's look and smiled. "Surprised I know their names? Your story probably works much better on those who don't know the delegates personally. I could toss a few more names at you, including the werewolves, but I doubt you'd recognize them, and they wouldn't appreciate me filling that void for you."

He paused, head tilted, feigning deep thought. "Oh, but I do have another name, one you might find infinitely more interesting. You know who Paige Winter-bourne's husband is, I presume. You can't possibly be that out of touch."

Tristan stiffened.

"Ah, you do know. A very nice young man. I did some work for him last year. Quite pleasant." Marsten frowned. "I hear his father isn't always so pleasant, though. A decent employer, I'm sure . . . unless he finds out one of his employees has been building his own little spy network behind his back."

"I haven't been doing anything behind Benicio's back. He knows all about my initiative. And he's very impressed."

"Oh? So this is a Cabal-sanctioned hit? Funny, I could've sworn it smelled like personal revenge. Well, what do I know? A Cabal kills a Pack werewolf . . . that shouldn't cause too much trouble. Or I suppose it won't if the Cabal doesn't know about it."

Tristan waved to the guards. "Get him out of here."

He turned, and Marsten started to follow. Then one of the guards spoke up.

"Sir? What about the girl?"

"Oh, I wouldn't worry about her," Marsten said. "She's quite resourceful. I'm sure she'll get herself free, if she hasn't already. But the security guard? Now that's a problem. You should—"

Tristan turned sharply. "Hope's still alive?"

"Is that her name? Of course she's alive. You didn't think I'd—" Marsten shook his head. "I suppose, considering who I'm talking to, I shouldn't need to ask. Oddly enough, I find the best hostages are the live ones. Yes, Hope is fine and, as I said, will almost certainly free herself, so there's no need—"

"Where is she?"

"The question is: where's the dead guard? The girl can take care of herself. That guard, sadly, is beyond—"

"Where is she?"

Marsten paused and rubbed his chin, as if realizing he wasn't going to talk his way out of handing me over. I'm sure he had some self-interested reason for not wanting to do so, but I was grateful for the effort nonetheless. I didn't know how I'd face Tristan, knowing the truth.

Oh God . . . the truth.

My stomach heaved. I've been tricked. The whole time I'd been up here, listening as the facts rolled out, I'd processed them without absorbing them. Without *letting* myself absorb them—

"She's in a janitor's closet," Marsten said. "Tied with her own handcuffs, which I thought was appropriate. I can take you there—"

"You'll wait here. I'll come back for you when I'm finished with her."

Finished with me? What did he mean by—?

I pushed the thought away and, as Marsten gave Tristan directions to the closet I'd used earlier, I scrambled for an escape plan. Yes, escape. Maybe I was being paranoid, and Tristan had only meant he'd return when he'd finished freeing me. Yet Marsten's life *was* in danger. And I'd put it there.

Tristan left with one guard. When he was gone, the second one backed up to the desk and, gun still trained on Marsten, slid his rear onto it.

I eased the vent cover out. Marsten's gaze shot up, but he looked away before the guard noticed, then flicked his fingers, telling me to stay where I was.

As quietly as I could, I moved the cover into the shaft, and laid it down beside me. Marsten's gaze met mine and he shook his head, in case the waving hadn't been understood.

When I grabbed the edge of the vent, he threw me one last glare, then cleared his throat.

"You do work for the Cortezes, I presume," he said to the guard, his voice loud in the small room.

The guard said nothing.

I gauged the distance between us, then pulled my legs forward, moving into a crouch.

"I've heard the Cabals frown on this," Marsten continued. "Employees taking outside jobs. Yes, I know, you're working for a Cabal AVP, so one could argue it's not truly moonlighting, but I suspect Mr. Cortez wouldn't be so quick to see the distinction."

I braced myself on the edge of the opening.

Marsten continued. "An AVP using Cabal resources for a personal vendetta? I'll wager Mr. Cortez would like to know about that, and would richly reward—"

I jumped. Marsten leaped to the side, out of the range of the gun. I hit the guard in the back. An *oomph*, and he fell forward. Marsten snatched the gun. Then he tossed it to me. The move caught me off-guard, and I scrambled for it but was too late, and my hand knocked it flying. The gun ricocheted onto the desk, and tumbled down behind it.

Marsten grabbed the guard around the neck. The guard flailed. Marsten swung him off his feet and bashed his head against the filing cabinet. As the guard's body went slack, Marsten looked over at me, still crouched on the desk, staring.

"Don't worry," he said. "I didn't kill him."

The last licks of chaos rippled through me. I shuddered, eyes rolling in rapture. Marsten's brows arched. I turned the shudder into a more appropriate shiver of fear.

"You're sure?" I said. "He looks—"

"He's fine." Marsten kneeled beside the guard as he pulled my handcuffs from his pocket. "Though I do hate to waste these on him." Another dig into his pocket and he tossed me my scarf. "Since you did such a good job tying this earlier . . ."

We secured the guard. Then Marsten waved me to the door as he double-checked my knot. My fingers brushed the knob, but Marsten yanked me back.

"I was going to look first," I said.

"You don't need to. I can hear them." He looked around. "You take the vent." He grabbed my arm and propelled me to the desk. "Go headfirst this time, and you'll be able to squeeze through."

"After you," I said.

"No time. Just—"

"After you."

He gave me a look, as if contemplating the chances of stuffing me in the shaft himself, then, with a soft growl, hopped onto the desk. He grabbed the edge of the shaft, and easily swung himself up and in, then paused in the opening, his rear sticking out.

"It's very narrow," he said. "I'm not sure I can—"

"Try," I said, and gave him a shove.

He wriggled through, then reached back between his legs, and helped haul me up. The door clicked. No time to replace the cover. I pulled my legs in, scrunched down on my hands and knees, and followed him.

8

In the movies, ventilation shafts are the escape route of choice for heroes trapped in industrial buildings. They're clean and roomy and sound-proof, and will take you anywhere you want to go all, like a Habitrail system for the beleaguered protagonist on the run. I don't know where Hollywood buys their ventilation shafts, but they don't use the same supplier as the museum.

We crept along, shoulders whacking the sides with every few steps. The sound reverberated through the shaft. I could feel skin sloughing off my knees as they scraped over the rivets, and imagined a snail's trail of blood ribboning behind me. And the dust? I sneezed at least five times, and managed to whack my head against the top with each one.

"Breathe through your mouth," Marsten whispered, his voice echoing down the dark tunnel.

Sure, that helped the sneezing, but then I was tasting dust, as it coated my tongue. Would it kill the museum to spring for duct cleaning now and then?

I resumed crawling, and smacked my face into Marsten's ass . . . again.

"Warn me when you stop," I muttered . . . again.

A low chuckle. "At the next branch you can take the lead, then you won't have that problem. I will . . . but I suspect *I* won't complain about it."

"You won't have an excuse. Werewolves have enhanced night vision."

"Mine's been a little rusty lately."

"You seem to be doing just fine." I head-butted him in the rear. "Now move."

After that, we did switch positions—three times—as we ran into three dead ends.

"I'm taking the next exit," Marsten said on the fourth about-face.

"Not arguing."

The next vent we hit, *he* hit, driving his fist into it and knocking it clattering to the floor. Guess I wasn't the only one getting claustrophobic.

Marsten crawled out. I started to, then my dress snagged on a rivet, and I tumbled out headfirst, floor flying up to meet me—

Marsten grabbed me and swung me onto my feet. I regained my balance and took a deep breath of clean— reasonably clean—air.

"Well, there goes two thousand dollars," he muttered, looking down at himself.

Both elbows of his jacket were torn, and the front of his shirt was streaked with dirt, as were his face, hands, and pretty much every exposed inch of skin. Cobwebs added gray streaks to his dark hair. His shoes were scuffed, as were his pant knees. While he surveyed the damage, he looked so mournful I had to stifle a laugh. Well, I tried to stifle it. Kind of.

"Don't snicker," he said. "You're just as bad."

"But I don't care."

As he brushed himself off, I looked around. We were in some kind of laboratory, with microscopes and steel tables and what looked like pots of bones in the middle of being de-fleshed. At any other time, curiosity would have compelled me to take a closer look. Tonight, only one thing caught my attention: the exit door.

As I strode to it, Marsten grabbed my arm.

"You can't go out like that," he said.

"Oh, please. My life may be in danger. You really think I care how I look? You stay here and pretty up, if you like, but I'm bolting for the nearest exit."

His grip tightened as I tried to pull away. I yanked harder. He squeezed harder.

I glared at him. "That—"

"Hurts. Yes, I know. But you'll hurt a lot worse if Tristan catches you."

"We don't know—"

"That he plans to kill you? He wasn't heading to that closet to congratulate you on a job well done, Hope. He wants me dead, and to do it safely, without risking his own life on the repercussions, he needs to clip off his loose ends. That includes you and, later, those guards."

"Kill four people because you *embarrassed* him?"

"There's more to it than that."

"What did—?"

"Whatever I did, it came after *he* retaliated because I turned down his job offer. It doesn't matter. To a man like Tristan Robard, killing four people to avenge his ego is perfectly reasonable."

He studied my face, then shook his head. "You don't believe me? Fine. But at least give me the benefit of the doubt by not strolling out that door and testing my theory. You don't think he'll have all the exits covered?"

"Uh . . . yes, of course, but there are plenty of other exits. I know my way around—"

"Good. But if we start wandering the halls looking like this, we're going to raise alarms. If not Tristan and his men, then a security guard or a concerned guest—"

"Who will cause a fuss, which will alert Tristan. Okay. Let's pretty up then."

Marsten declared his tux jacket a write-off. No big deal. It was nearing midnight, and jackets and ties would be coming off anyway as the party wore down. Under it, his shirt needed only a brisk wipe down. My dress had actually fared quite well, with only a rip under the arm and a smear of blood on the skirt. Take off my nylons, wipe down my dusty shoes and bloody knees with a damp paper towel, and I was fine . . . below the neck anyway. There were no mirrors, and my distorted reflection in the stainless steel table wasn't very helpful.

"Here," Marsten said. "I'll get your face if you can clean mine."

He wet a fresh paper towel in the lab sink, and walked over to me. I lifted my face. He raised the cloth to my cheek, then paused to brush cobwebs from my hair. When he finished, he smiled, took a stray strand, and wrapped it around his finger. As he did, I could see, out of the corner of my eye, that it was more than a "stray strand." It was a huge hunk of hair, which thirty minutes ago had been battened down in an upswept twist.

I groaned. "How bad is it?"

"It's a bit . . . tousled. Very sexy."

I lifted my hand to my hair and swore. At least half of it had come free. Beyond repair without a brush and a mirror . . . and a half-hour of styling time. I yanked out a handful of bobby pins, and gave my hair a shake, letting it fall down my back.

"Mmmm . . . very sexy."

"Down, boy. We're fleeing for our lives here, remember." I raked my fingers through my hair. "Any better?"

A wolfish grin. "Much. You look like you just crawled out of bed."

"Damn it—*not* the look I'm aiming for."

He caught my hands as I tried to smooth out the damage. "It's fine. Tousled, yes, but it looks intentional."

He put his hand under my chin and lifted the wet cloth again. Then he paused again.

"What now?" I said.

A low chuckle. "I was just thinking I've never seen a woman who looked so beautiful in dirt and cobwebs. Trouble suits you."

"You have no idea," I muttered.

"No, I'm sure I don't, but I certainly hope I get the chance to find out." He brushed his finger over my cheek.

"Fleeing for our lives, remember? Let's save the flattery and soulful gazing until *after* we escape."

"Is that a date?"

"Date!" I jumped so fast I knocked the paper towel from his hand. "Sorry. My date. Douglas. He'll be looking for me. I need to tell him—"

"Tell him what? Don't worry, I was held captive by a werewolf but I'm okay now . . . except for the deranged Cabal sorcerer on my tail?"

I glared up at him. "I'm serious. He'll be worried—"

"Let him worry. From what I saw, it's only . . . what, a first, maybe second date, and you didn't seem very enamored—"

"He's a nice guy. Kind of. He's not evil."

Marsten's brow shot up. "That's your dating criterion?"

"You know what I mean. He was worried, and I can't just walk out on him. Plus, if my mother finds out I abandoned the guy she set me up with—"

"Your mother sets you up blind dates? With guys like that?" The corners of his mouth twitched. "She doesn't like you very much, does she?"

"My mother—" I bit back at the rest, and started again. "My mother is just fine, which is why I won't embarrass her like this. I do that enough as it is."

His face softened. "All right. But, while I *do* understand, you're forgetting—"

"The whole 'fleeing for our lives' part?" I took a deep breath. "You're right. I'll have to—I'll work something out later. Apologize to my mother. Make it up to Douglas . . ."

"I don't think you owe Douglas anything." He paused. "If we need to go past the party, you can tell him. Make an excuse to leave, and call it even."

I nodded and we finished getting ready.

I was picking cobwebs out of Marsten's hair when I remembered something else.

"The gun," I said. "I should've grabbed the gun."

"I wouldn't worry about it. In my experience, guns are only good for threatening. In combat? I'm as likely to shoot my own foot. Best to avoid them altogether."

"Easy to say when you have super strength, super senses, fangs, claws . . ."

He glanced up at me as I plucked out another cobweb. "You *are* a . . . What's the word they use? A supernatural, aren't you?"

"Sure, but not all of us come with built-in defense mechanisms. Why do you think I carry a gun?"

"So what is your—?"

"Speaking of my gun, it's also still back there, in my purse . . . with my bracelet. Damn it."

"The bracelet—an heirloom, I presume."

"So you didn't mistake it for a 'cheap bauble' after all. And you still didn't try to nick it. I'm shocked."

He glowered as he got to his feet.

"What?" I said. "I've offended you? I should be ashamed of myself. Those pieces in your pocket just fell in there, didn't they? Damn museum displays. Stuff just drops off them—"

"Point taken," he said as he stood and smoothed his hair. "But, no, your bracelet isn't at risk. Valuable or not, it's worth more to you than to me. These—" He reached into his jacket and transferred the jewels to his pants pocket. "Worth something only to an insurance company. Which I realize is no excuse but—" He shrugged. "As for your bracelet, considering it's with your gun, and you'd probably feel safer carrying that, I suggest we make that office our first stop, presuming Tristan has moved on."

I shook my head. "Yes, I want it back, but I have to trust my purse will still be there when all this is done."

"I'll make sure I get it for you later."

Later? I hoped that didn't mean he planned to come back and steal something else. No, he'd been leaving when I'd first stopped him.

He took my elbow and propelled me toward the door. "Let's go before they find us."

It took a few minutes to get my bearings. The laboratories weren't part of your typical museum visit and thus were woefully lacking in directional signs. I knew we were on the first floor, which helped . . . except that most of the sprawling first floor *was* offices and labs, which didn't help. Nor did the lack of windows. I'd never noticed it before, but, the building was window-free. Great for security and artifact preservation; not so great for those needing to end their visit in a hurry.

"There," I whispered to Marsten. "That's the media room. I was there last month for a story."

"You're a journalist?"

I nodded, not mentioning I'd been covering the story of an "ancient curse" that a former worker swore was responsible for his herpes outbreak. That thought pinged another. Did all this mean I'd never cover another silly curse story?

An unexpected pang of panic followed the thought. I liked what I did. Once I'd worked past the "I'm too good for this" phase, I'd genuinely enjoyed tracking down UFOs and Hell Spawn sightings, far more than I'd ever liked covering drive-by shootings and political scandals. But if I wasn't working for the council and wouldn't be plugging supernatural leaks . . .

Had I ever been suppressing leaks? Helping my fellow supernaturals survive under the cover of secrecy? Or had I just been covering up a Cabal's messes?

My gut twisted. *Oh God, what had I done?* I thought I'd been—

Stop it. Not now.

I looked up at Marsten. "We're in the northeast quadrant, closest to the main doors, which I know we can't use, but there must be an emergency exit—"

"There's one along the west side, probably fifty feet from the front."

"Perfect. I'll watch for exit signs; you listen for company."

* * *

We found the exit. As Marsten strode toward it, I called, "It might trigger an alarm."

"A chance I'm willing to take."

I stayed at his heels, eager to be out of this place—

Every hair on my body leaped to attention, and I stopped short, lips parting in an involuntary hiss. Then I grabbed Marsten by the back of the shirt.

"It's trapped," I said.

"I said—"

"Not alarm-trapped. *Trap*-trapped. Magically. They must have a witch or a sorcerer—" I stopped myself. "Earlier, you said something about a Cabal sorcerer. You meant Tristan, didn't you?"

As Marsten nodded, I winced. Another unforgivable faux pas. Tristan had let on he was half-demon, but I'd never seen a display of his powers or even asked what those powers were. If I'd known he was a sorcerer, I would have been suspicious of his "working for the council" story.

Witches led the interracial council, and witches and sorcerers had as little as possible to do with one another. The Cabals were the great sorcerer achievement— powerful corporations staffed by supernaturals and run by sorcerers. I knew little about Cabals—every half-demon I knew stayed away from them and had warned me to do the same, but if I'd realized what Tristan was, I'd have had a good idea who I'd *really* been working for.

"What kind of trap is it?" Marsten asked.

I shook my head. "No idea. I can just tell that it's there, and it's trouble."

When I caught his frown, I said, "That's my so-called power. Chaos detection. Like you said, trouble suits me."

"Your 'power'? So you're a half-demon?"

When I nodded, his frown grew. "I thought—admittedly, my knowledge of demons is next to none, but I was under the impression that they were all chaotic. They feed off chaos or some such thing."

"Demons, yes. Half-demons, no. Half-demons inherit their father's special power without his affinity for chaos. Lucky me, I'm the one type that gets the reverse."

I walked toward the door and peered at it. "All I can tell you about this is that someone cast a spell on it, and I know as much about spells as you do about demons. It might just alert Tristan . . . or it could immolate us instantaneously."

"Having no great desire to end the evening in flames, I say we don't test it."

"Agreed." I paused. "I'm sure, then, that he'll have the other unguarded exits trapped, too. So now what?"

"We'll skip the 'fleeing' part and revert to the second mode of defense: hiding. We'll start by getting that gun for you, then find a safe place and try to outlast them. Eventually, someone is bound to realize a security guard is missing and sound the alarm."

"Making it too hot for Tristan to stick around."

"Or hot enough for us to escape out the front door in the confusion."

When we reached the hall adjoining the one with the offices, Marsten made me wait while he scouted. When he came back, I could tell the news wasn't good.

"Tristan left a guard behind," he whispered. "Either in case we come back or to forestall discovery of the crime scene."

"Maybe they're moving the guard's body. Getting rid of it."

He shook his head. "Tristan will want it found eventually. That's his backup plan."

"But you said—" I stopped. "That was a lie, wasn't it? About being part of the werewolf Pack."

"Not . . . entirely. I'm what you might call a quasi-member. But the Alpha—the Pack leader—knows I'm not a man-eater. My reputation in that respect is spotless."

"So why are you worried?"

"Some members—I've done things, in the past, to the Pack and while I've had a change of heart in that regard . . ."

"The ink on your reprieve is still wet, and you can't afford to test it yet."

"Exactly."

"Which is why you tried persuading Tristan to take care of the body."

"No, I was trying to divert his attention from you." He paused. "But yes, admittedly, I had a secondary goal in mind."

"Okay, so why don't we look after it now? Take out Tristan's guard, and we can move the body someplace safer, to dispose of it later, plus we'll have my gun."

One side of his mouth twitched. "For an amateur, you're remarkably good at this sort of thing."

"It's in my genes, remember?"

"But I suppose you want the guard disabled, not killed."

"Preferably. I'm not ready to completely give in to the dark side yet."

His smile broke through. "Let's see what we can do then."

9

I leaned against the wall, closed my eyes, and focused. The guard was a supernatural, probably half-demon. After a moment, I picked up his vibe, but it was too far away to be in the first office, with the body.

"He's in the second one, isn't he?" I whispered as Marsten returned. "The room we escaped from."

Marsten's brows shot up.

"Supernatural radar comes with my package."

"Oh? But you didn't detect me earlier." He smiled. "Not even when you ran right into me."

"I did. That's *why* I ran into you." I shook off the urge to explain. "I'm still practicing. The package doesn't come with a user's manual."

"Well, it worked fine this time. He *is* in the second room. Replacing the vent cover. Cleaning up, it seems."

"Good, then let's—"

"I'll look after him. You stay—"

He caught my expression and breathed the softest sigh. "Just stay clear then. As you said, I'm better equipped for this. Provide backup if you want but—"

"Don't turn this into a hostage situation."

"Exactly."

Marsten started to leave, then wheeled back to me. "He's coming."

He held his finger to my lips before I could answer. His eyes narrowed as he tracked the footsteps. A moment passed, then he shoved me in the opposite direction, prodding me to the next adjoining hall. We barely made it around the corner before the guard stepped into the hall we'd vacated.

Marsten pressed me against the wall, still listening, body against mine as if he expected the guard to veer around the corner and open fire.

The footfalls grew softer. The guard was leaving. That would certainly make getting into the office easier.

Marsten started to pull away from me, then froze.

"Was it okay?" a muffled woman's voice asked. She giggled. "I'm kind of tipsy—"

"It was great, babe."

Marsten winced as he recognized the privacy-seeking couple from earlier. Guess they'd found what they were looking for.

A door opened less than ten feet away. Marsten swore and looked toward the corner, but it was too late to run—we'd risk being seen by the departing guard. But if we stayed here, the couple would recognize him, and if the man got belligerent again, the guard would hear—

Marsten's mouth dropped to mine. He pushed me up against the wall, his hands wrapping in my hair and pulling it up to shield the sides of our faces. As he kissed me, I felt a stab of disappointment. His kissing was excellent, of course. Polished and perfect, just like the rest of him. For most women an excellent kisser is cause for celebration. But me? I prefer the ardent gropes and kisses of an enthusiastic, if less experienced, lover.

Behind us, the man laughed. "Looks like we aren't the only ones looking for a little diversion. There's an empty office right over there, guys."

Marsten raised his hand in thanks. The couple moved on. I let the kiss continue for five more seconds, then pulled away.

"They're gone," I said.

Marsten frowned, as if surprised—and disappointed—that I'd noticed. I tugged my hair from his hands.

"Okay, coast clear," I said. "Let's go."

He let out a small laugh. "I see I need to brush up on my kissing."

"No, you have that down pat."

"She says with all the excitement of a teacher grading a math quiz . . ."

"A-plus. Now let's move. Before someone else comes along."

We reached the office safely. This time, the door was locked, but Tristan hadn't trigger-spelled it. He must have assumed we wouldn't come back. The door lock was only for snooping partygoers or privacy-seeking couples.

Marsten gave the handle a sharp twist, and it snapped open.

"I'll find my purse," I said as we hurried inside. "You pull the body out."

"Yes, ma'am."

I flipped on the light and looked around. No obvious sign of my purse. It must have fallen—

"It's gone," Marsten said.

"No, I'm sure it just fell—" I glanced up to see him leaning over the desk. "You meant the body?"

A grim nod. He pulled the desk farther from the wall, then glanced at me. "Find your purse. I'll find this."

He leaped onto the desk, hopped into the gap behind it, bent and disappeared. I resumed my purse search. I looked under the desk, beside it, between the desk and filing cabinet—every place my purse could have fallen when Marsten yanked me off the desk earlier.

Marsten popped back over the desk, started to crouch, then noticed me watching.

"What?" I said when he paused.

"I have to sniff the floor."

"Then sniff the floor."

Again, he paused, as if trying to think of a dignified way to do it. I sighed, and turned my back to give him privacy.

A moment later, he said, "Nothing. They must've carried him out."

"Meaning you can't pick up the trail. Not of the security guard, at least. But what about Tristan's guard?"

"Questionable. I can try, but it's difficult to do in human form and without getting on the floor, close to the scent."

"Which is a whole lot tougher to do in a semi-public place."

He motioned for me to keep looking, and pitched in, checking the other side of the room.

He continued, "I'll still try tracking. I know a few tricks."

"Ah, so *you* did get your user's manual."

"Most werewolves do."

"Oh, right. Most of you are hereditary. So your father . . . ?"

"Raised me and taught me everything I needed to know about following a scent." A quick grin. "Although there was usually a diamond or two at the other end."

"Your father raised you to be a thief?"

His gaze chilled. "My father raised me to have a career suitable for a non-Pack werewolf who can't stay in one place without being rousted by the Pack or his 'fellow' mutts."

"The Pack doesn't let—?"

He cut me off with a wave, his anger receding. "It's not like that anymore. Not entirely. But in my father's day, a nomadic life was a must, and thieving skills helped."

"Tell you what, then. You don't slam my mom for setting me up on blind dates, and I won't slam your dad for teaching you to steal."

He laughed. "Fair enough. No jabs against well-meaning—if occasionally misguided—parents. As for your purse . . ."

"It's gone, isn't it? Tristan or his guard found it when they were cleaning up, and they took it to erase any sign of me being here."

"Most likely. As for the body, though—"

"Billy?"

The voice echoed down the hall. We both froze and turned toward the closed door.

"Billy? You down here?" Then softer. "Damn kid."

It was a security guard, looking for his dead colleague. Marsten waved for me to get behind the desk, and we both jumped on it just as the door opened.

"You!" the guard said.

A flashlight beam pinged off our backs. Marsten slipped his arm around me in an awkward, interrupted embrace. We looked over our shoulders to see the same older security guard who'd "helped" me open the janitor's closet. He speared Marsten with a glower.

"Get lost on your way to the bathroom again, *sir*?" he said. "This is bigger than that storage closet, but I'm sure the young lady would be more comfortable in a hotel. There are two right down the road."

"Uh, oh, yes, of course," Marsten stammered. "We weren't—that is to say, we wanted to look around the museum, see the sights—"

"Oh, I know what sights you wanted to see, *sir*." He waved us off the desk. "You're a long way from the dinosaur exhibits."

We complied, getting off the desk and pretending to straighten up. The guard continued to glare at Marsten, as if disgusted that a man wealthy enough to afford tickets to this gala couldn't spring for a bed.

"There's a Holiday Inn three doors down," he said as we walked past. "But I'm sure the lady would prefer the Embassy, which is—"

A movement at the door stopped him. One of Tristan's guards strode in. He'd swung around the right side of the door, meaning he hadn't noticed the security guard against the right wall. His attention—and his gun—were on us.

"I thought I heard voices," he said to us as the security guard stepped up behind him, surprisingly silent for a man of his size. "Good thing I came back. Tristan will—"

The security guard pressed the barrel of his gun between the younger man's shoulder blades.

"Didn't see me, huh?" the old guard chortled as the other man stiffened. "A word of advice, boy? Always check the room before you walk into it. Now, lower that gun—"

The younger man spun, gun going up, finger on the trigger. The security guard's eyes widened and he froze. Whatever ex-cop reflexes he had were buried under years of chasing kids off dinosaur displays and foiling amateur thieves.

The old guard stumbled back, as if forgetting he still held a gun. Marsten threw himself at Tristan's guard's back. I wish I could say I did the same. God, how I wish I could. But the truth was that I just stood there, shocked into impotence, like the old guard. It all happened in a heartbeat, not even enough time for me to feel the chaos rising, and not enough time for Marsten to make that five-foot leap. The young guard spun on the old, and fired.

Marsten hit the shooter in the side, knocking him away even as the silencer's *pffttt* still hung in the air, even as the old guard was still falling, bloody hole in his chest, even as I was reeling backward from the chaos explosion.

I hit the floor and, for a moment, could only lie there, system shocked by the high-voltage jolt. If there was any pleasure in that shock, I didn't feel it. I lay there gasping, mind blank. Then another shot snapped me from my shock and I leaped up, limbs flailing as if I'd been jolted again. Marsten was crouched over Tristan's guard, who lay in a heap, neck twisted, eyes open and staring.

"The shot," I said. "Did he hit you—?"

Marsten waved to a bullet hole in the wall, but didn't speak, just stayed crouched with his back to me, his breath coming in sharp, short pants.

I ran to the old security guard. Even as my fingers went to his neck, I knew he was dead. The bloody spot on his breast now covered half his shirt, and was still growing.

As I looked down at him, I saw him again sneaking

up behind Tristan's guard, eyes dancing as he imagined himself retelling the story of how he'd single-handedly apprehended an armed man. Again I heard his "see, I've still got it" chortle as he put his gun to the young man's back. The hair on my arms rose, and I rubbed them, trying to chase away the chill, unable to pull my gaze from his body.

My first murder. My first witness to death. And, only an hour earlier, peering behind this desk, I'd seen my first dead body outside a funeral home.

Before tonight I'd never even seen a dead body, and yet I'd fancied myself some kind of secret agent. What had Marsten said when I'd asked if he thought me a fool? Naïve, probably, but not a fool. *Probably* naïve? Dear God, could I have been any *more* naïve? I'd pulled a gun on a werewolf thief. I was lucky Marsten hadn't done what he just did to Tristan's guard, and snapped my neck.

"I need to hide the bodies," he said, his voice soft. "You can wait in the next room if you'd like."

"No, I'll clean—" I took a deep breath. "I'll clean up."

That's what I did. Cleaned up the crime scene. When I realized, really *realized* what I was doing, my blood went cold.

Oh-ho, so now you're worried. All this time, playing secret agent, and now that you're actually doing something illegal, you get scared.

I chased the thought back. Yes, I was scared, and yes, I'd been the biggest damn fool—

Enough of that.

As I wiped away evidence of a crime, and watched Marsten hide the bodies in the ventilation shaft— another handy vent shaft—all I could think about was what would happen to my family if I was caught. The shame, the embarrassment, the humiliation, but most of all the "why didn't we do more to help" bewilderment and grief. And what could I say? "No, no, you got it all wrong. See, I thought I was helping supernaturals with this interracial council, but really I was working for this sorcerer corporation, and then this werewolf . . ." I loved my family way too much to inflict *that* explanation on them.

"It's clean," Marsten murmured behind my head. When I tried to give the tile one last rub, he caught my hand. "It's clean, Hope."

"Out damned spot," I said, trying to smile.

"There's no blood on *your* hands."

"I wouldn't be so sure of that," I said softly.

I thought of all the cases I'd solved, the "criminal" supernaturals I'd turned in. I could see that one witch, so terrified she couldn't even cast a spell, begging me—*begging* me—not to hand her over, swearing it wasn't that council who wanted her but a Cabal—

"Hope?" Marsten grasped my shoulder, his grip hard enough to push back the vision.

"Sorry," I murmured. "Just . . . ghosts."

"Whatever you did, you thought you were—"

"Doesn't matter, does it? It's actions that count, not intentions. Ignorance isn't an excuse. That's what my ethics prof always said. Ignorance isn't—"

I champed down on my lip hard enough to draw blood, then pushed myself to my feet. "So no gun, no body, but one guard down." I paused. "*Three* guards, I should—" I shook it off. "*One* of Tristan's guards. One goal achieved out of three. Not doing so hot, are we? So what's next? Resume the plan and find a place to hide?"

He nodded. "We'll try that."

That didn't sound terribly optimistic but, considering our luck so far, I can't say I blamed him.

10

We discussed options and settled on hiding in one of the less "sexy" exhibits—those displaying artifacts unlikely to interest a bored partygoer conducting his own off-limits tour. The ceramics or textiles galleries seemed like the safest bets.

Both required passing the party, but we would take the back hall around it, rather than walk through. Seeing two people die had convinced me this wasn't the time to worry about my abandoned date.

We hurried into the hall skirting the gala, then veered left. We jogged through the looming skeletons of the dinosaur exhibit, and were crossing to the Greco-Roman wing when I picked up the twang of a supernatural vibe.

I grabbed Marsten's arm and told him. He listened for footsteps, then inhaled the scents.

"Tristan and the other guard," he said. "Coming right where we'll be going. Is there another—"

He stopped and answered his question by looking at the open doors down the hall. A quartet of men lounged in the doorway, ties and jackets off. Beyond them were more gaggles of partygoers.

"We could go back," I said.

"Too late," he said, and steered me toward the party.

"We'll cut straight across to the main exit," I said as we moved. "From there, the first left will take us to ceramics."

We squeezed past the drunken quartet who were ill-inclined—or too unsteady—to move out of our way. Once inside, I motioned to our goal across the room. We were passing the buffet table when I caught sight of Douglas, less than ten feet away, still talking to the Bairds.

Seeing me, Douglas blinked, and looked beside him. Figures. Here I was, worrying that he'd been searching for me, and he probably hadn't even noticed I'd been gone.

Marsten reached for my arm, to steer me away from Douglas, but I waved him back and veered onto a new course myself. Douglas only lifted his brows in polite question. When I gestured to the buffet table, he smiled, nodded, and turned back to the Bairds.

"Don't mind me," I muttered. "I'm just passing through, killers in hot pursuit. No, no, it's okay. You go back to whatever you were doing. I'm fine."

Beside me, Marsten chuckled. "Your mother knows how to pick them, doesn't she?"

As I rolled my eyes, Marsten's gaze shot back to the door, and I saw Tristan and the other guard brush past the drunken quartet. At that moment, Douglas turned and lifted a finger, motioning me over. Probably wanted me to grab him something from the buffet.

When I hesitated, trying to gesture back, Marsten grabbed the back of my dress and nearly yanked me off my feet. I backpedaled as fast as I could to keep from tripping, as Marsten dragged me into a large group of people and out of Douglas's sight.

"He's coming," he hissed by my ear, as I spouted apologies to the partygoers whose circle we'd invaded.

Tristan's guard was striding around the back of the buffet table, moving as fast as he dared without calling attention to himself. How he'd seen us in the crowded room, I couldn't imagine.

As we broke free from the group, Marsten gave me a shove, none too gently, toward the main door. With him behind me, I hurried out it, then left, toward the exhibits.

When I rounded the first corner, Marsten caught up and pushed something at me. A tuxedo jacket, which presumably he had grabbed from a chair in the gala.

"Take it," he said when I made no move to do so. "Put it on."

I almost said, "But I'm not cold," an automatic response that, under the circumstances, would have made me sound like an idiot. Instead, I settled for an equally idiotic "huh?" stare.

"Your dress," he said.

My . . . ? Oh shit. My canary yellow dress. How had Tristan spotted us in that crowded room? Well, duh. When I'd bought this dress, I pictured myself as a glowing beacon in the black night. Now, I had my wish.

Marsten steered me through around the next corner.

"No," I said. "The ceramics are the other—"

"I know. We're circling back. He won't expect that. Now put this on."

I took the jacket as we jogged into a room of Grecian urns. The coat fell past my short skirt, and wrapped around me easily . . . could have wrapped around me twice. The sleeves hung past my fingertips.

"A bit big," I whispered.

"No, you're just a bit small. Now move—"

He grabbed my arm and *stopped* me from moving.

Before I could comment, I caught the distant sound of footsteps—running footsteps, growing louder. Marsten pushed me into a gap between two stelae, and squeezed in with me.

When only one set of footfalls entered the room, Marsten's eyes narrowed, and his fingers flexed against my sides. As he tracked the steps, his face went taut and a glimmer of that icy rage I'd seen earlier seeped into his gaze.

What had Tristan said about a cornered werewolf? That they were ten times as dangerous as any other supernatural. Looking up at Marsten's face, I knew Tristan was right, and I knew why: no predator willingly accepts the position of prey.

So when Marsten's lips moved to my ear, I knew what he was going to say.

"Wait here."

I opened my mouth, but took one look at Marsten's eyes, and stopped. He was right. Things had changed since the last time he'd halfheartedly tried to keep me from following him into danger. Two men had died and I'd learned this wasn't some movie jewel heist caper. As much as I wanted to help Marsten and stop Tristan, now wasn't the time to redeem past stupidity.

So I nodded, and let him slip off into the darkness alone.

The footsteps had stopped as if our pursuer had paused to look around. Was it Tristan or his guard? I wished I could tell, but trusted Marsten's nose could. It would make a difference—facing a sorcerer versus a half-demon . . . presuming that's what the guard was.

I should have tried harder to figure out the guard's race when we'd been tying him up. I'd need to practice more.

Practice for what? You're not—

I stifled the voice and concentrated on listening. With the other man gone still, the room was silent, but Marsten managed to move without breaking that silence. I could see his white shirt gliding—

His white shirt? Why hadn't I offered him the jacket? I told myself he must have known what he was doing, and prayed I was right.

Pulling the jacket tighter around me, I eased forward enough to glance out. There, about fifteen feet away, by a gilt statue of Athena, was the guard we'd originally knocked out and handcuffed. He faced the other side of the room, his profile to me . . . and his back to Marsten.

Marsten crept forward, his gaze fixed on the guard, managing to skirt obstacles as if by instinct. His feet rolled from heel to toe, soundless. The guard's gaze swept a hundred and eighty degrees, and I fell back, but Marsten only froze in place.

The guard took three steps, then peered around another statue. Marsten kept pace less than five feet behind, so close I half-expected the guard to feel Marsten's breath on his neck.

Marsten took one last step. He tensed, then sprang. At the last second the guard turned, too late to fire his gun, but soon enough to throw Marsten off his trajectory.

Marsten checked his leap at the last second and smacked the guard's gun arm back hard and fast. The guard let out a hiss, part pain, part rage, and dove for the gun as it spun across the room.

Marsten knocked the guard flying. The guard crashed into a vase stuffed with replica scrolls. As he reached up, sparks flew from his fingertips, and I knew his power. Fire.

The guard's hand closed around the scroll. Even as

my lips were parting to shout a warning to Marsten, the paper burst into flame. The guard swung the fiery torch at Marsten, who was already in mid-leap, coming straight at him.

The scroll caught Marsten in the side of the face, and he fell back. The guard dropped the paper, now nearly ash, and dove for Marsten, his good hand going to Marsten's throat. Marsten drilled his fist into the guard's stomach. As the guard fell, he grabbed Marsten's arm, and Marsten yanked away, but I could see the guard's scorched handprint on his white sleeve.

It was then, as the two men launched into a full supernatural strength versus fire brawl, that I snapped out of my chaos intoxication and realized that I, too, had a weapon—a loaded gun lying, forgotten, less than twenty feet away.

So I left my hiding place. Instead of dashing across the open room to the guard's gun, I crept along the shadows, moving from exhibit to exhibit. While I'll admit I was worried about the guard seeing me and deciding I made an easier target, I was even more worried about Marsten seeing me out of my hidey-hole and being, if not concerned, at least distracted.

Whether Marsten *could* be distracted was another question. He fought with a single-minded purpose of someone who's done a lot of it. Not what I would have expected. But was I surprised? No. I'd seen that look in his eyes as the civilized skin sloughed away, and I hoped never to be on the receiving end of it again.

As the two men fought, I circled around the outside. The gun had slid under a scale model of Pompeii. I managed to get behind the low table, then stretched out on my stomach. I reached into the narrow opening until my shoulder jammed against it, then swept my hand back and forth, feeling nothing but gum wrappers and dust.

I peered under the display table. In the dim emergency lighting, I could see the gun, its barrel pointed toward me, still inches from my fingertips. I wriggled and stretched and twisted and finally brushed the gun's barrel. Another wiggle, and I got my index finger into the lip of the barrel. Not the safest thing to do with a loaded gun, I'm sure, but I managed to tug it forward an inch or two, enough to grab it from a safer angle and pull it out.

As my hand slid around the grip, I envisioned myself leaping from behind the table, gun trained on the guard, giving Marsten the kind of distraction he could use to get the upper hand.

I crouched, steadied the gun, then jumped up—

Marsten was sitting beside the guard's prone body, surveying the burn damage to his own shirt. He looked over at me. I was poised Dirty Harry style, gun drawn, hair wild, still drowning in the oversized tux jacket. His lips twitched.

"I, uh, have the gun."

"So I see."

"And *I* see you have the situation, uh, under control. So I'll just . . ."

I let the sentence trail off as I lowered the gun and moved from behind the table, ignoring his barely stifled laughter.

"If you can stand guard, I'll hide this one," he said as I approached.

I looked down at the dead guard, and pushed back the initial stab of "did we really need to kill him?" regret and doubt. This had long passed the point of "just knock him out" solutions. We already *had* knocked this guard out, and handcuffed him, and he'd still come after us, ready to kill. A solid justification, but still, if I *had* leaped up from behind that table, what if I'd needed to do more than distract him? Could I have pulled the trigger?

You've been carrying a gun for a year, and you don't know whether you could have fired it? What did you think it was? A fashion accessory?

"Hope?"

Still crouched beside the body, Marsten touched my leg, gently prodding me back to reality.

"If you are not up to it—" he began.

"Guard duty. Got it."

The burning scroll hadn't triggered any fire alarms, nor had the grunts and punches of combat been loud enough to bring partygoers running. As Marsten stowed the dead guard, I concentrated on both exits, looking, sensing, and listening. I caught a supernatural vibe just as Marsten looked over.

"Footsteps," he said. "Supernatural?"

I nodded. "Are they coming—?"

"This way," he said. "From the direction we did."

I glanced toward the far exit but knew without asking that Marsten had no intention of fleeing. Only Tristan was left, and when he realized he'd lost both his guards, he wouldn't walk away. He'd call in reinforcements.

"Hide back where you were. Keep the gun ready but—"

His eyes narrowed as he turned to track the approaching footsteps.

"More than one set," he murmured. "Probably partygoers. Can you tell?"

I concentrated, but my heart was pounding, reminding me with each rib-jangling beat that those footsteps were getting closer, and I didn't have time to dawdle.

My powers caved under the pressure, and I couldn't even pick up one vibe anymore.

"It doesn't matter," Marsten whispered when I told him. "We'll see them soon enough."

The last word was leaving his lips as Tristan came into view, flanked by what could only be two additional guards. Marsten let out an oath, biting it off mid-syllable. He propelled me back to our original hiding spot between the stelae. This time, when we heard footsteps into the room, Marsten didn't move. One opponent was fine, two maybe, but three at once? Not if we didn't have to.

As they passed, Tristan took his cell phone from his ear and scowled.

"Russell still not answering?" one of the guards said.

Tristan shook his head. "I'll try Mike. See if he can go look for Russell."

Marsten and I looked at one another, then at the spot where Marsten had hidden Mike's body—less than three feet from us. As Tristan finished dialing, Marsten tensed and I fumbled to get the gun from my pocket, then leaned out to see Tristan as he kept walking, phone to his ear. Seconds ticked past. He stabbed the disconnect button.

"Vibrate," Marsten whispered.

That made sense—that they'd have their phones set to vibrate. Nothing blows your cover faster than *The Ride of the Valkyrie* resounding through a supposedly off-limits hall.

When the three were gone, we headed back the other way, across the main hall and into the "biodiversity" wing, a.k.a. the stuffed animal gallery. On the other side was the ceramics exhibit. Halfway across the biodiversity room, we caught strains of a lively monologue coming from the ceramics gallery. The midnight behind-the-scenes tour.

Marsten frowned at the direction of the voices, as if debating joining them and taking refuge in numbers. That depended on how likely he thought Tristan was to avoid public confrontation. After a moment, he shook his head and prodded me toward the narrow opening between a pillar and the African savanna diorama.

When I stepped into the gap, he tugged me out, then backed in and crouched, sitting on a fan box. He motioned for me to turn around and back onto his lap. As I did, I knew why he'd picked the lower position—we'd be hidden from casual viewers by a nearby meerkat display.

As I shifted onto his lap, his arms went around me, holding me steady . . . or that's the excuse I let him have. We settled in for what could be a long wait. As things went quiet, I struggled to hold back all the thoughts I didn't want to think, all the regrets and self-recriminations I'd deal with later. My heart raced, filling the void by indulging in replays of the running, the fighting, those delicious spurts of chaos that only sent my heart tripping faster still.

As I luxuriated in the memories, other visions crept in: a vulture circling overhead, an ocean of long, dry grass whispering, a breeze bringing the heavenly scent of musk, my stomach growling, tail twitching in anticipation—

Marsten shifted, his fingers accidentally brushing my hardened nipples and I groaned, my breath coming faster.

He chuckled. "Not immune to me after all, I see."

"Hmmm?"

He cupped his hand under my left breast, and pressed it there as my heart raced beneath his fingers. When those fingers climbed to my nipple again, I let out a soft moan.

"Sorry," I said. "It's not you."

Another chuckle. "If you want to tell yourself that . . ."

I closed my eyes and saw the lioness crouch, hind quarters twitching, mouth watering in anticipation. I could feel her excitement, pulse racing, and my own raced to match it. I moaned again, as Marsten's hand slid up to my shoulder.

He hesitated. "Either you have some strange erogenous zones, or you're right. It's not me, is it?"

I opened my eyes. "It's—" I waved at the display. "I pick things up, from the past . . . chaos."

Another brush against my hard nipples. "And this is what happens?"

"Mmm, yes." My eyes closed again. "Strange, I know . . ."

"Actually, no, not to me, at least. Should I stop?"

"Mmm, no."

A soft laugh. He unzipped my dress and tugged it off my shoulder, pulling the bra down with it. A wave of cool air rushed over my bare breast and I shivered, backing against him as his hand went to my breast, lips to my neck, tongue sliding over the sensitive spot behind my ear, raising more shivers. I shifted again and he put his free hand around my waist and repositioned me on his lap. I felt his erection hard against my rear, and pushed against it, thrusting softly. He let out a low growl and moved his lips to my ear.

"Tell me what you see," he whispered.

When I hesitated, his free hand moved to my leg, pushing up my skirt, fingers tickling up the inside of my thigh. He traced the edges of my panties, then slid a finger under it. I parted my legs to let him in, but he only teased me with his finger.

"Tell me," he said.

"It's . . . a hunt."

"Mmmm." A growling chuckle. "Nothing like a good hunt. What do you see?"

I told him, the words coming hesitant at first, then flowing faster as his finger slid in, moving expertly as he thrust against me, egging me on when I slowed, my excitement feeding his. As the lioness sprang for the klll, I felt the first wave of climax—

Then he stopped.

"It's still not me, is it?"

"Wh—wha—?"

His lips moved down my neck. "It's insufferably vain of me, but if I'm going to seduce you, I want to be the cause of your arousal, not passive recipient."

"You don't seem all that passive to me."

He laughed, but shook his head, fingers on my thigh.

I craned around to look at him. "So you're just going to leave me hanging?"

He hesitated, then shook his head. "That wouldn't be very gentlemanly of me, would it?"

"Not at all."

"Hmmm."

He still hesitated, toying with the edge of my panties.

"Well . . . ?" I said.

"I'm trying to decide . . ."

"I say yes."

He laughed. "I doubt it, and I doubt we're thinking of the same question."

"Which is . . . ?"

"Control. As in, can I help you without helping my-self to you."

I stood, turned around and repositioning myself on his lap, facing him, squarely straddling him, hands around his neck. "What if I'm offering?"

He growled deep in his throat and reached for me, pulling me against him, hands tugging up my skirt as I unbuttoned his pants—

An alarm rang, so fast and sudden I almost toppled backward off him.

I looked around. Smoke wafted from the hall. I pictured the fire demon again, reaching for the vase of scrolls, sparks raining from his fingertips. A few must have fallen into the vase, smoldered there and caught fire.

From the other room came the shrieks of people hearing alarms, smelling smoke, and reacting as if the building had transformed into the Towering Inferno. I caught the first lick of chaos and shivered, then shut it off.

Marsten's arms went around me, pulling me back against him with a hard thrust and a soft growl. I rotated to face him, my hands going around his neck, mouth finding his, drinking in the chaos arising around us. Burning building? Who cared? I had a more urgent fire to put out.

Marsten growled again, this one harsher as he pulled his lips from mine.

"I hate to be the one to bring this up, but . . ."

"The building's on fire?"

"Unfortunately."

I slipped my hands under his shirt. "How fast can it burn?"

A low growling chuckle as he pressed against me. "You have no idea how badly I'm tempted to test that. But I have to remind myself that you're acting under the influence of something."

"Something *other* than you, you mean."

"There's that, too."

"Vain," I said, poking him in the chest.

He caught me up in a hard, deep, tongue-diving, groin-grinding kiss, then put me back on my feet.

"Time to go," he said, and started across the room.

"Tease."

He tossed a smile over his shoulder. "Just giving you something to remember, once all this interference is out of the way."

We reached the main hall to find it log-jammed with people. Marsten hesitated, then took my arm and led me straight into the heart of the mob. The crowd buoyed us along, and before I knew it, the cool night breeze was rippling through my hair. I looked up, and only then, seeing the stars winking against the city's glow, could I truly believe it.

We were out. Free.

If Tristan and his guards were here, they'd be watching with dismay as the museum expelled a steady river of white shirts and black jackets and nary a yellow dress to be found. The crowd was so thick that even if I hadn't covered my dress, they'd probably never have picked me out.

As fire engines and taxis competed for curb space, sirens and blaring horns rose above the din of partygoers yelling for their lost spouses and friends. A few taxis managed a passenger snatch-and-grab before the police cordoned off the area.

We let the crowd carry us across the road, where the taxis were regrouping. Marsten's grip suddenly tightened, and he ducked sideways, nearly plowing me into a white-haired woman with a walker. As I glared at him, a voice cut through the din.

"Hope? Hope!"

"Don't look," Marsten muttered by my ear as he steered us into another pocket of people. "Just pretend you don't—"

"Hope?"

Douglas cut between a couple. He smiled at me. There I was, bedraggled and dirty, hair flying everywhere, wearing a tux jacket, running from a burning building, and he only smiled, as if I'd just popped back from the buffet line.

"The Bairds have invited us for drinks," he said.

I stared, the words not penetrating, certain I was mishearing and somehow the din around us had turned "Oh my God, are you okay?" into an invitation for post-inferno cocktails.

"I—I have to go," I said finally. "The—the paper. The fire. I need to—"

"Oh, you'll need to write it up, won't you?" He smiled and winked. "For a cause, I'd go with spontaneous human combustion."

"I was thinking more of fire demons," I muttered.

"Sure. That's different. I'll let you go, then. Have fun, and don't work too hard."

Marsten yanked me backward again, as Douglas slipped off through the crowd. When we reached the sidewalk, Marsten body-checked a young man and shoved me through an open cab door, then crawled in after me and slammed it.

He looked over. "Your address?"

I gave it.

To the driver, though, Marsten just said, "Head east."

"Oh, Riverside is beside the river," I said. "Which is north."

Marsten didn't correct the driver, just shut the panel between the front and rear seats and buckled up.

"To be safe, you should spend the evening some-place else. Your mother's maybe? Is she in the city?"

"Yes, but if I'm in danger, I'm certainly not taking it to her, no matter how slight the risk."

"Friend, sibling, cousin . . ."

I shook my head. "Same thing. This is my problem, so until it's resolved, I'm keeping it that way. We should find a hotel or motel on the outskirts of town, and get some rest before we figure out how to resolve this, because I'm assuming Tristan won't just give up and go away."

"He won't. All right then. We'll find a hotel, and I'll make sure it's safe. Then, when I come back—"

"Back? Where are you going?"

He patted his pocket, where the jewels were. "I need to take care of these tonight. I shouldn't be more than an hour or so—"

"Just long enough to hunt down Tristan and kill him." When Marsten looked over sharply, I said, "I may be foolish, but I'm not stupid and, after tonight, not nearly so naïve. The only way to end this is to kill Tristan, so that's what you're going to do. That why you said you'd retrieve my bracelet 'later'—you meant once I was out of the building and you went back for Tristan."

He hesitated and studied my expression, then nod-ded. "I've tried walking away twice, and he refuses to leave it that. As much as I hate to bother with someone like Tristan Robard, I can't walk away again."

"That's why you asked for my address, isn't it? Be-cause you think that's where he'll go. Right now, I'm the more urgent threat, the one who could let his Cabal know about his extracurricular activities."

Marsten nodded.

"Well, you know I'm not going to any hotel." I held up a hand against his protest. "Have I interfered yet?"

"No, but—"

"And I won't. I am so far out of my league—" I shook my head. "Let's just say I won't embarrass myself further or endanger you by interfering. But Tristan wants me, and if you show up alone at my townhouse, he'll know something's up."

For a moment Marsten and I just looked at each other, then he nodded and gave the driver my address.

12

I live in a brownstone backing onto the river and surrounding parkland. Not your typical twenty-something, tabloid journalist digs. The house technically belongs to my mother. I say "technically" because her ownership is really only a technicality . . . and a contentious one at that.

My mother had bought the place while I'd been in J-school, only a mile away. She'd called it an investment, but when I'd graduated, she'd wanted to give it to me. College had been a struggle—not academically, but personally, coming at the worst time in my life, when I'd been dealing with my demon powers. I think the brownstone was Mom's graduation gift . . . and a hoped source of stability for a daughter sorely in need of it.

I love the townhouse, love the area, love my beautiful riverfront "backyard" with its winding forest trails—an escape route whenever I needed it, which seemed often. So I'd agreed to keep living there, as a property manager of sorts, maintaining the building and protecting Mom's investment. But I refused to take the deed, and insisted on paying all expenses and upkeep—though the property taxes alone were nearly enough to bankrupt me. Thank God I had two jobs—

Two jobs? As the taxi disgorged us on the front lawn, I stared up at my beloved brownstone and realized I no longer had two jobs, and probably not even one.

Of course my mother could—and would—step in and pay the bills. I so desperately didn't want that.

I'd given my mother enough sleepless nights to last a lifetime. I often wondered whether, at some level, she knew my problems were rooted in something she'd done, that brief post-separation encounter that no one could blame her for. Even if she didn't know the true nature of my trouble, I think she blamed herself, and I didn't want that. I wanted to be strong and independent and stable, and to be able to take her for lunches on my dime and say, "See Mom, I'm doing fine." And I *had* reached that point, stuffed with the newfound confidence my council job had given me—

"We'd better get inside," Marsten whispered as the cab pulled away.

He looked around, nostrils flaring, body tense, as if we'd just stepped into a trap . . . which we probably had. Definitely not the time to worry about my life's recent crash and burn. When this was over, I should just be thankful I still had a life to repair.

"Good security," Marsten whispered as I undid the dual deadbolt. "Are the other doors and windows—?"

"All armed. Motion detectors in every room, too. My mom worries."

I hurried in to disarm the system. It was still active. If Tristan had beat us here, he'd backed off when he'd seen the security. This wasn't the kind of neighborhood that ignored screaming sirens. Better to wait for us to disarm the system.

"What now?" I said as Marsten relocked the front door.

"Turn on a couple of lights, and stay away from the windows. Is that open land out back?"

"A park," I said. "Mostly forest."

"Good. That's where I'll try to get him then. Away from the houses. We'll stay here for a bit, give him time to arrive and stake out the house. Then I'll change and lead him into the forest."

"Change?" The words "but I don't have anything for you to wear" were on my lips when I realized what he meant. "Into a wolf."

He nodded. "By far the preferred way for dealing with these things. Easier to track, easier to fight and"—a quick smile—"a built-in disguise if anyone sees me."

I flipped on the living room and hall lights.

"What about the television?" I said. "Should I turn that on, too?"

A brow arch. "We escape death, flee to the safety of your townhouse . . . and watch television?"

"So what would Tristan expect?—" I followed his gaze to the stairs leading to the second level. "Ah, of course. You'd want a good night's rest."

"And that's probably all I'd get," he muttered. "Unless I set the place on fire first. From Tristan's point of view, though, we just had a harrowing evening, I saved your life—"

"You did?"

"Play along. You take me upstairs—"

"Oh, reward sex." I paused. "But for proper reward sex I wouldn't take you upstairs. We probably wouldn't even make it past the front door. I just push you against the wall, get down on my knees—"

He cut me off with a growl. "I'd suggest you stop there unless you plan to follow through."

"Oh, but I would follow through . . . if you'd saved my life." I swung around the banister onto the stairs. "Not that you'd *let* me, though. No sex unless it's *you* I want, remember? No chaos sex. No reward sex. That's your rule."

He muttered something and followed me up the stairs.

At Marsten's suggestion, the first thing I did was remove my dress . . . which sounds a whole lot more interesting than it was. As he pointed out, heels and a slinky yellow dress didn't make good late-night commando gear. While he cleaned up, I put on jeans, a T-shirt, and sneakers. Then we headed for my bedroom. Yes, I have a separate dressing room. It's a three-bedroom townhouse—I'm just trying to make efficient use of space. Really.

I walked into my darkened bedroom, flicked on the light, then made a face.

"Sorry," I said. "It's a mess. I wasn't expecting company."

"Poor Doug." Marsten walked to the unmade bed, plunked down on it, and gave it a test bounce. "Doesn't get a lot of use, I'll bet."

"I'm picky. Sorry."

A wolfish grin. "Don't be. I like picky." He pushed to his feet. "Well, no, usually I don't like picky, but this time, I think I do."

With a sidelong glance through the window, he put his arms around my waist, leaned down, and kissed me. It was a slow kiss, easy and relaxed, with none of the practiced attention to art of his first one.

"Setting the scene?" I murmured with a nod toward the window.

"A good excuse." He kissed me again, then sighed. "You really *are* immune, aren't you?"

"To what?" I caught his look and rolled my eyes. "Oh please. You really *are* vain, aren't you?"

"I already admitted that. I can't help it—I'm accustomed to having my attentions returned."

"Ah."

"Not even going to bite for that, are you?"

I stepped back and sat on the edge of the bed. "What? You admit that you find me attractive, so I'm honor-bound to return the compliment? Fine, yes, you have your charms."

A twist of his lips. "Oh."

"That's not good enough? Okay, let me try again. I think you're the most gorgeous thing I've ever seen and I can barely keep my hands off you . . . , well, not when there's a decent source of chaos around."

He growled and scooped me up off the bed, kissing me again.

"Enough already," I said, squirming free. "I admitted you were—"

"Charming."

"I said you had your charms."

"Which means you find me charming."

"No, well yes, you *are* charming, but I don't find that charming."

He laughed and shook his head. "All right, you find me physically attractive then."

"Yes, you are, but, no, I don't find that particularly attractive."

He bared his teeth in a quick grin and stepped closer. "My wit?"

I moved back and shrugged. "Witty enough, though not as witty as you think you are."

"Ouch." He gave an almost self-mocking grin. "Then it must be my undeniable sense of style."

"Because you can pick out a decent tux?" I snorted. "There's what, one color option and two or three styles?"

A feigned look of shock. "You mean you don't find me irresistibly suave, debonair—"

"Where I grew up, guys learn suave from the cradle."

His grin only grew. "Then whatever you find attractive about me has nothing to do with any of this—" He waved his hands over himself. "This infinitely polished package?"

"Nope. Sorry."

"Good."

"Good?"

"Very good."

He caught me up in a kiss. As he did, a distant vibe twanged through me.

"They're here," I whispered.

Marsten glanced out the window, his body blocking mine, gaze scanning the dark street.

"They're across the road," he murmured as he turned back to me. "They must have just arrived. On the count of three, I'm swinging you past the window and onto the bed."

He did. As soon as I hit the mattress, I rolled to the far side and dropped onto the floor. Marsten followed. We crawled into the hall, down the stairs, and to the back door, arriving just in time to duck behind the kitchen cabinets when we heard footsteps on the rear deck. The guard tested the door, peered in, then moved on.

"Quickly," Marsten murmured. "They'll be back in a minute. This is the safest place to break in."

As we slipped out the door, I started pushing in the handle, to relock it when it closed. But Marsten caught my hand.

"We want them to know we came out this way," he whispered.

Hunched over, and darting from bush to tree to garden shed, I led him across my tiny yard, and down the small hill to the woodland beyond. Marsten found a place for me to hide. He made sure I had my gun, and warned me to stay where I was, whatever happened. Then he gave me a card from his wallet, and told me if he didn't return in an hour, I was to run to a public place, call the hand-written number on the back, and explain everything.

A moment later, he was gone.

I stayed where I was. As impotent as I felt cowering in those bushes, I knew if I tried to help, I'd more likely get us both killed. So I hid and I listened.

I listened as the soft lullaby of cricket and frog calls went silent under the heavy footfalls and guttural muttering of Tristan and his guards. I listened as those mutters gave way to orders and oaths. I listened as those trudging footsteps divided and turned into running feet. I listened as a scream shattered the night, a scream cut off by flashing fangs.

That wasn't my imagination working overtime. I *saw* those fangs flash, smelled bowels give way, felt hot blood spatter my face, and the visions brought not a split second of chaos bliss. With every cry, every scream, every silenced pistol shot, I was certain Marsten had been hit. The death vision came twice, and still I heard multiple running feet and voices. My God, how many were there? How would he ever—

Another shot. Then the sound that broke my resolve: a piercing canine yelp of pain.

13

I broke from my cover then, but I resisted the urge to run pell-mell toward the noise, toward the laughs of triumph. Instead, I gripped my gun tight and slunk through the shadows until I was close enough to see a flashlight beam cutting a swath through the dark forest. The beam stopped, and my gaze followed its path.

A black mound of fur lay motionless at the end of that flashlight beam. A guard stood beside the mound, gun pointed down.

Oh God. God, no—

Something flashed near the top of the heap, a blue eye reflected in Tristan's flashlight beam. The eye rolled, following Tristan. I took another three steps until that dark mound became a massive wolf lying on his belly, his head lowered but not down, his ears and lips drawn back as he watched Tristan's approach. The fur on Marsten's shoulder was matted with blood. The guard had his gun pointed at Marsten's head, and I couldn't tell whether he was staying down because of that gun or because he was too badly injured to rise.

"Hope!"

Tristan's voice rang out so loud and sudden that I

jumped. Only the barest rustle of dead leaves gave me away, but Marsten's ears swiveled in my direction. His black nostrils flared. Then he let out a low growl, and I knew that growl was for me. As clear a "get the hell out of here" as if he'd shouted the words.

"Hope!" Tristan yelled again. "I know you're out there."

Marsten's muzzle turned sharply as the bushes across the clearing crackled. The top of a head bobbed from the darkness. Tristan waved for the guard to stand near Marsten.

"Hope! Don't you think you've caused enough trouble tonight? Two men dead and another to follow? All because you couldn't do your job and catch one man— a thief, no less. Isn't that what you'd signed on to do? Help us put away scum like Karl Marsten?"

As Tristan tried to guilt-trip me into giving myself up, I looked around for a better position. He had no intention of letting Marsten go—this was more about his vendetta against Marsten than about shutting me down—so I wasn't stupid enough to even consider turning myself over. Marsten was alive, and would stay that way until Tristan got me, too.

If I could find a better position, with a better view, I might be able to help Marsten. I still had the gun.

Oh, right, the gun . . . a weapon you've never even fired.

Didn't matter. It was still a plan . . . and the only one I had.

When Marsten had found hiding spots, he'd emphasized protecting my back. If your back was open, anyone could sneak up behind you. So where could I safely . . . ?

I looked up. The trees.

While Tristan shouted for me again, I scurried to the

nearest candidate, grabbed the lowest branch, and channeled my inner tomboy. In minutes, I was lying on my stomach on a thick branch about seven feet off the ground. Perfect. In the darkness, someone could walk right under me.

"Hope! You have thirty seconds to show yourself or I put a bullet in this mutt's head."

Yeah, sure. Kill the only way you have to get to me. Right.

My sight line into the clearing was less than ideal. I could make out heads and torsos, but nothing below waist level, including Marsten. I wriggled farther along the branch. Ah, there he was, still on the ground at the guard's feet, his head up, glowering at Tristan.

Tristan walked over to Marsten and lowered the barrel of his gun. Marsten tensed. The guard put his foot on Marsten's neck to hold him down, but the move was halfhearted. My gut twisted as I realized Marsten was badly hurt—he had to be if the guard was so unconcerned with restraining him.

"Hope? Last chance."

Tristan's finger moved on the trigger and even as I told myself it was a ruse, that he had no intention of pulling it, my mind washed back the reassurances with a tidal wave of doubt. Tristan wanted Marsten dead, wouldn't leave this forest until he was dead, so why not just kill him now—

"Wait!" The word flew out before I could stop it.

Tristan smiled and lowered his gun. "That's my girl."

Oh Christ. Now what? Maintain position and think. Think fast. And stall.

"I want to negotiate," I said. "I—I made a mistake."

"Yes, Hope, you did."

Tristan lowered the gun and hand-signaled for one guard to search in the direction of my voice.

"Uh-uh," I said. "I'm not coming out. Not yet."

Tristan jerked his chin, motioning for the guard to circle around from behind.

"And don't tell him to sneak up on me, either," I called, my voice ringing in the stillness. "I can sense him, remember? He comes anywhere near me, and I'll do what you threatened to do to Karl. Put a bullet in his head."

"Ah, a bullet," Tristan said with a laugh. "From your gun, I presume." He reached into his pocket. "This gun, maybe?"

I unscrewed the silencer and fired the guard's gun into the ground below. "No, *this* gun."

"So you have a gun. Wonderful. It would be even better if you knew how to use it. But they don't teach marksmanship in debutante classes, do they?"

I laughed. "Do you really think I'd let you get me a gun, and not even learn how to use it? I'm a keener, Tristan, remember? I was at the gun club an hour after you handed it to me. And yes, the West Hills country club *does* have marksmanship facilities. Excellent facilities. You'd like it . . . if they ever let you in."

Tristan stiffened. Found a weak spot there, didn't I? Now if only I had some clue what to do with it . . .

"I made a mistake," I said. "Karl tricked me."

Tristan smiled. "Charmed you, more like."

"No, he lied to me," I said as I looked around, babbling while I searched for a way to help Marsten. "He told me I wasn't working for the council. He said I'm working for a Cabal."

One of the guards shot Tristan a confused look, mouthing "Council?"

They didn't know . . .

The other two guards had been in on Tristan's scheme, but these ones had no idea what I was talking about. Marsten said Tristan was working on personal revenge, that the Cabal would never have sanctioned his death. The other two guards had known that, had been moonlighting outside the Cabal with Tristan. But these two weren't. Interesting.

I called down again. "I don't know what you hope to gain by killing me, Tristan." I pulled out the business card Marsten had given me. "We've already called—"

I squinted at the card. Earlier, I'd glanced at it just long enough to register the last name—Cortez—and I'd remembered Marsten saying he'd done work for Benicio Cortez's son, the one who wasn't part of the Cabal. So that's the name I expected. When I saw what was really printed there, my heart thudded.

I turned it over. A handwritten phone number. Oh God, was that real? What if it wasn't?

"Yes, Hope? You were saying?"

I'd been about to say that I'd called the person on the card and told him everything. But that wouldn't work now. Had I really called already, these guards wouldn't be here.

Think . . . think . . .

"Who am I really working for, Tristan?" I said. "Who sanctioned this job?"

His gaze shot to the guards. "The Cortez Cabal, Hope. You already said that."

"Yes, but I . . . I'm confused. You two down there. When you were called in, what did Mr. Cortez say Karl's crime was?"

The guards looked at one another.

"Wait," I said. "Mr. Cortez didn't give the order, did he? That came straight from Tristan. So what did *Tristan* say Karl's crime was?"

"He's a thief," Tristan said, between his teeth, surveying the forest as if trying to pinpoint my voice.

"Okay . . . but—well, he's been a thief all his life, right? And his father before him. But now, out of the blue, Mr. Cortez decides he deserves to die for it? Right after Karl joins the Pack. Right after the Pack joins the interracial council. Isn't that a diplomatic crisis in the making? I thought Mr. Cortez was pretty careful about stuff like that."

The guards turned to Tristan, their eyes narrowing, but still expecting a logical explanation.

"I don't question my orders," Tristan said.

"Maybe, but I do. I'm going to call Mr. Cortez. Got his card right here." I read off the office numbers, so they'd know I was telling the truth. "And, while I'm sure those numbers would get me through to some flunky eventually, I can probably save some time by using the number on the back. Benicio Cortez's personal number."

"How'd she get—" one of the guards began.

"She didn't, you—" Tristan clipped off the insult. "It's a stalling tactic. You really are a naïve little girl, aren't you, Hope? Where did you get Benicio Cortez's number? The phone book?"

The second guard snickered, but the first took out his cell phone.

"Here," he said. "Give me the number and I'll call."

Tristan smiled in my direction. "Yes, Hope. Give him the number."

I resisted the urge to rattle it off, and stammered it out instead, as if I was making it up. Where had

Marsten got this number? What if someone had given it to him as a joke? I looked down at him, trying to gauge his reaction, but his eyelids were flagging, as if he was struggling to stay conscious.

My hesitant delivery made Tristan smile, and he made no attempt to stop the guard from dialing, just leaned back against a tree and awaited my downfall.

Ten seconds after the guard finished dialing, his head jerked up.

"Mr. Cortez?"

Tristan chuckled and shook his head.

"This is Bryan Trau," the guard said. "SA Unit 17. I'm sorry to disturb you, sir, but we have a situation here."

Tristan jumped so fast he nearly tripped. His hand flew out, and he motioned for the guard to hand over the phone, but the guard stepped away. Tristan started to lift his gun, then stopped as the second guard raised his halfway, the threat respectful but clear.

The guard explained the situation, and I swore I could see Tristan sweating. When the guard finished, he listened, said, "Yes, sir," then held out the phone.

"Mr. Cortez would like to speak to you."

Tristan stepped back and looked ready to bolt. Then he caught sight of Marsten and must have, in that second, seen a possible way out, the elimination of the only person who could confirm the entire story. He lifted his gun.

A shot sounded.

I didn't think. I jumped from the tree. The second I started falling, my brain screamed "Idiot!" and I saw the gun still in my hand. I managed to fling it aside before I landed on top of it and shot myself in the gut.

I hit the ground hard, but scrambled up, grabbed the gun, and ran. As I made it to the clearing, I heard,

"Yes, sir." Pause. "No, sir. He's gone."

I flew into the clearing to see the guard kneeling beside a body. Tristan's body. In the guard's other hand, he held his gun.

"Yes, sir, I did. You said if he made a move—" A pause, then the guard nodded and glanced over at me. "She's here now."

The guard held out the phone. I hesitated, then took it.

"Is this the young woman who was with Karl?" a voice asked. A pleasant voice. Calm and alert, as if he hadn't been woken in the middle of the night.

He asked a few questions about me, whether I was hurt and what had happened, his tone mild but concerned, almost avuncular, not what I'd expect from the head of the most powerful Cabal. After a few questions, he said,

"You've had a very long night, and I'm sorry you had to go through this, but I can assure you, Mr. Robard was acting outside his jurisdiction. Since he is an employee, though, I take full responsibility for his actions, and will do everything I can to put things right, starting with looking after Karl. Is he badly hurt?"

Oh God, I'd been so shocked I hadn't even checked. I blurted an apology, and raced to Marsten. The second guard was already there, tending to Marsten, who was unconscious. He'd been shot through the shoulder, and his entire side was wet and sticky. Blood must have been pumping out the whole time he'd been lying there.

Mr. Cortez assured me a doctor, one from his local satellite office, would be on the way. Then he left me to help the guard bind Marsten's wound as we waited.

14

The guards took Marsten back to my house, then left me there to wait for the doctor while they returned to the scene to clean it up. They weren't even out of the backyard when the doctor arrived. He got the wound cleaned and covered, left antibiotics and painkillers, and told me to call if Marsten's condition worsened.

The two guards stopped back at the house to let me know everything was cleaned up. They brought something for me, too—my purse, left by Tristan in the van. My bracelet was still in there, as were my wallet and gun. Everything back in order, just as Mr. Cortez had promised.

We'd left Marsten in the living room, on a blanket. I found a second blanket and laid it over him. He looked ridiculous, of course, this huge wolf on my living room floor with a pink and white knit afghan tucked in around his muzzle. At least I didn't get him a pillow . . . though I did consider it.

I lay down on the sofa above him, intending to keep watch until he woke, but, within minutes, I was asleep.

* * *

I awoke to the sound of running water. Marsten was gone.

"Up here," he said when I called for him.

I climbed the stairs. He was in the bathroom, with the door open a crack.

I stopped a few paces from the door. "You need your clothing, don't you. Let me get—"

"Found and on . . . mostly. What's left of them, anyway. Now, if I can just—" He growled. "This bandage fit me better as a wolf."

"Here, I can—"

I started pushing the door open, then stopped, realizing he might not want the help. He kicked it open the rest of the way as he quickly shrugged on his shirt.

I laughed. "Feeling shy?" I gestured at the shirt. "I can't fix your shoulder like that."

He hesitated, then let the shirt fall off. His chest and upper arms were a loose patchwork of scars. He tensed, as if waiting for me to comment or react. I grabbed bandages and iodine from the closet, and set to work fixing him up.

"The Cabal sent a doctor over," I said. "I'm not sure he did a very good job. He didn't seem to know much about werewolves."

"That's fine. I know someone who does." He glanced at me. "So I didn't imagine that, then. You contacted Benicio Cortez."

I nodded. "And that's all it took. Tristan's dead, you're alive, the mess is cleaned up, and Mr. Cortez has promised to look after any fallout. Which, of course, led me to wonder, if you had that number, why didn't you use it right away. I think I know the answer, but I'm hoping I'm wrong."

"Probably not," he murmured.

I looked up at him. "As nice as Mr. Cortez was, I'm

guessing he didn't get where he is by playing Santa Claus. Cleaning this up for us wasn't a free gift, was it?"

Marsten shook his head. "We owe him. He wouldn't say that, because it would have been crass, under the circumstances, but it's a chit owed." He rubbed his shoulder, adjusting the bandage, and made a face, then looked at me. "When I turned down Tristan's offer, Benicio came to me and made one personally. *He* was much more persuasive—"

"He threatened you?"

Marsten laughed. "Benicio Cortez does not threaten. He knows a lollipop can be a better motivator than a swat on the behind. He made me a lucrative offer, and when I respectfully refused, unlike Tristan, he let it go, but gave me that card, in case I ever 'needed help.'"

"And now I've accepted it on your behalf, putting you in his debt. God, I'm *so* sorry—"

"If I hadn't wanted you to use it, I wouldn't have told you to. Given the choice between being dead and owing Benicio Cortez, we're better off with the latter, as uncomfortable as it may be. He will eventually call in the chit, but, in the meantime, you can go back to your life, including your job at the paper, assuming that's what you want."

"It is." I sat on the edge of the counter. "I'd like to—well, maybe I'm kidding myself thinking I could do anything on my own—"

"You could still monitor and report problems. To the real council this time. They have someone doing something similar, another journalist, and I know she'd love the help."

I shrugged, torn between not knowing if that would be enough and not knowing if I could offer more, if I still had more to offer.

Marsten stepped in front of me and leaned forward, a hand on each side of me, balancing against the counter. "It's a start," he murmured. "Take it slow and start there. The only drawback, I'm afraid, would be the pay . . . or lack of it. The real council isn't a group of white-haired philanthropists. Most of the delegates aren't much older than you, meaning it's pretty much a no-budget operation."

"That doesn't matter. I never even wanted Tristan to pay me. I get paid well enough—" I stopped and shrugged. "Well, you know . . ."

"In chaos dollars."

My cheeks heated. "I know that sounds awful, helping others because I get something out of it—"

He put his hands on my hips and leaned closer to me. "You need an outlet. Do you think I don't understand that?" He reached into his pocket and took out the jewels. "This is mine. A way to get my regular adrenaline shot without ripping apart strangers in alleyways. And, with you, it isn't all about the chaos. You have balance. The good impulses with the bad. Me?" He grinned. "A little more inclined to the latter." His eyes glinted. "Though not irredeemably so."

I laughed. "Something tells me that would be a fun, but futile challenge."

"Challenge is good."

I shook my head. "If you're happy with what you are, then anyone who wants you would need to accept that."

He ran his fingertips along my jawline. "Wouldn't be easy, I'm sure."

"No, but if you look hard enough, I'm sure you'd find someone willing to try. You know, my mom's great at finding dates—"

He growled and kissed me. When he pulled back, he

ran the tip of his tongue over his lips, as if sampling the kiss.

"The immunity is breaking down," he murmured. "But still has a ways to go." He leaned toward me again. "I'd ask if I should stay for a while, but I suspect the answer would be no. A reluctant no, maybe, but a no nonetheless. So instead I'll ask whether I can come back."

I smiled. "Yes, you can come back."

"Good. Better, actually."

"Better?"

"Much."

I laughed and shook my head.

Marsten stepped back. "I should go. I have a doctor to visit and goods to dispose of . . . not necessarily in that order. And I will make those calls for you—ensure the termination from your old job and the start of your new one go smoothly."

"Thanks. I appreciate that." I caught his hand and met his gaze. "I really do, Karl."

He leaned over for a kiss, little more than a brushing of the lips, but very . . . nice. When he pulled away, he backed up to the door, started to turn, then stopped.

"I'm too old for you."

"Too old for what? To come back for a visit?"

A dramatic sigh. He shook his head, and walked out of the bathroom. From the hall I heard a murmured "I'm going to make a fool of myself."

"It'll look good on you," I called after him.

His chuckle returned. I smiled and listened to his footsteps recede down the stairs, across the floor, and finally disappear out the back door. Then I took a deep breath. One life gone. Another on the way. Was I up for it?

God, I hoped so.

DEAD MAN DATING

Lori Handeland

1

On the day he died, Eric Leaventhall had a date that couldn't be broken, so he went. Dead and all.

Too bad I was his date.

Turned out dead dating was the only way he could get what he needed.

Sustenance.

Are you confused yet? I know I was.

Maybe I should start at the beginning. But I'm not quite sure when that was. Probably when I decided to become a client of *www.truelove.com*.

Pretentious? Maybe. But I'd hoped that any man who chose a service by that name might be a little more grown up than most—had at least moved beyond a desire to bang supermodels and begun to think about finding a life. Being a literary agent, I should have known that semantics were as dead as most people's belief in a soul mate.

The date itself started out well enough. We met at a martini bar near my office. A new place, kind of *Sex and the City,* which should have tipped me off right away. If not to the whole demon issue, then at least to his hopes for the evening. He wasn't after true love.

I hadn't been completely honest, either. In my bio I'd said I was "in publishing." I'd learned that the quickest way to a stack of manuscripts from the wannabe famous was to tell anyone but immediate family what I really did for a living.

Of course some people figured it out as soon as they heard my name. My mother had been one of the top agents in the business before she'd gone and died on me. Was I following in her footsteps trying to regain some of the happiness I'd enjoyed while she was alive?

You betcha.

However, that wasn't working out. I liked to read, but I didn't like to sell. Sadly, my degree in ancient civilizations made me fit to do little but teach, and I doubted I'd be very good at that, either. Kids kind of scared me.

At loose ends—in my job and my personal life—I'd decided to start searching for that soul mate I'd been dreaming of. Just my luck, the first candidate didn't even have a soul.

I should have caught a clue to Eric's intentions the instant I'd seen his photo on the web. He was dropdead gorgeous—dead being the operative word, although in truth, he hadn't been dead at the time. Still, what on earth would a man like him want with a woman like me?

One thing and one thing only. What's that horrible saying about all women being the same in the dark?

I'm not a hag, but I am short and just a little dumpy, with long, black hair that curls too much and the dark eyes and olive complexion of either my father's Sicilian ancestors or my mother's Hebrew ones. Take your pick. With a name like Mara Naomi Elizabeth Morelli, I'd never be mistaken for a Nordic bimbo, even if I'd had a prayer of looking like one.

Anyway, call me Kit. Everyone does. I was never able to carry off the Mara Naomi Elizabeth thing.

Now back to the date—if not from hell, at least from a place very near by.

Manhattan.

Rich, blond, and handsome, Eric was every plain girl's dream. He was not very tall, which I liked, since big men always made me nervous; his teeth were white and straight; his eyes deep blue. He was also a surgeon. Of course he was too good to be true.

"I'm so glad you came," he said, and his smile warmed the chill of the early spring night.

Eric led me to a secluded table, held my chair, let his fingertips drift over my hair. Sure he got a little too close, rubbed his knee against mine a little too soon, laid on the interest in my job, my future, and me a little too thick. But I was lonely, confused, unhappy, and here was this great guy hanging all over me.

"What do you say we take this to your place?" Eric murmured, stroking the back of my hand.

I hesitated, uncertain how to say no. I'd never been one for sex on a first date; I wasn't one for sex at all. I might be smart-mouthed, just a little sarcastic—blame my mother—but I was also shy with men. The thought of baring my body to a stranger—well, it wasn't a thought I entertained very often.

However, I was suddenly struck by the odd notion that tonight was the night I'd met the man I'd been waiting for all of my life.

"Okay," I said.

Had that word come out of my mouth?

I'd been raised on my mother's tales of love at first sight. She'd taken one glance at my Italian-Catholic, working-class father and defied her wealthy intellectual Jewish family to marry him.

They'd been happy until the day she died. I'd been in my last semester of college, uncertain of what I should do with my life.

Then—bam—my mother had died from a brain aneurysm. Life suddenly seemed so short. Her work wasn't done, and I had no pressing place to be. So I slid into her job, and two years later I was still doing it.

My father never recovered from her death. He'd passed away just this winter. I was so lost without him, I felt hollow inside. Which had no doubt precipitated my sudden search for true love.

Hand in hand Eric and I left the bar and strolled south toward Chelsea.

I had an apartment on West Twenty-fourth Street. My mother had been a *very* good agent. Throughout her married life, she'd made three times the money of my electrician father. They'd deposited the checks and never mentioned it. So when Daddy died, I'd nearly choked at the size of his bank account, which was now mine.

I'd spent the money on a condo, not too far from my Fifth Avenue office. Trying to live up to my mother's reputation meant I had to work harder and longer than everyone else. Saving commute time had seemed like the best way to invest my inheritance.

Eric's arm slid around my waist. Sighing, I leaned my head on his shoulder.

"This is nice," I murmured.

"It'll get nicer, I promise."

His palm drifted lower, cupping my bountiful butt, squeezing a little. His thumb slid down the center, and I jumped.

"I can't wait to get inside you. You'll die of the pleasure, baby."

Baby?

Uck. I was going to have to put a stop to that. He sounded like a used car salesman, trying to sell me a vehicle I did not want.

His thumb teased me again, and I decided later would be time enough to discuss endearments. Who'd have thought a guy's thumb could be so arousing. Of course, I couldn't recall ever being this aroused.

Eric must have felt the same way because he yanked me in between two buildings and shoved me against the wall, slapping his lips against mine a little too hard. I tasted blood when my teeth cut my lip, shuddered when he licked the blood away.

I should have been angry, disgusted, a little scared. Instead I felt . . . wanted. Something I'd never felt before. Sure, in a tiny sane portion of my mind I knew I'd lost it, but right now I couldn't summon the will to care.

Eric's body shielded mine from the night, his erection pressed against me too high to be of any help. I'd have to climb his body, wrap my legs around his waist if I wanted any relief. I was contemplating doing just that when the snick of a match made me still.

Someone else was in the alley.

I yanked my mouth from Eric's. His lips slid across my jaw, then latched onto my neck. My gaze went past his shoulder to the man hovering in the shadows. The glow of his cigarette did nothing to reveal his face. I got a sense of height, breadth, and darkness.

"Eric," I whispered.

He continued to rain kisses across my chest, then rooted at the neckline of my brand-new black dress like a nursing child. My nipples tightened in anticipation, even as the glitter of eyes from the shadows caused a tingle of unease to dance across my skin.

What in hell was wrong with me? I was definitely not an exhibitionist.

"There's someone here," I said more loudly.

"Doesn't matter," Eric muttered, fumbling with his pants. "Gotta do you now or I'll fade away."

That got through to me. I might be attracted, aroused, insane, but I was definitely not so far gone that I'd let a virtual stranger screw me in an alley while another one watched.

"No," I said.

He ignored me, sliding my dress up my legs, yanking at my pantyhose. The nylon went *ping* as his thumb popped through. A run shot down my leg, even as his erection beat a pulse against my stomach.

I began to struggle, becoming just a little afraid, yet in the midst of all that, I wanted him. And that scared me more than anything else.

"You'll die happy, baby," he muttered. "They always do."

A hand slapped onto Eric's shoulder. "She said no, *hibrido*."

Though the words were harsh, the tone was mellow, the accent south of the border. A voice that could haunt me for the rest of my life.

Eric shifted, his shoulders blotting out everything but him. Neither the hand on his shoulder nor the whispered warning even slowed him down.

The salt, however, did.

I wouldn't have known what had been thrown in

Eric's face, except some of it hit me. The grains burned my eyes like hellfire.

Eric made a sound that was half snarl, half shout, and shoved away from me so hard my shoulder blades scraped the brick wall.

He swung around and the other man shot him.

Right in the head.

2

The shot was muffled—*silencer,* I thought—yet the sound still bounced off the walls and echoed down the alleyway. Tensing in expectation of the blood splatter, my eyes slammed closed.

Nothing happened.

When I opened them again, I was alone.

No Eric. No stranger. No blood. What the hell?

I stepped onto the street. No one appeared to have heard the gunshot, or if they had, they didn't care, continuing on their way with the typical zombielike trance of lifetime New Yorkers. The tourists were too busy staring upward, either dazzled by the neon or trying to find their way to their hotels by way of the skyscrapers—a method similar to using the stars in places where stars could actually be seen.

I was dizzy with the adrenaline, both confused and frightened, so I wandered back into the alley, and I saw him.

Just a shadow, a slip of darkness against the light as he moved onto the street one block over.

I didn't think; I ran. If he vanished into the crowd, what would I do? How would I prove anything that had happened tonight? I didn't consider why I thought I needed to prove anything.

I burst out of the alley, and someone grabbed me around the waist. The force of my forward motion, and the sudden end to it, swung me about so fast, my feet lifted off the ground. A choked sound came from my throat, but I didn't have the air left to scream.

Even if I had, it wouldn't have mattered since he slapped his hand over my mouth and dragged me backward. I just couldn't win tonight.

"Why are you following me?" he asked.

"Why do you think?"

My lips moved, but the words were garbled. His body, rock-hard against mine, tensed.

"If I lift my hand, do you promise not to scream?"

Since screaming hadn't worked very well for me so far, I nodded, and the hand went away.

"You shot my date in the head!"

"What date?"

I blinked. "The guy in the alley."

"What guy?"

"Eric Leaventhall. Slim, blond, handsome."

He snorted.

"What does that mean?"

He didn't bother to answer, continuing to hold me aloft, my feet dangling near his knees. He was so much taller, so much broader, so much stronger, I felt helpless. And while that should have unnerved me, instead I got kind of annoyed.

"You mind?"

I swung my feet, almost cracking him in the shin, and he set me down but kept his arm around my waist. I could neither see him nor run away.

"There wasn't any man," he said.

"Of course there was. He bought me a drink. He—he—"

I ran my tongue across my lip, felt the telltale ridge where my teeth had ravaged the skin when Eric kissed me. I wasn't crazy.

But this guy was.

"Let me go," I ordered.

Amazingly, he did, and I scampered out of his reach and spun around.

My first thought: What a shame. He was too gorgeous to be insane. As if beauty and lunacy were mutually exclusive.

As dark as Eric had been light, bulky where Eric had been slim, this man was large, hard, his hair shaggy, his face shadowed by at least two days' growth of beard. The clothes had obviously been slept in, a lot, though even before that, they'd been years away from new.

His blue work shirt had faded nearly to white from repeated washings. With it unbuttoned to his sternum, I saw the hint of a tattoo, though I couldn't tell what the shape was. The jeans were ancient, too, the boots scuffed and dusty, his black leather jacket a relic.

His eyes were as dark as mine, but he had longer lashes. Isn't that always the way? High cheekbones, a fine blade of a nose. I wasn't certain, but I thought I saw the sparkle of an earring. Nothing fancy or swingy, just a shiny silver stud piercing one lobe.

He was so different from anyone I'd ever encountered—exotic and wild—I had to remind myself he'd just murdered my date in cold blood. Except . . .

Where was the blood?

According to him, there hadn't even been a date.

I was back to the eternal question—was he crazy, or was I?

"There was a man with me," I said, "and you killed him."

"If I had, you shouldn't be troubling your pretty little head."

My eyes narrowed, but he ignored me.

"That's the quickest way to getting it shot off," he continued.

"In other words, Eric troubled his pretty little head? About what?"

"I don't know any Eric. I walked through the alley. You were leaning against the wall. Figured you were high on something."

"I was—"

I broke off as I remembered what I'd been doing. Suddenly I was mortified. Why had I been making out with a stranger? Why had I been bringing him back to my apartment? Both behaviors were completely out of character.

With Eric no longer attached at the lip, I couldn't figure out why I'd been so enthralled by him.

"He was here," I repeated, "and you shot him."

The man cursed under his breath, a long stream of indecipherable Spanish that brought Ricky Ricardo to mind.

"Come along," he snapped, and stalked back in the direction I'd come.

On the opposite end of the alley he paused, knelt, peered at the ground. "No blood, no body." He lifted his gaze. "No shooting and no guy."

Joining him, I stared at the stained, but not with blood, asphalt.

"You want me to take you somewhere?" he asked.

I didn't answer as I inched closer to the wall. I'd been leaning here. Eric had been standing there. Crazy man with a gun had been there, so . . .

I peered more closely at the brick and found the bullet hole.

"Aha!" I stuck my finger into it and glared at the guy triumphantly.

"Aha, what?"

"A bullet hole. You shot him." I frowned, remembering the no blood, no body problem. "Or at least *at* him. You missed."

He joined me, then poked his finger into one, two, three other holes. "So did a lot of people."

I yanked my hand away, more miffed than scared. "I know what happened."

"Listen, *chica,* I didn't see any guy."

"I am not crazy. And I don't do drugs."

"Maybe you should."

At my glare, he lifted his hands in surrender. "I meant prescription ones. You need help."

Maybe I did. *Definitely* I did if I'd not only imagined Eric but also his murder. Did I miss my dad even more than I thought?

Frustrated, I shoved my hand into the pocket of my dress. My fingers brushed paper and I remembered. I'd printed out the last e-mail from Eric.

Withdrawing the sheet, I thrust it at the man. "I'm not nuts, and here's the proof."

The guy narrowed his eyes, read the words, scowled. Then he pulled out his gun and pointed it at me.

Why had I never learned to leave well enough alone?

"Let's go." He flicked the barrel of the gun toward the street.

"Wh-where?"

"Your place."

I shook my head. "I don't think so."

"You don't get to think."

"You're kidnapping me?"

"What was your first clue?"

If I wasn't so scared, I might have found him funny.

He lost patience and grabbed me by the arm. "Either take me to your place, or I'll take you to mine."

I doubted I'd care for his place. At least in my own I'd be surrounded by the familiar and have a hope in hell of escape.

"Mine," I murmured. "On West Twenty-fourth."

His eyebrows lifted. He obviously knew the neighborhood. Swell. Now he'd want money in addition to . . . whatever else he wanted.

My kidnapper set his left arm over my shoulders and I tensed, trying to inch away, but he wouldn't let me. Instead, he drew me close, then slid his right hand beneath his jacket and pressed the gun to my ribs. I guess there'd be no shouting for help. He'd obviously done this before.

"Who are you?" I asked as we stepped onto the street.

"Chavez."

"Is that your first name or your last?"

"Both."

"Right."

He shrugged, the movement rubbing his side against mine, making the gun skitter across my skin. I flinched, and he tightened his hold.

"*Relaje,*" he murmured in that voice that would have been seductive if he hadn't been kidnapping me at gunpoint. "I don't want to hurt you, *chica.*"

"Then why are you doing this?"

"You'll be safer with me. I promise."

I snorted my opinion of that, and I could have sworn he laughed. The sound became a cough as I glanced up.

As the neon lights spilled over us, his face resembled something carved on a western mountainside. Not a hint of emotion—no humor, definitely no compassion. How could I possibly be safer with him? Right now the most frightening thing in my world *was* him.

"What's your name?" he asked.

I debated ignoring the question, but since he was dragging me home, he'd find out anyway. And did I really want him to continue calling me *chica* in a voice that reminded me of tequila on a scalding summer night?

"Kit," I said, though not very nicely.

"What kind of name is Kit?"

"Nickname. My whole name is longer than your—" I paused and he stared down at me from on high.

"Arm," I finished, and his lips twitched.

"What is Kit short for?"

"My father called me—"

My voice broke suddenly, embarrassingly. My father's death was too new, too painful, too private to talk about with a kidnapper.

"Kitten," Chavez blurted.

I stopped walking. "How did you know that?"

"Fits."

No one but my father had ever thought I resembled a kitten. Strange, and disturbing, that this stranger saw it, too.

We continued on silently. Every once in a while I couldn't stop myself from looking at him. He was everything foreign to me; I should be frightened. Instead that foreignness had turned my fear toward fascination. Especially when his hair shifted, a streetlight blared, and his earring sparkled.

A tiny silver cross. How strange.

I lowered my gaze, saw where we were, and paused, indicating the building on the other side of the street with a dip of my chin. "This is it."

He scowled. "You've got a doorman."

"So?"

"Don't even think about tipping him off. Say I'm your boyfriend."

"Right. Out of the blue I come home with a boyfriend like you."

"What's wrong with me?"

"Besides the gun? The leather? The earring and the—"

I stopped short of mentioning his tattoo. I wasn't sure it was there, and I didn't want him thinking I'd been staring at his chest.

"The killing," I finished.

"I didn't kill anyone." His eyes narrowed. "Yet. If we're both lucky, I'll get what I want and be out of your hair in a few days."

"A few days?" I shouted, managing to startle several passersby.

"Shh!" He jerked me more tightly against him. "I won't hurt you as long as you help me out."

"That's what all the psycho kidnappers say right before they kill someone."

"You have a lot of experience with psycho kidnappers?"

"I think I'm going to."

His lips tightened. "I'm not crazy."

"Which is what all the crazy people say."

He glanced at the sky, as if asking for guidance. For some reason, that calmed me. If he believed in the divine, he couldn't be all bad.

"I'll tell you whatever you want to know." Chavez lowered his gaze from the heavens to my face. "Inside."

Since I didn't have much choice, and he had the gun, I let him lead me across the street.

3

I'd always been able to relax inside my home, protected by two deadbolts and an ace security system, not to mention that I lived on the tenth floor.

With Chavez taking up too much space in my winter white living room, I doubted I'd calm down anytime soon.

"You want a drink?" I blurted.

His dark brows lifted, and I wanted to take the question back. This wasn't a social occasion.

"I don't drink," he said.

It was my turn to look surprised. Chavez definitely seemed the drinking type. Of course, appearances were never reliable.

Eric had seemed like a gentleman, but he'd taken off and left me in an alley with a gun-wielding maniac. Guess he hadn't been "the one" after all.

You think? asked my increasingly sarcastic inner critic.

My eyes, scratchy from wearing contacts, ached. I only wore the lenses on dates—in other words, once in a blue moon—preferring my glasses for everyday use.

"I'm going to the bathroom," I announced, pausing

when he followed me. "I haven't needed help since I was two."

"Tough. I don't plan to let you disappear."

"There's only one way out."

"What about these?" He indicated the French doors that led to my balcony. I had another set in the bedroom.

"Ten floors down. Spider Woman, I'm not."

He almost smiled, caught himself, and scowled. "I'll be right here."

"I just bet you will," I muttered, and slammed the bathroom door.

While I was at it, I washed my face, changed into my sweats, then grabbed my glasses. I might as well be comfortable and kidnapped.

When I stepped into the front room, Chavez contemplated me for several ticks of the clock. I hated being stared at. Probably went back to those days in junior high, when being stared at was never a good thing.

"What?" I snapped.

"You wear glasses."

"I'm a short, dumpy, plain girl who reads books for a living. Of course I wear glasses."

He tilted his head. "You read books for a living?"

Of all the things he could have focused on in my statement he chose that one? I rolled my eyes. "Never mind. You said you'd answer my questions."

"Sure. But first, show me all the e-mails you got from this guy."

"So you admit he was there? I'm not nuts."

Chavez slid his weapon into a holster tucked under one arm. "He was there."

I'd known that, but I felt better having him say it. I also felt better now that he'd put away the gun.

"It wasn't very nice of you to try and make me think I was crazy."

"I'm not nice." He flicked a finger at the computer in the corner of my dining room. "The e-mails?"

He'd kidnapped me to look at e-mails? Who was this guy? And who was Eric? I started to concoct all kinds of conspiracy theories.

"Huh," he said when he'd read all of the messages. "Nothing weird."

"Should there be?"

"Considering what this guy is, yeah."

"Is Eric some sort of secret agent?"

And if so, what did he want with me? Besides the obvious.

"Agent of the devil," Chavez murmured, still staring at the computer screen. "Not much of a secret."

I frowned. "Is that code for terrorist?"

"Terrorist?" He glanced at me, amusement in his eyes, though nothing so lighthearted showed on his face. "You think I'm Homeland Security? FBI? CIA?"

"You're something."

"Got that right."

Considering his accent, his appearance, his innate foreignness, maybe *he* was the terrorist. Except we hadn't been at war—even a cold one—with any Hispanic countries for a long, long time. Of course, pretty much everyone hated us lately.

"DEA?" I blurted.

"You think the guy was a drug dealer? You've got quite an imagination, but you're way off base."

"Get me on base then."

"He's a demon, and for some reason he wants you."

"He's a *what*?"

"Fallen angel. Spawn of Satan. Minion of hell. Soulless, evil, creepy thing."

For the first time tonight, I was speechless.

I'd started to believe that maybe Chavez wasn't crazy. Maybe he was just a gung-ho member of one of the many law enforcement agencies in a country that had gone a little overboard on security after September eleventh. Who could blame us?

But demons?

"If Eric's a demon," I said slowly, "that makes you a—"

"Rogue demon hunter."

I blinked. "Lost in the Buffyverse, are we?"

"That show was a real pain in my ass," he muttered.

I was *not* having this conversation. Except I was.

"Not sure what kind of demon he is," Chavez continued, as if he hadn't just said something weirder than weird. "Salt didn't work. Neither did a silver bullet."

"Maybe because there's no such thing as demons?"

He turned a dark, placid stare in my direction. "Then what do you call your date?"

"A jerk. But that doesn't mean he's the devil in disguise."

"You didn't think he was such a jerk when you were letting him stick his tongue down your throat."

I stiffened, even as my face flooded with heat. "You shouldn't have been watching."

"If I hadn't, you'd be dead now." He tilted his head. "You don't seem the kind of girl who'd let a guy screw her against the wall of an alley."

"Gee, thanks. I think." I took a deep breath and admitted the truth, though I'm not sure why. "I don't know what got into me."

"It was almost Eric."

I ignored that. "I don't sleep with men on a first date. I just felt—"

"What?" He leaned forward, face intense.

I searched for the word to describe my bizarre lapse of character.

"Consumed," I said. "I couldn't seem to stop what was happening. I didn't want to."

Chavez jumped to his feet and began to pace. "He's some kind of incubus."

"Which is?"

He paused, surprised. "You've never heard of an incubus?"

"Of course. I'm just a little rusty on my demonology. Haven't had to use it in, oh . . . my entire life."

A slight narrowing of his eyes was the only indication that he didn't find me half as funny as I found myself. "An incubus uses sex the way the rest of us use hamburger."

I got some bizarre images on that one and made a face.

"I meant an incubus feeds on sex," Chavez muttered. "If he goes too long without it, he dies."

"So actually he's *just* like a regular guy?"

"Ha, ha. An incubus can also compel people to do what they normally wouldn't. Hence your humping him in the alley."

"I wasn't."

"You were going to."

Yeah, I was. That Eric had been a demon capable of influencing me to have sex with him explained a lot. If I could only get past the demon part.

But I couldn't.

"I don't believe any of this."

"You'd rather believe you were so overcome with

lust for a guy you'd just met that you were not only going to bring him back to your apartment after an hour in his company, but you were perfectly willing to do him in an alley with me watching?"

When he put it like that . . .

I still didn't believe Eric was an incubus.

"Why did *you*?" I blurted.

"Excuse me?"

"Why did you think Eric was a demon? He seemed normal to me. Does he have a tail I'm not aware of?"

"That's a myth. Tails on demons. Some have them, true. But not all. And not Eric."

"Then why him?"

He turned away. "Trade secret."

I stared at his back as he studied my collection of books on ancient civilizations. Most guys took one look at them and headed for the door. I hoped he'd do the same, but no such luck.

"Trade secret?" I repeated. "That's convincing. Shouldn't there be nice men in white coats searching for you somewhere?"

He faced me again. "Are you a librarian?"

My back stiffened as if I'd been slapped on the butt. "What?"

I wasn't even sure why I was insulted, except that I'd spent the better part of my afternoon off getting ready for the date from hell.

Literally, according to Chavez.

"You said you read books for a living."

"I'm an agent. I sell books to publishers."

"Oh."

Yeah, I kind of felt that way about it, too.

"I don't suppose you have any books on demons?"

"What do you need a book for?"

"Unless I know exactly what's necessary to kill a particular type of demon, they won't die."

A convenient excuse to explain why his methods didn't produce results. I recalled reading somewhere that the insane often constructed elaborate delusions with rules that actually made sense to the not so crazy.

"You're the demon hunter, why don't you have a book?"

"There are way too many demons to fit in a single book, and I can't exactly carry twenty or thirty books with me everywhere I go, nor memorize all the types and the methods."

"What are the chances that the demon you're searching for would be listed in a book I might have?"

"Good point."

"You kidnapped me because you thought I was a librarian?"

"I kidnapped you because you had info from the demon."

"Now that you've seen it, you can leave."

"The book?" He gestured at the case.

"I don't have anything on demons. Never studied them. Wasn't interested."

Disappointment trickled over his face like water down a windowpane. "You can't help me then."

"You need a different kind of help than I can give you."

"You think I'm insane."

"Big time."

His smile was as sad as his eyes. "I hope you never have a reason to change your mind.

He left without any further attempt to convince me that there were demons in the world. He also left without a good-bye, going straight to the front door, then closing it quietly behind him.

After that, the night got boring.

I certainly couldn't sleep. So I made myself some tea and settled down to work. I had a stack of manuscripts with my name on them. I always did.

Reading was how I spent my free time, and that wasn't so bad. I loved books; I just hated selling them.

I'd been an agent for two years, and I was beginning to get the drift that I wasn't any good at it. Another depressing tidbit to add to a long list of them. What was I going to do if I didn't do this?

I'd come to believe that selling books was like selling a sunset or a lake or the bluest blue sky. How do you put a price on perfection?

Whenever I found a really great story, all I wanted to do was share it with the world—at any price. Which made me a shitty agent.

I was no good at my chosen profession. I felt as if I were letting my mother down. The only time I was happy was when I lost myself in another reality, one of adventure and romance, a life I craved but would never have.

I turned to the stack of manuscripts I'd brought home from work. Unfortunately, the first one was more boring than peeling paint with my fingernails and did nothing to get my mind off Chavez. Interesting that I found myself unable to stop thinking about him instead of Eric.

"Tattooed homicidal maniacs are always more fascinating than slim, blond surgeons," I muttered.

And why was that?

I forced myself back to the book. One good thing, it made me sleepy. Just after midnight I gave up and went to bed.

All the excitement had revved me up, and now I was crashing hard. Everything went black not more than an instant after my head hit the pillow.

I had a doozy of a dream.

The French doors opened. A breeze fluttered the curtains. The quilt waved like wind across water as it slithered off my bed. The sheets soon followed.

My body was hot, almost feverish. I yanked off my sweat suit and lay naked to the night.

A shadow slid from the balcony and into my room; like a spreading stain the gray darkness crept across the carpet, up the side of the bed, and spilled over me.

I was no longer hot, but pleasantly cool, the rapidly chilling sweat causing goose bumps to rise on my skin.

My sigh was arousal, desperation, need. Writhing, I cried out, and the shadow took the shape of a man. No more than a shade really, impossible to see who he was, or even *if* he was.

The wind was a whisper all around me, a language I didn't understand, yet words that encouraged me nonetheless. The air touched me everywhere, a caress that I welcomed.

I'd been waiting for this all of my life. Did I mention that I was a virgin?

The feather-light stroke of lips to the pulse at my throat, a tongue trailing over one breast, then the other, teeth grazing my nipple, then my stomach, then my thigh. Heated breath brushed the curls between my legs as a clever tongue did things that made me both limp and tense, tantalized and tortured.

I came awake, panting and gasping, my dream orgasm still rocketing through my body. I glanced around my room and stifled a scream.

The balcony doors were open, and a man stood on the other side.

4

I fumbled for the phone, knowing it was too late for 911, but I had to try. Unfortunately, at the first press of a button, the first tiny *beep*, the man on the balcony walked into my room.

I dropped the phone.

"You!"

Chavez bent and picked up the bedspread from the floor, then calmly flipped it around my shoulders and turned away. I hadn't gone to bed naked, but I was now. How much of that dream had been real?

"What are you doing here?"

"I thought—"

"We've been over this. There aren't any demons, Chavez. Go away."

"I couldn't just let him come back and murder you."

I nearly dropped the bedspread. "Murder me? Since when does he want to murder me?"

"What part of incubus didn't you understand?"

"The part where he kills me."

"He feeds off of sex."

"Still not hearing death anywhere in that explanation."

"After he's through with the women he's chosen,

they . . ." He paused, stuck his fingers into his pockets, and shrugged. "They're sucked dry."

"Which means?"

"He has sex with them until they turn to dust."

Chavez had an answer to everything. I still wasn't buying any of it.

"Thanks for the info," I said, "but you don't need to stay. I'll be extra careful. Besides, I've got great locks and an even better security system."

"I got in."

That stopped me.

"How?"

"Breaking and entering. The demon will have an even easier time."

"Because . . . ?"

"They can teleport."

"That's it!" I pointed to the door. "I'm sick of your fairy tales."

"Fairies aren't my department."

"Out!" I shouted.

Chavez was unimpressed with my theatrics. His gaze wandered over the room, over me. I pulled the bedspread tighter across my breasts.

"I wanted to watch for a while, just in case he was nearby. Then I saw someone moving around in your apartment."

"You mean someone like me?"

His dark, serious eyes met mine. "Definitely not you."

Despite my brave words, I glanced toward the bedroom door.

Chavez laid a hand on my arm. "I searched the place. No one's here."

His touch, in my bedroom, in the night, with me wearing nothing but a blanket, should have been unnerving. Instead I found it comforting. My reactions to men tonight were nothing short of bizarre.

"No one except you," I muttered.

The room was dark, his figure shadowy. I was reminded of the dream, and my skin suddenly felt too small for my body. I shifted, and he stepped back quickly, as if he didn't want to get too close to me, almost as if he were afraid.

I glanced up, and his eyes glittered in the small amount of light from the half moon that spilled through the open French doors. What time was it? How long had I been asleep?

I was so confused—going from unconscious to conscious, from fear to safety, from arousal to . . . arousal all over again. With Chavez looming over me while I was still naked, my body humming from an orgasm that had seemed pretty real, my head spun. I swayed and he grabbed me by the shoulders.

"*Chica?*"

That voice trilled along my flesh like warm water in winter. Both familiar and foreign, I could listen to him all night.

"Did you touch me while I was sleeping?"

I hadn't meant to ask that, but now that I had, I wondered.

Instead of an answer, he kissed me, and I forgot the question.

He was so tall my neck crackled as I leaned back, so good at kissing I automatically went onto my tiptoes to get more.

His mouth was soft, sweet. Now that I was closer I caught the tang of the cigarette he'd no doubt been smoking on my balcony. He must have chewed gum to get rid of the taste.

I shuddered as his tongue tested my lips. Opening, I let him all the way in. I wound my arms around his neck, and the quilt slid to the floor.

I'd never been kissed the way Chavez kissed me, as if I were the only woman in the world, the only woman he'd ever wanted. Foolish, I know, but that's how he made me feel, and I began to wonder, in a far corner of my mind, exactly who was the sexual demon.

Even though my naked body was pressed against him, he did nothing but kiss me. He didn't slide those big, hard hands over my skin, no matter how much I might want him to. In fact, when I ran my fingers across his shoulders, down his arms, I discovered he was clasping those hands behind his back as if to keep them under control.

I don't know how long the embrace would have continued, how far we would have gone. I was certainly in no hurry to end it. But Chavez stepped back, shook his head when I would have followed, then snatched the blanket again and covered me.

"*Lo siento,*" he murmured. "I don't know why I—"

He glanced away, and the movement pulled the collar of his shirt in a different direction. He *did* have a tattoo on his breastbone, but I still couldn't see what it was.

My fingers touched my lips; they felt swollen, sensitive, needy. I craved the taste of his mouth.

Was not having had sex, ever, turning me into a nymphomaniac? Although I had to say that what I'd felt while kissing Chavez had been far and away better than what I'd felt with Eric. Then I'd been out of control; this time Chavez had been.

I liked that he had been fighting the lust. I was not the kind of girl who inspired it. When we weren't talking incubus demon anyway.

"I shouldn't—" he continued. "You're a—"

I stiffened. "A what?"

"A job."

My eyes narrowed, but he still wasn't looking at me. "I'm supposed to take care of you, not take you."

"So why did you?"

His glance snapped back to mine. "I didn't! I wouldn't." He sighed. "I can't."

"Can't?"

Chavez's lips twisted. "That's not true, as you can easily see."

My gaze lowered to his jeans. He definitely could.

"I mean I can't and still live with myself. You've been influenced by an incubus. They mess with your mind. All you want is sex."

"That doesn't sound like me."

"Exactly."

"The incubus hasn't influenced you."

"What?"

"*You* kissed *me*. Why?"

"I couldn't help myself. You were so small and lost." He shrugged. "And those glasses . . . All those books."

"I—what?"

"I never finished school. I don't read that well. I like women who do."

"You're attracted to women who read?"

"Yeah."

I shook my head. This was all still insane and so was he.

"Maybe you're the one whose mind has been messed with," I muttered.

He gave a short, humorless bark of laughter. "I haven't had sex in a very long time. I kind of forgot how much I missed it."

"Forgot?"

Even I, who'd never had sex, certainly didn't forget about it.

"Until I saw you, on the bed, with him."

I stiffened. "I wasn't with him."

That had been a dream, hadn't it?

"He's in your head now. He'll haunt you. He'll make you so insane with lust you'll have no choice but to—"

"I don't believe this," I interrupted.

"I do." He pulled a cigarette from his coat, which he'd laid on my unused exercise bike in the corner. "I'm going to—"

He nodded toward the balcony.

He seemed so sad, so defeated somehow. Even though I thought he was crazy, I still wanted to soothe him.

Chavez thought my glasses were sexy, my dumpiness cute, my penchant for reading on a Friday night attractive. No wonder I wanted to keep him around forever.

Which only made me as nuts as he was. But I was starting to wonder if that wasn't the case.

"You want some coffee?" I blurted.

"Yeah." He slipped out the doors and into the night.

Quickly I threw on my sweats, grabbed my glasses, and hurried through the darkened apartment. In the kitchen I reached for the light switch, and someone grabbed my hand.

I drew a deep breath to shriek, and another hand slapped over my mouth. This was happening to me with far too much regularity lately.

"Did you think I'd let you go?"

The voice wasn't Eric's. Come to think of it, the guy was too tall to be Eric. His body was pressed to the length of mine and then some.

Whoever he was, he really, really liked me.

I tried to speak, but he tightened his hold, pulling my neck backward until I thought he might break it. I went silent; I had no choice.

"You're mine now. I need what only you can give."

He kissed my neck, scraped the throbbing vein with his teeth. A weird lethargy came over me. My blood seemed to thicken and slow; my pulse beat in my ears as if I'd been running for miles, or making love for a long time.

I was suddenly free—to scream, to fight, to escape. I did none of those things. Instead, I turned around and flicked on the lights.

As I'd suspected, the man in my kitchen wasn't Eric. I'd never seen him before. Taller, broader, his hair was dark blond, his eyes brown.

He shrugged out of his shirt. The garment slid down his arms and spilled onto the floor.

His skin was glaring white, like marble, the muscles shifting and bunching as he moved. I was seized with a sudden urge to lick every one of them as he rose above me, came into me, took me over and over, until I—

I shook my head, hard, tempted to slam it against the countertop until I found myself again.

"Wh-who are you?" I asked.

"You know."

His fingers slid down his chest, caressing himself, lowering to the zipper that bulged over an erection my mouth went dry at the notion of seeing.

The sound of the zipper being opened made me start so violently my skin tingled.

"You'll die willingly in my arms," he whispered. "They always do."

As if from a long way off, I heard his words, puzzled over them, discarded any unease. The sex would be amazing. I'd come screaming. I'd beg him to do me again, and he would. He'd keep at it until I was—

Chavez loomed behind him. His presence brought me back to myself, so when he snapped, "Get down!" I did, hitting the floor just as a sheet of flame streaked from his hand.

I cried out as the strange man in my kitchen, the one I'd been willing to screw seven ways from Sunday, became a burning ball of fire.

My smoke detector went off; the sprinklers rained water on us all. The man, whose name I didn't know, stopped burning. There wasn't a mark on him.

He stared at Chavez. "You again."

"Me always."

The stranger turned to me.

"We aren't finished," he said.

And then he disappeared.

5

"**Y**ou believe me now?" Chavez asked as we dripped all over the carpet from the kitchen into the living room.

He'd turned off the alarm, which had shut down the sprinklers, while I called security and lied. "I burned some toast."

No one asked why I was making toast at 3 A.M. One of the perks of living in a building like this—money not only got you attention, it got you left alone.

"The guy disappeared." My voice sounded as dazed as I felt. "Poof."

Chavez gave me a slight push, and I collapsed onto the couch. Water darkened his hair, ran down his cheekbones, dotted his eyelashes. "Towels?"

"Hall closet."

He retrieved a stack, divided them, and sat in a chair as he began to dry his hair.

"That wasn't Eric," I said.

"No."

"He also wasn't human."

"No. Shape-shifter most likely."

I tried not to gape, but failed.

"Like a werewolf?"

"In a way. Demons shift into different people. Were-wolves change from a man, or a woman, into a wolf, then back again."

"You say that as if they exist."

He lifted a brow.

I lifted my hand. "I don't want to know."

Chavez went silent for a moment, then said slowly, "Why did he come back?"

"I'm irresistible?"

"Sure, but . . ." He trailed off.

I was still stuck on *sure*. Was he being a smart-ass? And why did I care? Why did my chest, which had felt like a cow was sitting on it, suddenly feel like butter-flies were twirling merrily inside?

Because of that damn kiss. I couldn't stop thinking about it.

But I had to. Maybe he wasn't crazy anymore, actu-ally he never had been, but that only meant he was a demon hunter. He was *so* not for me.

"He's an incubus," Chavez murmured, thinking out loud. I yanked my eyes and my mind from his mouth and listened. "He needs sex to live. But there are a million plus women in this city. Why not get it somewhere else?"

"Yeah, why not?"

His head tilted. "What did he say to you?"

"That we weren't finished. He needed something only I could give."

"What?"

"Got me."

I was new at the whole sexual demon gig.

"If I can discover why he's obsessed with you, I might be able to figure out exactly what kind of in-cubus he is."

"There's more than one kind?"

Chavez nodded. "The heading *incubus* covers a wide range of sex-feeding demons. Each one of those has its own particular method of death."

"Terrific," I muttered.

"As soon as I know exactly what he is, I can find out how to kill him." His dark eyes met mine. "You'll be safe as soon as I kill him."

Funny, I felt safe now.

An hour later we'd cleaned up the apartment, cleaned up ourselves. I was dry and dressed. Unfortunately, so was Chavez. I'd kind of enjoyed the short period when he'd worn nothing but a towel around his waist and another looped around his neck as his clothes tumbled around the dryer with mine.

We sat in the living room, lights blaring against the remnants of the night. I'd made the promised coffee, and we both sipped from the largest travel mugs I had in my cupboard. I needed more sleep, but since I wasn't going to get it, I'd have more coffee.

"What do we do now?" I asked.

He glanced up. "We?"

"We," I said firmly. "I don't plan to sit around waiting to be demon raped."

His hands jerked, sloshing hot liquid very near the rim. "He won't rape you; he'll make you want him."

"*Make* being the operative word. Even if I think I want him, I really don't. Which means he's raping my mind as well as my body."

I set down the cup. My hands had begun to shake at the thought of what was after me, of my complete lack of control whenever it came near.

"I want him dead." I lifted my chin. "Preferably last week."

"Okay," Chavez murmured, staring at me with new-found respect. "I guess it's we."

"What do we do now?" I repeated.

"You know where Eric lives?"

"No. And he wasn't supposed to know where I lived, either. That's the beauty of Internet dating."

"Not exactly. If you know what you're doing, an address is pretty easy to find. Can I use the computer?"

Moments later, we had Eric Leaventhall's address on the Upper East Side.

"Let's pay him a visit." Chavez glanced at the window. The sun was just coming up. "We've got only so many hours of daylight."

"What difference does daylight make?"

"Dark spirits arise at sunset."

"Seems like there's too much evil in the world all day to have demons only available at night."

"Just because the demon is sleeping doesn't mean it isn't still whispering."

Which actually explained quite a lot.

Not too long afterward, we paused on the sidewalk opposite Eric's building. He had a doorman, too.

"Now what?" I asked, but Chavez was already cutting across the street.

I hurried after him, catching up as he slipped around the corner and headed for the service entrance.

Chavez stopped and handed me a pair of plastic gloves. After donning a pair himself, he withdrew a long, thin strip of wire from his pocket.

"Done this before?" I asked.

Chavez didn't bother to answer as he jimmied the lock. At Eric's door he used what appeared to be a pocket calculator and a squiggly power cord to disable the security system. My feeling of safety was rapidly disintegrating.

"Where did you learn this stuff?" I asked. "Rogue demon hunter school?"

He shook his head and used the wire again, popping the lock as if it were a toy. "On the streets like everyone else."

"Everyone?"

Chavez glanced over his shoulder and smiled. His teeth were so white they blinded me. Or maybe I was dazzled by the excitement in his eyes. He was having fun, and at the moment so was I. I couldn't recall the last time I'd felt this alive.

Was it because I might be dead soon? Or was it because I was with him?

"Everyone *I* knew," Chavez answered. "In Mexico City there were way too many people, not enough houses or jobs."

Mexico City explained the accent. I doubt Chavez would ever be able to completely explain his occupation. How did one become a rogue demon hunter?

Chavez pushed open the door, motioned for me to stay in the hall. I was about to argue, but did I really want to be caught breaking and entering? Of course just being here was probably enough to get me arrested. Nevertheless, I stayed behind. For about thirty seconds.

When Ricky Ricardo–like cursing erupted, I trailed the sound to where Chavez knelt next to Eric's dead body.

"Oh-oh," I muttered.

I was suddenly *not* having fun.

Chavez glanced up. "He was dead when I got here."

"The cops are *not* going to believe that."

"Which is why we won't tell them."

I blinked. "But—but—we have to."

Chavez examined Eric, hands still covered in the plastic gloves. "Where is that written?"

"In the code of common decency."

"Never read it."

Why wasn't I surprised?

Chavez went on with the examination. Pushing at Eric's skin, turning him this way and that, ruffling through his hair before leaning back. "There's no visible means of death."

"What difference does that make?"

"Could help to reveal what kind of demon this is. For instance, if the demon killed Eric, then inhabited the body, he'd want to kill him so as not to leave a mark."

"Okay."

"But if he inhabited him, then killed him when he was finished, no reason not to cause graphic bloody death." At my sharp glance he shrugged. "Demons are evil. They like to make a mess."

"Wait a second." I was suddenly so dizzy, I had to sit and I didn't want to do so next to the body. With no convenient chair nearby, I made do with leaning against the nearest wall. "Are you saying I had a date with a dead guy? I *kissed* a dead guy?"

"Sorry."

"Not as sorry as I am."

I dragged the back of my hand across my mouth and got a good taste of plastic glove. At least it made me stop tasting Eric.

"Look at the bright side," Chavez said. "At least you didn't screw a dead guy."

Hey, there was a silver lining to every cloud.

"If Eric was dead on our date, how could he seem so alive?"

"When demons animate a body, the postmortem

changes are frozen. Once the demon exits, the decomposition begins."

He lifted Eric's arm, or tried to. Eric was stiff as a . . . corpse.

"By the state of rigor mortis, the demon has been gone less than eight hours."

"Why bother to exit at all? He'd found a perfectly good body."

"Several reasons. One—I'd seen his face, and he knew I'd be searching for it. Two—decomposition can only be stopped for a few days. Demon reanimation or not, dead is dead."

Chavez stood, but continued to stare at Eric, thinking out loud. "A demon inhabiting the newly dead makes me think night wanderer—a Rakshasas."

"Hindu," I said.

His gaze flicked to mine. "How do you know that?"

"I have a degree in ancient civilizations."

"Why?"

A question I'd often asked myself.

"I was interested."

"So am I. What else do you know about Rakshasas?"

"Squat. I remember the name, but I didn't spend too much time on ancient religions. I was more concerned with the rise and fall. Weapons and wars."

"I wouldn't think that would be up your alley at all."

I shrugged. "I do recall that one thing most civilizations have in common is a belief in a greater good, as well as a greater evil."

His gaze sharpened. "Exactly. Demons by any name are still demons."

"And God is still God. If you search long enough you can find a similarity even in the most disparate societies."

"Too bad no one ever takes the time to look."

"Too bad," I echoed. "Now tell me about the Rak-shasas."

"A Hindu demon that reanimates corpses. Except the Rakshasas isn't interested in sex. Unless it's with the dead. Or maybe they eat the dead." His lips tightened. "I can't remember. Either way, fire is how you kill them, and it didn't work on this one."

"You didn't use fire on Eric, that was on the other guy." I frowned. "Whoever he was."

"Has to be the same demon inhabiting different men. Otherwise why did he come back for you? Why did he say, 'We aren't finished'? Why did he know me?"

I shrugged since I didn't have a clue. "Why do demons inhabit people anyway? Why don't they just come to earth and do their thing?"

"Demons in their natural form are so hideous, humans can go mad from the sight. Their voices are so god-awful, eardrums rupture. People can die from the shock before a demon ever gets its jollies. As terrible as possession is, the alternative is worse."

We went silent for several moments just contemplating it.

"Any other ideas on what kind of demon we're dealing with?" I asked.

"No. Every one that I know of would turn to dust at the touch of salt, fire, or silver."

"Which means?"

Chavez lifted his gaze to mine. "We've got a demon I've never heard about."

"Does that happen a lot?"

He lit a cigarette and took a drag.

"Never."

"Never?" My voice rose so high, he flinched.

"Here." He held the cigarette to my lips.

I jerked back. "I'm not so hysterical that I need to start smoking. But thanks anyway."

"Smoke keeps the demon from possessing you." He glanced at the body. "I think this one's gone, but it never hurts to be cautious."

He stuffed the unlit end between my lips with a little too much force. The filter smashed against my teeth. I shoved him away, then took a drag. I wanted to avoid demon possession as much as the next person.

"There." I let the smoke trail out through my nose— hey, I'd gone to college. "I thought this demon only inhabited dead people."

"Since I don't know for sure what type of demon this is, it could do just about anything."

"Terrific," I muttered.

"Mmm."

My curiosity was piqued by something else he'd said. "Possession really happens? That isn't just in the movies?"

His face went still, his eyes hard. "Demons inhabit anything and anyone they damn well please."

I'd been curious, but suddenly I didn't want to know what he'd seen, what he'd done, what he'd killed. His eyes were haunted for a reason.

Chavez stared at me for several seconds, as if he planned to say something else. Then he took the cigarette, pinched the lit end between his fingers in a macho display that I refused to acknowledge, and placed the butt into one of his pockets.

Without another word, Chavez trailed around the apartment, picking through the mail, then moving on to the phone messages. Not wanting to be left alone with dead Eric—I had the nasty suspicion he'd open his eyes and try to seduce me again—I tagged along.

"We need to find the other guy," Chavez murmured.

"According to you, he's already dead. What's the rush?"

"Maybe the demon is still inside him. We could save the next poor sap on the dead dating parade."

I hadn't thought of that. Which was why he was the demon hunter and I was the one being hunted by the demon.

We left the apartment, and Chavez glanced at the security camera on the wall.

"We may as well call the police," I muttered. "They'll be calling me soon enough."

"I checked it when we came in. The light's not on. Whoever was here before us disabled the camera."

"That was nice of him. I think."

"I doubt *nice* had anything to do with it." Chavez headed for the service entrance. "This demon's a lot smarter than most."

"Are they usually stupid?"

"No. But they're not exactly savvy with the ways of the world. Kind of like a bull in a china shop—flailing around, obsessed with getting whatever it is they came here for. They don't worry about security cameras, police, or demon hunters. They think they're invincible."

"But they aren't."

"Not invincible, no, but hard to kill. Only one, maybe two, methods will work, and the trick is to figure out what before the thing kills you."

The trill of excitement returned. Life and death. Good versus evil. The stuff of really great books—and Chavez was living it. Too bad I might be dying from it.

"You must be very good at your job," I said.

"I'm the best."

"How did I get so lucky?"

Chavez checked the alley, then motioned for me to follow him. "Lucky?"

"How did you find me?" I paused. "Actually, I guess you found Eric. Is there a demon hunter hotline?"

"No."

He didn't elaborate, just stalked off so fast I had to move double time on my short legs to catch up. His face, when I reached him, was stonelike, unwelcoming. Wrong question, I guess, so I tried another.

"Are there a lot of demon hunters? You have a club or something?"

The look he shot my way would have scared me several hours ago. Now it intrigued me. There was a whole world out here I'd never known about. No one did.

"Rogue means I don't play well with others," he said. "I don't like rules."

"There are rules?"

"I've heard there's a society of monster hunters. Had a few approach me about a demon-hunting unit. I guess they've got government funding."

"The *U.S.* government?"

"Hard to believe, isn't it?"

"After being kissed by a dead man dating, not really."

"Funny how a little thing like that changes your whole perspective."

"I wouldn't call it funny. Why didn't you throw in with the monster hunters?"

"Even though getting paid would be nice—" he began.

"You don't get paid?"

"*Chica,*" he said with infinite patience, "who would pay me?"

"How do you live?"

"Very carefully." At my frown, he lifted one hand. "I do odd jobs for cash."

Cash?

"Are you an illegal alien?"

"Yes."

"Oh." I couldn't think of anything to say to that. "Wouldn't it be easier to get paid for what you're already doing for free?"

"The money would be nice," he repeated, "but the government would want to know where I'm from. How I got here. What I've been up to for half my life. I don't want to tell them. And I don't like being told what to do. I ask no one's permission. I never will. I eliminate evil from this world no matter the cost."

"Sounds like a good policy to me."

"I doubt you'd think so if you were part of that cost."

I stopped and stared at him. "You'd sacrifice an innocent person to eliminate a demon?"

He kept walking, but his answer drifted back on the early morning breeze.

"I'd sacrifice anything and anyone."

6

So much for any dreams I might have had about Chavez and me. Not that I'd been having any. I wasn't that stupid. But I *had* felt safe with him. Until he'd admitted he'd toss me over a cliff to rid the world of one more demon.

Well, he hadn't actually said that but I could read between the lines pretty well. Occupational hazard.

"Mind if I use the computer again?" Chavez asked when we returned to my apartment.

The place smelled wet. I opened a window, lit a candle, turned up the heat.

"Go ahead." I yanked the newspaper out of my mail drop.

"I want to find out who that second guy was."

"I don't think you need to."

I turned the paper in his direction. The face of the man Chavez had lit on fire last night was all over the front page.

He appeared to be missing. Or at least his body was.

"Malcolm Tanner," I read. "Stockbroker. Hasn't this demon ever heard of street guys? Their deaths and disappearances would be less noticeable."

"Would you date one?"

"I didn't date Malcolm."

"True. You didn't even know him. Which might be the point."

"You lost me."

"If he picked people you knew, sooner or later the police would be knocking on your door. But random guys? Hard to connect."

"Why bother setting up a date in the first place? Malcolm just popped in here, uninvited."

"Some demons need to be invited in first."

"Like a vampire?"

"Now you're catching on."

"But Malcolm—"

"—was the same demon as Eric, just a different body."

"So since I invited Eric—"

"Malcolm could enter."

"How do you know this stuff?" I asked. "Is there a *www.demonology.com*?"

"No. What I've learned is mostly by trial and error." He lifted one shoulder. "A little half-assed, but all I've got."

"You've tried salt, fire, silver. What's next?"

"Holy water, the Hail Mary, the Lord's Prayer, sacramental wine, the host."

"I'm seeing a pattern."

"Christian symbols." He sighed. "The problem is, there are a lot of demons that aren't Christian in origin and some that predate Christianity."

Since I'd studied plenty of ancient civilizations, I was aware of this. Still, the idea that something could predate time as we marked it had always creeped me out. Probably an American phobia. In countries that had been around for a few gazillion millennia, people didn't get wiggy over a little pre-Christian demon or ten. Did they?

"How can you kill something so ancient?" I wondered aloud.

"It ain't easy."

My gaze was drawn to his earring. "If Christian symbols don't work, then what's with that?"

"I didn't say they don't work. They do. More than most." He fingered the cross in his earlobe. "Every little bit helps."

"What can I do?"

"Any good at research?"

"Actually, yes."

Research was what had brought me to my major. I loved looking things up, finding answers to questions only I cared about.

His gaze traveled from the tip of my overly curly hair, past my black-rimmed glasses, to the ample breasts and hips ensconced in an oversized sweatshirt and equally oversized jeans.

"I've always had a thing for librarians," he murmured. "They're so . . . helpful."

Considering his face, that hair, the body, I just bet they were.

"I'm not a librarian," I said stiffly.

"We could pretend."

I stared at him for several seconds. Was he trying to make a joke? It was hard to tell when he never cracked a smile.

Chavez turned away, and the strange, charged moment was gone. "I'm going for supplies before it gets dark."

"What supplies?"

"Holy water, host—"

"Where do you get stuff like that? At the discount holy water and host shop?"

"A church."

"They give it out because you ask?"

"Because *I* ask, yes."

My skepticism must have shown on my face because he continued. "Priests believe in evil, Kit. If they didn't they wouldn't have a job. They've seen amazing things—great good and great bad."

"And you? Do you ever see any good?"

His eyes met mine. "Not until just lately."

"What'd I do?"

"You chased me out of the alley. You wouldn't stop questioning me. You weren't afraid to stand up to the insane man you believed had shot your date."

"You *did* shoot my date."

"But I didn't kill him."

"There is that." I tilted my head, curious. "What else?"

"You let me into your home."

"At gunpoint," I muttered.

"Not all the time. You went breaking and entering with me. No one's ever done that before."

"No one?"

He shook his head. I got all warm and fuzzy.

"So your interpretation of good is . . ."

Pretty damn broad. Basically I hadn't screamed, called the police, or kicked him out of my house. Give me the Nobel Prize.

"You're courageous, unselfish, a risk taker," Chavez said.

That didn't sound like me at all. It sounded more like the me I wanted to be.

"And then there's that kiss."

I looked up and he smiled.

"Good?" I asked.

"More like great."

Hours passed. The sun moved across the sky and began to descend. I began to get nervous.

Where was Chavez?

If I were a demon, I'd put my death on hold and go straight for the demon hunter. The thought made me unable to sit still, so I paced from the bedroom to the living room and back again.

"I'm sure Chavez has had demons come after him before," I told myself.

Hell, that was probably what he wanted.

Nevertheless, I was close to frantic. The first man who thought I kissed great—or at least the first who'd told me so—just my luck he'd walk out of my life and never come back.

I'd just completed my fifty-fifth pass into the bedroom when a soft footfall from the living room caused me to freeze.

I bit my lip, then glanced at the window. The sun was still up, though not for long. Nevertheless, daylight was daylight, and we still had it.

"Chavez?" I hurried into the front room and stopped dead at the sight of a strange young man with a huge pot of daffodils.

"How did you get in?"

"The doorman. He thought you were gone. Should I set this here?" He indicated the floor.

"Sure. Fine. Whatever."

I wanted him gone. I cast a quick look over my shoulder, down the hall, heard the slight thud of the pot hitting the carpet and turned around.

The kid was right next to me.

"Freakishly fast," I murmured.

In a not quite human way.

"You're so pretty," he whispered.

His eyes were hypnotic blue, his hair golden curls. Way too young for me, but I didn't care. He was pretty, and he thought I was, too. What more could a girl ask for?

A soul?

I took one step back and his arm snaked around my waist. His full, soft lips brushed mine.

"Souls are overrated," I whispered.

"You got that right."

His mouth moved down my neck; his hands moved up my ribs. My knees wobbled. The desire pulsed in my blood with the beat of a thousand ancient drums. I couldn't think straight.

"A virgin." He lowered his hands to the small of my back and ground us together. "The best time there is."

His words penetrated the haze. "How do you know I'm—?"

He pressed his nose to my neck and inhaled. "You smell all fresh and new. Never touched. You've been waiting for me."

I hadn't been waiting for him. I'd been waiting for true love. I knew that.

Of course I knew I wasn't a slut and look how that was working out.

"Virgins taste the best."

He licked my cheek and I didn't mind. Since I was a little Howard Hughes about germs, another reason I was probably still a virgin, that should have disturbed me. I fought against the lustful lethargy and focused on what he was saying instead of what he was doing.

"Taste?"

"Sex is food for me, baby."

Baby again. Wish I could find the will to care, or to kick him where it counted.

"Only virgins can keep me alive. So, you want it against the wall, on the bed, the table, the counter, the floor? I'm easy."

Actually, *I* was.

He fumbled with the zipper of my jeans.

"I'll consume you," he whispered, "and no one will ever know."

"I will."

At the sound of Chavez's voice, the lust I'd been unable to fight, fled. I managed to shove the flower boy away.

Chavez tossed a vial of burgundy liquid into the young man's face. I flinched, half expecting him to shriek as his skin dissolved. I should have known better.

"Sacramental wine?" Laughing, he shook himself like a dog coming out of a lake. "You have got to be kidding me."

"Ave Maria," Chavez intoned. *"Gratia plena."*

"Latin." The boy shook his head. "That language is as dead as I am."

"Our Father, who art in heaven."

"Way after my time, dude. Nothing will help you. I'm gonna have her. You can watch if you want."

Chavez socked the kid in the mouth. Blood spurted. "Don't touch her; don't look at her; don't come near her again."

"She's mine." His steadily fattening lip muffled his voice. "There aren't a lot like her left in this city."

Chavez glanced my way, and the demon took the opportunity to escape. *Poof.*

"Why didn't he disappear as soon as he saw you? Did he want a fat lip?"

"Teleporting is a tricky business. Sometimes they have to recharge before they can do it again."

That made sense, in this weird, new, demony world I was living in.

"Why bother with flowers?" I indicated the pot with a flick of my finger.

"You let him in?"

"No. He was just here when I came out of the bedroom. I knew something was weird, but he said the doorman let him in."

"Probably didn't want you to scream and alert me before he could get into your head."

"Where have you been?" My fear made me shout. "How long does it take to get Christian paraphernalia these days?"

"Not that long. I've been waiting for him to show himself."

"You used me as bait?"

Chavez cast me a quick, wary glance. "I wouldn't have let him hurt you, Kit. I was right outside."

He didn't deny he was using me. I'd known that, yet it still hurt.

"He was just here—like Malcolm. You couldn't have seen him—"

"I did."

Chavez strode to my bookcases and removed a tiny camera from between two books. No wonder he'd been so damn interested in them.

"He came out before dark," he said, "which makes him a lot more powerful than I thought."

Silence fell between us, but my mind was full of questions, thoughts, disappointments. When Chavez spoke again, I was glad for the distraction.

"He said there weren't very many like you in the city. What did he mean?"

I didn't want to tell him, but I had to.

"I'm a virgin."

His eyes widened. "You didn't think that was something you should tell me?"

"That's not something I've ever told anyone."

"Mudre de dios, he'll never stop chasing you."

"Why?"

"Because these days, *chica,* there aren't that many virgins to be had."

7

"**S**pectacular," I said. "Try to save myself for marriage and end up demon bait. The story of my life."

Well, not exactly. My life had never been this exciting.

Or weird.

Or terrifying.

Lucky me.

"You were saving yourself for marriage?"

I glanced at Chavez to find him staring at me. I suppose I was an oddity—in this century as well as the last.

I shrugged. "Or at least true love."

"You should have been born in another age," he murmured, eerily echoing my thoughts.

"Today I wish I had been."

"Get your coat," he ordered.

I gaped at the sudden change in subject.

"Zip your pants."

I blushed to realize the flower boy had started undressing me, and I had barely noticed. Not only was I scared of the demon; I was starting to be scared of myself.

I closed my pants with an annoyed *snick*.

"Where are we going?" I asked as we stepped onto the street once more.

"To someone who can help us."

"They couldn't help us before?"

"I only use this source when I have no other choice."

"Since when don't you have a choice?"

"This demon is more powerful than any I've ever faced. I don't know what to do."

That Chavez, whose life had been devoted to ridding the earth of demons, would admit he had no clue how to kill the one that wanted to kill me frightened me more than anything else ever had.

I stopped and was nearly run over by the usual suspects—tourists, street people, locals—the throng of Manhattan. Someone cursed and gave me a little shove. There's no place like home.

Chavez grabbed my arm and tugged me along. "I'll take care of you."

"You keep saying that, yet I'm still not feeling all warm and cozy." I ignored the dark, warning glance he slid my way. "Where are we going?"

"Near the World Trade Center."

I slowed, though I knew better than to stop. "There is no World Trade Center anymore."

"That's why my friend is so dangerous."

"I don't understand."

"She lost her son there. She's never gotten over it."

Stories like those were far too commonplace. So many people had lost so much.

"Has she tried a support group?" I asked.

"She's got her own way of dealing."

"Which is?"

"She talks to him."

The night shot an icy trickle down my suddenly sweaty shoulders.

"Talks to him," I repeated dumbly.

"Samantha is a psychic."

"Okay," I said.

Why not? I thought.

"The anger and grief changed her."

"Changed her how?"

As we walked in the direction of the water, the Statue of Liberty, Ellis Island, the crowd thinned.

"She channeled her pain into power. She wasn't psychic before."

"Is that why she's dangerous?"

"*She* isn't dangerous, but sometimes what she brings out is."

"Brings out of where?"

"You'll see."

"What if I don't want to?" I muttered.

Chavez just kept walking.

I'd only been to the World Trade Center site once—in broad, sunny daylight. The place had been cool, gray, haunted even then.

At night? I'd rather have a root canal.

Amazingly, there was no one standing at the fence that encircled the great, big empty. Maybe I wasn't the only one who found that hole in the middle of all the skyscrapers obscene.

We were searching for a demon? I was of the opinion that several of them had knocked down these buildings one Tuesday morning in September.

As we approached, I heard a slight whisper. Half believing the dead spoke, I hung back.

A woman stood at the fence, staring into the crevice

and murmuring. Her skirt was long, billowy, and black, her sweater loose and pale gray.

Had she been there the entire time and I hadn't seen her, or had she just appeared? It didn't matter. She was here now, and I knew without asking that she was the one we'd come to see.

Her hair flowed to her waist and shone stark white in the faint light of the moon. The air around her seemed to hum.

Chavez moved forward, leaving me behind. I didn't mind. There was something about her that disturbed me almost as much as that hole.

"Samantha," he murmured, and the air stilled.

"Chavez," she said without turning around. "You have a question for the spirits?"

"Yes."

She faced us, and I couldn't help but stare. Samantha didn't appear a day over forty. She might be well preserved, except for the hair. Premature electric white? Or had a terrible shock caused the change? I'd heard such things could happen but hadn't believed them. Of course I hadn't believed in demons, either, until yesterday.

"Who's this?" she asked.

"She's being hunted by a demon."

"So it's demon hunter to the rescue." Samantha's smile was a little bit sad. "You must be desperate if you've come to me."

"I don't like to disturb you."

"The only thing that disturbs me is people who need help but are too afraid to ask for it."

Chavez went silent and her expression softened. "Never mind. I live only to help, and I've never regretted my sacrifice."

I must have made a small sound, a slight movement, because she tilted her head and her eerily light blue eyes seemed to look straight at me, then right through me. "Chavez didn't tell you?"

"What?"

"To see the other side she had to sacrifice her earthly sight," he murmured.

Samantha was blind?

I lifted a hand and waved. She didn't blink, just continued to stare slightly to the right of my shoulder.

"A minor price to pay to see my son again," she said.

"What else do you see?" I asked.

"Whatever you ask."

I glanced around at the deserted cement slab. "I can't believe there isn't a line of people waiting to do just that."

"I see the truth, and the truth is often unpleasant. Some, actually most, would rather not know. After I saw enough horror, word got around, people stopped coming."

"Maybe if you weren't—"

Chavez shot me a glare, and I bit off the comment I had no business making. But that didn't stop Samantha from hearing it, apparently.

"Here?" she asked. "You think if I spent my days in a park filled with children, a candy store, riding a merry-go-round that then I'd see happiness?"

"You might."

"Truth is truth, Mara."

I jerked. How did she know my real name?

Chavez cast me a sideways glance and shrugged. I was starting to see why he only consulted her when he had to. The woman was spooky, and she hadn't even called the spirits yet.

"I come to this place *because* of what it is." Samantha spread one hand in an all-encompassing gesture. "A graveyard."

The wind—cool and damp—shrieked in off the water. Dirt flew up from below and swirled above our heads.

"If you want to call the spirits," Samantha continued, "it's best to go where there are a lot of them."

"Which must be why all those houses built on Indian burial grounds have so many problems."

"Exactly. The spirit energy is off the Geiger counters." Samantha turned her attention to Chavez. "What is it you want to know?"

"I thought the demon that is after Kit was an incubus, but I haven't been able to kill it in any of the usual ways. I discovered the beast is reanimating dead bodies, so I considered Rakshasas, but fire didn't work, either."

"I see your problem." Samantha faced the fence again. "Ready?"

"Yes."

The wind lifted her hair, fluttered her skirt, but left us untouched. A faint glow began all around her, like a banked flame, though no warmth flowed. When she turned, her eyes were even lighter than before, nearly white.

"Are you a godly spirit?" Chavez asked.

The voice that slithered from Samantha's mouth was not her own. "No."

"That can't be good," I murmured.

Samantha's weird gaze slid in my direction. No longer blind, whatever was inside her saw me and smiled.

That saying about your blood running cold? It can happen.

"No!" Chavez waved his arms in front of her. "Deal with me."

"Chavez." The creepy white eyes flickered back to him. "It's been too long."

The voice brought to mind a snake—somewhat sibilant—but so deep, so sluggish it seemed to be coming from a tape recorder with severely low batteries.

"Not long enough," Chavez said. "What have you unleashed this time?"

"Wouldn't you like to know?"

"If I ask, you must tell."

"The rules. I hate them."

"What have you done?" Chavez repeated.

"You should be thanking me. If I didn't unleash them, what would you do with your life?"

"Answer," Chavez snapped.

"I've made something new."

"New?" Chavez said. "Since when can you create new demons?"

"I could always create them. I had to have something to do while I whiled away several thousand millennia. What's changed is that now I can set them free."

"Why now?"

Samantha began to laugh—a deep, wicked sound that would have been comical—like the laughter that spewed from a plastic Halloween skull—if it hadn't been real.

"Didn't you get my hint?" He/she/it swung out Samantha's hands to encompass the gray, silent crater. "The beginning of the end. My time is coming. Mark of the beast. Six-six-six. Four horsemen. Is any of this ringing a bell?"

"End of days," I whispered.

"Now you're talking," Samantha said in a voice that I was starting to believe was Satan's. "Anyone up for an apocalypse?"

8

"I'm Jewish," I said. "We don't do the apocalypse."

Samantha's body swayed to the side and something very un-Samantha peered back at me. "Armageddon is nondenominational. What falls on one falls on all. Besides, you're not completely Jewish. You don't go to Temple and you eat Gyros."

"That's lamb."

"Damn." She smacked herself in the head with the heel of her hand. "I never could keep those cloven-hoofed animals straight."

"And you with such nice ones, too." I glanced at Chavez. "Does she always channel the Prince of Darkness?"

"Smart girl," said the sonorous voice. "Too bad she has to die."

"Enough," Chavez snapped. "I want to know what you've sent and how I kill it."

"He's Satan, the inventor of lies," I said. "We can't trust him."

"When he inhabits Samantha, he has to tell the truth."

"Fucking Ouija board rules," Satan in a Samantha suit muttered.

I'd never done the Ouija board, being easily freaked out, but I'd heard stories. The spirits who chose to answer were compelled to tell the truth. However, the truth could be told in many different and confusing ways.

"*What* did you send?" Chavez ground out from between clenched teeth.

"There's no name." Samantha's head tilted. "This demon is very hard to kill. Hard to detect, too. No one cares these days about gratuitous sex. Promiscuous behavior on a first date has become the norm."

She peered at me, and I ordered myself to stare right back. I refused to feel guilty about what I'd done while I'd been under the influence of a demon.

"A few things need to be tweaked," Samantha continued. "I combined an incubus with a Rakshasas, which requires a dead body. But they don't last very long, and all those dead bodies are going to pile up. Now, if I could have the demon take the form of a human—"

"Possession drives a human being insane," Chavez said.

"You should know."

I looked toward Chavez just as he flinched. Then his mouth tightened, as did his fists. I touched his arm. Slugging Samantha would do us no good.

"But you're right," the deep, slithery voice flowed from Samantha's pretty mouth. "The longer I saw it, the creepier it became. "Too many stark, raving crazy people would tip off the white hats, as well. What I need is for the demon to be able to look human, but not actually *be* human. That would work."

"Focus." Chavez clapped his hands in front of Samantha's face. "How do I kill the one you already sent?"

Samantha smirked. "You're going to love this."

"Somehow I doubt it."

"The demon feeds on sex with virgins."

"Been there, know that."

"In the good old days they sacrificed virgins to appease the beast. Man, I miss those days."

Chavez made a whirling motion with his index finger—*Get on with it*—but I already knew what was coming.

"All right, all right. To save her from a fate worse than death, all you have to do is sacrifice her."

A rumbling began. At first I thought there was a train coming, maybe a tornado, a tour bus. But the sound was coming from Chavez's chest. Pure fury.

"Get out," he shouted. "Leave this place."

"Too late." Samantha's eyes rolled back. "I'm already here."

He caught her as she tumbled, but only a few seconds later she struggled upright. "I'm okay."

Her voice was her own again. So were her eyes. I was so glad she couldn't see me. I was shaking and no doubt as pale as the pavement. I didn't want to scare her. Then again, she'd been the one speaking with the devil's voice.

"What did I do?" she asked.

We were both silent and she sighed. "The devil?"

"Yeah," Chavez said.

"I hate it when that happens." She stuck her tongue out and made a face. "I can taste the brimstone for days."

"I'm sorry I had to ask," Chavez murmured. "But I had to."

"What did I say?"

"Heard any whispers about the end of the world?"

"There are always whispers. Especially since this." She jabbed her thumb in the direction of the empty space. "The spirits have been restless. There's a lot of evil going on, and it seems to be getting worse with every passing day."

Chavez and I exchanged glances. That would follow if there were new and old demons being released at an unknown rate.

"He said the apocalypse is coming," Chavez murmured.

"He's probably right."

Samantha refused to let Chavez and me take her home. "I have too much to do here. We need to be prepared."

"You really think the end is near?" he asked. "They've been predicting that for centuries."

"Sooner or later, they've gotta be right."

When she wasn't speaking with Satan's voice, Samantha made a lot of sense.

"Could I talk to you privately, Chavez?" Samantha tilted her head in my direction—though slightly to the left.

"Sure," I said. "I'll just be"—I glanced around the depressing cement walkway—"over here."

I hadn't gone very far when Samantha began to whisper furiously. Chavez's deep tones answered with equal fervor. I couldn't hear what they were saying, but not for lack of trying.

"Hello."

I jumped. Heart thrumming so loudly I could hardly hear, the beat slowed at the sight of the tall, slim, beautiful blond woman near the fence. I must have been too preoccupied with Samantha and Chavez to notice her.

"Hi," I returned. "I didn't mean to disturb you."

"You weren't. It's lonely out here."

"I'll say." This place had given me the willies, even before Satan showed up.

"He'll kill you."

I jumped again. "Wh-what?"

She indicated Chavez. "He's a warrior. He understands that sometimes one must be lost for the good of many."

My eyes narrowed. "Who are you?"

She smiled, and the familiar low, thrumming sexual need began—the need that was brought on by a demon.

"I don't do women," I said.

"You will."

She was probably right. I opened my mouth to shout for Chavez.

"He's obsessed. Ever since the unfortunate incident."

My mouth snapped shut. Did I really want to know this?

Uh-huh.

"What incident?"

"Possessed by a demon. Poor baby."

I glanced at Chavez, who was still speaking with Samantha. If he looked my way he'd only see me talking to what appeared to be a harmless woman.

I remembered what Chavez had said to Satan. "Possession drives humans insane."

"Exactly."

"You're saying he's crazy?"

She shrugged. "Crazy is a relative term."

Not in my book.

"What happened?"

"He was possessed. His mother did everything she could think of to drive the demon out."

She licked her lips and gave an "mmm" of pleasure.

I gritted my teeth against the response that tugged in my belly.

"She was quite creative."

My eyes narrowed. "What the hell does that mean?"

"Have you seen his tattoo? She gave it to him herself when he was fifteen."

I frowned. "And then?"

"She whipped him, starved him, locked him in the basement. The usual things people do to get rid of the devil."

"Sounds like the things people do who *are* the devil."

"Ignorance. Fear. They're my master's domain."

"He had Chavez possessed so his mother would hurt him?"

"That's what he does."

My fingers curled until the nails bit into my palms. The pain eased both the anger and the infuriating sexual arousal. "How did they get the demon out?"

"Exorcism."

"Those are still done?"

She scowled. "Every damn day."

I found that hard to believe, but what did I know?

"Once Chavez was clean, he became the most feared of all the hunters. He was young, but he was thorough. He'll do anything to defeat one single demon. He hates us."

"News flash—everyone does."

"Not you."

"When you aren't messing with my head I do."

"Messing with heads is in my job description." Her gaze swept over me. "Among other things. He *will* kill you, you know?"

Chavez's face was fierce as he listened to Samantha. He did seem capable of anything. Even murder.

"And you won't?" I asked.

"I didn't say that. But you'll die happy. I promise."

I was tempted to run, except where would I go? No matter where I went, if Chavez didn't find me, the demon would. Wouldn't it be better to die easy at the hands of a friend, than horribly at the hands of evil?

"Chavez," I shouted. "Bring the salt."

I give him credit; he came running. But she was already gone.

"That was a woman," he said.

"Sex is sex."

"A comment only made by someone who's never had any." He went silent for a second. "A woman is a succubus."

"Thanks for the tip."

"Our demon is supposed to be part incubus."

"I think this one is a lot of things."

"True. What did she say?"

I hesitated. If Chavez had wanted me to know about his possession, about the abuse at the hands of his mother, about the exorcism, he'd have told me. I wasn't going to bring it up. I also wasn't going to bring up my imminent death. From the look on his face, he was upset enough already.

"The usual," I lied. "Sex until I die. Never give up. Yada-yada. The powers of evil need a new tune."

He stared at me for a few seconds, and I managed to stare right back. Amazing what a little Armageddon can do for one's lying skills.

"You ready to go?" he said at last.

I glanced at the fence, the concrete, the hole. "Definitely."

Chavez hailed a conveniently trolling cab, then gave the driver my address. Silence fell between us. What did we have to talk about? His method? My funeral? Damnation. Forgiveness. I preferred the quiet.

The doorman, already accustomed to Chavez's presence, nodded as we got on the elevator. *Oh-oh.* I didn't want Chavez arrested for my murder. He'd be needed in the coming days to keep the demon horde down to a manageable level, if not thwart the coming Apocalypse.

I let us into the apartment, moved into the living room as he locked up behind us. Not that locking up had done much good so far.

"There's a service entrance," I blurted. "Do you know how to short-circuit the security cameras?"

"What the hell are you talking about?"

"You'll need to get out of the building unseen."

He crossed the room, stopping so close I could feel the heat of him calling out to the sudden chill in me. "You think I'd hurt you?"

"Hurt, no. Kill, yes."

He threw up his hands, then stalked away. "That damn demon!"

"Redundant, I think."

I surprised a laugh out of him.

"I'm not going to kill you, Kit."

"You have to. I understand. Although . . ."

My voice faded as a thought took hold—an insidious thought, but a very tempting one. I'd changed over the last few days, probably because the whole world had. Or rather the world had always been far different than I realized.

I'd saved myself for marriage, true love, but I wasn't going to find either one in the next five minutes. Did I really want to die a virgin?

"One request," I blurted.

He sighed impatiently. "Kit, I am not going to—"

"Make love to me."

Chavez stared at me for several seconds, then slowly shook his head. My hopes died.

He crossed the room and I tensed, knowing this was the end.

"Make it quick," I said.

Gently he reached out and slid my glasses from my nose, folding them, before setting them aside.

"It will definitely not be quick, *querida*," he murmured.

Then he kissed me.

9

The single kiss we'd shared had come in the depths of the night as this did. Then I'd still believed in a world without pure evil. Then I'd believed I had a life ahead of me, that I still had a shot at true love.

Now I knew better. That knowledge made the kiss no less mind-bending. Maybe the knowledge made it more so. If tonight was my last night, I wanted to spend it like this. With him.

I opened my mouth, deepened the kiss. He tasted of mint—fresh, cool, new. I licked his teeth and he moaned.

My fingers managed to pop several buttons of his shirt before fumbling in their haste and becoming unable to finish the job. Instead, I latched on to the lapels and tugged.

He stumbled forward, almost knocking me down. "*Lo siento*. I—"

I kissed him again. "No talking."

If we talked too much, I might lose my nerve. If we waited too long, he might lose his.

Grabbing his hand, I practically dragged him to the

bedroom. There I yanked my shirt over my head and tossed it into a corner. My bra followed just as fast. His dark gaze wandered over my breasts. I might be short, and I might be dumpy, but my breasts were pretty darn good.

He kicked the door shut behind us.

His shirt hung open, framing his chest. The ripples and curves, all that bronzed skin . . . I wanted to run my hands everywhere; so I did.

My thumb skated over the tattoo on his breastbone. Very small; without my glasses I had to get closer to make out the tiny cross inside of a circle. I wondered what it meant, then I wondered if I'd ever have time to ask.

I leaned forward and ran my tongue over one nipple, then the other. They tightened against my lips so I scored them with my teeth.

He grabbed my hair and I stilled, ready to fight for the right to taste him. But instead of pulling me away, his palm cupped my head, urging me on.

I suckled him, the tiny bud of his nipple hard against the roof of my mouth. His free hand smoothed over my back, up my ribs, then settled onto my breast where his thumb teased me into a similar state.

My knees wobbled, so I let them collapse, sliding my cheek down his stomach, rubbing my mouth against the front of his pants. I'd always wanted to open a guy's zipper with my teeth.

It didn't work as well as I'd hoped. My teeth ached; the zipper stuck. Too much pressure from the other side.

Impatience flared, and he wrenched the thing open, taking himself in his own hand and jerking his palm over the length just once.

I shoved him out of the way and took him in my

mouth. No time to be shy, no time to learn all the nuances. I wanted to experience everything, and I only had one night.

His palm at my neck, he showed me how it was done, throwing his head back, his hips flexing in an ever-increasing rhythm. When he pulled away, I pulled him back. But he lifted me to my feet and kissed me so roughly our teeth clashed.

He was hard and hot against my stomach, wet from my mouth. I gave an involuntary shimmy, and the resulting slide made us both groan.

He tore his lips from mine and pressed our foreheads together. "Where did you learn this stuff?"

"I'm making it up as I go along."

The soft breath of his laughter brushed my cheek. "I love a woman with an imagination."

After inching me backward several steps, he put a hand to the center of my chest and shoved. I tumbled onto the bed. He stared at me with a strange expression—as if he'd never seen me before.

"What?" I asked.

"You're so pretty."

I snorted. "Don't bother, Chavez. I'm a sure thing."

"Bother?" His head tilted; his hair swung free of his shoulders and his earring winked in between the dark strands.

"I'm not pretty. Never have been. I never will be. Don't care."

Or at least I didn't anymore. What would be the point?

The realization was freeing. I *didn't* care about my rounded belly, my wide hips, the stretch marks that resembled a road atlas across my butt. None of that mattered anymore. Only this did.

Him. Me. Together just once.

He shucked his pants, then removed mine and joined me on the bed. I lifted my arms. He came into my embrace and brushed his lips across the slope of one breast.

"I know where beauty lives," he murmured.

His dark fingers drifted over my skin, gentle and sure as he aroused me. He learned what I liked as I did. His clever mouth wandered; his devilish tongue arrowed in on erogenous zones I'd never heard of, as well as those everyone had.

His beard had lengthened past the rough stage and become almost soft. The texture both tickled and tormented, another sensation to add to so many. He teased me to oblivion more than once, and then he teased me to the precipice again.

"I can't," I gasped.

"You will."

His body slid up and over me, nearly into me. I opened for him and he stopped.

"Ahhh!" I smacked his back with my fists and he choked on stifled laughter. The sound rumbled all the way to my toes, making me hum everywhere, making me want to laugh, too. To be laughing now was both a wonder and a gift—a downright miracle.

"This might hurt a little," he said.

"What did I tell you about talking?"

His smiled deepened, and he kissed me, the way I was starting to crave. Hot, wet, lots of tongue. The man knew what he was doing.

While I was preoccupied with his talent at tickling my tonsils, he drove forward, burying himself inside.

It didn't hurt. I felt . . . full. A tiny bit uncomfortable maybe—

I shifted, and something went *ping*. That hurt a little, but I forgot all about it when the very earth seemed to move. I know that sounds so dumb, but there you go.

Warm and alive he filled me. His body moved to an ancient rhythm—a rhythm echoed in the beat of my blood. I rocked against him; he rocked against me, and for that moment there were only the two of us.

His face was fierce, his eyes dark, intense as they stared into mine. I'd always thought sex an act better performed in the dark, but we'd left on all the lights, enjoying every sight, every sound. I couldn't help but reach up and touch his cheek.

"Chavez," I whispered.

He slowed, staring down at me with such an intense, searching expression, warmth spread through my chest. Something had changed, but I wasn't sure what.

"My name is Zac."

"Zac," I repeated.

At the sound of his name on my lips, he pulsed inside me, the force of his release inciting my own. The orgasm went on and on—him, me, us—there was nothing and no one else, just the way the world ought to be.

When it was over, we lay tangled together. He stroked my hip; I played with his hair. I didn't want to let him go, and that was a very dangerous thing to want.

"Did the world move?" I asked.

"Oh, yeah."

He lifted his head, kissed the tip of my nose. I got that weird feeling again—the sock in the gut, the warm, gushy swirl. My eyes burned.

"What's the matter?"

I glanced at the window. Still night, but not for long.

"You think we can do it again?"

He rolled off me but grabbed my hand as he went,

tangling our fingers together, then playing footsie, too. "We can, but not right this second."

I drew one finger over his tattoo. "What does this mean?"

He stiffened. "You know what a crucifix is."

"Yes. But the circle?"

"Eternity."

"Your mother—"

I bit off the word, but he already knew.

"It told you about my mother?"

"I'm sorry."

"Don't be. She did her best."

"Hurting you was her best?"

"She didn't know any better. I was possessed by a demon. What was she supposed to do?"

I wasn't sure. What would I do if my son had a bit of Satan inside of him? I hoped I never had to find out.

He touched the tattoo with his fingernail. "She gave me the cross. I did the circle myself."

I thought of the pain he must have endured—at his own hands and those of someone he trusted. I wanted to take that pain away, but it was too late, and I didn't know how.

"Why did you do it?" I asked.

"So I'd never forget what I'd sworn to do. If it takes eternity, I *will* kill every demon on this earth."

I shivered, knowing that meant he'd kill me, too.

"Cold?" He pulled me closer. "I'll keep you warm while we sleep."

Oh-oh, said a tiny panicked voice in my head. I was in serious trouble now.

I'd vowed not to have sex without love, but what was I going to do now that I'd fallen in love because of the sex?

Not love. *No.* I was just dazzled by the orgasm. Once he killed me, everything would be different.

I pulled away. I couldn't sleep in his arms and wake up to a gun, a knife, or whatever he planned to use.

Getting out of bed, I yanked the sheet along with me and wrapped it around my chest. Chavez didn't even try to cover up, merely stared at me with wary, confused eyes.

"When are you going to do it?" I demanded.

"You have to give the equipment a rest, Kit. I'm not seventeen."

"Not it, it. When are you going to kill me?"

His brows drew together; his mouth turned down. He sat up slowly, and I took a step back at the violence in his expression.

"What do you think I am? A monster worse than the ones I hunt?" He climbed off the mattress and began to stalk me around the room. "You think I'd make love to you, then murder you?"

"You have to, Zac."

"Don't call me that!" His voice broke, anguish washed over his face. "You can't call me by that name and think I'd hurt you."

I let him get too close and he grabbed me, then gave me a good shake. "I wouldn't kill you. Not for any reason."

"You won't need to," said a strange voice from the door.

I yelped and spun around. No big shock to find another stranger in my house. This guy was nondescript—not too tall, not too short, average weight, dishwater hair, gray eyes. But there was something strange about him that I couldn't quite put my finger on.

"Does a person have to be dead to find some peace around here?" I muttered.

Of course being dead didn't seem to mean what it once had. According to Satan, the dead would soon be dating all over the place.

Chavez shoved me behind him, facing the latest demon wearing nothing but a scowl. "What do you want?"

"To set the record straight. I guess you didn't tell her."

Chavez's shoulders tensed and I got a bad feeling.

"Tell me what?" I asked quietly.

Average Joe grinned. "There's more than one way to sacrifice a virgin."

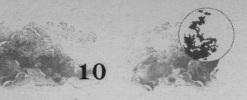

10

I put my hand on Chavez's shoulder and spun him around. "You knew that sacrificing the virginity would work as well as sacrificing the virgin."

No wonder he'd been so insistent that he wasn't going to kill me. He'd known he wouldn't have to.

I'm not sure why the truth hadn't occurred to me before now. Just because I'd been told the sacrifice would be my life didn't make it true, especially since I'd been told that by a demon.

"Don't listen to him," Chavez said. "He wants to put a wedge between us. I'm just not sure why."

I wanted to believe he hadn't known. Really I did. But there was that voice in my head that kept saying, *Did you really think he wanted you? Look in the mirror, then look at him.*

But there was another voice that insisted Chavez was different. He knew about the ugliness that lived beneath the beauty. He killed it every day. He'd said he liked women with glasses, women who read. Of course that sounded like a bigger lie than any of the others.

"What were you talking to Samantha about all that time?" I asked.

Anger flared in his eyes. I couldn't believe Chavez had the balls to be angry. "What did you think we were talking about?"

"Where to bury my body?"

"I told you, I've killed a lot of things, but I don't kill people."

The demon snorted. "Men. They'll say anything, won't they?"

I didn't even glance his way, instead holding Chavez's eyes. "You should have shot me."

It might have hurt less.

He winced. "Just because Samantha suggested that removing the virginity the demon craved might be the answer doesn't mean I don't care about you."

The demon in the doorway began to laugh.

"You shut up!" Chavez snarled.

"Why is he still here?" I demanded. "You sacrificed the virgin. Shouldn't he be demon dust?"

"That isn't a demon."

I switched my attention to the now giggling stranger, and I realized what was different. I didn't want to jump him. I only wanted to slug him—and every other guy in the room. The sexual obsession was gone. You'd think I'd be happier about it.

"What is it?" I asked.

"Beelzebub."

I glanced at Chavez. "Again?"

"He seems to like me."

For a minute I sympathized. Imagine spending half your life chasing evil, killing it, and enjoying periodic visits from Satan whenever things got really rough.

Not much of a life, but that still didn't excuse him.

Chavez had betrayed me in the worst possible way a man could betray a woman. He'd pretended to want me, but he'd only been using me. Not for sex, but to save my life and the lives of others. I still wasn't going to thank him.

"So the earth moved for you, Kit?" Satan asked.

I could feel the blood drain from my face. He'd been *watching*?

I glanced at Chavez, who appeared as horrified as I was.

"I hate to be the one to break it to you, Chavez, but that wasn't a result of your prowess. The demon was dying."

Chavez ignored him, reaching for me. I stumbled back. I didn't want him touching me. Not now or ever again.

Pain flickered in his eyes, turning quickly to fury when the devil snickered. Chavez spun toward him.

"You did this. You sent the demon; you made it so I'd have to hurt her in one way or another."

"What's your point?" Satan asked.

Cursing, Chavez snatched his pants from the floor and withdrew a vial of holy water. The devil rolled his eyes. "That isn't going to kill me."

Chavez tossed the contents into Satan's face. Steam, the scent of cooking flesh, the hiss of flames, for an instant I saw the monster behind the mask.

"I know it won't kill you," Chavez murmured. "But it sure does sting."

The devil writhed for several seconds. I was hoping he'd begin to cry, "I'm melting!" then do so. Instead, he straightened and lowered his hands from his face. I tensed, expecting something ugly, but he appeared exactly the same.

"Quit being childish," he snapped. "I came to offer you a deal."

"A deal with the devil? Hmm, let me think." Chavez tapped his fingernail against his chin. "No."

"Don't be so hasty. The end is here. Demons are pouring out of hell even as we speak. You're the only chance the human race has got."

"Why me?" he asked.

"As you said—I like you. Always have. When I was inside you for that brief time, I felt at home."

"Fuck you," Chavez snarled. "I cast you out. And you aren't getting back in."

He yanked a cigarette from his pants and hurriedly lit the end. His hand shook, causing the devil to smirk and me to take a single step closer. I might want to stick a sharp implement repeatedly into Chavez's eye, but I wasn't going to let Satan hurt him.

"What is he talking about?" I asked. "I thought you were possessed by a demon."

"He's the father of all demons. In every one lies a little of him."

"You're more like me than you want to believe," Satan whispered. "That's why you're so good at killing us. You can smell evil a mile away, can't you?"

Chavez took a deep drag and blew the smoke in the other man's face. Instead of coughing, the devil inhaled it like ambrosia.

"That's what I thought," he murmured. "Here's the deal, if you can kill everything I've released before the end of the world, I'll call off the apocalypse. It'll be like a video game, except real."

"Since when is he in charge of the apocalypse?" I asked.

Neither one of them answered.

"When's the end of the world?" Chavez took another drag.

"That's for me to know and you to find out."

Now who was being childish?

"What happens if I lose?"

"You know."

The devil began to laugh again, then he disappeared.

I stared at the place where he'd been for several seconds before I lifted my gaze to Chavez. "What happens?"

"He gets my soul."

Ask a stupid question . . .

Chavez began to gather his clothes.

"You're going?"

"You heard him. I don't have much time."

"Or maybe you have plenty. No one knows when the end of days actually is. And what if he just decides to finish things when there's only one demon left to down?"

"It doesn't work like that."

"How *does* it work?"

"There *is* an end of time, except no one's been able to figure out the exact date. There are a lot of theories."

"The apocalypse is a Christian belief, and not all Christians believe it."

"Not believing it doesn't make it any less real."

"Sixty-seven percent of the world isn't Christian," I pointed out.

"Where do you get all this information?" Chavez asked.

"I like trivia."

"I like smart women."

I narrowed my eyes and he went on.

"Satan does come out of the Christian legends, but remember . . . all religions believe in good and evil. Just because he isn't called Satan doesn't make him any less the leader of the underworld. You saw him. He's real."

"Which makes the apocalypse real?"

"Even if he's lying, it won't hurt to kill all the demons. It's win-win."

"Unless you lose."

"Someone's got to do it."

Quickly he dressed, then it was time to say good-bye. I didn't want to.

What I'd felt for Chavez had been genuine even if what he'd pretended had been . . . pretend.

"You must have found my last request"—I sighed and turned away—"hysterical."

"I found it flattering." He inched in front of me. "And arousing."

"As well as convenient."

"Kit—"

"You were going to seduce me." I shrugged. "You didn't have to."

He took a breath as if to speak, and I lifted my hand to stop him. I'd had an epiphany. They didn't happen often, but when they did I listened.

"It doesn't matter if you knew or you didn't. You saved my life."

My anger had faded. Chavez did what he had to do for the greater good. I didn't like what he'd done to me—

That was a lie. I'd liked it a lot.

I couldn't throw stones. I'd slept with him when I thought he planned to kill me. The ultimate one-night stand. I'd sworn to hold out for true love—then at the first sign of an apocalypse I'd thrown away my vow for a good time.

That I'd discovered I loved him later did not excuse me in the least.

I couldn't stay angry with him when he'd only done what I asked—and what was absolutely necessary.

"Do your job," I said. "Save the world."

His gaze softened. My stomach flip-flopped. I couldn't believe I was giving him up, but then I didn't have much choice, either.

"I knew you were special from the beginning," he murmured. "Can I have a kiss good-bye?"

"You can have two."

The kiss and the one that followed were everything I'd ever dreamed of in a farewell embrace—the heat of lust, the gentleness in caring. My eyes stung, and I fought not to let the tears fall. He had to go, and I had to let him.

Chavez lifted his head. "If the world wasn't about to end—"

I put my fingers over his lips. "But it is."

"Yeah." He stepped back; I clung just a little. "If the world *doesn't* end . . .

"Give me a call."

He never would. A guy like him, a girl like me— heat of the moment and all that. As soon as I was out of sight, I'd be out of mind. But it sounded good—as if I didn't care, as if I weren't dying inside.

"Hasta luego, chica."

The tears were blinding me. I wiped them away, but he was already gone.

The *snick* of my apartment door closing echoed in the suddenly silent room. I was alone again.

Just me and my big fat boring life.

11

My life didn't get any better. Without Chavez in
it—there was nothing worth getting up for.

I'd never liked my job. Now I loathed it. What
good was trying to sell books to people who were only
promoted for paying far less than what they were
worth? What good was any job when the world was
about to end?

I drifted, waiting for something to happen, but I
wasn't sure what.

Three months later, I was still waiting. I fell asleep
late one night while reading a manuscript. Just another
Saturday and I didn't have anybody.

Because I didn't want anybody but him.

I dreamed of Chavez all the time, and in my dreams
he was with me. His touch gentle, his eyes full of love.
Definitely a fantasy, but all I had.

"Kit. Wake up."

His voice sounded so close. His fingers were so
warm as he removed my glasses. I fought against sleep
and opened my eyes.

"Hey, *chica*."

I closed them again, squeezed tight, and tried once more. He was blurry, but he was here.

I struggled upright, and manuscript pages spilled from my lap, cascading onto the floor. I let them go. "Is the world saved?"

Chavez shook his head. He appeared tired, drained, defeated. Not the man who'd left on a quest only three months ago.

"Why did you come?"

He hesitated. "I—I need you."

"Okay." I tangled my fingers with his and started for the bedroom. I'd take whatever I could get.

"No!" He snatched his hand away. "That's not what I meant."

"What did you mean?"

"I—I've seen some terrible things. The world is a mess, Kit."

"I've noticed."

"Through everything, I remembered you. You're what kept me going."

I wanted to believe him, but I wanted to be sure, and I wanted him to be, too.

"We had one night, Chavez. Manufactured intimacy in exchange for the death of evil—or at least one little piece of it."

"We had sex."

"I know."

"For me, it was more."

My eyes widened; my breath caught. I couldn't speak. He didn't seem to have that problem.

"I was crazy for you from the first moment I saw you, but I couldn't touch you. I had to—"

"Protect me." I smiled, and some of his tension eased. "You did. I'm safe now because of you and I'm grateful."

"I don't want you to be grateful," he growled.

"What do you want me to be?"

He glanced away and muttered, "Mine."

"Huh?"

He took a deep breath and looked back. "I want you to be mine. I want to have someone, somewhere, who's waiting for me. I'm sick of being alone and lonely. The only time I felt as if I belonged anywhere was when I was here with you."

"What are you saying?"

"I love you. I can't live without you. I hope you feel the same way."

I hesitated and his shoulders sagged. "I know a girl like you and a guy like me—you probably forgot about me the instant I walked out that door."

I let a small laugh escape. "You're kind of unforgettable."

Hope lit his eyes. I didn't want that hope to die.

"I love you, too, Zac."

He smiled at my use of his name. For him, the gift of his name went deeper than the gift of his body.

"My life without you isn't much of a life. I hate it here when being here means I'm not with you. I want to help you save the world."

Chavez shook his head so hard his hair flew and his earring caught the lamplight and flashed bright sparks into my eyes. "I won't let you risk yourself."

"But you can risk yourself?"

"I hunt demons. That's what I do. It's all I've ever done."

"Seems to me that the last demon took both of us to kill. Without me, you'd still be flailing around with your salt and your holy water and your sacramental wine."

His brow lifted. "Don't forget the silver bullets."

"How could I when they worked so well?"

His smile turned shy. "I was thinking—love has always been stronger than anything."

"I agree."

"Maybe it wasn't so much the sex that killed that demon as the love."

"You could be right."

"So the more love we make—"

"You don't need an excuse, Zac."

"Then . . . ?"

"Together we fight; together we win or we don't."

"You can't fight," Chavez scoffed.

"I meant in a 'pen is mightier than the sword' kind of way."

"Research," he said.

I reached under the coffee table and pulled out a stack of papers that I'd written. "Without you here, I've had a lot of time on my hands."

I offered them to him and his eyes wandered slowly over all that I'd learned, then lifted to mine. The excitement was back.

"This is great, Kit."

"I told you I was good at trivia."

"This isn't trivial." His hands clenched on the papers. "This is world-saving."

My face heated at the praise and I ducked my head. He inched in close, put a finger to my chin, and lifted.

"It'll be dangerous," he said.

"You'll protect me."

"I will."

His words were a promise, one that he kept.

Did the world end?

Not yet.

RETURN TO THE HOLLOWS WITH
NEW YORK TIMES BESTSELLING AUTHOR

KIM
HARRISON

WHITE WITCH, BLACK CURSE
978-0-06-113802-7
Kick-ass bounty hunter and witch Rachel Morgan has crossed
forbidden lines, taken demonic hits, and still stands. But a new
predator is moving to the apex of the *Inderlander* food chain—
and now Rachel's past is coming back to haunt her . . . literally.

BLACK MAGIC SANCTION
978-0-06-113804-1
Denounced and shunned by her own kind for dealing with
demons and black magic, Rachel Morgan's best hope is life
imprisonment—her worst, a forced lobotomy and genetic
slavery. And only her enemies are strong enough to help her
win her freedom.

And coming soon in hardcover
PALE DEMON
978-0-06-113806-5

PROWL THE NIGHT WITH
NEW YORK TIMES BESTSELLING AUTHOR

KIM HARRISON

DEAD WITCH WALKING
978-0-06-057296-9

When the creatures of the night gather, whether to
hide, to hunt, or to feed, it's Rachel Morgan's job to keep
things civilized. A bounty hunter and witch with serious sex
appeal and attitude, she'll bring them back alive, dead . . .
or undead.

THE GOOD, THE BAD, AND THE UNDEAD
978-0-06-057297-6

Rachel Morgan can handle the leather-clad vamps and even
tangle with a cunning demon or two. But a serial killer who
feeds on the experts in the most dangerous kind of black magic
is definitely pressing the limits.

EVERY WHICH WAY BUT DEAD
978-0-06-057299-0

Rachel must take a stand in the raging war to control
Cincinnati's underworld because the demon who helped her
put away its former vampire kingpin is coming to collect his due.

Visit www.AuthorTracker.com for exclusive
information on your favorite HarperCollins authors.

Available wherever books are sold or please call 1-800-331-3761 to order.

HAR 0908